Y0-BSL-120

Stephanie
expect it!
Then allow it!
Las Vegas 2001 NFR
James
Romero

THE SPITTING IMAGE OF MY FATHER

An American Cowboy Novel by James Pomerantz

Acknowledgements:

Gary Leffew...without you, this book doesn't happen.
The bull riders of the Professional Rodeo Cowboys Association and the PBR.
Dennis Schaffner...Aloha, my friend.
Steve Eastin...Castle Rock Police Department.
Fred Hoffman...Ala Carte Entertainment, Chicago.
Jim Earley...Ala Carte Entertainment, Chicago.
The residents of Castle Rock, Colorado.
Ned O'Brien...it's time to get e-mail.
Peter Garin...Denver attorney.
Bob Greene...Chicago Tribune columnist. Your insight and persistence has brought much needed attention to the child abuse that happens every day in this country.
Gwen Herndon...Handlebar J's, Scottsdale, Arizona.
Carl Schock...The Professional Rodeo Cowboys Association.
Richard Pomerantz...thanks, again.
Jeff Steinback...attorney and friend.
Sgt. Job Hernandez...Chicago Police Department.
Paul Stickney...United States Magistrate Judge...Dallas, Texas.
Chris LeDoux...for the songs that inspire a generation to live life with their spurs held high.
Earl Silver...my sincere gratitude for all your support.
Joey...rest in peace.
To my family...we're gonna' get there!

Edited by Jerry Gross, Croton-On-The-Hudson, New York

Cover design by James Pomerantz and Bill Holloway.

Kye Publications, L.L.C. Visit our web site at kyepub.com.
Printed in the United States of America.

A thin layer of dirt covered the worn out pair of Justin Boots.
The daily rush hour gridlock of I-94 and the Kennedy Expressway were memories.
Chase the hands of a clock until time chases back.
The dogs always tired before the property fence lines appeared.
Children learn how to lower the reins and give more left.
Relatives and friends shake their heads and question what was thrown away.
George Strait sings a ballad about the best day in a child's life.
All is right, at last.

Dedicated to Joey

During the autumn of 2000, a Chicago Tribune columnist ran a series of columns on the tragic death of a small boy in Ohio. The columns detailed the unimaginable sequence of events that began with the beating death of the three-year old boy. Joey (not his real name) was beaten and battered repeatedly by two adult guardians. Under the guise of discipline, Joey's brain bled internally from the severe blows. According to police, Joey's caretakers had bitten the boy numerous times, leaving clear bite marks deep into the skin. The assailants were accused of dragging Joey by his ears, which appeared disfigured and bruised when the scene was discovered. Joey was hog-tied, gagged and left to die. Just three years old and less than forty pounds, Joey died from the attack. There was Joey's blood splattered around the kitchen floor and cabinets. The medical reports determined that Joey drowned in his own blood. The accused killers were his natural father and his girlfriend. The columns pointed to the statements at the time of the arrests. Joey's father and girlfriend claimed that they put the boy to bed because he wouldn't eat his eggs. In the morning, the boy just wouldn't wake up. The tape and a mouthful of his own blood that closed his throat had nothing to do with it.

The killers were freed after they plead guilty to involuntary manslaughter and served three years. A judge ruled that because the killers did not mean to kill the boy, they should have been given another chance. I never met Joey. I never met thousands of children who have fallen asleep each night wondering how they could have behaved better to make the ones they loved, stop hurting them. The Ohio judge, having freed the killers in Joey's case, said what they did to the child was "fraught with ignorance, immaturity and inexperience, more than malevolence." Malevolent...arising from ill will. A court ruled the child was not treated with ill will. What part of the torture lacked ill will?

When has a psychiatric evaluation concluded that a suspect was evil and not "fraught with anything?" Has a psychiatric evaluation ever determined that a suspect was "fraught with culpability?" The courts have provided more avenues of extrication for unfit parents than Elmer Gantry gave to the crippled on a Sunday afternoon. Responsibility should have been stricken from the dictionary and buried forever like the concept it previously stood for. Are adults now allowed to torture children and feign remorse? Remorse is the modern Queen's English synonym for getting caught. Spare me the remorse of those locating morality only after the police have located them.

When did the paradoxical characterization of child abuse crimes borrow the adage, *size matters?* Crimes against small children are treated as smaller crimes. In many courts, killing a child is not murder because the parent has convinced a judge, the intent was not to kill the child. The discipline simply got out of hand. The morning papers remind us, again, of another child, doused with gasoline and set afire by his father. We all gasp, in between gulps of a half skim latte. Then, we skip to the sports page and move back into a more comfortable world. The nation cries out, appalled by the astronomical salaries in professional sports and the exorbitant ticket prices to attend the games. Blasphemy! A national debate ignites. Are we a dedicated nation of priorities?

~ PROLOGUE ~

Autumn 1989

Dana Davenport sat in the hallway of the Douglas County Municipal Building. Dana continued to fidget with her hands, nervously rubbing them together as if she were washing. The Douglas County Municipal Building served as home to one courtroom, the city manager's office and the Douglas County School Board. Assistant Principal Dana Davenport was waiting to see Principal Martin Hollis. The snow fell early in the fall and through the window at the end of the corridor, Dana could see the frosted alpine energy of the Rocky Mountain perimeter surrounding Castle Rock. Dana Davenport was the Assistant Principal for South Street Elementary School and Castle Rock Elementary School. Dana was forty-eight years old and had been with the Douglas County School District for nine years. She had never been married, more by circumstance than choice. Dana was not an attractive woman. Overweight and appearing much older than her years, Dana loved her work with children, especially the very young children. This day was not one she welcomed or planned. The resignation letter had been delivered on Monday afternoon. On Wednesday, Mr. Hollis requested the meeting. Dana would finish the term and resign at the Christmas break. She pulled a copy of the letter from her purse and began to read it again. The nausea returned instantaneously.

November 7, 1989
Mr. Martin Hollis / Principal
Douglas County School District
South Street and Castle Rock Elementary
Douglas County Municipal Building
Castle Rock, Colorado

Dear Mr. Hollis,

I hereby tender my resignation regarding my position as Assistant Principal for South Street and Castle Rock Elementary Schools effective on December 18, 1989 or the last day of classes before the winter break. The past nine years have been the position of a lifetime for me with the one exception that has ultimately forced my decision to retire from my post. For the past four years, we have witnessed the systematic destruction of the most precious part of life itself, a child. The meetings, the counselors, the social workers, DCFS, the police and the doctors have continuously echoed the same tired song. "My hands are tied" is not an adequate response. The response was not adequate on day one and it remains a flaccid, feeble excuse in the face of the horrific treatment brandished upon one little girl.

Before I walk away from my job, I must remind the school board of the egregious actions we have ignored under the guise of legal complications. These legal complications will prevent me from using the girl's name in this letter. I have been reminded on more than one occasion that any specific allegations could be construed as slanderous and therefore may place the school board in jeopardy of costly legal action brought on by the girl's father.

Four years ago, the school board dealt with a young child stealing food from other classmates as a disciplinary problem. The matter was handled through the parents and the girl began to grab scraps of food from the garbage as an alternative. My assessment that the child, age eight at this point, was being deprived of food at home was dismissed as ludicrous. The young girl was the daughter of a high school hero in Castle Rock. The blind eyes and deaf minds began early. She was reluctant to go home at the end of the day and would often find the most menial tasks after school to prolong her stay. Many afternoons, I found the young girl walking the playground picking up small bits of paper or discarded gum. I told her that the school employed people to do that. She asked if it would still be all right to continue?

During fourth and fifth grade, the young girl was brought to the emergency room on nine separate occasions. I checked with the local hospitals because of the girl's physical appearence. Our high school hero had apparently learned a few things along the way. The emergency room visits were spaced throughout the region. Multiple visits to any emergency room normally generate red flags for child abuse. Visits were made to Aurora, Colorado Springs, Parker, Evergreen, Boulder and more. Those visits documented very unusual interpretations of childhood injuries. Duct tape adhesive was found on her wrists and ankles. Human bite marks marred her shoulders and abdomen. The parents explained that when their daughter got angry, she lashed out by biting her parents. To teach her a lesson, the father explained that he would bite her back. These doctors accepted an explanation that showed a father biting a twelve year-old girl repeatedly on the shoulders and the stomach.

At the most benevolent level, these measures would still require a father to remove the blouse from his daughter and place his mouth in any number of inappropriate places. Blunt trauma from a baseball bat caused three broken ribs one year ago. I spoke to the attending physician in Parker. He told me that there were no signs of abuse. I asked him if he thought the young girl ran into the bat on purpose. The doctor pulled the file and recited the father's account of how the girl was riding a bike and fell into a metal playground apparatus. She almost died from "accidentally" ingesting a combination of Tabasco sauce and human urine during fifth grade. According to the little girl, her father insisted on absolute obedience. Punctuality to the minute was demanded. Three minutes late from school or a walk to the Plum County Fairgrounds on Saturday afternoon to watch the rodeo, always resulted in isolation. The girl would be bound by duct tape at the ankles and wrists. She was placed in a closet. The girl was not gagged, because her father used an unusual method to assure silence. When the girl cried or begged for food from the closet, she was forced to ingest a glass of Tabasco sauce causing the girl to vomit and choke. The cries ceased from the closet.

Often, the girl sat for twelve hours before the tape was removed. After the family ate dinner, my young student was given eight minutes to clear the table and wash the dishes. If she was one second late, the disciplinary action took on frightful proportions. A beaker of human urine was forced down her throat after one particular pan from dinner took longer to scrub, thus pushing the clean-up time past eight minutes. When the results ended with a trip to the hospital, alternative solutions were enacted. One month later, she was brought to a Boulder hospital with food poisoning from bad meat. The father claimed she ate the meat before they had a chance to throw it away. Another emergency room visit in the Springs was caused by "accidentally" ingesting dog feces. Often, disciplinary action by the father included forcing his daughter to eat dog feces. The other trips to the emergency room were due to the child's "clumsiness". Each visit was explained and the mother refused to press charges against the father. Our Castle Rock hero was systematically killing his daughter.

We have an obligation to protect those in our care. I came to win a degree of trust from our young victim. By now, we had a ten-year old girl that weighed forty-one pounds. This frightened little girl told me that her father would not allow her to eat for days at a time following any kind of disciplinary action at home. She was punished for not finishing the dishes in a specified amount of time, punished for leaving her bike on the wrong side of the walkway, punished for having a friend over. Before long, there were no friends. The father was the sole administrator of the disciplinary decisions. Her mother was reduced to a catatonic state of fear. The family lived in fear of the drunken arrival of the father. Enough liquor and the man would pass out shortly after returning home. Unfortunately, most evenings, the liquor was only enough to blame a failed life on the only child in the house. Nightly beatings often became directed at the spouse when the young girl went to bed.

Women are treated as if they have provoked the husband in most cases of domestic violence. They are asked why they refuse to leave. In most cases, they have left or attempted to leave. The solitary fear for the children can erase any plans for an escape. In a society that has been raised by veterans, we forget that POW's have been afforded the compassion brought on by years of manipulation at the hands of the enemy. The enemy begins the process of mental manipulation as the captor and a hated adversary. Imagine the damage done to a spouse entering a relationship with love and trust. We know that a hated captor can brainwash an unwilling prisoner. Yet, we refuse to see the carnage done by husbands aided with love and trust. The Department of Children and Family Services from Denver has made numerous visits, all pre-planned. The results were laughable. The father paints a picture of a harmonious family. His wife and daughter echo every reference to a loving family.

When school started this fall, the young girl told me that she counted the days of summer. The start of school was her only haven. The father grew more calculated over the years. The torture became less evident. As the girl grew and the drinking continued, our father began taking sexual advantage late at night. Knowing sexual intercourse was easily detectable, the man forced his young daughter to satisfy his needs orally. By starving his daughter, the father would bring food into her bedroom during his late night visits. The food was used as a reward for the functions he demanded. A dog is trained to respond to food treats. Any comments to the mother or the school would be dealt with accordingly. Her confessions to me were under the conditions that if I made them public, she would deny them. Her father would beat her mother often and he assured the girl that her mother would bear the brunt of any allegations. Anyway, he told her, the authorities have never done anything about his abuse to date. He assured his daughter that the authorities take the word of an adult over the word of a child every time. I have looked into the eyes and faces of many, many children, but the eyes of a child have never taken my breath away. The emptiness in these eyes strangled my wind-pipe.

I faced a terrible dilemma. On one side, the young girl yearned to know that someone believed her ordeal. On the other side, she was petrified that the story would get out and her father would conduct reprisals against her mother. My attempts to convince the young girl to allow me to bring the matter to justice were dismissed. After hearing about the sexual abuse, I could no longer stand by and allow this to continue. I taped my conversations with the young girl and brought the tapes to the District Attorney's office. After one week, the Castle Rock Police Chief came to my home. He informed me that the girl denied ever speaking to me concerning any matters relating to her home and family. When I asked the Police Chief if the voice on the tape was matched to the little girl's voice, he informed me that the DA's office was considering filing charges against me. The girl has ceased speaking to me and I am certain that repercussions are immanent.

We all know the family and the circumstances in question. I can no longer work for a school board that chooses to ignore these abuses. I will pursue all avenues in Denver to pull this child from the nightmare she endures daily. Trust me, copies of those tapes are safe. You all have children and yet the nightmare continues. Blind eyes and deaf minds. With regrets, I will end my tenure in Douglas County.

Respectfully,

Dana Davenport

After folding the letter on her lap, Dana Davenport was informed that the Principal would see her now. Dana rose and walked into the office of Martin Hollis. Mr. Hollis was seated at his desk. He held a copy of her resignation letter. Suddenly, Dana froze. Seated in front of the desk and holding a copy of the letter was Billy Don Barrett, Devon Barrett's father. Devon Barrett was the young girl in the letter.

"I believe that you may have met Devon's father, Billy Don Barrett, at one of the parent/teacher nights." Martin Hollis remarked to the startled administrator.

"I have never met Mr. Barrett." Dana answered softly, feeling very nervous.

"There are some very serious charges in your letter and in this country we get to face our accusers, Ms. Davenport." Hollis chided his soon-to-be former assistant.

"What else you been doin' to my daughter to make her tell you things that you wanna hear?" Barrett got closer to Dana. His breath reeked of cigarettes and liquor.

Dana Davenport, betrayed and frightened, turned and ran from Hollis' office.

* * *

~CHAPTER I~

Winter 1978

The apartment building at 444 Nahua stood twenty stories. The one-bedroom unit on the seventh floor was home to Buddy Peak and Cody Law. Buddy and Cody had transferred to the University of Hawaii from a two-year stint at Fort Lewis College in Durango, Colorado. On any given afternoon from the small lanai facing north, the sun would break through the ominous dark clouds hugging the Koolau Mountain Range and sprinkle the Heights and the Manoa Valley with a shower of warm yellow rays. Buddy Peak enjoyed the neon streaks from the cobalt blue wash in the sky. The elusive sunlight danced down the mountainside like an avalanche of flashbulbs while the trade winds played havoc with the cloud cover.

Honolulu was a picturesque city regardless of the commercialization. The crowd on the seventh floor began to grow through the evening, making Buddy Peak even more nervous than usual. Buddy was a twenty-year old student at the University of Hawaii. Buddy stood six-foot five and weighed a trim one hundred ninety pounds. Buddy was not particularly athletic, but the washboard stomach and deep tan never gave away a thing. Buddy's hair was long and very wavy, bleached naturally from endless hours on the beach. Buddy lived at the beach during the day and occasionally went to class when the rains came. Buddy's roommate was at work.

Cody Law worked as a bartender at the Red Lion and Cody did not care for Buddy's friends, especially Kurt Holloway. Buddy's smile was engaging, as bright as a summer sunset over the Hilton Towers at Kahanamoku Beach. Buddy trusted his friends. Trouble was, he didn't know who they were. Kurt Holloway was a celebrity in his own eyes and a cocaine dealer for a sizeable section of the resident haoles in Waikiki.

Kurt Holloway met Buddy Peak on Waikiki Beach. The beach was the order of all business in Waikiki. The Diamond Head point on the island of O'ahu was separated from the rest of Honolulu by more than the Ala Moana Beach and the H-I freeway. Waikiki and Diamond Head may have been the tourist capital of the Pacific, but they were also home for the nocturnal postscripts to thousands of young people, who for one reason or another had decided to step off the planet for a prolonged stay in paradise.

Holloway arrived in Hawaii in 1975 from Los Angeles. With no intention of pursuing employment or school, Holloway began selling quarter ounce bags of cocaine on the beach at Waikiki. Kurt initially did not step on the product, satisfied to make a c-note per quarter, which more often than not went up the nose of a stewardess on holiday, anxious to barter a couple grams for some sandy copulation.

Holloway's business flourished. The quarters became half ounces and the half ounces became full ounces in a matter of months. The import pick-ups at the airport were now measuring up to four or five kilos. Full ounces sold on the street for $1300 or $1400 with a profit margin exceeding forty percent. The drugs came into Honolulu from Los Angeles, shipped with the normal movement of luggage and parcels making the trip on commercial airlines. The major airlines flew into Honolulu at least a dozen times daily from LAX. Kurt and Buddy often went to the airport together for the weekly packages. Cocaine smuggling from the mainland was not a highly visible priority for Hawaiian law enforcement officials in 1978. The focus for the Honolulu Police Department and the DEA was the growing presence of the yakuza, Japan's own version of La Cosa Nostra, in Hawaii.

Tattoos and missing fingers comprised the most obvious features of the new criminals. The tattoos were magnificent, full-color designs of samurai warriors, flowers and dragons that stretched completely across the body. The severed extremities were ceremoniously chopped off and the smallest finger was presented to the gang leader as a sign of atonement. The growing Japanese presence in Hawaii surely meant the yakuza would begin to flourish in the islands. Yakuza membership in Japan approached nearly twenty times the estimated members of the American Mafia.

Strolling along Kalakaua Avenue in Waikiki, mixed among the Japanese shopping boutiques, Pizza Huts, hotels and Woolcos were a gaggle of massage parlors, porno movie houses, adult bookstores and strip clubs. All had a relationship to the yakuza. Many businesses were fully financed by the yakuza, while others simply paid for the protection and privilege of operating in Waikiki. The 1978 estimates bantering about the DEA and HPD began at $100 million for yakuza funding already in Honolulu. The state's major industry, tourism, provided cash and victims for criminal organizations. The yakuza in Hawaii by 1978 had vilified interests in gunrunning, gambling, drugs, pimping and money laundering. The Far-Eastern hedonism was now firmly implanted within the island structure.

The Japanese gangs, their oyabun (godfather) and the rising number of yakuza would push the small haole drug dealers down the priority ladder in the eyes of the police. Japanese investment firms, funded by the yakuza, were the major players in the acquisition of prime real estate holdings all along the Waikiki shoreline. The fine line between rebuilding the islands as the premiere vacation destination for the mainland and waging a drug smuggling war at Honolulu International Airport rode the wave of discretion.

Cody Law was five-feet, eight inches tall and weighed one-hundred fifty-seven pounds. Cody's blond hair crept down to his shoulders. Cody's father was Scandinavian and Cody's facial structure carved the profile of the mythical Norseman, more at home wielding a broadsword than riding a surfboard. Cody Law was a striking youth evolving into a magnificent man. Cody's mother was Old English, the family immigrated from London after the first World War. Cody's physique was commanding with a small waist and wide shoulders like a gymnast. Years of weight-training, running and skiing triple black winter runs from Vail to Telluride, left no excess weight on the five foot eight inch frame. Cody concentrated on muscular definition rather than bulk in strenuous ninety-minute weight training sessions, four times per week.

The routine in Honolulu developed quickly after Buddy and Cody located an apartment, two blocks from the beach at Waikiki. Expenses were reduced by the absence of any vehicles. No heating or A/C expenses were incurred, while a variety of visiting roommates shared the rent. Friends from home came and stayed for weeks at a time. Cody looked for work immediately. Buddy fell into the sedentary lifestyle enjoyed by the resident beach wise guys.

Ground zero was the beach in front of the Royal Hawaiian Hotel, a pink relic preserved immaculately amidst the palm trees of Waikiki. Servers dressed in colorful Hawaiian attire carried flour dusted scones on silver trays to the morning arrivals at the beachside cafes. The main beach was crowded with tourists scrambling to spread the suntan lotion over pale skin. The Japanese accounted for well over fifty percent of the tourist dollars. Fathers staked out parcels near the ocean, while small children discovered their first taste of salt water. With bad shorts, pastel-flowered shirts and big stomachs, an army of Tommy Bahamas pondered how their wives had talked them into any vacation at all, much less Hawaii.

The University of Hawaii was located in Manoa Valley, a short fifteen minute bus ride from Waikiki. Cody and Buddy were not regulars on the morning 707 city bus that rolled down Kuhio Boulevard and stopped at Nahua, beginning the circle that dropped the handful of students living in Waikiki at the University. Heavy rain was a prerequisite for any plans to spend the day in class. Light rain and clouds almost always cleared. Often, Cody and Buddy rode the bus to campus, only to notice the cloud cover breaking over the mountains. The pair remained on the bus and continued the ride back to Waikiki and the beach. The beach became their vocation and their education.

Cody walked toward the Royal Hawaiian Hotel. He had an arrangement with most of the pool and health club attendants working at the Royal. Cody was given unlimited access to the pool and the weight room in exchange for a heavily discounted status at the Red Lion, Waikiki's premiere after dark watering hole. A dip in the Royal pool was the most refreshing aspect to the afternoon. A cool, fresh water plunge purged the body of all saltwater residue.

Cody finished a thirty-minute iron session at the Royal Hawaiian by completing a burning curl routine with eleven sets at twenty repetitions of decreasing weight from 110 pounds. On his way from the pool, Cody stopped for a brief encounter with Kurt Holloway, who stood at the enclave of grass blankets and Frisbees situated about fifteen feet from the Royal Hawaiian pool. Kurt had his face buried in a towel, dripping from a stint in the ocean. When the towel dropped, Cody Law was uncomfortably close. The two young men stood toe to toe.

"Fucking wind kicked those Frisbees onto the deck of the Royal. Did you see those ladies scatter?" Kurt asked, uneasy with Cody and no one around.

"The next time that I hear about you dealing in my apartment," Cody replied, ignoring the opening small talk. "I will break every bone in your face. Jaw, cheekbones, orbits, nose, you name it."

"Talk to your roommate. I was invited." Holloway was not certain that this was a wise response, but they were on a crowded beach. Holloway's eyes twitched slightly and he began to rotate his jaw reflexively.

"You heard me. Buddy is my friend. I cannot stand you. It is that simple." Cody finished and walked away. Kurt Holloway did not want anything to do with an angry Cody Law.

Cody showered and arrived at the Red Lion by 5:00 p.m. Cody worked as a bartender at the Red Lion, a tremendously successful bar located on the lower level of the Outrigger West Hotel. The hotel was located at the corner of Kuhio and Walina, across the street from The International Marketplace. Cody walked through the marketplace on his way from the Royal to the Red Lion. The parasitic salespeople ignored the locals. Tending bar at the Red Lion became the most sought after bar position in Waikiki.

The entrance to the Red Lion was street level on the corner. The large teak doors opened to a small entryway featuring a wood-burning pizza oven and three young men behind the counter struggling to satisfy the pick-up pizza orders. The phone at this early hour rang constantly. The stairway to the lower level began just to the right of the small prep kitchen area. There were no chairs or tables on the upper level. Customers picked up the pizzas and left. The only other traffic was from a pizza runner. One young Polynesian boy ran pizzas from the prep area to the bar during the night.

Downstairs, the bar was typical island fare. Nautical artifacts hung throughout the space. Dark, weathered wood covered every inch of the facility. The one indelible characteristic of the Red Lion was the aquarium behind the bar. The saltwater tank stretched thirty-six feet from one end of the bar to the other. The tank rose from just above the floor to the top of the eight-foot ceiling. The backdrop to the busiest tavern in Waikiki was a dazzling display of underwater foliage and a kaleidoscope of brilliant corral. Swimming slowly and gracefully through the seascape maze were seven, five-foot Tiger sharks.

Tiger sharks are one of three main shark species known to attack man. Tiger sharks are considered sacred under traditional native Hawaiian beliefs. The animals possess "Auma kua" or ancestor spirits. The sharks moved menacingly throughout the tank and seemed to provide security through a subconscious jurisprudence. The steely eyes and slithering confidence produced an unusual aura within the club. The seven centurions seemed to say, *don't fuck with my club.*

Tuanni Kapo had worked as the club manager at the Red Lion since the club opened seven years ago. The club space was leased from the Outrigger, Inc. The owner of the Red Lion was a California corporation with similar properties in Long Beach, Santa Barbara and Monterey. A thirty-seven year old Samoan, Tuanni stood five foot, seven inches tall and weighed two-hundred and seventy pounds. The man was a barrel with thick, long black hair. Tuanni possessed the finest sneer in the business. Deep, onyx eyes broke up more fights over the years than most doormen accomplished with strong-arm tactics. Tuna's hands were the size of Sasquatch lore. Forearms appeared to be Sequoias with hair.

Job openings were rare at the Red Lion and the waiting list for employment was endless. Bartenders never left. Even the pizza counter job was coveted because of the women. Cody Law's quest for employment had barely begun. Two weeks after his arrival to the islands and a couple weeks away from a serious job hunt, Cody Law met Tuanni Kapo, on the beach at Waikiki. Cody and the resident Frisbee clan were in full gear. The crowd began to swell as the participants grew farther apart. Tuanni watched from the Outrigger East pool. Tuna's wife worked at the Outrigger East as the banquet manager.

An errant Frisbee sailed high into the growing throng of onlookers. A frightened four-year old was accidentally barreled over by the churning onslaught in the sand. After a brief apology to the parents, the exhibition continued. Cody walked over to the young boy, still crying from his encounter. With a father's nod, Cody hoisted the boy onto his shoulders and walked to the water. With one hand locked around the boy's ankles, Cody motioned for the disk. A white spinning blur came hurtling above the sand. Cody spun in place and caught the disk behind his back with the four-year old firmly planted on his shoulders. In the same motion, Cody spun the disk back across the beach and out over the water. The diagonal ribs on the disc caught air the moment of launch. The whoosh was unmistakable.

The waves broke knee high to Cody and his ride. The Frisbee sailed thirty feet above the water and curled around to follow an exaggerated hook, landing square into the hands of T.J. Cole. MTA (Maximum Time Aloft) is a competitive event where the thrower attempts to keep the disc aloft for as long as possible. The MTA record was 17 seconds. Cody's throws with the boy on his shoulders hung in the air for every bit of 15 seconds. After each throw, the young boy riding on Cody would follow the disc intently with a wide-eyed glow and wait patiently for T.J. to yell out the time aloft while sailing the disc back. The crowd caught on and began to time the disc in the air along with T.J. Cody finished a fifteen-minute run with the young boy and returned him to his father.

Tuanni Kapo made his way onto the beach. After introducing himself, Tuanni asked Cody to stop by the Red Lion that night. Within three days, Cody was training with Tuanni behind the bar. At twenty, Cody Law entered a business that would dictate his life for the next twelve years.

Cody worked the third station behind the bar on this particular Thursday night. Three bartenders rang an average of $2,000 per night at each of three registers. Two bar-backs took care of all glasses, restocking the coolers, cutting fruit, refurbishing the tropical ingredients for fourteen varieties of blended tropical drinks. Each station behind the bar featured four blenders and twin speed rails with eight base mixes and an array of fruit accents. Thirty-four flavors of bottled beer, a dozen draft beers, twenty-four specialty shots, one-hundred forty brands of vodkas, rums, bourbons, scotches, gins, and liqueurs kept three bartenders whirling in an organized frenzy of motion behind the backdrop of seven serene gladiators floating from one end of the bar to the other.

Thursday night at the Red Lion was like any other night. Every night was Friday night. Cody liked to work the entire evening shift, beginning at 5:00 p.m. and ending at 2:00 a.m. One bartender opened and had the option of leaving an hour before closing. The other two bartenders came in at 7:00 p.m. Cody learned fast that it was ludicrous to work the entire night and leave for the last hour. Some bartenders doubled their tips in the last hour.

Tuanni worked with Cody for one week. Tuanni stressed the consolidation of motion behind the bar. Condition every movement to accomplish more than one task. Bartenders at the Red Lion were not there to absorb the trials and depressions of the clientele. The clientele had few trials and fewer depressions. They were in Hawaii to let go. Bartenders at the Lion had to pour at kick-ass speed or they were gone faster than a Sunday morning thunderstorm over the Pali Pass.

At 8:00 p.m. on a warm, windy January night, four young women entered the lower level of the Red Lion, two days after the quartet had arrived on their fifth or sixth trip to Hawaii. Travel agents received constant complimentary trips in exchange for favorable booking recommendations. The bar was typically crowded. The Red Lion was not a dance club, but a matrix of energy, an anomaly in the choreographed world of cloned entertainment. After eight, there was a five-dollar cover. No clubs could charge a cover without live music. The lines began to form after 11:00 p.m. Locals rarely ventured out to the clubs before midnight.

Kirsten Myers and three friends from the Mile High Travel Agency in Denver finally found a spot at the bar. Kirsten Myers was only five-foot two inches tall and weighed no more than one hundred pounds. Kirsten carried a slight bronze to her skin. Long, full auburn hair fell seductively on bare shoulders. A chartreuse beaded bra hidden under a Calvin Klein white, silk lace blouse was buttoned only once at the bra line. Tight, blue jean shorts rode up the back of both thighs and pulled the shorts tight within the backside curves. The shorts hung low in front and followed Kirsten's flat abdomen well below her hips. The colorful outline beneath the white lace teased the eye with erect silhouettes leaving little to the imagination. Kirsten's sophisticated sensuality cast a profile of sweat provoking chic. Kirsten exuded confidence, free from silly games. She flashed a smile that was all about winning over anyone to do anything gladly and without reservation. Kirsten's bedroom blue eyes and the natural beauty of a windy day caught the eye of Cody Law.

Kirsten Myers was born and raised in Castle Rock, Colorado. Located roughly thirty miles south of Denver, Castle Rock had been home to Kirsten's father, Dale Myers. Dale grew up the son of a stock contractor down on Crowfoot Road. Dale Myers drove eighteen wheel loads cross-country for thirty years. Kirsten's mother, Christine, tolerated the absence of her husband and found comfort in gin. Kirsten graduated from Douglas County High School in 1976. At the age of 18, Kirsten moved to Denver, ostensibly to be on her own and save for college. Actually, Kirsten wanted to move to New York City and take a flier on modeling. Initial inquiries expressed doubt due to her height. Torn between an untapped source of adventure and the comfort of Castle Rock's resident bad boy boyfriend, Billy Don Barrett, Kirsten relocated in Denver.

Cody was quick to address the four females at the bar. Bartenders at the Red Lion wore white tank tops and red shorts with the bar's logo sewn on the back pocket. Cody's long bleached hair, dark skin and ripped physique moved gracefully under the haunting neon light cast by a myriad of beer company signs. Every other bar and lounge on the island deemed it necessary to require the obligatory floral printed Hawaiian shirt as mandatory work attire. The girls ordered a Planters Punch, a Blue Hawaii and two

Quervo margaritas. Kirsten stood on the barstool to search her rear pocket for the money to pay for the drinks. Cody enjoyed the search. Before Kirsten could finish, a mangled hand slammed a fifty-dollar bill on the bar.

"The drinks are on me. Keep the change, *Amekoh*." A male voice announced with a slight Asian accent, referring in Japanese to Cody Law. The man was from Tokyo and rather large. His name was Seikichi Tokashiki. Two other men entered the club with Tokashiki. "What is your name, young lady?" The question was directed to Kirsten.

"My name is no thank you." Kirsten reached onto the bar and gave the fifty-dollar bill back to the Japanese man standing behind her. She handed a twenty to Cody. "Is that enough?" Kirsten asked.

"Plenty." Cody lied.

Seikichi Tokashiki moved closer to Kirsten. He did not appreciate the abrupt dismissal. A loose Hawaiian shirt on each member of the Japanese trio revealed a kaleidoscope of colors on their chests and arms. Cody had been schooled on the yakuza.

"Do you always speak for the others in your group?" Tokashiki asked. Thick black hair, layered stylishly long hung deep into his eyes.

"Did you hear anyone arguing?" Kirsten had developed an instinctive wit to combat the constant advances that always accompanied her travels.

"Maybe they were just about to speak up." The persistent patron placed the fifty back down on the bar. "I'll get the next round. Hey, *ketoh*, ring up the next round and keep the change." Tokashiki's menacing stare never left Kirsten.

"The ladies declined, sir." Cody politely responded. "Move on."

The tone climbed a notch. At the same time, Cody hit the small button under the front bar. A very bright strobe beam began to spray a light show across the walls of the club. The light was not overwhelming, yet deceptively intense while streaming in rhythm to the music. The light did not arouse any suspicion. The light did, however, alert Tuanni Kapo of a problem at the bar.

"Move on means move on. The ladies aren't buying the Kokuruyu-kai or Black Dragon thing." Cody repeated while leaning closer over the bar. Over the months, Cody Law had become fascinated with many aspects of the Japanese culture and history. Cody could see Tuanni Kapo approaching from the back of the club.

"Fuck you, my little bar friend. We will move on when we fucking feel like moving on. Do you know who we are?" Tokashiki spoke louder and his companions stood like painted mannequins poised for trouble.

"If I guess wrong, do I still get to keep the fifty." Cody answered sarcastically while picking up the fifty and smiling. Tuanni Kapo arrived behind the confrontation at the bar.

"Back away from the bar, sir." Tuanni Kapo sternly ordered. Teki Hana arrived with Tuanni Kapo. Teki was an assistant manager at the Red Lion, a former offensive tackle for the University of Hawaii and the New Jersey Generals of the World Football League. The tattooed man at the bar turned slowly toward Tuanni Kapo.

"I find it hard to imagine that hospitality is treated so rudely in your club, my friend. A man offers a lady a drink and this is the result? You are making a mistake, my friend." Tokashiki stepped away from the bar and slowly slid back his loud Hawaiian shirt. Tucked neatly in his trousers was a 1972 Redhawk 357 Magnum pistol. The subtle move was designed to freeze the massive presence of Tuanni Kapo.

In a moving sequence of extraordinary speed and split-second precision, Tuanni Kapo reached down and pulled the pistol from his guest. With his other hand, Tuanni grabbed the man's throat and lifted him against the bar. With the weapon, Tuanni slammed the barrel of the gun into Tokashiki's gasping mouth, breaking three teeth. Tuanni shoved the barrel deep down the man's throat causing him to choke and gag. The two yakuza at the doorway turned and ran up the stairs and outside, heading west on Kuhio Avenue.

"Cody, find Yoho and Bryant on the street." Tuanni barked in reference to the two officers working Kuhio and the marketplace on Thursday nights. "Call the district before you leave. Teki, search this prick for any more toys."

Sekichi Tokashiki now hung by Tuanni Kapo's gargantuan left arm. Tokashiki had been stunned by the swiftness and force that had him pinned against one of four twelve-inch bar support beams. His feet were at least six inches off the floor. Kapo's arm felt like a sledgehammer while keeping the 357 barrel jammed deep into Tokashiki's mouth. The steel shank began to cause his body to shake in a convulsive impulse to regurgitate.

"Don't you fucking throw up on me, mother fucker." Tuanni commanded.

The girls had moved away. Cody was just reaching the foot patrol in Waikiki. Teki had begun to search the man for more weapons. Kapo's grip tightened. He did not like to be intimidated by anyone, especially the yakuza. Normally, the Japanese underworld figures did not create this type of public disturbance. Kapo suspected the men in his club were unaccepted or unsponsored factions of the closed Japanese underworld. Yakuza in full standing would not degrade themselves or the organization in the manner these men did.

"Ahhhhhyyyyy...." Teki Hana screamed at a sonic level, jolting everyone in the club. The scream uprooted the music and Hana jumped back holding his arms up in a catatonic frozen stare. "The mother fucker went to the bathroom." Hana yelled while staring at his hands.

"Don't you piss on my floor." Kapo turned to the man he continued to hold upright.

"He didn't piss on your floor!" Teki Hana yelled back. "The mother fucker shit in his pants while I was frisking him! I felt it come out. Get him the fuck outside, now, Tuanni."

Tuanni Kapo turned to Sekichi Tokashiki with a look of horror. "Did you shit in your pants?"

The question came fast and the gun remained jammed down Tokashiki's throat. "Tell me, you did not shit in your pants."

Kapo kept repeating the same line as he pulled the man upstairs toward the door, never releasing the gun jammed into Tokashiki's mouth. The answer to Kapo's questions became rather obvious. Tuanni Kapo turned his face from the malodorous load he carried up the stairs.

"Yattenai...yattenai." Tokashiki's muffled, emphatic denials kept coming. Tokashiki could barely utter a sound with the better part of a seven-inch gun barrel wedged into his mouth. "Yattenai, yattenai. (Japanese for denial, not me)"

"Oh, man. I don't fucking believe this." The last statement Tuanni Kapo could be heard uttering before they reached the doorway and the waiting police.

The commotion ended with Seikichi Tokashiki handcuffed and placed in the backseat of an HPD squad car. Two very unhappy officers wrote the complaint and contemplated dropping their cargo into the Ala Wai Canal. The squad car pulled away from the club at 9:10 p.m. Unfortunately, the rear windows in the squad did not roll down. The small crowd gathered outside the entrance to the Red Lion dispersed quickly. Kirsten Myers and her friends returned to the bar rather anxiously. Cody Law slipped underneath the bar after reminding Teki Hana that his face resembled something from the Exorcist at his moment of discovery.

"Interesting club." Kirsten Myers commented to Cody Law. "What's next?" Kirsten smiled.

"Stick around." Cody smiled back.

"Am I supposed to thank you or is that just part of your job?" Kirsten coyly inquired.

"Part of the job, my ass!" Cody replied mischievously. "Hell, I risked my life to thwart the clear and present danger that reared an ugly head tonight. According to ancient Hawaiian tradition, you are obligated to repay the gesture."

"Amazingly convenient tradition, isn't it?" Kirsten was interested.

"Hawaii is an amazing place." Cody laughed. "Fortunately for you, there is a way to alleviate your obligations."

"I'm listening." Kirsten sipped the new Pina Colada, frothing over the pineapple rimming the hurricane glass.

"Two days ago..." Cody stopped and addressed the new customers approaching behind Kirsten and her friends. Cody made the drinks and returned to Kirsten Myers.

"Two days ago, we were jamming in front of the Royal, when one of my friends tells me that the Eagles are staying at the Royal Hawaiian. Not all of them, but Glenn Frey, Joe Walsh and Timothy Schmit are guests at the Royal. Don Henley was staying with friends on the North Shore. This guy is telling me this because Frey and Walsh want to join the frisbee toss on the beach. Two hours later, I'm sitting at the bar in Davy Jones' Locker, drinking Heinekens with Glenn Frey and Joe Walsh from the Eagles. Frey gives me two tickets to a midnight show inside Diamond Head tonight. I'll have to clear this with my boss, but would you be my guest to a special Eagles concert at midnight inside Diamond Head Crater. Chances are good that you may be relieved of all Hawaiian traditional obligations after attending the concert." Cody waited while he spun the gin and vodka bottles up in the air simultaneously beginning a Long Island Iced Tea.

"You drank beers and played frisbee with Glenn Frey, yesterday?" Kirsten lost a bit of her cover girl cool.

"I think it was Tuesday." Cody raised his eyebrows. "The concert? Are we on? I've got to clear it with a very large man, so I may need some time."

"You want me to go to an Eagles concert inside Diamond Head Crater with you, tonight?" Kirsten stumbled.

"Is everyone from Denver, this sharp?" Cody leaned closer across the bar. The twenty year-old beauty from Colorado looked at her girlfriends.

"I'll go." One of Kirsten's girlfriends spoke up. Cody smiled and looked back to Kirsten.

"Love to." Kirsten folded her arms and sat back in her barstool. "Will I arrive like Cinderella in a horse-drawn carriage?"

"Nope, a Kawasaki 750." Cody called Tuanni Kapo from the bar.

Diamond Head Crater lies along the southeast shoreline of O'ahu. Normally concerts are held at the Waikiki Shell in Kapi'olani Park directly next to the crater. On this Thursday night, the stage was built at the north end, inside the crater. Four thousand folding chairs were arranged with military precision in front of the stage. The remaining seating comprised the rising slopes along the inside of Diamond Head's ocean lip. The setting was spectacular. The clear, windy night pushed the trade winds down from the mountains above Honolulu. The winds cooled the floor of the crater to a pleasant seventy-four degrees. Tuanni Kapo had not only agreed to cover for Cody, Kapo offered his motorcycle for the evening. Kapo was grateful for the way Cody handled the yakuza problem.

The ride to Diamond Head was short. Cody spun up into the Heights for the long way around. With Kirsten's arms wrapped around his waist and her chest pressed up against his back, Cody was not in a tremendous hurry to arrive. Kirsten and Cody left the Red Lion at 11:15 p.m. They arrived at their seats just before midnight. Kapo had slid a bottle of cabernet into the saddle-bags on the bike. The bottle, a corkscrew and two plastic cups were all they carried into the crater. Cody never imagined the seats that Glenn Frey gave out were first row, center stage. Cody Law and Kirsten Myers were led to the stage and their seats, not five feet from the front of the security line. At exactly midnight, the lights were suddenly shut off. All stage lights, security lights and overhead lights were turned off in unison. Thirteen thousand fortunate fans began to scream, whistle and applaud in the darkness. The noise grew quickly in anticipation of the opening act. All concerts began with an opening act. The rumor circulated that a Chicago trio called Aliota, Haynes and Jeremiah opening for the Eagles. An acoustic sound from the north side of Chicago, Cody looked forward to the set.

Figures could vaguely be seen running across the stage. Small red lights led the musicians to their perch. The crowd was clapping in pounding sequence for the music to begin. A petulant cloud of cannabis swirled in the trades within the crater. The stars began to brighten the sky. The darkened strings of a classical guitar echoed through the twin speaker towers. The Spanish riffs were unusual and exotic. The crowd grew silent while trying to grasp the direction they were being led. The rifts slowed to a single note. Henley hit two staggering snare drums. The stage lights flashed on with the strength of runway floods. Don Henley was kissing the microphone. The verse began unmistakably.

On a dark desert highway,
Cool wind in my hair...

The Eagles were on stage. There would be no opening act. At precisely midnight, the most popular band in the United States, opened their show with *Hotel California*, arguably the most popular song of the decade. The crowd stood in shock. Kirsten Myers espied the stage in disbelief. Suddenly, chills ran down her arms. Cody Law stared in stoic admiration as one band had the audacity to begin a concert with the biggest hit of their careers.

The Eagles did not gavotte on stage. There would be no narcissistic hysteria on stage. The Eagles exude confidence from the opening song to the acoustic rendition of *Best of My Love*, closing the show at 1:45 a.m. With Don Henley, Glenn Frey, Joe Walsh and Timothy Schmit all seated on tall stools to close the show, the audience sensed they had been witnessing a very special show.

Cody leaned over to kiss Kirsten at the first bridge in the closing song,

Best of My Love, a romantic anthem even when heard in the most mundane surroundings. Inside Diamond Head, the closing song thrashed the libido inside two strangers. Cody began slowly, lightly touching Kirsten's lips. Cody pulled back and kissed her again, gently. This time he did not pull away. They finished two minutes and thirty seconds later when the song and the concert ended.

Southeast O'ahu meanders around the base of the Ko'olau Mountains to form the treacherous and scenic bodysurfing venues some twenty minutes outside of Waikiki. H-I evolves into Kalanianaole Highway, which hugs the coast to the windward side of the island. On the ocean side of the road, Cody and Kirsten flew aboard the nimble motorcycle accelerating through the low volcanic pulchritude along the sea. The concert kept replaying song after song under the half-moon dancing along the coastline. Cody laughed as his right hand gunned the Kawasaki, pulling Kirsten even closer.

The turquoise lagoon of Hanauma Bay laid dormant in the darkness. The underwater wildlife preserve was desolate in the early morning hours. Tour buses, diving companies and snorkeling companies threatened the very existence of a sanctuary bordered by Witches' Brew and Toilet Bowl. The Kawasaki slid along the Kalanianaole, while Kirsten marveled at the moonlit white sandy beaches and the lava shores. The Halona Blowhole spewed a geyser of ocean water through an irregular chimney of lava on the shelf below the highway. The motorcycle downshifted past Sandy Beach and climbed the last mile to Makapu'u Point and Makapu'u Beach, the most famous bodysurfing beach in the islands. Surfboards were not permitted.

Makapu'u means bulging eye, named after a stone image with eight protruding eyes in a cave at the base of Makapu'u Point. The waters were extremely dangerous and unpredictable. With no protecting reef, enormous swells rolled in slowly before crashing near the shore. Bodysurfers have a long ride before the fear of hitting the coral rushes in. Red lifeguard flags signify no swimming.

Makapu'u Point is a craggy palisade rising 420 feet above the turbulent seas. On the summit, facing the perilous Ka'iwi Channel is the Makapu'u Light House, land-fall light for vessels bound for the mainland. The light is clearly visible from the deck of a ship twenty-eight miles off shore and has been reported from as far away as fifty miles. The Makapu'u Light House oversees the white sand and black lava cliffs of Makapu'u Beach. The beam hovers over the deserted swells and pounding surf. Cody and Kirsten walked slowly down to the ocean's edge. The trade winds had died and the summer breeze barely moved the spray from the breaking waves. Headlights above slid effortlessly past the point. Kirsten gripped Cody's hand.

"Have you been here before?" Kirsten asked.

"We come here for the bodysurfing. When the red flags are out, the rush is phenomenal." Cody answered. "I wanted to show you my favorite spot on the island."

"The question still stands. Have you been here before, at this time...you know?" Kirsten probed, seeking an answer and not wanting to hear the answer.

"What was your favorite part of the concert?" Cody changed the subject. They were standing face to face. Cody gripped both of Kirsten's hands. Her body stiffened.

"That bad, huh?" Kirsten smiled.

"Stay with me. What was your favorite part of the show?" Cody repeated.

"I don't know. I liked the entire show, start to finish." Kirsten didn't follow.

"I have never brought anyone to this point for any reason other than bodysurfing." Cody pulled Kirsten closer and kissed her. The waters crashed around them, running up over their knees.

"This night is extraordinary. Occasionally, we are fortunate to find ourselves in an uncomfortable position that we have sought forever. It will end Kirsten, but it has to finish first. Remember, start to finish. You are going home in a day or two. I don't know much about what is destined to happen, but I can believe past my own dumb luck that you did not just happen to walk into the Lion tonight. I told you before we left, that you would be freed from all traditional Hawaiian obligations after the concert. I lied. There are only two fantasies that I have had during my life that did not involve sports or something to do with an engine. The first has come true. It has to do with being in a place like this with a girl like you." Cody's hair hung over his eyes. Kirsten could see the clear white outlines beneath the sun-bleached blond hair.

"What's the second?" Kirsten's breath was becoming shorter. The ocean calmed as if on cue.

"The second fantasy is about to come true." Cody replied assuredly.

"Really?"

"Absolutely."

"Damn, you may be right." Kirsten ran her hands up under Cody's shirt and lifted the white tank top over his head. Cody unbuttoned Kirsten's white lace cover, removing it slowly. Kirsten unhooked a beaded bra and let it fall to the water. She kissed Cody and pressed hard into his mouth. Cody and Kirsten fell to their knees in the wet sand about fifteen feet from the water. The waves rushed over the sand, an intermittent stream of frothy white salt water. The storybook ambience of the isolated setting cushioned the sand against Kirsten's back. The infinite grains retained warmth from the daytime sun. The lighthouse beacon beamed silently above. Kirsten guided Cody's entrance. The sand rolled with each slow penetration. Kirsten arched her back and felt the sand fill her hair. The warm tumbling water enhanced life's most pastoral pleasure.

* * *

One year later

Cody Law was looking forward to returning to the Chicago area after being on the island for nearly eighteen months. Cody dropped out of school at the University of Hawaii near the end of spring term, 1978. Less than four weeks before finals, he had not purchased the books for three of his classes and was terminally behind in the other two. Cody had begun to work more hours at the Red Lion during the spring of '78. Tuanni Kapo lost one assistant manager and turned to Cody to pick up the responsibilities. By late summer, Cody was doing all the ordering for the bar. Tuanni conferred with Cody on all new hires.

In the restaurant business, young managers enjoy the title. While the actual hourly wage bordered on minimum wage, a twenty-eight thousand dollar salary tag sounded progressive at age twenty. The daunting task of scrambling to catch up in all five classes, two of which Cody had never attended, proved untenable. Cody left school in early May, 1978.

The months that followed were an epochal marathon between working tremendous hours and the plethora of women shuffling from the Lion to 444 Nahua. The Red Lion position began to approach seventy-five hours weekly by the fall. Work had deteriorated into a hedonistic whine-athon from a generation, too selfish to even hide behind a cloak of social consciousness. Timothy Leary had created a monster. Leary gave an army of brats that existed solely on Daddy's dime, a nihilistic excuse to get fucked-up. Cody grew to loath the sniveling underachievers that arrived in the islands daily. Cody would work through New Year's, take a couple weeks to visit some friends on Maui and head back to Chicago in late January, 1979. After an afternoon workout at the Royal, Cody was shuffling through the mail prior to leaving for the Red Lion. The date was January 6, 1979. The letter was addressed to Cody. The return address was Castle Rock, Colorado under the initials, KMB.

Dear Cody,

It has taken awhile to write this letter. By now, you have probably moved to some beachfront house on the windward side of O'ahu. My one letter may never find you, but there have been many written and rewritten in my mind.

I will never forget the Eagles concert at Diamond Head and I will never forget the Point at Makapu'u. I lived the night most women only read about. I will always hold you in my heart for that one night. You gave me a past that neither brings sadness or regret. You gave me a daughter on a deserted beach in paradise. Her name is Devon.

I moved back to Castle Rock after I found out I was pregnant. I knew it was yours. Not having the baby was never an option. My former boyfriend welcomed me back without question. We moved in together and I never spoke about Hawaii. The pregnancy seemed natural and Billy Don Barrett welcomed the news that he was about to become a father. We were married a month later. Billy Don Barrett is Devon's father on her birth certificate. We are doing fine. I am not writing you because I want or need anything. Billy Don is doing great. He's about to take over his father's business, a huge brickyard halfway between Denver and Castle Rock. They have over one-hundred employees and supply bricks and concrete to half the state.

I'll never forget what happened between us. I wake up to her every morning. Our daughter has sunshine in her eyes. You did good, haole boy! Thank god for old Hawaiian folklore, hey Cody Law?

Kirsten Myers Barrett

* * *

~CHAPTER II~

Early, 1990

The building at the corner of Dearborn and Ontario in Chicago was built in 1892. The architect was Henry J. Cobb, whose many contributions to the city landscape included the main campus at the University of Chicago. The new home for the Chicago Historical Museum at Dearborn and Ontario stood nearly six stories tall. The building was constructed entirely of Wisconsin granite without the use of plywood, wood support beams, oak flooring or any wood products whatsoever. The aforementioned, growing as an aberration from the recent Great Chicago Fire.

Cody had been following the rumors in the trade publications about Desperado Entertainment, Incorporated, an emerging restaurant and night-club conglomerate started by Law in the early eighties. The trade papers had Desperado Entertainment., Inc. purchasing the property at the corner of Dearborn and Ontario. The Chicago Historical Museum had long since departed. The building sat vacant for years before the River North explosion in Chicago. The property had been purchased some years ago by Sandy Gallen and opened as The LC244 Nightclub in Chicago. While the LC244 in New York remained cutting edge, the club in Chicago faded after the initial curiosity eroded. The eerie caged dancers amidst a maze of private little rooms held fascination from Soho down to Central Park, but fizzled in the windy city.

Law kept reading about his impending deals with Gallen, a man whom he had never met. Finally, Law became intrigued by the speculation and placed a call to Gallen in New York. A starker trade was hammered out between the attorneys, culminating with the exchange of properties. Starker trades involve real estate swaps. Law gave up a suburban three-acre site in a real estate swap for the granite icon across from Chicago's Hard Rock Café. Starker trades have been employed as popular loopholes to capital gains taxes, primarily in real estate.

Cody knew what he wanted in the space and the transformation began immediately. Desperado Entertainment, Inc. owned ten different venues in the city and suburbs. The venues included fine dining, sports restaurants and bars, country music clubs, a blues club, and trendy late night bars where covers get you in only if the guest list bears your name. Cody Law had drawn the new club in his head for years.

Over the years, Cody had learned that instincts became stale within every firm. Outside ideas were often needed to jumpstart new directions. Not this time. The new stepchild for Desperado Entertainment was born from CEO and President, Cody Law's imagination. Renovation of the LC244 began after New Year's, 1989. The final party of the year at LC244 was for the employees. They left an indelible message carved into every room of the club, *FUCK LAW*. The message energized Cody during the renovation period, lasting nearly one-year.

To the financial advisers and accountants of Desperado Entertainment, Law was placing the firm in harm's way. Halfway through the reconstruction, the budget was tapped for the club. Cody and Gary Deitz, Desperado's Vice-President of Operations, had woefully underestimated the spiraling costs. Contractors were made aware of the financial problems. They had been paid for the work to date, but any future work would be solely dependant on the club's completion and success. The contractors chose to stick it out, meaning to roll the dice on completion and success.

The format was massive. The main level would house three separate bars. The predominant room on the main floor was a museum for motorcycles. Hanging or perched on specially built platforms were vintage Indians, BSA's, Nortons, Triumphs, BMW's, and a variety of early Kawasaki crotch rockets, Honda's four-stroke front-loaded imports, and two rare Ducati's. The room was about the bikes. There was little in the way of cluttered paraphernalia. Strategically hung leather jackets marked the walls and an array of helmets from across the country, dotted the ceiling. Each helmet had been customized to represent a specific region or sponsor.

The main floor featured a blues bar, a comedy club, and a dueling piano bar. The ground floor, one level below the main floor, was devoted to billiards, darts, televisions, and over one-hundred video games. Food was served on the lower level and the main floor. The ground floor boasted four different bars, four tub stations, and numerous shot girls. The upper level, accessible only from the main floor, was the heart of the club. The first two levels drew the tourists and suburban crowds. These patrons were crucial to the success of the club, especially given the enormous dimensions involved with a six-story club.

The personality of the club began on top. Access to the top floors was restricted and pricey. Covers started at $10 on weeknights, escalating to $30 on Friday and Saturday night. Drink prices had no breaks for wells and calls. All drinks were $8. All beers were $6. The top club housed three separate levels to the same dance floor. A tiered set of balconies hung precariously over the dark pulsating dance floor. Cody's promoted theme was defiance and the upper club was the backdrop for the Hell's Angels Motorcycle Club. The upper club featured motorcycles as well. The only bikes displayed in the upper club were Harleys. The winged skull of the HAMC (Hell's Angels Motorcycle Club) hung over the stairway. The words, *Live To Ride, Ride To Live*, were carefully inscribed on the doorway to the club. Cody Law carefully planned this nightclub.

The club's attraction, as explained by Cody Law, would be simply based on the premise that rebellion and some degree of danger or uncertainty will attract all ages. Women have always been attracted to bad boys. The principal is not complicated. Society has always condemned the non-conformist. The Hell's Angels represented the ultimate expression of rebellion. The Angels placed a draconian enigma on the back of a loud machine and society backed away. They managed to exist within their own set of rules and laws based on numbers. Mess with one Angel and you will encounter the entire chapter. One particular by-law of the Hell's Angels calls for the immediate expulsion of a member who does not stand up and fight for another member regardless of the circumstances.

They are the "one percenters" as referred to by the American Motorcycle Association. The AMA called the outlaw motorcycle gang the unwelcome one percent of all decent and law-abiding motorcycle riders in this country. Cody wanted the club to glide the edge of acceptability, to embrace the nefarious and to inject the city with audacious insurrection. The lower levels were holding tanks to a separate world upstairs. The club featured exclusively Harley Davidson Motorcycles. Cody cut deals with the two Harley Davidson dealers near River North. They provided most of the bikes in exchange for prominent plaques as to where the bikes came from. Some long time employees of the dealers provided bikes for display.

The Chicago Chapter of the Hell's Angels provided vintage 74" Harley Choppers. Hung precariously from a thirty-foot ceiling over the main bar, a 1965 Harley chopped panhead, hovered like a licentious pagan deity. Invisible wires cast the stripped down, eight-hundred pound mass of chrome and iron as the holy grail. FXR's, FXRT's, Sportsters, Electra Glides, and Softails reigned above like clouds of masculine imagery. Cody spent over one hundred thousand dollars in securing the design to support the motorcycles.

The club used the custom designed FXR Harleys with extended forks, small front wheels and elaborate chrome additions as the station seating for tub girls clad in thongs and tiny bathing suits. Doormen were actual members of the Hell's Angels. Working alongside Cody's internal security men, the Angels served back-up roles behind the full-time security staff in the event of a fight. Fights occurred often. Every nomadic bad-ass with a few drinks wanted to take on an Angel. HAMC colors were worn on cut-off blue jean jackets. No one wore the colors and patches of the Hell's Angels except members of the motorcycle club itself.

This was not a nightclub with a gift shop. Most HAMC members worked without shirts under the patched jackets. Arms and chests were covered with tattoos. Even as the nineties approached, HAMC members continued to sport long hair, long beards and the general appearance of a marauding Hun. The publicity created by the comparison to the Stones concert at Altamont, California in 1969 was precisely what Cody had hoped for. Why would Cody's new club employ members of the Hell's Angels. A fan was stabbed to death at Altamont because the Hell's Angels lost control. Had the HAMC miraculously transformed itself into a responsible entity suitable for employment in a volatile industry? Of course not.

No other timeless symbol emphatically represents defiance as the motorcycle. The loud, masculine, Harley-Davidson testosterone machines, thundering at high speeds on the highways driven by an unkempt mass of hair and tattoos brought the door locks down every time. The Hell's Angels survived as losers who apologized for nothing. They traveled in numbers and the numbers counted for the freedom and the fear that followed them. The Angels did not submit quietly to the expectations of upward mobility in society. Their future consisted of self-gratification for the day. Exploit the framework of acceptability and then create one's own society complete with rules, by-laws, officers and traditions.

The Hell's Angels would not wear leather jackets or allow any leather jackets to be displayed within the upstairs club. Leather jackets were a symbol of weakness because they absorbed a great deal of damage in a fall from a motorcycle. Angels wore denim or nothing. The Angels colors would not be displayed on any leather jackets.

The press devoured Cody's new club. Lines often stretched three blocks long and many customers never got in after waiting all night. Guest list passes to the main floor were coveted. The upper club was even harder to reach. The music exploded through a two-hundred thousand dollar sound system. The club was simple. Loud, dangerous and women loved it. Club success on any level has to attract females. Cody Law named his new club, *Fat Boys*, derived from the newest addition to the Harley Davidson line-up of beefy road bikes.

The enormity of Fat Boys placed Desperado Entertainment, Inc. in jeopardy. Six floors of operation, twenty-two bars, countless tub stations and a twelve-hundred square foot cooler for beer demanded a mind-boggling up-front cash outlay. The bars alone needed forty thousand dollars in change to open. The bars and coolers needed an opening COD beer order of thirty-one thousand dollars. Cody Law was forced to take on a one-million dollar lease for cash. A leasing company would front Cody and Desperado Entertainment one million dollars. Cody personally guaranteed the lease. Cody needed the money to purchase everything from glasses to toilet paper. The payments incurred would work out to twenty-two thousand dollars per month for five years. The club opened with three hundred forty employees. Weekly grosses were exceeding $150,000. The gamble worked. Fat Boys became the hottest club in Chicago almost immediately after the doors opened in January, 1990.

In 1979, Cody Law returned from Hawaii. Plans were sketchy at that point, but Cody had intended to seek employment for the immediate future in the Rush Street area of the city. Shortly after his arrival back on the mainland, Cody ended up tending bar at the Lodge, a 4:00 a.m. joint on Division Street in Chicago. The popular bar was small, but unusually crowded throughout the evening. The doors opened at 4:00 p.m. The Lodge served no food except for an endless supply of salted peanuts in the shell. The steady crowd grew markedly after the 2:00 a.m. bars closed.

The Lodge was an icon on the Gold Coast for employees in the restaurant and bar business. The destination of choice after work for scores of wound up waiters, waitresses and bartenders possessed with a pocketful of cash and the need to make up for lost time. Tips reflected the self-aggrandizing need to stuff an evening into less than two hours. The earlier crowd, blended a general mix of Werner Erhard sheep, pseudo-existential sissies searching for the elusive inner child, and the delusional, over-dressed fossils chasing a chimera of youthful nymphomaniacs that were attracted to thinning hair combed over a bald palate. The peanut shells on the floor grew like a January snowstorm, while the pin-striped neophytes thinned out around midnight.

Desperado Entertainment, Inc. was born on North Avenue in the fall of 1979. Cody Law had saved $10,000 in eight months since returning from the islands. Cody convinced the jukebox operator at the Lodge to front $25,000 for the exclusive game rights to the new club and a percentage of ownership. Electricians, plumbers and carpenters donated time for a small percentage and free suds. On Halloween, 1979, Cody Law opened Law and Order, a small tavern located at 5340 West North Avenue.

Cody worked the bar himself. The joint did over $300,000 during the first year. Cody worked every night, packing a Browning revolver in the back of his pants. Law and Order was anything but law and order. The first year, the working class tavern averaged one major fight every other night. Cody never pulled his gun, but lost track of the fractured jaws courtesy of a short nightstick he used often. Cody never tried to reason with a mean drunk. Off-duty cops began to discover Law and Order, a proprietor's dream.

The Roadhouse, Cody's second establishment, opened in 1980 in Edison Park. The Roadhouse quickly became the proto-type success wagon for the eighties. A somnolent end to the seventies, opened the door for an operator wise enough to sense the prevailing musical trends and the advent of multiple television monitors throughout the club. The residential neighborhood surrounding Law and Order had grown tired of the late night fights, drunks urinating on lawns and vehicles, and the general deterioration of the business community. By the time the residents along and near North Avenue voted the Ward dry in late 1980, Cody Law and the Roadhouse were approaching two million dollars for the first year in Edison Park.

Cody emulated Chicago nightclub icon, Butch McGuire. Butch McGuire's tavern on Division Street was often referred to as the first true singles bar. Butch always poured a myriad of unique draft beers, preached immediate beverage service and kept a simple, affordable menu available at all times. If customers left to eat, they rarely came back. The Roadhouse served half-pound burgers for $1.95 and all-you-can-eat sea baskets for $3.95. Liquor drove the apple cart. Ten years and eleven locations later, Desperado Entertainment, Inc. opened *Fat Boys.*

Cadrell Easley paced the small stairwell landing. *Fat Boys* was crowded on a Thursday night. The line up to the upper club stretched down the stairs and into the main floor bar. Cadrell was in Chicago for an officer training class at the Northwestern Center for Public Safety. Cadrell was an officer with a Colorado Police Officer contingent in Chicago to attend a three-week class on drug enforcement tactics. The thirty-member troupe was housed in the Orrington Hotel in Evanston, Illinois. Two NYPD Narcotics Detectives and two DEA Agents presented the current class. Many other sessions were presented by Chicago Police Detectives, as well as, visiting officers from numerous Law Enforcement Federal Agencies. Seasonal classes at Northwestern included administrative classes, homicide classes and the current narcotics classes. The sessions drew from police departments all over the country.

After one week of classes and room service, Cadrell and a number of other Colorado Police Officers decided to venture into the city for an evening out. The answer to every question as to where to go in Chicago included Cody Law's new club. The group arrived at 9:30 p.m. The Colorado visitors paid the initial cover of five dollars each to enter the club. They enjoyed a couple of beers at the main bar, but were somewhat taken aback by the price. At any Colorado liquor store, one could pick up a twelve-pack for six dollars, the Fat Boy's price for one beer.

The line upstairs intrigued the visitors. The scenery on the stairway beckoned more than curiosity. Even in the midst of a Chicago winter evening, the females in line mirrored the runways of a Versace fashion parade. Trendy neophytes hugged the stairway, fresh from Elizabeth Arden Salons, sporting drinks and filled with attitude. The clothes left little to the imagination. Cadrell, happily married, was born with cowboy charm and a wandering eye. After waiting nearly forty minutes, Cadrell and his friends arrived at the door to the upstairs club. The doormen included two of Cody Law's security staff and one member of the Hell's Angel's Chicago Chapter.

The cover to the upstairs club on a Thursday night was twenty dollars. Six rural police officers from Colorado were astounded at the cover.

"That will be $120.00 for your group to enter the club." A security employee announced.

"We just paid a cover to enter your club." A surprised police officer stated.

"The five dollar cover is for the main floor, sir. The upstairs club requires an additional twenty-dollar cover." The same security man explained.

"Twenty bucks a head after we waited forty minutes. Forget it boys, nothing in there is worth another twenty bucks." Cadrell blurted out.

"Move it along Flicka, you're holding up the line." The comment came from the bearded member of the Hell's Angels. The reference obviously reflected the Justin Ostrich boots and a prominent gold belt buckle Cadrell wore.

"What did you say?" Cadrell asked in response to the abrupt comment.

"If you do not want to pay the cover, sir, then we need to keep the line moving." A Fat Boy's security guard interjected.

"I'm sorry, I just waited forty minutes to find out we have to pay another twenty-bucks a head to enter this club. At the same time, the fat-ass behind you calls me Flicka and tells me to move along. Now, honestly, I'm not all that concerned about the progress of the line, but I am curious about why we are being asked to pay another twenty dollars while this bloated relic of a third-rate Ann-Margaret movie is insulting me?" Cadrell asked while moving up to the entrance.

"We told you once to move down the stairs. Now, trust me Tex, you are going down the stairs, one way or another." The HAMC member announced and moved into Cadrell's face.

"Is that a fact? Why do people east of the Mississippi River find it necessary to refer to all men wearing cowboy hats as Tex. All I get is *Howdy, Tex, What's up, Tex, What can I do for you, Tex.* You see, in a perfect world, I don't even like it when my friends call me Ace or pal. So you can imagine the way I feel when a scumbag like you calls me, Tex?" Cadrell replied.

At that moment, with Zen-like agility and surprising speed, Cadrell Easley locked into a handful of ratty beard and rendered a similar vice-grip on the Hun's groin. In one thunderous motion, with the exultation of a shot-putter, the overweight antagonist was launched down the stairs. The tumbling oaf barreled over scores of well-dressed patrons creating an avalanche of bodies on the stairway below. The two remaining security guards barked into walkie-talkies and rushed to restrain Cadrell Easley. Easley's stunned companions froze. Career suicide flashed among them and his remaining companions scattered. The commotion at the bottom of the stairway gave way to an onslaught of security men rushing up the stairs. Easley offered no resistance. Three security men led the Colorado police officer down the stairs. As he passed the bearded HAMC member, apparently injured from the fall, Cadrell Easley smiled and bent down, straining against the security men holding his arms.

"Hey, dick-head!" Easley barked. "Tough is a state of mind. Fuck's like you talk blood but few want to give it up. Mindless shit-heads buy big bikes, ride around with other mindless shit-heads and think they're tough. We spit up crap like you where I come from. Don't come looking for me because you won't like what you find."

"You're fucking dead." The fallen doorman grimaced through the broken ribs. Cadrell Easley smiled again while security pulled him away.

Cody Law walked outside the Fat Boy's main entrance. Cody had been inside the club when the fight on the stairs erupted. While the disturbance in itself posed nothing unusual, Cody was summoned outside because the disturbance was caused by a police officer. Cody's security team was trained to remove any individuals involved in a fight from the club. The Chicago Police Department parked a transport wagon in front of the club. The wagon served the entire River North District, although Fat Boys always provided the most customers.

When the security team brought Cadrell Easley to the officers out front, they discovered that Easley was a police officer. At this point, Cody Law was summoned. Law could decide to drop the issue and allow Easley to walk. As a fellow police officer, the Chicago uniforms on duty wanted Cody to make the call. Normally, they were instructed to assume the club would press charges on all incidents.

"My staff tells me that you threw one of our employees down the stairs because the high cover charge offended you. Is that true?" Cody asked Easley while the officer stood handcuffed in the cold. Cody lit a cigarette.

"Absolutely." Easley answered. "Do you mind if I grab some chew? It's in my left front pocket."

"Do police officers in Colorado believe they are above the law when they travel, Mr. Easley?" Cody asked while reaching in Easley's pocket and pulling out a package of Skoal. "How much of this crap do you want?"

"A chunk, if you don't mind?" Easley replied.

"You didn't answer my ..." Cody started to say.

"Please don't patronize me." Cadrell Easley interrupted. "They told me that you own this place. Your own employees goad patrons into a hostile confrontation and then threaten them. That fat fuck on the ambulance gurney they just wheeled away should be going to jail, not me."

"My club is unique, Mr. Easley. It can also be offensive to some. My apologies if one of my employees contributed or caused the disturbance." Cody stated with no intention of pursuing any charges. "Where in Colorado do you call home, Mr. Easley?"

"I live and work in Castle Rock, Colorado. I have been with the Castle Rock Police Department for two years. I am thirty-two years old." Cadrell answered. "I was born and raised in Colorado Springs, but moved to Castle Rock for the job."

"Before that?" Cody asked.

"Before Castle Rock, you mean?"

"Yes, I'm sorry. I wasn't very clear." Cody muffled voice was the result of a brisk wind blowing off the lake and slicing through each man like a knife. Both men had turned to avoid the brunt of the icy blast.

"Before Castle Rock, I rode saddle-bronc on the PRCA (The Professional Rodeo Cowboys Association) circuit for ten years. I was home sporadically and the body pounding began to add up. Never jumped into the top ten. Never made it the NFR Finals. I won less money in ten years than my father-in-law loses on vacation in Las Vegas every year. After my wife found out she was pregnant with our second child, the ultimatum came. It was time to find a real job." Cadrell Easley beamed when he spoke of chasing what his wife referred to as the endless mistress, dressed in boots and mud, while mocking their family with infinite entry fees and eight second dreams.

"Please unlock Mr. Easley." Cody instructed one of the police officers on the street. The police knew Cody Law. In fact, Cody was one of the more recognizable faces in the city. Cody's accomplishments had been the subject for numerous magazine cover stories.

"The firm will not be pursuing any charges against Mr. Easley. If you need to speak to Mr. Easley regarding any reports necessary, he and I will be in the club at the main bar." Cody turned to Cadrell Easley.

"Will you join me for a beer? The main bar will have to suffice. I can't stand the music upstairs."

"It sure beats jail." Cadrell Easley did not like the feel of handcuffs. He rubbed his wrists as the two men headed for the main entrance. "Mr. Law?"

"Cody, call me Cody. I guess we are about the same age."

"Cody, Thank you for what you did back there. My wife can attest to the fact that the incident on the stairs was not my first exposure to bad decisions. Since becoming a police officer, my meltdowns have decreased substantially, but there is a little roadhouse cannon inside that tends to reload every now and then."

" Let's go have a beer. It's getting too fucking cold out here." Cody Law pulled the main door open and two doormen scrambled to open the doors inside the vestibule. The two men settled at a small table near the Ontario Street side of the main floor. The club was bustling. Many of the patrons followed Cody with their eyes. Cody had redefined the club and restaurant venues within the city. Cody's forty-fourth floor capacious condominium at Lake Point Towers was the focus of a special Sunday Section in the Chicago Tribune during the fall.

The patrons in Fat Boys continued to follow Cody and his guest. A nervous waitress brought a couple of Bass Ales.

"You seem to be a marked man, Mr. Law." Easley observed.

"Cody, man. Remember. Every time I hear Mr. Law, I have the desire to turn and look for my father." Cody smiled.

"Cody, excuse me. I was brought up to call strangers Mister or Ma'am. That's not a cliché where I live. It is the way children are raised. Anyway, Cody, I read about you last year in People magazine. People is about the extent of my literary adventures, but I remember the article because you quoted an old Willie Nelson song in describing a rise to the top of your profession. The phrase stayed with me because I always felt the same words could have been written about my life;

My heroes have always been cowboys
And they still are it seems
Sadly in search of and one step in back of
Themselves and their slow moving dreams.

"You were quoted in the article by using these lyrics as best describing your ascent to the business success you now enjoy. I found it odd that you would use them. They are the lyrics of frustration. They represent a nomadic search guided by the heart for some Holy Grail that the mind must know does not exist. The way the magazine described your success, at thirty-two years old, frustration would hardly be the first thought one would conjure up." Cadrell Easley remarked.

"People want to see the narcissistic aspect of success. I can't go there, yet. What have I accomplished? I control a string of clubs and restaurants that may depend more on disconnected indulgence than understanding quality. My clubs cater to almost everything I detest, but they make a shit-load of money. I've got enough money. Most men spend the better part of their adult lives worried about making money. When they achieve financial success, they spend the remainder of their lives wishing they hadn't wasted the first part of their lives worried about money."

"Evolution is watching your father live the cycle and listen to yourself vow never to fall prey to the same thing. In the next act, you have taken the cycle to the next level. I turned shallow into an art form. I have had more meaningful relationships with my projects than the people I spend time with. How pathetic is that? Shit, you know the one girl that I always think about was from Castle Rock, Colorado." Cody finished his Bass Ale and corralled another round. The crowd watched Cody and Cadrell watched the crowd.

"I'm sorry, Cody. I didn't hear what you said about Castle Rock." Cadrell turned back to Cody after drifting momentarily. The background noise was growing steadily and the years of getting slammed into a dustbowl by an angry Mustang did not help any of his sensory functions.

"I said the only relationship that I still think about was with a girl from Castle Rock. Do you know a girl named Kirsten Myers? I only knew her for a couple days about twelve years ago. She might have married some guy from Castle Rock. I forget his name. Maybe Billy Bear, Bobby Joe, I don't remember. I know it sounded country, like a two-name first name. Kirsten was from Castle Rock. I remember that. I was tending bar in Hawaii when I met her. She was on vacation with some girlfriends. She was beautiful, but her eyes, I remember those eyes more than anything else. She had the eyes of an angel. I remember wondering, how do you talk to an angel? There are more things in my life that remind me of Kirsten Myers than I care to admit. I guess there will always be the ones we regret losing. Do you know if she is still around Castle Rock?" Cody asked and waited for Cadrell to respond. The boyish fascination associated with the evening thus far disappeared from Cadrell's face in an anguishing split-second.

"What is it?" Cody asked. The sudden change in his guest was disconcerting.

"You know Kirsten Myers?" Cadrell had hoped Cody mispronounced the name.

"That's right. Kirsten Myers. That was her maiden name. I cannot remember what her married name would be. She was planning to marry this guy when we met." Cody stopped again. The body language and the sullen demeanor of Cadrell Easley closed down the entire room.

"What is it, man? Your face and your silence are telling me that this girl has got to be dead." Cody waited.

"She may as well be, Cody." Cadrell began. "Kirsten Myers married a local high-school stud named Billy Don Barrett. Barrett was a football wonder boy in high school. Unfortunately, Billy drank himself into a permanent state of suspended animation. You know the type, Cody. Living on a quart of Jack and a resume filled with a first-team selection to a high school All-American team in 1976. Billy Don Barrett got mean in a hurry. From what I've been told, Barrett could have gone scholarship at CU or CSU in a heartbeat, but he drank himself off the list during the recruiting season." Cadrell grabbed his beer and took a long swallow.

"Kirsten told me that this guy was from some well to do family in Castle Rock. She told me that Billy Joe or Billy Don, whatever his name is, would be working for his father. The father owned some kind of large construction company?" Cody was lost.

"Billy Don Barrett's father took off when he was seven years old. Alvin Barrett is serving a life sentence at Rahway State Prison in New Jersey for beating a man to death during a gas station robbery. For the past ten or eleven years, Billy Don Barrett has been a fixture at the Rascal Flats, a dive tavern on the corner of Wilcox and Fourth Street in downtown Castle Rock. Cody, Billy Don Barrett married Kirsten Myers. He beats her on a regular basis. I have been called to the house on more than a dozen separate occasions during the past couple years. Each time, Kirsten refuses to press charges. The woman is petrified. My boss seems to turn his head. My chief and Barrett's old man go way back. We have been instructed to allow the family to work out their own problems." Cadrell stopped. Cody Law was visually uncomfortable.

"You all right?" Easley wanted to know.

"What about kids? Were there any kids?" Cody focused and spoke quickly, as if to avoid the answer.

"One child, a daughter, Devon, eleven or twelve years old. The motherfucker has beaten this child into a frightened shell. This family has become the single most frustrating aspect of my short career as a police officer. The little girl is a miniature replica of her mother. A striking pair with the same lost eyes. During each call to their home, Kirsten's hands trembled as she spoke. Her eyes never rose from the ground as she defended her husband on each visit. Devon sometimes stood next to her mother with her own eyes focused on something that was not there. There have been many dispirited calls to 222 Gilbert Street. We tame the moment, but we all fear the one call that will find someone dead. I'm sorry, man. How well did you know Kirsten?" Cadrell Easley finished.

"How well did I know Kirsten?" Cody repeated. He stared at Easley while taking deep breaths. Now, the real connotation of success made him want to vomit. "How well did I know Kirsten?" The question became recurrent.

"Devon is my daughter." Cody answered.

* * *

Gary Deitz was on the phone with the Chicago Sun-Times Entertainment Editor, Marsha May. Apparently, the Times ran a story in the Friday Section of the morning paper in which a source had reported that Cody Law and Desperado Entertainment, Inc. were in negotiations to purchase the five-star restaurant called LaBoheme, operating inside the Ritz-Carlton Hotel. The hotel is located a block off the Magnificent-Mile and behind Water Tower Plaza. The restaurant has been a Chicago icon for fifty-seven years, moving from the original location blocks away when the Ritz was built.

"Marsha, Marsha." Gary Deitz was laughing. "Cody has no more interest in LaBoheme than the doorman in your building. Desperado's definition of fine dining is to throw the largest side of beef on a plate and make sure the knives are sharp. You need to re-evaluate your sources, Marsha. Honestly, that property holds no interest for our firm and we are not negotiating with the Poussiere family to acquire their restaurant." Gary smiled and nodded on the phone.

"Thank you, Marsha. Please call me when you want any information on Desperado, Inc." Gary Deitz hung up. Cody Law was standing at his desk.

"How the fuck did she find out we are negotiating for La Boheme?" Cody knew the answer, but as CEO, he could vent.

"Poussiere's attorney had to leak. You know the owners wouldn't." Deitz replied.

"Whatever. I don't care. I need to talk to you, now." Cody sat down at Gary's desk. Cody never sat down at Gary's desk.

Desperado Entertainment, Inc. kept their corporate offices very separate from any of the club venues. DE, Inc. was headquartered in a nineteenth century brownstone located on N. State Street. Cody purchased the structure in 1984. Badly in need of rehabbing, the cost was $467,000. During the expansion of DE, Inc., Cody made use of the carpenters under contract for each venue. Over the course of two years, the property on N. State was completely gutted and had recently been appraised at $2.7 million.

The third floor belonged to Cody Law. Cody held court in an impeccable walnut enclave. Burgundy leather furniture was imported from Denmark. Cody's desk was used by William Jennings Bryant more than a century ago. Bookshelves lined the walls, floor to ceiling. The dark overtures were sprinkled with brilliant lines of sunlight dancing off an array of crystal glassware and the beveled glass skylight. Cody had not been afraid to show success.

"I'll be taking some time away from the business." Cody began. Gary Deitz knew the setting had to be a prelude to something unusual. Why else would Cody be at his desk?

"Man, I have never known you to be the vacation type?" Gary commented while certain Cody would not be heading to Atlantic City for a stroll down the boardwalk. There had to be another venue in the pot.

"Are we looking out of state?" Gary asked referring to expansion.

"We are most certainly not looking out of state. Trust me on this one. My time off does not have anything to do with the firm. I may be gone a week. I may be gone a month. Tell Poussiere's attorney that we are pulling back and are not prepared to proceed on any deal at this time. If he pushes, tell him that is all the information that he needs. If anything, the move will scale down their pedestal. If and when we decide to resume negotiations, the meetings will be on our terms. Henry Bolotin works for the Ritz Carlton. He was not hired by the Poussiere family. I wouldn't pay one hundred and twenty dollars per square foot for a location in the White House. I never liked that guy anyway. I hate guys with monogrammed shirts. What is that all about? Do we need our fucking initials embroidered on our cuffs? We are out. Bring Helton and Warring in for daily updates."

Brian Helton and Alexandra Warring worked directly beneath Gary Deitz. Each held the position of General Manger. Brian was General Manager/Restaurant and Catering. Alexandra had been brought in eighteen months prior as General Manager/Nightclub Division. Each club or restaurant had one Senior Manager and a staff of Assistant Managers, the number based on the size and volume of each venue.

"Change the mangers meetings from bimonthly to weekly. I'll talk to you daily, if I can. At the present, my plans are to be in Castle Rock, Colorado by tomorrow. I have a daughter living in Castle Rock, Gary. I never told you about the girl because I always believed that she was part of a well-to-do family in Castle Rock. I met her mother in Hawaii twelve years ago. I was with her once. Kirsten Myers was something very special. Before I left Hawaii, I received a letter from Kirsten. She gave birth to my child. Kirsten assured me that her new husband came from a wealthy local family and everyone would be fine. In my infinite compassion, I left things alone. Do you remember the catch phrase from many of the staff meetings?" Cody asked.

"There have been many, Cody. You can pull a quote from a book or a film like no one I have ever met." Gary smiled and shook his head.

"There have been many, you're right. I stand in fucking judgement of everyone on my staff and pontificate with every nickel and dime cliche. I told Brian last week that he did not listen as well as he hears. Brian should have told me to look in a fucking mirror. Twelve years ago, a girl wrote me a letter with one simple message. Kirsten asked for nothing. I was a father, but not to worry. The baby's life would be happy and the white picket fence was already being erected as the words were typed. Shit, Gary, I read only the ink on the paper. Kirsten was asking for my help simply by writing to me. Twelve years later, I can see that."

Cody got up and walked to the front window. He continued. "Rudy T.

got bounced down the stairs at Fat Boys last night. We were about to throw the launcher in jail when I discovered that he was an off-duty policeman from Castle Rock. They were in town to attend one of those seminars at Northwestern. I met him at the wagon on Dearborn. Christ, I wanted to congratulate the man on his performance. Rudy T. ended up at St. Viator's Emergency Room with some broken ribs and a broken wrist. We talked over a couple beers inside when the subject of Kirsten Myers came up. Kirsten married into a bad situation, not a wealthy local family. She tried to tell me this twelve years ago. Kirsten gave me the opportunity to change the direction of her life, yet I was only concerned about the direction of my life. I don't listen. I hear what I want to hear. Am I that way with my own people in the company?"

"All the time, Cody." Gary answered matter-of-factly.

"You're right, but you answered way too fast." Cody shook his head. "I am going to Castle Rock. I don't know anything more than what I have told you. I want to see Kirsten again. I want to meet my daughter."

"What do you think you are going to do, Cody?" Gary stood up. "You can't fix everything by ordering it fixed. There is a family that now, all of a sudden, you decide to become involved with? They may have something to say about that. Arrogance in business is tolerable and often rewarded. Bring it to Colorado and you may experience some catastrophic consequences. I think you have been on your own so long that you actually believe these people are waiting for you to arrive and save the day. You're my friend Cody, but don't walk into a room with the lights off and a blindfold on. You should be smarter than that now." Gary finished and was standing across the desk, eye to eye with Cody.

"I am going to Castle Rock in the morning. I expect you to handle things here until I return." Cody Law announced again.

"You know I will. You said it, Cody. You hear what you want to hear. For the record, you are going about things the wrong way. That's all I'm going to say." Gary sat down.

"What is for the record? Would you like to have this conversation typed up so we can sign it? I made a mistake twelve years ago that two people are paying dearly for. If I make another mistake, do you think we will need a signed affidavit to prove your intuitive hands off approach may have been the wiser road to follow? I am not going out there to watch. Too many people are doing that already." Cody reached out to shake hands with Gary as his second-in-command left the room.

* * *

Arriving in Colorado had always been a treat for Cody Law. Memories bore a smile from the days of visiting friends in Durango and the short trips to Telluride. Denver International Airport was a marriage between a P.T. Barnum mirage and the nightmare of Tokyo's Narita Airport. DIA is fifty-three square miles, more than twice the size of Manhattan. The airport inhabits more land than the city limits of Boston, Miami or San Francisco. Cody felt like he could nap between the terminal and the rental car agencies. The transit van pulled up to the Budget complex, Cody looked up to the infinite prairie surrounding the terminals and longed for the days of Stapleton.

Cody took the rented Jeep Wrangler down the access roads to Interstate 25 South. The winter had been mild and the roads out of Denver would be clear. The mountains painted a fading light show to the west, reminding Cody of the Thomas Kincaid paintings in his office on North State. Castle Rock waited thirty-two miles away.

" At the bend of Plum Creek stands a large flat-topped round rock resting on a pyramid-shaped base. It is an isolated part of the original rock formation, the softer part below being worn away. We find a crevice through which we climb to the top, fire off our guns and christen the place, "Castle Rock'..."

from "Across The Plains" in 1858: Diary of David Kellog, as published in The Trail, Volume 5, No. 8, January, 1913.

Cadrell Easley was waiting at the Castle Café, a renovated remnant from the 1890's. The small café was nestled into the corner space at Wilcox and Fourth Street inside the Castle Hotel and Bar. In those days, the hotel and bar would hire security men for paydays. The security was responsible for limiting the brawls to the bar and preventing the inebriated cowboys from riding their horses through the bar and hotel lobby. Cadrell was leaning against the squad car when Cody pulled up. Their greeting was cordial, yet not overly friendly. The information Cadrell was to pass on would not be pleasant.

Cadrell agreed to meet with Cody under certain ground rules. First, their conversation was off the record. The case records were classified documents and Cadrell would jeopardize his employment to pass copies in public. The documents would be waiting at the hotel. Cadrell would not risk passing the reports in public. Also, waiting at the hotel would be a case history on Billy Don Barrett. Secondly, Cody's trip to Castle Rock would not bear the intention of vigilante retribution. Cody's first impulse had to be translated into a controlled effort to assist Kirsten in extricating herself from the abusive environment and removing the child from the home on a permanent, legal basis. Less than two weeks had passed since Cody Law met Cadrell

Easley in Chicago.

"Did you have any trouble finding your way?" Cadrell asked as the two men pulled up stools at the Castle Café Bar.

"No trouble. We have suburbs in Chicago farther than Castle Rock is to Denver. Could I get a Coke?" Cody asked the bartender. Easley held up two fingers indicating that he would like the same thing.

"Anything new since we last spoke?" Cody inquired while keeping his voice low.

"Two things. First, Barrett is in jail. It is a misdemeanor charge, but we can hold him until midnight tonight. Seems as though Mr. Barrett got himself tanked last night and put a brick through a Lexus windshield while parked at a relatives home not far from Barrett's home. Barrett usually has some beef with almost every one of his neighbors. Apparently, the neighbor's father and owner of the Lexus had given Barrett a disgusted look while searching the block for his daughter's address earlier that day."

"Barrett told us the guy pulled up and asked for directions early in the morning. Barrett was standing outside his house at 7:45 a.m. wearing a sleeveless shirt, holding a Budweiser and smoking a Camel. Billy Don Barrett looked like an unmade bed that just got caught in an Oklahoma dustbowl. Barrett's entire upper left arm from the elbow to the shoulder is covered with a satanic tattoo. Hard to imagine anyone frowning at that sight, hey Cody? Last night, the dumb-fuck made so much noise that a patrolman heard the incident from the station-house parking lot seven blocks away. The squad car found Mr. Barrett scrambling down the sidewalk in a futile attempt to navigate the short distance to his home. No one actually saw him do it, so we can only hold him for twenty-four hours. We told him that we pulled his prints from the driver's door and window, but he knows the dance too well."

"He called Kirsten for bail, but she didn't have the cash. So, he'll sit for twenty-four hours before we actually have to charge him. I pushed for it on the small chance that he would own up to it in exchange for retribution to the vehicle owner. My boss told me that I had a better chance of running for the Senate."

"Secondly, school started again after winter break. Devon missed the first two days. Her mother called to inform the school that Devon wasn't feeling well but that she should be back in a day or two. I don't know if Devon is back in school today. Something doesn't feel right. Devon's only solace from that home was school. While she had few friends, Devon could exist unharmed within the confines of the school. I do not believe that Devon would miss school on her own accord. The case records are waiting for you at the hotel. Cody, there is a small window. Go see Kirsten before we release Barrett." Cadrell Easley was all business.

The Castle Hotel and Bar became a rest haven for weary travelers between Denver and Colorado Springs as early as 1910. A dance hall was built over the bar and served as a community center for much of the twenties and thirties. The original main street in Castle Rock had remained virtually intact since the structures were erected near the turn of the century. The hotel was a weathered granite monument to a faded era. Guests entered the three story treasure through the beveled glass double doors erected of solid oak, cut and hauled form the base of the Rockies nearly three quarters of a century before. Cody tapped the bell at the hotel's registration desk. An expansive mural depicting the territory prior to statehood hung prominently behind the check-in desk. Cody was given a plain brown package upon checking into the hotel. The hotel clerk did not say a word. The package contained no identification, but the clerk knew precisely who to give it to.

The guestroom was straight from the annals of Tombstone and Doc Holiday. A small cherry wood table held a painted china wash basin near the antique chest of drawers. Two large brass spittoons guarded each side of a century old desk. Cody wondered how much Redman had been drooled into those brass buckets over the years. A hardwood floor creaked beneath the lone bearskin, musty and full of age, lying as a throw rug next to a four-poster bed. Renovated bathrooms hardly fit the scheme.

Cody Law threw a large duffel bag on the floor next to the bed. After a quick shower, Cody pulled on a pair of jeans and the same pair of Luchese boots. The wet hair hung long across his shoulders. Shirtless, Cody sat on the edge of the bed and pulled open the brown package left by Cadrell Easley. The package was larger than Cody expected. How big could a file be, he thought? The box contained a stack of case files. There were sixty-one. Each file was marked by the date and the complainant.

Examples included, April 5, 1986; Kirsten Barrett against Billy Don Barrett, October 13, 1987; The Douglas County School District-Castle Rock Elementary School against Billy Don Barrett and Kirsten Barrett. Cody had to reread some of the complaints to fully comprehend the allegations. Two hours elapsed and the long wet hair had long since dried. Each complaint was stamped "Complainant refused to prosecute. No custody required."

Cody read the allegations, many reaching draconian levels of barbarism. Devon's age kept beaming across the pages. Kirsten's crying echoed in the walls. Cody's penitent regression soothed nothing. The room shrank with each chilling file. Cody began to perspire in the winter chill of a barely heated hotel room. The fourth to the last file contained a copy of the resignation letter dated 1989, written by Assistant Principal Dana Davenport, Castle Rock Elementary School / South Street Elementary School. The letter was crisp and rigid. The paper remained stiff, as if new. Cody read slowly, enunciating each incomprehensible word.

Cody dropped the letter on the bed upon finishing. He walked slowly to the bathroom and looked into the mirror. Cody vomited in the sink. The purging erupted wave after wave. His stomach was empty and the heaving continued. Cody turned off the light and stood gagging on his own phlegm. He kept spitting while unable to generate any saliva. Cody reached for the water handles on the sink and turned them on full. The faucet coughed and spit. The water was a murky brown. Cody jumped back and the water ran clear.

* * *

The Castle Hotel and Bar sat across the street from the new Douglas County Courthouse. The old one was burned down in 1972 by an irate housewife whose husband had been thrown in jail for the night. The Thursday morning air was crisp. The jutting peaks surrounding Castle Rock cut clean lines against the blue sky. Cody grabbed a cup of coffee at the diner next to the hotel and scribbled down some directions from a waitress who was eyeing more than the morning paper. Cody drove his rented vehicle up past the Castle Rock Feed & Supply on Third.

Castle Rock Peak is in the profile of an Indian. Folklore has it, that at the right time of day, the Indian will look back at you. After hearing that from Cadrell, Cody kept looking up at the rock formation that stood like a Roman Gladiator shielding the town. It was just after 8:00 a.m. Cody drove up Third and turned onto Lewis in a seedy residential section located at the base of Castle Rock Peak. Cody pulled over across from the Castle Rock Elementary School.

Cody began to tremble as if the caffeine had been shot into his veins. The children were all on the playground before school started. Cody had only seen the photographs of Devon from the police file that Easley gave him the night before. Packs of laughing children filled the basketball courts and the playground sandlots. Castle Rock Elementary School held grades Kindergarten through eighth. The total enrollment for the school was ninety-four kids. The school was built in 1917 and mirrored the brownstone facades of Main Street. Black wrought iron fire escapes hugged the building from front to back. In the far corner of the school property was an old rusty red swing set, maybe forty or fifty years old. The monkey bars were deserted. All of the children were congregated near the other playgrounds.

Of thc four long swings that hung from the overhead bar, only one held the soft slow rhythm of a child floating like a pendulum. Cody stared at the rusty red swing set. One child in a white tee shirt under blue denim overalls sat quietly alone, oblivious to the chaos of her classmates. Cody froze in his vehicle and even his breathing became silent. Cody got out of the Jeep and walked to the edge of the fence. Cody's eyes caught the face of an angel and for that split second, the eyes beneath him on Mokapu Point twelve years before were as clear as the sky above. Devon's hair tumbled down her shoulders. The thick auburn hair framed the slight features on Devon's expressionless face. The twelve-year old girl was thin and pale. She was beautiful. Cody watched his daughter for nearly five minutes until a school bell broke the silence. Devon rose slowly off the swing and walked toward the school entrance. For a moment, she stopped and gazed up at the stranger standing against the fence. Cody almost waved. Devon turned and proceeded to her classroom.

The neighborhood adjacent to the school yard consisted of overgrown lawns thick with weeds and assorted engine parts. Small one and two-bedroom houses dotted each street with many inoperable vehicles littering the driveways and causeways. Cody pulled up to 222 Gilbert Street and spied the 1500 square foot home with the sudden epiphany that he did not have any business there. The house sat up from the street. Twelve concrete steps leading up to what appeared to be a completely sealed off residence. A beat-up 1970 Ford Bronco sat in the driveway. The rust had to come from the Midwest or the East Coast.

Each house appeared more pitiful than the next. Paint had to be regarded as a foreign concept. Stepping out of the Jeep, Cody imagined the year to be anybody's guess. Chicago was a microcosm of everything cutting edge, the hub of fashion, capital of the loft condominium and a sophisticated outlet for the arts and theater. In Castle Rock on Gilbert Street, one perpetual time warp prevailed. Neighbors bore the hairdos and clothing from years gone by. Homes were a by-product of the post-war boom in the early fifties. Nothing had seemed to catch up.

Cody got out of the Jeep in front of Kirsten's address. A dozen or so, forklift crates were scattered on the side of the garage. A short hair mutt, possibly a cross between a Doberman and a Whippet, barked wildly from behind the fence adjacent to Kirsten's home. The neighborhood canines joined in unison to announce Cody's arrival. Cody knew Billy Don Barrett was not home. Cadrell Easley assured Cody that Barrett would remain in jail until the afternoon. Cody Law reached the front door and looked for a doorbell. Three attempts to depress the bell yielded no response. Cody assumed the bell did not work and knocked on the inside door. The outside screen door was resting along the front façade of the home, dislodged from the hinges long ago. Still, no answer. Cody tried to look inside the home. Every curtain was closed tightly. Nothing was visible from the outside. Cody tried the door. It was unlocked.

Cody Law closed the door behind him.

"Kirsten, anybody home?" Cody called out. "Hello....."

The house was dark, even for a bright morning. The house reeked of fetid air. Cody could only think of cat piss. Cody walked toward the kitchen, fully expecting a rabid mutt to attack at any moment. The living room was vintage trailer trash. It looked like a set from an off-Broadway play about rural insurance scams. The kitchen was barren. Cody walked with trepidation in every step. Even though Easley had assured Cody that Barrett was in jail, Cody pictured the mug shots from the file. He envisioned Barrett suddenly appearing with each step. Cody moved slowly down the hallway.

The hallway was darker than the house. The dogs had stopped barking outside. Cody pushed the door open to one bedroom. He froze in disbelief. The room was carpeted from floor to ceiling. Mismatched scraps of discarded carpeting were tacked throughout the room. A single light bulb hung from the ceiling. One single bed in the corner of the small room held a stripped down mattress on a white metal frame. Hanging from the bed frame was an odd looking rope with a cowbell attached. On one post of the bed hung a weathered straw cowboy hat. One small dresser stood in the far corner of the room.

Cody proceeded to the closet, trembling with each step as the odious surroundings began to close around him. The only light in the room came from the edges of the shade pulled over the window. Cody pulled the closet door open. A single white string hung from the light bulb above. Cody turned the light on. A clothes rod held three tattered dresses. One pair of Sunday shoes appeared shiny and very small. Cody immediately imagined that the shoes had never been worn. Inside the door was a life-sized poster of Lane Frost. Cody read the name of the young man at the top of the photograph. The poster had what appeared to be dried flowers taped across the figure.

The inside walls of the closet were plastered with the pictures of at least ten other cowboys. Cody knelt to read the photographs. The ten or more photos were surrounding another photograph collage of Lane Frost. The photos read Tuff Hedeman, Jim Sharp, Cody Custer, Clint Branger, Cody Lambert, Ted Nuce and Charles Sampson, etc. Cody Law had no idea as to the identity of these men. There were photographs of rodeo events scattered on the wall. A newspaper dated July 31,1989 hung alongside the photographs. The Cheyenne paper blasted a headline that read: *"Lane Frost Death Mares Frontier Days...the nation's most beloved bull rider is killed by the bull named "Takin' Care of Business."*

Cody's eyes followed the cutout magazine standings, articles and tributes to Lane Frost. A copy of ProRodeo News laid on the floor of the closet. Cody backed away from the closet, feeling like he invaded a shrine. The letter that Cody had read the night before and the face of the little girl alone on the playground fit the unthinkable. The need to find Kirsten immediately was now overwhelming. Cody turned to leave. The ice-cold metal of the revolver was shoved up under his nose. The distinct cocking noise echoed in the room as the trigger was pulled back and locked. A sudden fear invaded Cody's body like an avalanche of nausea climbing the back of his throat.

"Give me one reason why I should not shoot the intruder in my home." Kirsten Myers Barrett asked while holding the Colt 357.

"Kirsten, I'm Cody Law. Remember Hawaii, about twelve years ago?" Cody did not move.

"Oh, my God!" Kirsten pulled the gun away from Cody's face. She backed away slowly, not able to handle the emotions that had been dormant so long.

"Cody, what are you doing here? Better yet, what are you doing breaking into my house?" Kirsten did not abandon the corrosive tone.

"I did not break into your home. I came here to see you. No one answered and the front door was open." Cody moved away from Kirsten.

"I don't recall inviting you." Kirsten replied defensively.

"Kirsten, I came to meet Devon and to see if there is anything I can do. When you wrote me twelve years ago and told me about Devon, I took your letter on face value. The marriage, an ecstatic father and a bright future were all things telling me to back off. I didn't think through it, Kirsten. If you did not want me to do anything, it should have been so obvious. There would have been no letter."

"Last week, I ran into a Castle Rock Police Officer in Chicago for a seminar. He happened to visit one of my clubs. Our first encounter was rather dubious, but we got along and began to talk over the course of the night. When your maiden name came up, I had simply mentioned to this man that I once knew a girl from Castle Rock. In fact, the conversation was about women and relationships, when I told him that the only relationship that I had ever regretted not pursuing was a girl from Castle Rock named Kirsten Myers." Cody could see he was not connecting. Kirsten was agitated and pacing. The gun was held tightly at her side.

"Kirsten, the Police Officer from Castle Rock knew you and your husband very well. He detailed an incredible history of violence and abuse towards you and Devon. Last night, I read an account about Devon's abuse from one of the administrators at her school. I can help you. You have to get Devon and pull away from this guy, now. What is this room? Carpet from floor to ceiling? Do you know why anyone would carpet an entire room?

The only reason anyone would carpet an entire room is to deaden the sound coming from the room. This looks like a god damn torture chamber. I don't know what this guy has done to you, but it is not too late to get out of here. I stopped at Devon's school and watched her from the street. Christ, Kirsten, the girl is a lost soul."

"Stay away from my daughter!" Kirsten screamed and startled Cody with the abrupt ferocity of the response.

"What is this guy doing to you? I am not the police, the schools, the county or the courts. Everyone's failure is not mine." Cody implored.

"You just don't get it. Everyone's failure began with you." Kirsten looked at Cody differently for a split second. Kirsten's nose curled and her eyes closed to a squint, the way a cat feigns a polemic, superior glare.

"Kirsten," Cody pleaded. "Let me help you and Devon. This guy is a cancer and he'll destroy you unless you stop him."

"Excuse me, but you have to leave now!" Kirsten shouted while not looking at Cody directly. "We are fine and you do not know what you are talking about."

"Kirsten, you are not fine." Cody looked around the darkened room.

"If you don't leave now, I will fire this gun and claim that I shot a prowler." Kirsten struggled for the words. It was clear she was reaching.

"Kirsten, no one will believe that I came from Chicago to break into this house and rob you." Cody was careful.

"Get out Cody!" Kirsten yelled. "You don't belong here and your visit can only make things worse. You have to get the fuck out of this house now! This is my family. You have no daughter here. My husband will be here soon. You have to leave."

"Kirsten, I know your husband is in jail for the afternoon." Cody announced confidently.

"I just bailed him out, god damn it! Leave Cody. Billy is picking up his truck at a garage not far from here. You have no idea how much worse things will get if Billy comes home and you are here. This not your family. Get out and leave us alone." Kirsten ran into the living room and pulled open the front door.

"Go back to Chicago, Cody. You cannot see Devon. You are way out of your jurisdiction. Don't you remember, that ended in the sand twelve years ago." Kirsten was literally bouncing near the front door. She was afraid to peer outside and implored Cody to hurry. Kirsten was nervous and terrified. Cody stopped at the door before he left.

"Kirsten, do you want to live like this?" Cody asked.

"This is the way I live, Cody. Stay away from my family, please." Kirsten never found Cody's eyes.

"What's with the cowboy closet?" Cody turned and asked while on his way down the walk.

"My daughter has an obsession with bull-riders." Kirsten eyed the ground. "She sneaks out to Crowfoot Road and watches the bulls on the livestock spreads. Devon walks from school sometimes to the Plum Creek Playgrounds to watch the local rodeos. In June, the Elizabeth Stampede comes to town and Devon lives for the bull-riding event at the end of each day. Devon cried for a week when that Lane Frost fellow died." Kirsten drifted, but came back suddenly.

"Good-bye Cody. Go back to Chicago. You have no place here." Kirsten turned and disappeared behind the door.

* * *

Cody drove to the Castle Rock Police Department. First, he wanted to verify if Billy Don Barrett had been bailed out. Secondly, Cody wanted to find Cadrell Easley. The Castle Rock Police Department was located in a newly constructed building on the south end of Castle Rock. The gray concrete structure brandished the personality of a remedial architecture class fumbling through the first week of concept design. Cody Law walked through the first set of eight identical metal doors facing the street. The doors resembled a cellblock from the outside. Approaching the doors, Cody almost expected the eight doors to open simultaneously. The inner lobby was deserted and the doors to the station itself were locked. Cody dialed the number on the phone next to the inside doors. The procedure was identical to the security at most high rise residential buildings in Chicago.

"Can we help you?" A female voice inquired through the speaker.

"My name is Cody Law. I am here to see Cadrell Easley." Cody answered.

"Let me see if he is in. I believe that Officer Easley is on patrol." The female dispatcher could be heard calling Easley. Cody imagined a greater degree of procedure had been exercised over what was actually necessary. "Officer Easley will be up in a couple minutes. Please wait."

Cadrell Easley walked up through the main lobby. Cadrell greeted Cody and the two men sat down in a deserted police station lobby at mid-morning on a Thursday in January. The meeting began remarkably different than their first encounter at a nightclub in Chicago.

"I just found out." Cadrell Easley announced. "I was out looking for you when the call came in that you were here."

"I thought you said that Kirsten could not raise the bail?" Cody asked although fully cognizant of the futility within any response.

"Did you go to the house?" Easley skipped a pointless argument.

"Yes. Kirsten pulled a gun on me." Cody answered. "Kirsten made it clear that I was not welcome and that her family was fine. The fucking house is a prison. Barrett has mind-fucked Kirsten into being some kind of Islamic slave, content the beatings are not fatal. Why can't anyone get them the fuck out of his reach?"

"They won't go." Cadrell sounded defeated. "The law prohibits any real action unless the wife signs a complaint. Kirsten has steadfastly refused to sign any complaints naming her beloved husband. The state can file charges without spousal consent, but the District Attorney's office and the police chief have to be on the same page. In Castle Rock, the District Attorney blocked for Billy Don Barrett in high school and the Chief of Police grew up with Billy's father and took over that role when his real father took a fall for murder out East."

"She is scared to death!" Cody was angry. "The house itself has to be enough evidence to indict this fuck?"

"You know that is not the case. Bad taste and circumstantial isolation don't carry felony consequences." Easley began to raise his voice.

"We have pulled Barrett out of that house on six separate occasions. In Douglas County, assaults against wives and girlfriends are treated as misdemeanors. Kirsten has left on two occasions. Leaving will not protect these women. The courts actually gave Barrett the address and phone number of where Kirsten and Devon were staying. Colorado statutes provide that the accused is not deprived of any parental rights. "

"What about the letter to the school board?" Cody was clueless.

"Unproven charges. Non-substantiated claims and the unwillingness of the mother and the daughter to co-operate." Easley rattled off the excuses.

"Cody, my hands are tied by the law. Why they don't just leave is simple. We won't let them leave. Go back to the letter from Dana Davenport at Castle Rock Elementary. We successfully treat victims who are taken hostage by foreign nations or kidnapping victims held against their will for long periods of time. Our courts due not find justifiable similarities between those victims and the women taken hostage in their own homes. They are out there by themselves, my friend. The fucking courts just see most of this shit like a family squabble. That is, of course, until someone winds up dead."

"That's it?" Cody stood up.

"What do you want me to say? You walk into this mess less than a week ago and come here belching your indignation about frustrations with the law and the systems in place. DCFS has been a fucking joke. The Douglas County School Board President still talks about Barrett's 97 yard punt return against the Springs in the State semi's more than a fucking decade ago."

"Meanwhile, Devon is sitting in a closet with duct tape on her mouth, wrists and ankles because she was a half-hour late from school. She doesn't eat at home for three days and she knows that reporting this will only make matters worse. No one has ever showed her otherwise. That's it? Yeah, that's it. That's been it for a few years. I'm sorry for the frustration you feel. Where were you, my friend. That is your daughter and she is twelve years old. You just saw her today for the first time. Did you ride in to save the fucking day? Well, be my guest, save the fucking day." Cadrell had tired of Cody's condescending assumptions.

"I'm not going back to Chicago anytime soon." Cody did not ignore Easley's remarks. He would get back there soon enough. "I need a favor, Cadrell."

"Don't ask me to break the law, Cody. If I were going to do that, it would have happened a long time ago. I've got a family to protect and provide for. This is the first real job that I have held. My wife enjoys the life here and I am not about to allow a fuck like Barrett to dictate my future." Cadrell scowled and his dander rose.

"I don't want you to break the law for me, Cadrell." Cody assured his angered friend. "I want you to teach me to ride a bull."

"What did you say?" Cadrell was taken off-guard.

"I want you to teach me to ride a bull. You told me that you spent years in the rodeo, right?" Cody countered.

"I spent years in the rodeo riding broncs, you know, horses. I did not ride bulls. What is this all about?" Easley was baffled.

"I'm still young and in better shape than most people I know. I want to ride bulls."

"Competitively?" Cadrell raised his eyebrows

"Yeah, on the circuit." Cody declared.

"What circuit?" Easley pushed.

"I don't know. The PBA or PCA, whatever circuit there is for professional bull riders. I want you to teach me how to ride bulls. "

" The Professional Bowler's Association? Cody, you are either dumber than you look or this is the wrong time for a joke." Easley was not smiling. "How do we go from Kirsten Barrett to bull riding?"

"This is not a joke, Cadrell." Cody shot back. "If you can't do it, then let me know."

"Do you know how to ride a horse?" Easley asked.

"No. I've been on a couple during my life, but I wouldn't say I know how to ride a horse." Cody summarized. "It's the bulls I want to ride."

"Cody, this is ludicrous." Easley spoke with authority. "I did not ride bulls so I cannot teach you how to ride bulls. Cody, most bull riders begin knee high to a newborn colt. They learn to ride before they can talk and they ride something with horns before they can walk. Thirty years old is creaky for a bull rider. You are thirty-two. Most crappy bull riders on the PRCA circuit have been winning local rodeos since they were old enough to be a Cub Scout. The good ones took state and high school titles on the way to collegiate championships. Bull riding is the most dangerous sporting event known to this country. You want to sit atop fifteen hundred pounds of pulsating, spinning muscle, with one skinny rope as the only link holding you from snapping your spine like toothpick. A bull is a diesel engine gone berserk, a lethal testosterone machine that is not tamable or predictable. You want a hobby? Learn to ride horses. Most of them don't object to you sittin' on their back."

"Do you know anybody that can teach me to ride bulls?" Cody asked as if Cadrell had been silent.

"Did you hear anything I just said?" Easley wondered what this had to do with Billy Don Barrett.

"No." Cody shrugged.

"Follow me, Mr. Law." Easley got up and walked towards the stairway. "You are going on patrol with me."

Crowfoot Road spiraled outside of Castle Rock and disappeared into Richlawn Hills. The road was scattered with stock contractors from just outside the city limits to Cherry Creek. Stock contractors are ranchers. They raise livestock and provide the rodeo industry with the tools of the trade, animals. In rodeo, there are seven standard events. Four of the events are timed events and three of the events are roughstock events. The timed events include calf-roping, team roping, barrel racing and steer wrestling. The roughstock events are saddle bronc, bareback, and bull riding. The animals for these events are provided by the stock contractors throughout the country.

Cadrell Easley drove the Castle Rock Police car through the farms outside of town. Cody and Cadrell were content to be silent in the squad car. Cody did not know where they were going, but assumed that the destination must have something to do with their prior conversation.

Cadrell pulled the car onto the dirt drive of the Beacom/Winthrop Ranch, a seven thousand-acre estate, known for quality livestock from Calgary to Cheyenne to the National Finals Rodeo in Las Vegas every December. The entrance drive to the ranch was slightly over a half-mile long. The Beacom/Winthrop Ranch consisted of twelve buildings on the complex. The main house was a photogenic masterpiece of Western architecture.

Allen Beacom was a third generation rancher and currently the majority owner of Beacom/Winthrop, Inc. The squad car pulled around the main house and headed for the nearly 100,000 square feet of barn and feed storage. More than one thousand cross-bred bulls roamed the acreage. Beacom/Winthrop mixed the offspring of Brahma sires with "red and gray Brahmer crosses", mainly Black Angus cows. Brangus bulls, the mix of Brahma and Angus, are traditionally quick and agile. Purebred bulls tend to freeze in the chutes or quit on the rider. The investment for the rancher in each bull is substantial. The contractor's bread and butter usually lies in the slaughterhouse. His passion is the arena.

On average, a good bucking bull is not mature until they are five years old. Three more years and they are tainted, robbed of the ferocity they carried thirty-six months prior. Allen Beacom was standing on the third rail of the North fence when Cadrell and Cody pulled up.

"Easley, I just can't get used to you in that uniform. Man, you couldn't stay on a good bronc to save your life, but you looked fucking good in a Stetson and a pair of custom made Luchese lizards. Those dark blues and the patent leather shit-kickers don't fit you. What's up, cowboy? Shoot anybody today?" Beacom's North Texas roots had long since dissolved at prep schools and an Ivy League education. The drawl, which echoed in every word, was as misplaced as an English riding saddle in Cheyenne.

"Just a couple red Brahmas, loose by the front gate." Cadrell and Allen shook hands and the friendship came through the good-ole boy greeting.

"Meet Cody Law, Allen. Cody is a friend of mine from Chicago. Cody owns some big, big nightclubs in Chicago. Came out to Colorado to visit me. Cody wants to learn how to ride bulls, competitively. I'm not sure that Cody has ever seen a bull, but he wants to ride them, now. I brought him down here to see if there is any action in your arena today. I believe that Cody may be in for a change of heart."

"Cody wants you to teach him how to ride bulls? Has he ever driven with you before?" Allen smiled.

"You're in luck boys. Billy Shoulders is in from Missoula. He's helping with something down at the Hall in Colorado Springs. Called me yesterday and asked if he could come out and ride. A month off has left him a little rusty. Follow me."

Allen Beacom walked around the white metal warehouse building mainly used for feed storage. Two large grain silos rose seven or eight stories to the rear of the structure. Next to the grain storage was the rodeo arena, a full sized venue complete with seating for three-hundred spectators. There were five chutes along the west-end of the arena. Billy Shoulders was straddling one of the chutes. Billy stood five-foot nine and weighed a buck eighty, stockier than most bull riders. Billy finished third in 1988 at the NFR Finals. He rode six out of ten rides.

In 1989, Billy Shoulders finished seventeenth in the PRCA standings. The top fifteen go to the NFR Finals. Slumps occur in bull riding just like baseball, tennis or golf. The air was clear with the winter temperature hovering near forty degrees. The animal in the chute below Billy Shoulders churned a bit. Billy waited for the agitation to subside. Shoulders positioned himself on the bull's back. Another man pulled the bull rope with most of his weight. The hand was wrapped. Billy pushed his hat down low. The animal began to churn again. Billy nodded. The chute burst open. A sixteen hundred pound demon spun out into the arena. The bull's hind quarter whirled up into the air more than six feet off the ground.

"Left, Billy, left." A man shouted from the chutes. "Stay with him, Billy!"

The brindled four-year old fussed like a pro, spewing snot up over his whirling head and feces fragments from his ass end. Billy slid back too much on the bull's back. The control now belonged to the animal. The bull threw Shoulders to one side and then ass-whipped the rider to the turf less than six seconds from the start of the ride. Shoulders crawled like a toddler on a caffeine binge to avoid the post-party stomping the young bull had planned. Two ranch hands played the role of bullfighter while steering the aggressive tundra to the exit lanes. Cody Law looked down at his expensive boots and pressed jeans.

"This ain't no George Strait ballad anymore." Allen Beacom addressed Cody. "Billy was riding an easy stud compared to what competition brings. I'm from Texas and an old Dallas Cowboy fullback and ex-bull rider put it best. Walt Garrison said riding a bull was *like reachin' out with a hay hook and grabbin' a freight train goin' sixty.* You are out of your league, Mr. Law. Eighteen is too fucking old to start learnin' about bulls. Something tells me that you ain't eighteen. Forget about riding bulls."

"You're right, Einstein. I'm not eighteen." Cody pulled on a cigarette while getting the attention of Allen Beacom.

"I'm too old to listen to advice that I didn't ask for. I came out to Colorado to make a difference somewhere. Seems like the window is much smaller than I imagined. I am a green city-boy bent on becoming a laughing stock or a paraplegic. I can't ride a horse, throw a rope or line dance. I hate chewing tobacco and Wrangler jeans just suck. The closest that I ever got to a rodeo was watching Electric Horseman with Robert Redford and Jane Fonda. Somebody's going to teach me to ride bulls. I probably won't get much farther than the nearest orthopedic surgeon, but somebody is going to teach me to ride bulls. There are two things that I would advise to avoid when assessing my character. Don't ever think I am soft and don't ever assume that I will listen to anyone who tries to tell me what I cannot do. As

I've been saying, I need someone to teach me to ride bulls. Can you help or not?"

"Your friend is eloquent, if nothing else. He also sounds rather determined, Cadrell." Allen Beacom beamed.

"I'll call Gunner. That son-o-bitch owes me more favors than I can remember. The Gunner McGarrity Bull Riding School in Santa Maria, California is the Cadillac in a sea of Toyotas. Tell your friend about Gunner."

"Gunner McGarrity owns a Gold Buckle, the 1970 World Bull Riding Champion." Cadrell began. "Gunner placed in the top ten on a regular basis during a seventeen year run riding bulls in rodeo. Gunner's school is the catapult for collegiate stars making the transition to professional rodeo. The school is the oasis for established riders to break out of a prolonged slump. Billy Shoulders will be heading to Santa Maria, next week. If Gunner can't help you then you best start searching for a new line of work."

"Gunner calls it a bull riding boot camp. The full course is a twenty-one day barrage. The students stay on Gunner's ranch. The enrollment will eat, drink, sleep and crap bull riding for the duration of the camp. McGarrity works on mind control as well as body control. Gunner is a full-blown disciple of Maxwell Maltz and Psycho-Cybernetics. A Marine Corps curriculum and meditation make for strange partners. Welcome to the world of Gunner McGarrity. All of this is based on the premise that the student is an accomplished rider to begin with. Gunner takes you to another level. I don't know if Gunner will even consider teaching Cody?" Cadrell held McGarrity with an unmatched reverence. Most cowboys reserved a special place for Gunner McGarrity.

"He'll take Mr. Law." Allen barked. "Hell, I sent McGarrity's school two dozen mean-ass bucking bulls when he first got that thing off the ground. I send him four or five good bulls a year. Shit, Gunner's good for the industry. Gunner McGarrity will have your friend's ass back on a plane to Chicago after a week in the mountains. You ever been there, Cadrell?"

"Hell, no. I heard about it. Some bronc riders even went there during the years I was riding. They all came back with the same conclusion." Easley recalled. "Those fucking bull riders are crazy and Gunner McGarrity sets the standard. Good luck, Cody." Easley smiled back at Beacom.

* * *

Smack in the middle of Castle Rock, at the corner of Fourth and Wilcox, sat the Rascal Flats. The Rascal Flats is a beat-up, died in the wool, shitkickin country ass tavern. The place smells of greasy onion strings, stale beer and rancid cowboys, who can't smell each other because one reeks worse than the other. Only thirty miles south of Denver, the Rascal Flats blends Abilene, Texas, Lawton, Oklahoma and Big Fork, Montana into a Merle Haggard/Bob Wills emporium.

The owner of the Rascal Flats is mindless fat alcoholic named Curly King. The Rascal Flats opens at early in the morning or somewhere in the vicinity. Curly rolls in sometime in the early evening and works the bar until closing at 2:00 a.m. Curly wears one of the same three pair of overalls every night. It is anybody's guess how often the tee shirts are washed underneath the overalls. Some things are better left unknown. Two televisions frame each end of the bar. Twnety-two stools line the oak, inlayed bar. The back bar came from Canada during the thirties. The Rascal Flats was opened by a Canadian lumber company, with a large operation in the Colorado Rocky Mountain region, south of Denver.

Through all the years, the bar has remained an oasis drowning the overworked, underpaid, unemployed prophets plotting the next high school reunion revenge date. The regulars shared a misogynistic bonding, blaming everyone and everything for their own despondent mentality. Yeagermeister, Jack Daniels and Budweiser comprise the extent of Curly's expertise behind the bar. A single pool table is the conference room. The table, an antique drop-pocket design from the days of Buffalo Bill Cody, received a new layer of felt whenever the cigarette burns and broken bottles rendered the surface unplayable.

Billy Don Barrett leaned against the bar with both elbows resting comfortably behind him, facing the pool table. In one hand was a beer. A cigarette dangled precariously from the other. Billy's eyes began to nod. The bar was closing and a dozen beers churned with a half dozen Yeager shots. Charlie Malloy drove the seven-ball into the right corner pocket.

"That's it, Billy. I'm out of here." Charlie announced as they are the only two remaining patrons.

"Curly don't care, Charlie. Right, Curly?" Barrett let the cigarette fall to the ground. Billy Don Barrett was now looking out from the top of his eyes. Drunks have a way of attempting to look past the body's desire to call it quits for the night.

"Wrong, Billy, my boy." Curly belched from the corner of the bar. "This fat boy is going home, so you boys need to vacate the space, like pronto."

The lights had been up for ten minutes. When Curly sat his big ass down at the end of the bar, the night was done. Curly was not getting up. Last call at the Rascal Flats was Curly King filling the end stool after 1:45 a.m.

"Goin' home? Shit, Curly, you fucking live upstairs." Barrett had played the same tune more than Andy Williams has sung Moon River in Branson, Missouri.

Billy Don Barrett had been at the Rascal Flats since just after seven. Billy had been drinking for the better part of seven hours. When Kirsten bailed him out of jail, he went to the Ninth Street Garage and picked up his 81' Malibu. Dinner was brief. Kirsten cooked meat loaf and mashed potatoes. Not a word was said about jail or the bail money. Devon was allowed to eat after Billy and Kirsten had finished. Devon was given an allotted time period to clean the kitchen and finish the dishes. Having completed her task, Devon was given two small slices of meat loaf on a paper plate. Devon heard the door slam when Billy left. She was relieved. Tonight, she would not be timed at the kitchen table. Billy allowed for only so much time to eat. If Devon exceeded the time, the consequences included another day without dinner.

The Rascal Flats door locked behind Charlie Malloy and Billy Don Barrett. The Colorado night was glimmering with stars. The shadows on the spit-stained sidewalk emanated from streetlights. The moon was a simple passenger in the sky. Charlie Malloy pulled open the door to a weathered Ford half-ton, parked in front of the bar.

"You workin', Billy?" Charlie mumbled while climbing into his truck.

"Naw." Billy methodically answered. "Raynard thinks the eighteen wheel runs will open up as soon as the snow hits. Most of his dickhead drivers will pass on the winter runs. If we ever get some fucking snow, I'll make some money." Barrett was referring to the movement of livestock to the West Coast.

"Later, man." Malloy's truck rumbled the still night.

"Yea..."

Barrett continued walking. His car was parked behind the Rascal Flats. The storage yard for the Castle Rock Feed and Supply was adjacent to the rear parking lot serving the Rascal Flats and the Fourth Street merchants. The 81' Malibu was the only vehicle in the lot. Barrett turned the corner and watched a Castle Rock patrol car cruise slowly by. Barrett flipped his middle finger in the air long after the vehicle had passed. Billy located his keys and placed the leather key strap in his mouth while he unzipped his pants.

Barrett relieved himself under the stars. A steady stream splattered the blacktop while the white vapors rose from the warm body fluid into the cold night air. Barrett closed his eyes and exhaled. He would manage the few blocks to his home in any condition.

Barrett reached down to pull up his zipper when the baseball bat slammed into his groin, catching his hand along the way. The small bones in his hand shattered immediately and the force of the blow crushed his testicles. In a tenth of a second, Billy Don Barrett exploded in pain. A second blow from the wooden, thirty-six ounce bat imploded Barrett's face, breaking his jaw and cheekbone simultaneously. Blood erupted from Barrett's mouth and ear. He dropped to the ground, his body convulsing with agony and struggling to grab some air. The flow of blood muffled his cries. The footsteps of his attacker echoed around his head.

Suddenly, the boot heel landed full throttle into Barrett's temple. The alcohol was the only thing keeping Barrett awake. The force of the boot slammed Barrett's head back against the pavement and Billy made a feeble attempt to turn away from the attack. The baseball bat came back down into Billy's kidneys. The backside blow found the mark while snapping two ribs above the targeted organs. Billy Don Barrett was near death. His body twitched in volcanic pain. The blows subsided. Barrett was clinging to life, gurgling in pain, while writhing on the pavement. He was in shock. In what may have been one final conscious memory, someone grabbed Barrett by the hair, now matted in blood and urine.

"Greetings, Billy Don Barrett. The festivities here will not stop until I have your undivided attention. Are we clear on that, Mr. Barrett?" The voice was unfamiliar and clear. There was no response except for the garbled groans of agony from Billy Don.

"You will not ever harm your daughter or your wife again." Barrett heard the voice coming from behind the black ski mask. "I am going to tell you a story, Mr. Barrett. You will stay with me because this is your story. Last year, a man in California killed his three year-old son. The three year-old boy was choked, kicked, bitten, bound and burned. The boy was alive when the paramedics came to his home. When the boy's beatings caused the tiny body to go into convulsions, the father devised a fool-proof plan to cover his tracks. The father left his son quivering on the living room floor and sprinkled gasoline around the room. The father then ignited the trailer and called the fire department. The boy died choking on his own burned flesh and blood. The hospital found seventy-seven human bite marks on the boy. The father and a friend had made a game out of torturing the boy. Stay with me, Mr. Barrett, because this has everything to do with you." The attacker shook Barrett's head and leaned closer.

"The father in California was convicted of involuntary manslaughter. He tortured a three year-old to death and they gave him a seven-year prison term. He was paroled in three years. The judge ruled at the parole hearing that the crimes were so heinous that they were unlikely to be repeated. Listen to me! A man tortured a child and the authorities figured that because the crime was so gruesome, the man would be hell bent to try that again. The courts failed that little boy. They have failed Devon and Kirsten. Stay with me dickhead, the courts are not going to fail any more. I am here to introduce you to jurisprudence by committee. Stay awake, tough guy. You are not going to die mother-fucker. I am going to bring you as close as possible to what Devon feels every time you force your filthy fucking way with her. Then I am going to push you past it." The ski-masked assailant stepped on Barrett's broken hand. The pain pulled Barrett from the edge of passing out. His screams bubbled in the blood.

"Who....are...?" Barrett tried to talk but his face was swelling uncontrollably.

"Who am I? I am fuck you, that's who I am. I am this town. I am coming back, is all you have to be concerned with. If you touch Devon or Kirsten again, then I will do this again and again and again. There will be no repercussions from tonight. If you decide to blame Kirsten or Devon for this attack, then I will assume that all lessons from tonight have been forgotten. If anyone reports the slightest outburst from you, if Devon or Kirsten display any marks whatsoever, if any of my friends in Castle Rock just feel that you are thinking about an attack, then I will extract from you enough pain to make you plead to be allowed to die. Do you hear me, you miserable fuck?"

The voice from behind the mask was inches from the mangled face that once belonged to Billy Don Barrett. Barrett was fading, but he could feel the white hot breath of his attacker. Barrett wanted the man to leave him alone.

"Help me..." Barrett muttered to his attacker.

"How many times has Devon thought about help that would never come, Billy? How many times has Kirsten wanted to scream those words? I keep asking myself what she must have been thinking when you were biting her, taping her arms and legs, and forcing your own urine down her throat. Do you ever think about Devon wondering why she had to go through that? How many times did she think about what she had done wrong? How many times did she think about why no one came to help her?"

"When you finally get out of the hospital, you best remember our little encounter tonight. I will repeat myself, no repercussions. Devon and Kirsten will be allowed to live without fear from you. An ambulance will pick you up as soon as they can drag someone out of bed at the fire station. As God is our witness, you better remember every fucking word that I said."

Billy's attacker rose and gazed down at the shivering, blood soaked figure beneath him. He reached up and pulled the mask from his face. Billy's eyes tried to focus. The man turned and stepped over the trembling body. Billy's unbroken hand flailed at the blood in his eyes. Billy could not see. The man holding the ski mask reached down and pulled Billy's good hand away from his face. With an iron grip, he snapped the first and second finger in one more agonizing reprisal for the years of abuse. Barrett's body jolted in one paroxysmal reflex. Billy Don Barrett lost consciousness.

"Good-bye, Billy Don Barrett." The attacker exhaled, stood over Barrett's body and walked to the edge of the parking lot. A thick wooden bat soaked with blood hung from his right hand. Through the corner of one eye, he could see the fat face of Curly King peering through a window above. The man stopped and the face in the window disappeared instantaneously.

* * *

The telephone rang in Cody's hotel room at 5:00 a.m. Cody waited for a second and third ring, then picked up the receiver.

"Hello." Cody answered with the muffled coarse voice of someone predisposed to sleep.

"Cody, It is Cadrell Easley. Can you come downstairs?" Cadrell was direct.

"I do not remember leaving a wake-up call with you, Cadrell." Cody replied sarcastically.

"Cody, Billy Don Barrett was found beaten to within an inch of his life tonight. He is in surgery at Douglas County Hospital right now." Easley reported the details. "Someone took batting practice on Mr. Barrett. The doctors at Douglas County told us that Barrett has sustained a variety of injuries, possibly fatal injuries. The injuries include a broken jaw, a fractured cheekbone, a crushed eye socket, multiple broken bones in each hand, multiple broken ribs, unknown internal damage, the possible loss of vision in one eye, massive swelling in the facial region and extensive damage to the inner ear on the right side. Barrett may not make it through the night." Easley was reading the list.

"That would be a terrible loss." Cody commented.

"Can you come downstairs?" Cadrell repeated.

"Sure." Cody welcomed any visit that was precipitated by a grave injury to Billy Don Barrett.

The walk downstairs was cold. The hotel management failed to see the need to provide heat in the lobby and the hallways. The Castle Rock Hotel and Bar would never be confused with Chicago Four Seasons Hotel. Cody could see the lights from the stairway. The clear moonlight on a Colorado night was broken by the red and blue lights atop the Castle Rock squad cars. The kaleidoscope of colors illuminated the dark lobby through the plate glass windows facing Fourth Street. Easley leaned against the first car.

"Why the late night entourage?" Cody asked Cadrell after stepping onto the sidewalk.

"Procedure." Cadrell answered.

"Procedure when doing what?" Cody inquired without hesitation.

"Cody, I just came from the hospital." Easley moved closer to Cody. The two men were speaking face to face. The other officers present appeared uncomfortable with the exchange. "Kirsten Barrett was at the hospital. Kirsten told me about your visit to their home. Kirsten thinks you beat up her husband. She told me that you appeared angry and full of allegations. Cody, Devon was with her mother." Cadrell leaned in very close to Cody Law. Close enough so no one else could hear his words.

"I told you Cody, that I was not going to give you those files so you could pull some Charles Bronson, Death Wish bull-shit. I was trying to help you find a way to get next to your daughter." Easley backed up a foot or two.

"Kirsten thinks I did it?" Cody asked redundantly.

"Kirsten is certain." Easley shot back.

Cody Law took the space back. He leaned in close to Cadrell Easley. "I think you did it." Cody whispered to Officer Easley.

"I didn't do it." Cadrell shot back.

"Neither did I." Cody countered emphatically. The two men stood inches from each other, glaring. One man had brutally beaten a man into an unrecognizable mess, only a few hours earlier. The other man wished he had done it himself. The blows were calculated. Neither man had any marks on his knuckles or hands. Cody raised his hands up and wiggled his fingers.

"How stupid would I have to be to go after Barrett, tonight? I know you are not here to arrest me. You would have had someone else come if I were going to be charged. In a quiet town like Castle Rock, I imagine that someone may have seen or heard an attack like you describe?" Cody stepped back.

"Well, old Billy had spent the evening at The Rascal Flats, a worthless shot and a beer joint owned by Curly King. Mr. King said that Billy and Charlie Malloy were the last patrons to leave. Charlie told us that Billy was fine when he left the parking lot a few minutes before 2:00 a.m. Malloy claims that he drove off first and Billy was walking around back to get his car. Charlie Malloy claims that he saw nothing. The only resident in the apartment above the bar is Curly King. Mr. King claims to have witnessed no attack on Billy Don Barrett. Mr. King is lying." Cadrell Easley smiled.

"Why is he lying?" Cody played the role.

"Mr. King is lying for his own reasons. Also, most everyone in this town has feared Billy Don Barrett at some point in time. This is especially true for the alcoholic cheering section at the Rascal Flats. Thirty year-old adolescents on their way to becoming forty year-old failures." Easley raised his eyebrows.

Cadrell Easley turned and took the driver's seat in the Castle Rock patrol car. Easley leaned on the window of the squad car." I guess we go back to the hospital and wait for Billy Don Barrett. If he survives the night, then maybe Mr. Barrett can shed some light on the subject?"

"I doubt it." Cody commented.

"Why is that, Mr. Law?"

"My guess is that if Mr. Barrett may want to clean this up on his own." Cody turned to re-enter the lobby. "Good luck, Cadrell. It would be ironic if the man responsible for the savage beating on Billy Don Barrett was the first man Billy laid eyes on when he woke up. Shit, that alone might scare the mother-fucker to death. Regardless, we may reach a pleasant impasse." Cody pondered.

"How's that, Cody?"

" Barrett may not wake up."

* * *

In the three days since the attack on Billy Don Barrett, the Castle Rock Police Department made every effort to extract a description or a sketch from the victim. First, Billy Don Barrett could not or would not aid the investigation surrounding the attack. Although the injuries to his face and jaw prevented Barrett from speaking, the police photographs that were shown to the victim, all received by the same response. After each photograph, Barrett slowly shook his head from side to side. The same reaction occurred when the photograph of Cody Law was placed in front of Barrett. Billy Don Barrett had never seen Cody Law, never met Cody Law and did not know of any connection between Law and Kirsten Myers.

Two Castle Rock detectives spent time at the hospital. They asked a series of questions designed to give them a blueprint of the attack. Barrett could respond to the questions by nodding his head. Billy Don Barrett was attacked from behind. The man wore a mask. Did Billy Don Barrett get a look at the suspect? The response was positive. Cody Law's photograph caused no response. Barrett simply passed over the picture and continued with the stack. Detective Monty Price had been sliding one photograph after another in front of Barrett. At day's end, Monty Price informed Cadrell Easley that Cody Law was not the man they were looking for.

Next, if Cadrell Easley committed the offense, the Castle Rock Police Department would be the last to know. Cody Law never voiced his opinion concerning the matter and no one in the Castle Rock Department broached the possibility. Billy Don Barrett had no reaction to Easley when the officer entered his room on the day following his attack. Cadrell Easley stopped at Douglas County Hospital to question Billy Don Barrett, alone. Easley brought a separate photograph of Cody Law. Barrett was only allowed occasional visits. Other than the police and his wife and daughter, there were no other visits.

Cadrell Easley showed the photograph to Billy Don Barrett. Barrett resembled a bad make-up job for a costume party. The nine shades of purple and black on his face surpassed hideous. Stitches curled underneath Barrett's chin where the jaw was wired shut. Both hands were wrapped in plaster and immobilized on a wire pulley system from above the bed. Easley asked Barrett if he knew the man in the photograph, while holding the photograph of Cody Law. Barrett slid his battered head from side to side. Cadrell Easley held his contempt in check for the length of his visit.

The two men in the hospital room had exchanged words on numerous occasions. Officer Easley drove the responding police vehicle on three separate domestic violence calls to Barrett's home. Every rationalization or justification held out by women as to why they stay with men that beat them and their children is irrelevant to a police officer. AMA statistics prove that domestic violence cases cause more injuries to women than auto accidents and rapes combined. Barrett's response on each occasion was one degrading male stereotype that truly does exist in alarming numbers. *This is a family matter. Why do you insist on making this into a felony. Interfering in a private discussion in my home is a violation of my civil rights.*

On each trip to the Castle Rock Police Station, Kirsten Myers failed to press charges. While most people believe that it is wrong to strike a woman or child, many believe that under certain circumstances, the violence is inevitable. Officer Easley watched a robotic child and a terrified woman climb into a car with Billy Don Barrett after each arrest was nullified. Cadrell Easley placed the photograph in his pocket.

"Can you hear allright from the good ear?" Easley asked while waiting for a visual response. Barrett turned his head to the good ear.

"Outstanding, Billy." Easley continued. "No one is going to look very hard for this fellow, Billy." Cadrell Easley smiled and left the room.

Easley's information had not been a surprise. Cody had agreed to stay in Castle Rock for an undetermined length of time to clear the matter of his possible link to the beating of Billy Don Barrett. During the past three days, Cody had been in contact with Allen Beacom on four separate occasions.

Beacom had managed to reach Gunner McGarrity on the third day. Gunner's wife took messages but they rarely got to Gunner within the first twenty-four or forty-eight hours. McGarrity led weekly trail rides into the Sierra Madre Mountains of Central California for wealthy businessmen and women. Line dancing and the emergence of Garth Brooks found a shallow generation searching for another way to spend the growing cyber-space investment accounts emanating from Silicon Valley to Orange County. Gunner McGarrity remained a strand of weathered leather amidst the widening waistline of a sedentary society. Allen Beacom salivated at the prospect of sending Cody Law to Gunner McGarrity. Beacom set the stage with facts that did not matter to Gunner.

Cody Law was a wealthy business owner from Chicago. Beacom described Law as a wealthy, arrogant city shit from Chicago, resurrecting some repressed cowboy fantasies, while deciding that becoming a bull-rider may fill in the gap where masculinity has been circumvented by an asexual lifestyle. Beacom felt that societal trends regarding men and women were erasing the basic difference within both genders. Men like Cody Law were searching for what Beacom and McGarrity held as a way of life.

"Gunner, hoist those pretty-boy blue jeans onto any Black Angus on your spread. I'll give three to one that Mr. Cody Law pisses on that bull's back before the gate swings open." Allen Beacom mused. "Your new student will quickly re-think his new career plans."

"Did Mr. Law give you a specific reason for his desire to pursue bull-riding?" Gunner asked, oblivious to Allen Beacom's sarcasm.

"No, I do not believe that he did." Beacom responded. "You know the drill, Gunner. These fucking guys come and go. They want to find themselves because fine wine and cocaine have become boring."

"I will contact Mr. Law." Gunner announced while the only thing boring at the moment was the conversation with Allen Beacom.

Allen Beacom was a silver-spoon fed contracting imposter. Beacom was a third generation rancher with as much barbed wire in his blood as Ethel Merman. Beacom had provided the background information concerning the relationship between Cody and Cadrell Easley. McGarrity remembered Easley from his PRCA days, describing Easley as a hybrid spirit that simply fought the animals instead of confronting the demons within him first.

"Rodeo is not a contest between man and the animals." Gunner said during his initial call to Cody Law. McGarrity was not offended by an outside interest in the profession he loved. "Rodeo is the ultimate test of man against himself. The animals provide the purest arena. Bulls are not corrupted by motive."

From *The Picture of Dorian Gray*, McGarrity quoted Oscar Wilde. "All art is quite useless. That is, it exists for its own sake as art and not for some moral purpose. Rodeo is art, plain and simple. Mr. Law, you can accomplish whatever your mind will allow. Any bad-ass can get on a bull. Few can ride with respect. Many riders lose the fear, but never come close to attaining their goals. *Cowardice and conscience are the same thing. Conscience is the trade name of the firm.* Bulls are ridden with the head. I can teach anyone to master the mechanics. I cannot teach men to conquer the contest. Either they get it or they don't."

Cody was packing for California. He was thoroughly perplexed as to why McGarrity had not inquired about the reasons or the background behind such a decision. Surely, one does not wake up at thirty-two and decide it is now time to ride bulls for a living. In the first conversation that they had together, McGarrity quoted Maxwell Martz, Immanuel Kant and Oscar Wilde, yet never asked why. Cody felt like he was talking to a cross between Terry Bradshaw and Gore Vidal.

Gunner McGarrity's twenty-one day bull-riding school began in two days. McGarrity ran one such session per month with the exception of December for the NFR Finals and January for a two-week trail ride that netted more than half his yearly income. The bull-riding school had not been a tremendously profitable venture. Many of the students attended on a "McGarrity Grant." College students with no more in their pocket than a half-empty tin of Skoal, make the trek to Nipomo and pleaded their case to the guru of professional bull-riding. Migrant workers sent their sons with a down payment on the course and a backpack stuffed with dreams and promises. They paid when they earned enough to reimburse the school. The students lived on the ranch and McGarrity provided meals as well. McGarrity told Cody that he could not guess how many weeks or months would be needed to get him ready to enter a PRCA sanctioned event.

"The timetable does not exist." McGarrity reiterated. "Yours may have passed, Mr. Law. Most men wrap up their bull-riding days well before they reach your age. To say your efforts will be viewed with skepticism is to grant you the kindest analogy imaginable. Cybernetics tells us that we have all experienced times when instead of being bullied by anonymous forces, we do feel in control of our actions, masters of our own fate. On those rare occasions, we feel a sense of exhilaration and enjoyment that is cherished and becomes a landmark of what life should be like. To each man, however, motive is everything."

The police personnel came and went during the first three days. Castle Rock was not a community accustomed to violent crime. Billy Don Barrett aided no one during the initial search for a suspect in the brutal beating he received. Kirsten Myers assumed the role of dutiful wife. Conspicuously absent from the hospital was Devon Barrett. She did not make the trek to the hospital. Billy never asked about Devon and hoped she would never see him in the weakened state he occupied. At her quiet home on Gilbert Street, Devon spent the peaceful hours with the snacks she so seldom enjoyed. No one could tell Devon Myers that life did not begin with a Strawberry Pop-Tart. Kirsten told Devon that Billy was hurt in an automobile accident. The police were not allowed to question Devon. Kirsten forbid any questioning that involved Devon. As was the case with the entire matter, the police were not fervent in their attempts to question the girl. Billy Don Barrett's attack would remain unsolved.

On a misty Sunday morning, while Kirsten Myers sat dutifully at her husband's side, remiss in the absurdity of the misogynistic man she married, Devon rode a wobbly bicycle to the Plum Creek Playgrounds on the edge of town. The boys were at play on this morning. Devon leaned against the fence and could smell the animals in waiting. Seventeen and eighteen year-old boys readied themselves for the task at hand. Devon swallowed hard and wriggled into a perch atop the fence. The bulls waited in line as the gates closed one after the other. In sequence, the boys took their turns on the rankest stock afforded the Plum Creek Fairgrounds. Frozen in freedom for the first time in years, Devon Myers screamed like her little lungs had never screamed before.

Cody walked the seventy-five yards from the street to the arena. The Plum Creek Fairgrounds had not been a difficult venue to locate. Cody had watched the parking lot at Douglas County Hospital. When it was clear that Kirsten Myers Barrett arrived to visit her husband, Cody drove to their home in search of Devon. Against every thread of common sense in Cody's genetic blueprint, the man desired to meet the daughter he brought into the world. Cody remembered Kirsten speaking of the fairgrounds as a place where Devon often visited. Cody eyed the small figure on the fence clad in overalls and a white tee shirt. Cody approached in view and leaned on the fence a safe distance from the girl as to not arouse concern. He watched the activity in the arena and shivered each time the little voice atop the fence yelled at the participants.

"He's goin' to spin left on you." Devon yelled to the rider in the chute. "Remember, Lethal Bill comes out high and throws his head back from the get go. Don't fall away from your hand. The bull will stomp you like a ladybug in June if he feels you fall down his back."

Devon Barrett took on a new persona at the fairgrounds. Sometimes the crew would let her time the riders, clutching that stopwatch like it was Christmas in the palm of her hand. "Time" Devon would yell at the onset of eight seconds.

On this day, a bevy of riders from a nearby Junior College were working out with the school's rodeo coach, so the timing duties were not in Devon's hands. Cody Law watched his daughter from thirty feet away. Devon's features were fragile and tender. From a distance, the girl was thin and small. Frozen against the majestic peaks surrounding the ranch, Devon, clad in overalls clung to the fence. A delicate, turned up nose was sketched on a face as yet unlined from the sun, but marred from a profusion of trauma. Scars from thirty feet were visible in the saline white texture of silk lost in her cheeks. Cobalt blue eyes, innocent and rich, searched for nothing.

Focused on the action at hand, Devon Barrett had taught herself to enjoy what she could, avoid what she knew and survive the rest. Cody Law's voice startled her attention even though she had noticed the man when he arrived.

"You have to be a little crazy to get in there, huh?" Cody asked.

"Yes, sir." Devon eyed the stranger to her left. There had been little advice from her mother about talking to strangers. Devon often dreamed of abduction, a senseless fantasy she embraced wholeheartedly. The chute opened and the rider appeared helpless as the bull thrashed inside the chute, erupting in mid-air as the gate spun free. The bull-rider bounced on the hind quarter, sending his body airborne. Devon grimaced and screamed.

" Re-ride, he never had a chance!" Devon leaned over the fence and continued the tirade. "They pulled the chute before he was set." The lone spectator filled the arena with the sentiments of a full-blown rodeo.

"Do you know these guys?" Cody asked from his perch along the fence.

"Sure." Devon countered. "They come from Castle Rock, Parker, Woodland Park and as far away as Colorado Springs. Big shot riders where they're from, but that won't help them make a rodeo team in college. Half of them will split their gut on bulls too unpredictable for any respectable event." Devon's command of the vernacular astounded Cody.

"How do they score these guys?" Cody asked while walking closer to the young girl.

"Don't you know nothing about bull-riding?" Devon bluntly asked the stranger.

"Well, I'm kinda learning." Cody chimed in. "Could you fill me in on the basics?" Cody's inexplicable charisma was not lost on the child. The trepidation to strange men did not exist in Devon due to the foundation of Devon's upbringing. Fear began at home for Devon and evaporated as the physical distance grew from her stepfather.

"Riders are judged on a combination of the bull and the rider's ability." Devon began searching for a willing ear. "Fifty points belong to the bull and fifty points come from the rider. If the rider pulls a lame bull, there is nothing he can do to pull a score higher than the mid-sixties. Riders get a re-ride when the bull quits. Nobody gets anywhere in this business if the bull is a bust."

"Why did you yell re-ride on the last ride?" Cody began to respect Devon's unusual knowledge. Adult men rarely spoke to Devon and they most certainly, never listened. Suddenly, Devon had command. The words flowed.

"The yokel on the gate pulled the rope before the rider nodded. A rider gets a re-ride when the gate is pulled before he is ready. Any rider gets a re-ride if the bull is not on all fours when the gate opens. That animal was airborne when the gate opened. That guy could have had a re-ride on two counts." Devon absorbed the unusual attention to her prowess.

"How many rides is a contestant allowed during each rodeo?" Cody asked immediately.

"They just try to get to the short go." Devon answered and had no connection with Cody Law. "The size of the rodeo sometimes determines the number of rides. Each rodeo narrows the field for the final round or the short go."

"How many events are involved at a rodeo?" Cody continued.

"You really don't know nothin' about rodeo, do you?" Devon enjoyed directing the conversation.

"Not much." Cody shrugged.

"There are seven events at most rodeo. The events are split between the timed events and the roughstock events. The timed events include calf-roping, team roping, barrel racing and steer wrestling. The roughstock events are saddle bronc, bareback, and bull riding." Devon rattled off the facts like a reporter for PSN. (Prorodeo Sports News)

"Do you have any other events that you like?" Cody asked innocently.

"What do you mean?" Devon's guard rose.

"I mean, do you enjoy watching any events other than bull riding?" Cody didn't connect.

"How do you know that bull riding is my favorite event?" Devon's voice dropped and she slid from the top of the fence.

"I don't." Cody caught it. "I see you watching bull riders and I just assumed that you enjoyed watching this event. I'm sure the other events are just as exciting." Cody stumbled to backtrack. Devon did not answer right away. Cody let the silence hang.

"They aren't." Devon announced after nearly two minutes of silence.

"They aren't, what?" Cody forgot where they had left off.

"They aren't as exciting." Devon stared at the arena and the rider, thrown from the mount, scrambling to avoid a determined bull bent on kissing the shorts of his departed passenger. "Bull riding is THE event. The others are the opening acts. That's why the bull riders are always last."

"Thank you for the information. What's your name?" Cody wandered into dangerous territory.

"My name is Devon." The young girl replied without hesitation.

"My name is Cody. I am very pleased to meet you." Cody extended his hand to the daughter he could not afford to acknowledge. "I have to go now.

Thanks for your help."

"Where you from, mister?" Devon wasn't ready to end the conversation. She stared at the arena and did not extend her hand.

"Chicago. Have you ever been to Chicago?" Cody asked knowing the answer.

"Been to Denver a couple times." Devon responded to a city only thirty miles away. Chicago could have been a foreign country within the answer that never came.

"I'll see you again, Devon." Cody uttered while he walked away. Cody reached his vehicle and watched the young girl glued to the fence. She never turned around.

* * *

~CHAPTER III~

The plane landed in Santa Maria in the early afternoon. The middle of February in the region called Central Coast California was crisp and bright. The smog-filled bedlam of Southern California was an afterthought. Santa Maria, which lies some three and a half hours north of Los Angeles by car, was a rural community one hour south of San Louis Obispo.

The humidity was light for a location so close to the ocean. Pismo Beach was a thirty-minute drive. The region of Central Coast was bounded on the north by the historic property at San Simean and to the south by the city of Santa Barbara. The inclusive counties were San Louis Obispo County and Santa Barbara County.

Cody drew his bags from the baggage claim and proceeded to the taxi stand in front of the airport. While Cody was waiting for the cab to pull up, he glanced down at the two Nike bags near his feet. Cody wondered what does one pack for bull-riding school? The thought rattled in his head as grabbed a taxi. Cody instructed the taxi driver to take him to the nearest used car lot, where he could find a used pick-up truck. Cody had no idea how long his stay would run. Damned if he was going to pull up to an isolated ranch and spend a couple months with a powder blue rented Corolla. There were still some things he could control.

Cody shelled out a couple grand for a Ford one-ton pick-up truck. The white truck had seen some work, but the mileage was decent and there appeared to be no discernible engine noises to cause concern. Cody's destination was the Gunner McGarrity Bull-Riding School located just outside of Nipomo, California. Nipomo was a short drive up Highway 101 North to the Los Berros exit. Cody drove east to Dana Foothill Road, which ran alongside the foothills of the Sierra Madre Mountains. Dana Foothill Road eventually became a dirt road.

The ranch laid some nine miles up into the mountains, away from the paved sanity of a rural neighborhood. The manicured mailboxes and landscaped acreage along the paved highways gave way to the dust bowl progress of a country road. Those nine miles would take forty minutes to drive. The road took Cody through a microcosm of dirt poor farmers and wealthy ranches. The road belched and buckled in a seemingly endless journey. The apparent circuitous journey gave way to many thoughts of making a serious mistake. Cody was entering a world that made him nervous before he reached his destination. The longer the drive took, the more agitated Cody became.

Suddenly, the dirt road swung around hard left and fell off into what amounted to a small lake. The road continued some thirty yards beyond the water. Cody stopped and had no idea how deep the water would be. Slowly, Cody lurched forward in the truck. The water did not cause a problem for the pick-up and as Cody was climbing the bank to reconnect with the road, another obstacle froze the moment. Standing in the dirt road, not six feet from the hood of the truck, were two red Brahma bulls. Cody stared at the animals he would be mounting in the very near future. Any doubts that may have popped up during the trip regarding uncertainty, now posted up like the neon Mirage billboard on the Las Vegas strip. The smaller Brahma weighed in at sixteen hundred pounds. Big brother tipped in at nearly nineteen hundred pounds. The truck didn't move. The bulls finally lumbered out of the way, while Cody began to wonder about fences. Shouldn't these animals be confined?

Cody drove the truck up past the first signs for Gunner's school. Before the main house and bunkhouses, the road pulled past the full-sized rodeo arena. At the top of the gates, sat a large hand carved wooden sign that read, The Gunner McGarrity Championship Bull-Riding Schools. The arena was empty.

The large wooden structure fell naturally into the landscape of the Sierra Madre Mountains. Rows of bleachers, badly in need of paint, rallied high into the clear sky. Well-worn gear hung sporadically around the inside fences of the arena. Bull ropes, assorted gloves and vests could be seen dotting the chute area. A small tractor used to rake the infield sat unattended outside the bull-ring.

The main house and the barns were visible now. Cody pulled up the last part of the drive and stopped in the center of the structures. The main house stood to the left, a moderate ranch home that could have easily been supplanted from a sub-division in Santa Barbara. Two large barns stood at the center of the property. Redwood siding gave way to the two dozen horses housed inside. Two or three mechanical bulls could be seen inside the barns. The bunkhouse for students were made up of two converted trailers. Another trailer served as Gunner's office. Cody parked the truck and climbed down in front of the two men he could see struggling with another vehicle. Cody stood silent for a minute or two. One of the figures on the large trailer-truck, popped his head above the rails. The man smiled under a white straw Reisistol.

"Hey, you must be the fellow from Chicago?" Gunner announced. "What'd you do, boy? Did you roll old Gunther Sulley? You got his truck, man." Gunner knew every vehicle in the county, especially if that vehicle had spent any time at the taverns in Nipomo.

"My name is Cody Law. Allen Beacom and Cadrell Easley may have spoken to you about me?" Cody walked over to the truck. Gunner and a young man were struggling to tie two bulls into the back trailer of the truck.

"These two mother-fuckers have been tearing up the fences on the east half of the ranch. I took them down from Frank Farley's spread last month. I called Frank yesterday and told him that I was taking these worthless animals to the auction in Arroyo Grande today. As soon as we get these ropes secure, we'll all take a ride." Gunner smiled as if he knew something.

Gunner McGarrity was fifty-two years old. He had a wealth of thick white hair tucked under his hat, longer than most cowboys wear their hair. Gunner was five foot seven inches tall and weighed no more than a buck fifty. His arms were well-defined and his waist remained at thirty-two inches. Gunner's hands bore the years of competition. More than two decades of competitive bull-riding, left Gunner's hands scarred and curled from the countless broken bones sustained under the bull's weight. The most engaging feature on the rough man was his smile. Gunner could charm the skirt off a nun and she would hang it up for him. McGarrity was tanned and wore a white tee shirt with blue Wrangler jeans. A worn out pair of Dan Post boots and a belt buckle the size of Rhode Island finished the look.

Men envied the richness of the past they knew he lived. Women just fell for the country twinkle in his eyes and the boyish innuendo in every sentence. Gunner and his traveling fellow bull riders found life ripe with Buckle Bunnies or rodeo groupies. From Handlebar J's in Scottsdale, Arizona to the Dew Drop Inn between Cheyenne and Laramie, Wyoming, Gunner lived the life most men are intimidated reading about. Gunner McGarrity won the World Professional Bull Riding Championship in 1970. Gunner placed in the top ten from 1966-1976, culminating with the title in 1970. The Gold Championship Buckle brings respect with every step for each recipient. To be the best in the world at the world's most dangerous event is an accomplishment not taken lightly by the millions of rodeo fans. Men, like Gunner McGarrity, pride themselves on being called a cowboy.

"Yeah, Beacom called me a couple times about you, even after you and I talked. He's a pinhead. Helps me out with some stock now and then, but that is just so he can stay in the loop with bull riders. Most of my boys don't care for him much. Cadrell is a class act. He could ride a bronc better on sheer stubbornness than anyone I knew. Trouble was, Cadrell didn't use his head. You can't ride a bull or a bronc between your legs. You have to ride them between your ears. Let's go, man. I want to get these worthless hides to auction now, because we are going to Los Angeles this afternoon to watch my youngest son ride bulls in the PRCA rodeo at the Equestrian Center next to the Disney studios. Jason was ranked nineteenth on the Jack Daniels/Copenhagen Cup points leader board. The top fifteen go the NFR Finals at the end of the year. Jason finished out of the finals last year because he was having too much fun. It's early in the year, but he seems to be a bit more focused. We'll see. You'll get a chance to work the chutes and see what it's like close-up. " Gunner pulled the last rope and instructed the young man with him to secure the back gate.

"Are these some of the bulls your students ride?" Cody asked while climbing in the truck.

"The only riding these bulls are going to be doing, is to the bologna factory." Gunner replied as a matter of fact.

Gunner pulled the caravan slowly down the dirt road leading away from the ranch. As they passed the barns, Cody noticed the endless pastures rising from the barbed wire fences behind the barns. The feed silos and the water troughs dotted the well worn acres. Amidst the sporadic trees and countless herding dogs, Cody eyed the better part of two hundred bulls on Gunner's ranch. The truck wobbled and shook with the gyrations from nearly four thousand pounds of angry bulls.

"You know." Cody remembered. "You've got some bulls running loose. I almost ran into a couple on the road coming up here."

"Must be Fahrenheit Point." Gunner pulled off the white Resistol and placed it in the back seat. "Our sandwich treats in the back trailer did a number out on the point. A few old Brahmas know their way back down to the lower spread. They won't go anywhere, but they make some pretty mean watchdogs, hey Cody?" Gunner laughed.

The young man in the back seat was Russell Den, a Native American, eighteen-year old bull-riding champion from a small reservation in northern New Mexico. Russell came to the ranch a week before his session with Gunner to work one on one with the man. Russell was planning on turning pro after his twenty-one day session was completed.

Cody sat in the front seat, watching Gunner maneuver the twenty-year old truck at seventy miles per hour on Highway 101. The back trailer slid across the lanes as the bulls banged and fought to free themselves from the ropes. The truck felt like it would flip over at any moment. Cody looked down at the passing cars and wanted to flip them his middle finger. The fine foreign cars could hardly imagine what kind of trash was driving a beat-up dinosaur down the highway like an oversized demolition derby. Cody looked down at the passing BMW and saw himself there a week before. Cody flipped the driver the bird.

"Everybody from Chicago as friendly as you?" Gunner asked as he watched Cody extend the universal middle finger greeting.

"That prick was looking down his nose so far, I'm surprised he didn't hold up a sign telling us to remove the trash from the road. I don't know shit about bulls, but I know a dickhead when I see one." Cody responded defiantly.

"We gotta get you a fucking hat, my friend." Gunner laughed and tossed the empty Sprite can on the floor.

Gunner dropped the bulls at the auction yard and headed back to the ranch. There, they would clean up before the drive to Los Angeles. Cody followed Russell Den to the bunkhouse. The bunkhouse held eight beds set up as four bunk beds. The converted trailers were a conglomeration of saddles, bull ropes, chaps, fourteen different throw rugs, and a bathroom that had long ago seen the flaccid end of a mop. Russell had his gear hanging from a saddle post next to his bunk.

"Take your choice, my friend." Russell announced as they entered the room. Cody surveyed the room and thought about the Holiday Inns and the Ramada Inns he passed on the way to the ranch. The place looked like a western version of fraternity row. The refrigerator held two cans of Diet Coke, a bottle of ketchup, and what else, a half-empty package of bologna dated from sometime before Halloween.

"Can I smoke in here?" Cody asked, never envisioning a possible reason not to. The place smelled like a barn and there were spittoons scattered in every corner of the bunkhouse.

"Sure, I guess." Russell actually didn't know. Everyone in rodeo chewed tobacco. Few smoked anymore. "I'm going to jump in the shower. You wanna go first?" Russell Den was polite, as Cody was considerably older.

"Naw, you go ahead. I'm fine." Cody answered and lit a cigarette. Cody walked outside and looked down at the bull-ring. The arena sat well below the bunkhouse. Sitting on the edge of the slope, Cody could view the entire arena and the pens holding the animals before a match or training session. The pens were empty. The wind blew the long grass across the hills and made waves of shimmering vegetation gyrate throughout the valley. Gunner's ranch was surrounded by new wineries. Wealthy traders and entertainment industry executives purchased large blocks of available land in the Central Coast region.

A concentrated effort was in progress to supplant many of the misconceptions about Napa Valley. Central Coast was much closer to Los Angeles and the grapes could grow every bit as full as they grew north of San Francisco. The missing link was time. Wineries need time to develop a name for themselves and the region. Central Coast was in the incubation period when compared with the Napa Valley and Sonoma wineries. The tranquil setting framed acres of vineyards, hatching a myriad of delicate Chardonnays, robust Cabernets and bold Merlots. Miles and miles of wine country roamed the training grounds for the world's most dangerous sport. Amidst a backdrop of smoked mango pear crepes and Beverly Hills bank accounts, a couple hundred battle-scarred bull-riders tweaked and honed their craft each year.

Occasionally, an ambitious reporter or a frustrated cowboy wanna-be ventured up to the ranch for a quick check on his testicular tolerance. Reality doses came full circle when the mechanical simulators became eighteen hundred pounds of flesh between their legs. Gunner was never one to force a ride. Many a well-intentioned efforts ended before the rider could climb into the chute. Gunner had schooled his staff never to snicker or laugh when the wet trail of fear stained the jeans of a potential rider. Cody stood up and envisioned the same. Cody had never been in the military. His age launched him past the Vietnam era and away from the draft. Resolve resonated at odd times. Cody stood outside the bunkhouse, now. Whether he spent twenty-one days or six months with Gunner McGarrity, this was Cody Law's boot camp.

The ride from the ranch to the Equestrian Center in Los Angeles would take more than three hours. Gunner walked out of the main house at the ranch with his hair still wet from the shower, wearing a crisp clean pair of Wrangler jeans, a matching Ariat faded denim jacket and a pair of eight-hundred dollar natural colored, J. Chisholm Ostrich boots. Gunner carried a black, 20x, four-hundred and fifty dollar Stetson hat, while the Championship Buckle sparkled against the red western sky. "The Buckle" is the pinnacle of success, the crowd-stopping accessory throughout the twenty-three states west of the Mississippi River. From Edmonton and Calgary to Mexico City, the "Gold Buckle" bestowed royalty on the individualistic renegades known as cowboys. The premonitory aura surrounding the gold buckle revolves around mortality. Most acquisitions involving ten-karat gold, sterling silver and multiple diamonds emanate from Tiffany's. The small, tight, middle-aged body of Gunner McGarrity carried the over-sized buckle with one message-World Champion. Gunner McGarrity spent the bulk of his life defying the odds against earning a living through bull-riding, bucking the odds against surviving in one piece through the seventeen years of bull-riding, and walking away with the rodeo equivalent to the Holy Grail. No one could ever take away the moniker, "World Champion."

They would drive Cody's "new" truck to Los Angeles. Cody drove with Gunner in the shotgun seat. Russell took his place in the small second seat behind the main bench. There was no discussion. Everyone seemed to know where to go. Gunner McGarrity evaporated the three hours to Los Angeles. The man could talk the ears off an elephant. Gunner began the trip by talking about the popularity of rodeo.

"You know." Gunner liked to skip about. "The Cowboy Downhill each year in Steamboat Springs draws more spectators than all of the World Cup Races combined in Colorado." McGarrity was referring to the annual ski gathering of Rodeo Cowboys at the Colorado resort.

"On any given weekend, there may be two dozen sanctioned rodeos going on across the country. Riders can choose the location they enter based on the animal draw, the prize money and the proximity to their home. "

"What got you started in bull-riding?" Cody asked. The Pacific Ocean raced by the banks of Highway 101.

"My daddy owned a farm in Texas." Gunner loved talking about his father. "That man was the toughest son of a bitch that I ever met. He never made it big in rodeo. Daddy rode mainly bareback, but he worked nearly one-hundred twenty hours per week on the ranch. Given that there are only one-hundred sixty-eight hours in a week, Daddy had less than seven hours per day to sleep, eat three meals, take a bath, fix anything around the ranch or the house that needed fixin' and teach me and my brothers to ride, hunt, fish and fight. We had fifteen hundred head of cattle on that ranch most of the time. Before I was ten, I could ride anything with four legs."

"My older brother, Mark, and I used to have a contest to see who could find more strays before lunch. I was ten and Mark was thirteen. I knew where the steers hid. They thought they had their own secret path to freedom. I corralled each and every one of them. Kicked Marks' ass every time." Gunner pointed to a spectacular home on the outskirts of Santa Barbara.

"The guy that lives there owns a production company in Los Angeles. Stephen Davis got me started in commercials. So far this year, we have Coors Light, Pontiac, Pepsi-Cola and Wrangler contracted. When the commercials call for horses and someone that knows how to ride, they bring me in. Stephen Davis and his friends pay a king's ransom to go on one trail ride each year. Shit, they drop more money in a week than I earned in sixteen years on the circuit. "

"Did you know Lane Frost?" Cody asked and looked over at Gunner. Gunner paused before answering.

"Sure, I knew Lane." Gunner spoke slowly. Russell Den sat up from the rear seat. Everyone listened when the subject fell on Lane Frost. "I retired from riding years before Lane made such an impact on bull riding. Lane connected with the crowd. The little hand waves after a successful ride. The long hair and gregarious aura bucked the rodeo trends. But Lane was different, in other ways. Lane made more than one appearance at the Bull-Riding School. Lane Frost was my guest instructor for three different Christmas seminars that we put on for free. Kids from all over California were invited to the ranch for a full daylong seminar on bull riding. At the end of each day, even the smallest kids, got to ride on a bull. Of course, these bulls were softer than most horses I own. They might lope out into the arena for a few feet and stop. Myself or Lane would be right next to them. It was always a tossup as to whose smile was larger, the kids or ours." Gunner McGarrity spoke with a genuine reverence for Lane Frost.

"What happened to him?" Cody continued for obvious reasons.

"Lane was killed in Cheyenne, Wyoming last year. After having won the World Championship in 1987, Lane became the most popular rider in the sport's history. The guy was just likable. Lane had a smile that transcended generations and genders. At Cheyenne Frontier Days in 1989, Lane had completed a successful eight-second ride on a bull named " Takin Care of Business." Lane dismounted from the bull, when the bull quickly pivoted and hit Lane twice from behind. Lane had not gotten to his feet, yet. The second hit with the bull's horns severed a main artery. Lane died within minutes. We all know the risks." Gunner's voice trailed off. "Why do you ask about Lane Frost? Seems like he is the only rodeo competitor that anyone from back East has ever heard of. Was he well known in Chicago?" Gunner asked.

"Wasn't there a guy named Larry Mayan in rodeo? I knew he had some boot line or something?" Cody simply reflected the general knowledge of rodeo held by most mid-westerners.

"Larry Mayan was a six-time PRCA All-Around Champion between 1966-1973. Larry set the standard that no one has been able to match. Lane matched or exceeded Larry's following, but not the scope of his talent. Mayan rode saddle bronc, bareback, and bulls. Larry was the most focused cowboy that I ever met." Gunner knew him well. "Do you know what core is, Cody?" Gunner McGarrity asked.

"In what context, Gunner?" Cody followed. Cody Law was not intimidated by McGarrity, yet fascinated by the foreign territory.

"Core is what great bull riders possess. There is an infinite risk in what they do. Core is where the crossroads of trends miss the mark. Let me give you an example. The association of great numbers lack core. Harley Davidson owners are the epitome of this concept." Cody smiled. McGarrity had no idea the association loomed so apropos. Gunner continued. "Harley owners buy big bikes and immediately cling to the notion that they belong. They purchase expensive leather chaps, leather vests and jackets. The bikes come with everything from stereos and telephones to custom running lights. The motorcycles look more like circus bikes than road bikes. The Harley owners may be passionate about their hobby, but hobbies are not where men are defined. Motorcycle clubs resonate the perception of camaraderie. When no inherit risk or sacrifice exists, core is not relevant. Bull-riding is the essence of core. Rodeo breeds from the wealth of participation. That participation cannot exist without risk and sacrifice. Other clubs are inclusive by means of money. Rodeo doesn't care how much money any contestant may possess. You are a member through dedication and the core of your commitment. Lane Frost or Larry Mahan could have come from

Martha's Vineyard or Odessa, Texas. Participation is not the result of a choice, but the result of dedication. Results are not measured by the latest sought after apparel or the fancy machines purchased as an afterthought to one's youth. Results are measured by actions. The difference between a club and rodeo is the difference between painted perception and putting yourself in harm's way. Lane Frost and Larry Mahan exuded core. Most men never come close. " Gunner reveled in the fraternity of his sport. The message eluded most. Gunner continued with his mantra.

"Where I was raised, Cody, you have to earn someone's respect. The wealthy and famous get to skip that stop. People are instantly your friend because of who you are or what you have. Cowboys make you earn it."

"Gunner, I did not come here to argue the virtues of what your profession requires from the participants. Truthfully, I had never heard of Lane Frost before a few days ago." Cody admitted. "Someone I know in Colorado was a big fan. She kinda had a shrine set up in her room for Lane Frost. We never spoke about him, so I was curious."

"Who was your friend?" Gunner inquired naturally.

"A girl I know from Castle Rock." Cody was a bit evasive.

"Your daughter?" Gunner knew when to get to the point.

"Easley talked to you about my daughter?" Cody shot back.

"Cadrell had some thoughts about why you wanted to pursue bull-riding. He really didn't tell me anything more than the set of circumstances that brought you to Castle Rock. You just told me what I wanted to know." Gunner went on.

"Cody, I do not run a wealthy, mid-life crises, dude ranch. For me to get involved with a thirty-two year old, Chicago businessman, there has to be a whole lot more than Allen Beacom calling me to ask for a favor. For some reason, Allen is under the illusion that I owe him. I don't owe him squat, but if letting him believe that myth will bring a couple good Brahmas each year, well then let him believe. You want to connect somehow with your daughter through bull-riding. She is part of a nightmare back in Castle Rock. Cadrell gave me some background. Remember Cody, my school is not a vehicle for anyone's personal vindication or penance. What we do is too dangerous to bounce in and give it a whirl." Gunner preferred to bruise an ego in exchange for a broken neck.

"I believe that the sub-conscious does not know the difference between where you are and where you want to be. If you can imagine yourself next to your daughter, protecting your daughter, then you must practice whatever it is that will get you there. Don't dream it. Live it. That is the only way for you to arrive where you want to be. Do I think you can get there through bull-riding? Fuck, no. But, it does not matter what I believe." Gunner finished, not looking for a reply. "Remember Cody, I told you on the phone that honorable motivation is the fuel. Without it, the engine simply will not run."

The entrance to the Los Angeles Equestrian Center was located only blocks from the Disney Studios in Burbank, California. Cody guided the truck with Gunner's directions to the guards at the Center's entrance. Admission to the parking lots cost ten dollars. Cody reached in his wallet.

"Wait." Gunner exclaimed. "All we have to do is show my PRCA Masters Membership Card. That will take care of any fees." Gunner rifled through his wallet and then the pockets of his jacket. "Shit, I know I have that card somewhere." The cars and trucks began to line up behind them.

"Fuck it." Cody said. "The ten bucks is no big deal." Cody reached for his wallet, again.

"Yes, it is a big deal." Gunner announced emphatically. "Here, young man. This is my membership card." Gunner leaned across the truck and stuck his World Championship Buckle in front of Cody and visible to the gate guard. "1970 World Bull-Riding Championship. My name is Gunner McGarrity."

"Not a problem, boys." The guard perked up. "Please, go right in." The yellow and white gate rose quickly.

"Do we need tickets?" Cody asked naively.

"No." Gunner answered with authority, yet somewhat surprised the guard responded to the buckle. Judging by the guard's age, Gunner took a flyer on whether the buckle or the name would generate a reaction. "Cody, pull the truck all the way around to the back where the stock trucks are located. We will enter through the contestant doors." Cody drove the truck to the rear of the structure. The lot was a mass of pick-ups, mobile homes, horse trailers, and semi-trailers for stock transport. There had to be more than a thousand vehicles in the rear lot, all larger than the truck Cody and Gunner pulled up in.

"Most of the riders compete and travel together. The camper back-ends on most of these trucks will house three or four cowboys for months at a time. They all pool travel expenses, while one guy takes care of all entry forms and collects the entry fees for each rodeo." Gunner, Russell and Cody approached the back gates. A long row of iron fences was erected to lead the animals to their specified holding pens. The bulls seemed rather docile in the pens.

"They seem pretty calm." Cody observed as the trio entered the arena.

"Some of these guys will let you pick their nose out here in the back pens." Gunner explained. "Put a rope on their nuts and a rider on their back and you'll understand what rank means."

Gunner McGarrity was an attraction inside the arena. Fans yelled, livestock hands tipped their hats, and contestants reached out to shake Gunner's hand. A World Champion had entered the building. As Gunner approached the bull chutes, a collective rush to greet the man began. Gunner held court behind the chutes. Strewn about in a sea of cowboy rigging bags, ropes, chaps, special boots, spurs and Tiffany deerskin gloves, Gunner McGarrity greeted his son, Jason, and the other riders for the evening. Gunner McGarrity would work the chute for Jason, while the other riders would jostle to catch a glimpse of the Gold Buckle, although none would admit to such quick peeks. Cody and Russell were pulled up to the support plank behind the chute.

"Stay up here with us." Gunner pronounced. Gunner made all the introductions. Russell Den longed for the day he would be the one stretching and tightening the chaps. Russell knew his time would come. Cody Law felt like a Sherpa in Kansas. The bulls were led into the chutes. The smell was horrific. Each chute held a half-dozen support staff to assist the riders. The seats were filled to capacity. On this night, the attendance capped seven thousand.

The first introductions were made for the bull riders. Bull riding was always the last event at a rodeo. Gunner timed the trip to bring them in at the exact time the bull riders would begin. Cody eyed the chute next to them. The agitated bull bucked repeatedly in the chute. The rider had to sit up and pull off the bull twice. A large cowboy pulled the rope with the force of three men. The rider pounded his fist, strapped against the rope. Each rider wraps the rope twice around his riding hand after the slack has been pulled tight. The wrap was complete. The bull rider pushed his hat down hard on his head and nodded quickly.

The gate swung open and nearly one ton of angry muscle and bone burst into the arena floor. The bull jumped and spun hard away from the rider's hand. The unusual move caught the rider by surprise. This bull had a history of spinning into the rider's hand right out of the gate. The initial move pulled the rider too far to one side. The bull bucked the rider on his next kick. The time frame covered less than four seconds. No score.

Cody dodged the steady stream of tobacco juice shooting from almost every male participant or spectator behinds the chute area. Gunner had explained during the trip to Los Angeles, that all PRCA rodeos had a dress code. Contestants were required to wear long-sleeved shirts, jeans and hats.

"Hey, Gunner." Cody leaned over while standing next to the center of attention. "What's with all the Wrangler jeans." Cody gazed quizzically about the chute area.

"Cody." Gunner turned and smiled. "Levi's are like a cheap hotel. No ball room." Gunner shook his head because he knew that every cowboy from Amarillo to Calgary had heard that line and he was certain that Cody had not.

Jason McGarrity was up next. Gunner did not say a word. Any advice or critique may come after the ride but never before. Gunner pulled his son's rope to the desired tension. The bull was small, by all standards, but carried the reputation of wildly agile and active.

Two weeks ago, a rider named Troy Lawton, scored an eighty-nine on the same bull. Gunner never believed in scouting bulls, but many other riders devote tremendous attention to the scouting reports and habits of the bulls in the circuit mix.

Jason McGarrity was introduced as the son of World Champion Bull Rider, Gunner McGarrity. The hat came down hard and the chute was pulled open. The reports were accurate. The bull spun so fast out of the gate, Jason's hat was jerked off on the first move. Jason held court. He stayed up on the bull's back, riding high up over the front shoulders. Jason's spur action bought him a secure position briefly and then hung on, as the bull did not tire during the full eight seconds. Jason held his seat and did not fall into trouble once during the ride. The acrobatic animal scored well with the judges. Gunner's presence didn't hurt. A rider forced to make a miraculous save may ignite the crowd, but the judges will dock the rider for slipping out of position in the first place. Jason McGarrity's score was eighty-one, good for third place and a twenty-six hundred dollar paycheck.

The back parking lot at the Los Angeles Equestrian Center began to empty. After the completion of the bull-riding, the stands emptied like the two-minute warning in a football game where the score separation exceeded three touchdowns. The spectators, lined up in a procession. Four-wheel drive SUV's and expensive foreign cars, filled the main exit road leading out of the Equestrian Center. The rodeo contestants, for the most part, loaded pick-up trucks, campers and minivans congregated in the muddy back parking lot of the arena. Stock trailers lined up to retrieve the animals. Scores of bulls, horses, steer and calves would be hustled up ramps, down make-shift iron fenced corridors, and slotted into trucks ready for transport to the next rodeo.

Dusty, Copenhagen stained rigging bags were thrown into equally dusty vehicles. Some traveling contestants had lawn chairs set up near their trucks. The weary cowboys sat in the mist of the cool California night. Hours and hours of cramped travel and service station meals led to the eight-second window of opportunity they all sought. A mouthful of California clay, courtesy of a one-ton locomotive with horns was mostly what they got.

Small enclaves of rodeo cowboys shared a beverage or two, compared notes on the upcoming preferred road selections, or arranged a detour to the nearest honky-tonk before departing for the next stop on the PRCA Tour. Most of the Equestrian Center contestants would be headed to Sacramento, California. Others were en route to San Antonio, Texas. A bag of pretzels, a six-pack of A & W Root Beer, and a pressed out tin of chewing tobacco comprised a full load and signified departure was eminent.

Cody Law, Russell Den and Jason McGarrity walked back to the extended cab Ford pick-up that served as traveling home to Jason McGarrity, Sonny Wright and Dale Dunaway. The trio mirrored the old rodeo adage, *too lazy to work and afraid to steal. Essentially, rodeo cowboys are lazy fuckups, who fear danger less than they hate work.*

Gunner would require forty-five minutes to eventually make it out of the arena. Everyone, from the ushers to the bullfighters, clamored for a bit of time with the former World Champion. A small contingent of young females clung to the moving entourage of Gunner McGarrity. The girls ranged in age from nineteen to twenty-four. A tall brunette wore a Stetson "Turlock" 4x hat and a black berber frock coat with rose design ribbons on the collar and shoulders. Fringe epaulets hugged each arm. Painted-on jeans with concho insets lined each leg. The captivating young ladies had bull-riders on their minds. A formidable World Champion would present an unexpected trophy. Gunner played a game of eye contact throughout the evening.

Outside the arena, another group of contestants began shattering the late evening quiet with a bull whip contest in the parking lot. Alternate cowboys took turns attempting to strike a variety of target balloons with an ear-splitting bullwhip. Jason smiled at the ineptitude displayed by some of his fellow riders.

"How long will Gunner take?" Cody asked Jason.

"Anybody's guess?" Jason laughed and threw his hat in the back of the truck. "That man can seduce more women at fifty-four years old than the collective twenty-something talents combined throughout this parking lot. My mother miraculously still puts up with the man. Through twenty-nine years of marriage, my mother left Gunner four times and tried to shoot him once." Jason often referred to his father by his first name.

Gunner McGarrity was the actual name on the birth certificate. Jacquie Moore married Gunner McGarrity when she was nineteen years old. Gunner was a young rodeo junkie and never pretended to be anything more or anything less. Jacquie stopped traffic in her younger days. A pretty brunette with a figure to rattle the bravado at Central Coast High School. Two children and one miscarriage added weight. More than the weight, Jacquie bore the stress of motherhood with an absentee father. Gunner's rise in the rodeo ranks left the time at home more infrequent and the influence on his son's subliminal. The boys worshipped an absent enigma. Jacquie battled the everyday storms of two boys struggling through adolescence inside the mirror of a burgeoning icon.

In 1976, Douglas Hall wrote of Gunner McGarrity and his brethren, *they craved a special freedom; and once they gained that freedom they were proud enough and jealous enough of it to guard it with their lives one moment and reckless enough to turn right around and risk it in the most foolish way the next moment.*

"My father was an absentee myth during my childhood." Jason continued. "Gunner came home long enough to heal whatever injuries he happened to be nursing at the time. Gunner made sure that my older brother, Tyler and I were playing baseball, football, basketball, or any other organized sport outside of rodeo. The checks came sporadically from all the county fair rodeos and tour stops where Gunner made the short go. When Gunner left after a short stay at home, my mother would cry and curse the last time she would allow him to return. During my first ten years, the nicest thing my mother ever said about my father was that he was a *dull-witted, whippet-sniffing, cheater.*"

"What brought you into bull-riding, if Gunner kept pushing you into other sports?" Cody asked while eyeing the arena's back entrance. Gunner was nowhere to be found.

"Gunner started building the school when it became evident that his competitive days were numbered." Jason pushed a wad of tobacco into his mouth. "My brother and I were still in junior high at the time. Gunner was a martyr in Santa Maria. The majority of local kids idolized Gunner. The magazine covers and commercial stills covered the house. My friends knew Gunner's ranking before I did. Gunner was the Antichrist force within each member of our family. My father played by no rules and everyone worshipped him. My mother played by all the rules and we all resented her discipline. Gunner never took the heat at home. My mother was driven down every road of deception, infidelity and broken promises. She drove back up the road, back to Gunner every time. My brother and I were programmed to become something else. My mother was determined to raise the antithesis to Gunner McGarrity. What she got were two clones hell-bent on following some elusive footsteps into the world Gunner loved."

"Hey, Jason." Gunner yelled from the exit ramp leading to the stock pens. Gunner climbed the grade to the rear parking lot. Fifteen years ago, Gunner McGarrity would have been all over those conchos. "I funneled a lovely young princess over to Sonny and Dale. She has two friends, both

Mexican from south L.A. Ooouuueee!" Gunner whistled. "They make cute puppies, but ugly dogs. Go on, and bale those boys out, Jason. I've got to get back to the ranch. We have three plus hours to drive tonight. Jason, nice ride, tonight You rode him high and never lost your free hand. The score reflected the size of the bull. That was a ninety-point ride on an eighty-point bull. I told Sonny, he looked like a prairie puppy on a tranquilized sheep. Cody could have rode his bull. Good luck, son. Let's go, boys." Gunner hugged his son walked to the white pick-up.

"Thanks for coming, Dad." Jason waved as he headed for the trio of young ladies. Jason was more like Gunner than Tyler. Jason began moving up the PRCA rankings during the year and had a realistic chance of making the NFR Finals at the Thomas and Mack Center in Las Vegas. Jason joined Gunner in many of the commercials they contracted for. Jason had the McGarrity wandering eye and the charm to match. Tyler was married with one young son and living on the ranch in Santa Maria. Tyler rode bulls competitively for two years after high school. The money never justified the hardships of the road. It rarely does. Tyler consciously tried to be like his father. The match never blended. Tyler supported a soft soul and a kindred connection to his mother. Tyler's concerted effort to become his father failed outside the arena.

Actually, Tyler had more talent than Jason. Tyler stuck on the bull like he was meant to be there. Tyler often took the lead role at the school when Gunner was out of town. Jason would never attempt the position. Tyler's decision to pursue life outside of the PRCA, was pragmatic, not steeped in cowboy folklore that hails the nomadic solitude and emotional wastelands breeding on the rodeo tour. Tyler didn't like to drink and he possessed Jacquie's non-aggressive disposition, not an attribute at midnight in a Montana tavern stuffed with over-served, shit-faced, wandering egos looking for a fight.

Jason was a loose cannon from the age of three. Jacquie knew she had a miniature version of the husband she loathed and worshipped. Jason grew up with the sparkle in his eye and the trigger on his fist. Jason painted Gunner's shadow on a cloudy day, and he swelled with pride throughout every visit Gunner made to watch him ride.

Russell Den fell asleep in the back of the truck some twenty miles outside of Burbank. Cody drove. The miles didn't matter. The time didn't matter. It would be nearly three o'clock in the morning when the trio would finally arrive at the ranch. Cody could have driven to San Francisco while listening to Gunner expound on the virtues surrounding rodeo life. Renegades rarely grow up, they simply grow old. The beards became flecked with gray. The chest and shoulders moved south as the middle widened. But they would all choose one more ride aboard a piss-ass Brahma bull over a decade to talk about it.

"Gunner, explain the physical process to get me into a rodeo?" Cody asked, unfamiliar with the realm he would novitiate.

"You are asking me what the physical process at the school entails?" Gunner tried to clarify.

"No." Cody explained. "I want to know how I go about entering a rodeo once I complete the necessary training at the school."

"Cody, this is not a place that I wanted to go so soon." Gunner garnered a more serious tone. "I can try to teach you to ride a bull. Maybe, if you're an exceptional athlete with the right mindset, we may get you ready to compete at a local rodeo. But, boy if you are trying to make a name for your self in bull-riding for the sole purpose of attracting the attention of your daughter then you need to explore other methods of attracting her attention. Son, you saw what these boys were doing tonight. They have been riding bulls for most of their lives. Not one of them is in the top ten. Dale and Sonny grew up on ranches. They have been grabbin' earth since they were crawlin' in it. Jason used to ride the steers on the ranch when he was six years old. I'd take him to local rodeos that I competed in. Jason was sittin' on bulls in diapers. Rodeo is not a play station where college kids work off steam. Rodeo is a way of life. Most men give up families to pursue it. Any women blind enough to fall in love with men whose sole ambition revolves around a gold belt buckle will learn once and then avoid rodeo men like a grizzly in a fire storm. I believed the trip to Los Angeles would dowse the fantasy swimming in your head. " Gunner wasn't preaching. He spoke like a man and expected the same.

" Gunner." Cody replied quietly. "I have spent my whole life pursuing things that I thought were important or at the very least, pursuing things that I thought made me happy. A twelve-year old girl, who does not know me, has taught me that a human being can endure anything if they believe in something out there. I'm not sure what my daughter believed in to get her through what she has lived through but something is out there. You told me on the way down to Los Angeles that a bull-riders mentality has to endure pain and injuries. You told me that a true bull-rider is able to endure anything for eight seconds. Devon's eight seconds have lasted twelve years. I am not going to give this up just because I didn't grow up on ranch and the chances for success seem a bit remote."

"Fair enough, Cody." Gunner smiled. "You need to obtain a PRCA permit to enter a rodeo. The requirements are slim at the local level. You must be eighteen-years old and pay a permit fee. I believe the permit fee is somewhere around one hundred and fifty dollars. Once you have obtained a permit, the goal is to "fill" the permit. Filling the permit entails winning a specified amount of money during one year. Once the permit is filled, the permit is converted to a full-time membership to the PRCA. Full-time members can compete at any sanctioned PRCA Rodeo. Permit contestants are limited to the rodeos accepting permit entrants. Most big money rodeos attract too many full-time contestants, so the permit slots are non-existent in high-profile rodeos. If you are going to make a name, it's going to start in two-stoplight towns and with rodeos that pay a top prize of five hundred dollars. There are some eight hundred rodeos across the country sanctioned by the PRCA. About twenty-five will offer total purses worth enough to justify a career. Rookies that make a name are rare. Training starts in the morning. Sleep in and we'll begin with meditation at ten o'clock."

"Meditation?" Cody was perplexed.

"My rules, my methods." Gunner proclaimed.

"Meditation." Cody nodded. The trio arrived at the ranch early in the morning. Cody and Russell slid into the musty beds inside the student bunkhouse. Russell was snoring instantaneously. Cody laid awake, lost in the impossible task he had embarked upon. Cody's thoughts raced back to Castle Rock. He fell asleep, curled up like a child.

* * *

Billy Don Barrett was not a stranger to the emergency room at Douglas County. Devon's visit for the "self" ingested ammonia two years before was followed by a visit from her mother. Kirsten was brought in eighteen months prior for abdominal pains and a concussion sustained in a fall down the basement stairs. Basement stairs have been exceptionally treacherous for female spouses.

Other visits to the Douglas County Hospital emergency room included a fight at the Rascal Flats where an argument between Barrett and another patron left Billy with a fork in his right forearm. The current stay at Douglas County Hospital may have been longer than one week, except that Billy was less than the ideal patient. Barrett sustained a unique plethora of injuries. The cumulative effect became life threatening. The two broken ribs punctured the right lung. Broken ribs are generally left to heal themselves. If the jagged bones lacerate the lung then the chest cavity becomes an air pocket. A chest tube was inserted for three days to relieve the pressure from leaked air inside Billy's chest. The ear injuries would heal over the course of three to four weeks. The broken bones in one hand required the surgical placement of eleven pins to support the small breaks throughout the hand. Sixty-seven stitches closed a wealth of cuts inside Billy's mouth. The worst injury could be categorized as a cranial facial dislocation. Barrett sustained a Leforte II fracture of the left and right upper maxilla or a broken jaw. The multiple fractures within the facial structure allowed a physician to place his thumbs inside Billy's mouth and his index fingers along side Billy's temple, while at the same time, moving freely the facial bone structure. The maxilla is the upper bone on the jaw where the upper teeth are attached. The right and left maxilla separated completely from the hard palate called a fracture line or palatial split. Interdental wire ligatures were used to attach and secure the bone structure within the jaw. The wires stayed in place for four to eight weeks.

Billy Don Barrett required surgery to reconstruct the remaining facial damage, but the doctors had to wait until the facial swelling subsided and the punctured lung was stabilized. An IV drip slid eight to ten milligrams of morphine into Billy's arm every three hours. At the end of three days, Billy had stabilized. He was no longer considered critical.

Four days later, Billy Don Barrett was released from Douglas County Hospital. Billy was fed a myriad of nutritional supplements, the equivalent of Carnation Instant Breakfast, but the supplements were much harder to pronounce and much more expensive. The daily dosage of Vicodin couldn't compare to the morphine.

Kirsten and Devon spoke little of Billy's absence. Both reveled in it emotionally, but tempered any elation because they knew the absence was very temporary. Devon re-connected to the fairgrounds. She was able to walk up town and collect every new issue of Pro Rodeo News that she had missed. Billy did not allow magazine subscriptions, so the owner of Regal Drugs, Casey Willard, at the corner of Fourth and Main saved the occasional left over copies of the PRN's previous month's issue. Casey had a spot in his heart for Devon Barrett. Castle Rock knew something was wrong on Gilbert Street, but few wanted to explore a road they preferred to close. Relating to the situation at home, Devon was able to visit Casey on only rare occasions. During the week of Billy's hospital stay, Devon saw Casey every day.

Kirsten's sphere of emotional strangulation had closed slowly over the years. The obvious effects within Barret's reign of domination had been the absolute disintegration of Kirsten's self-esteem and the ability to make her own decisions. Kirsten's solitary thoughts or dreams of a better life had vanished. The systematic suffocation grew steadily. The majority of domestic violence is assigned a low priority in the eyes of the police, the neighbors, the schools, family and friends. The limited visibility of Billy Don Barrett's barbarism flourished within the blind eyes and deaf ears of Castle Rock. Domestic violence or child abuse when carried out by an intimate member of the family is often news the community would rather ignore than confront.

These are traditional boundaries more often protected by the police.

The immune definition surrounding "family dispute" continued to widen with alarming consequences. Acquired helplessness is a notion destined to trivialize domestic violence. Kirsten had been exposed to the progression of helplessness, a notion, thought by many to be learned along the way. In addition to the beatings, which Kirsten could have walked away from, she had acquired a veil of helplessness. Both were avoidable and theoretically her fault. Reality was that Kirsten had been forced into submission by constant intimidation and constant physical violence. The relentless oppression had quite methodically induced low self-esteem and difficulty in acknowledging her partner's behavior as criminal. Kirsten's inability to testify against Billy were not actions of choice, but reactions to the emotional breakdown inevitable given that no credibility had ever been accorded to any of Kirsten's fears. Devon's silence was driven by the fear of reprisals against her mother. Kirsten's silence was the reciprocal equivalent of imagining Devon's life alone with Billy.

Kirsten and Devon spent a week at home as they never remembered. No one spoke of the absent demons or the restoration of life without the restrictions associated with constantly watching the clock. The reprieve ended when Kirsten drove her husband home from Douglas County Hospital. Billy Don Barrett came home one week after the savage beating he received behind the Rascal Flats tavern. No suspects were in custody and the likelihood rose daily that resolution to the crime was remote.

Billy Don Barrett spent the first days at home in a medicated state of unusual calm. Barrett received the pampered treatment accorded any injured spouse under extreme circumstances. Devon stayed in her room, cut off from the only television located in the living room. During Billy's hospital stay, Devon was able to watch evening programs forbidden during her upbringing. Devon plowed through the magazines piled in her closet like an exiled playwright deprived of his imagination.

Billy was somewhat stationary in the house. The injuries seemed to prevent the physical mobility necessary to resume the abuse immediately. Kirsten knew the savage beating of her husband was not a bar fight. She prayed the messenger delivered the message. The wired jaw silenced the explosive tirades, so predictable on a daily basis.

The first week of Billy's homecoming ended without incident. While he was able to walk, the broken ribs coupled with the wired jaw kept Billy remarkably quiet. Within a week, however, Billy's behavior began to take on vengeful consequences. Billy's left hand sustained two broken fingers. The right hand required surgery and was immobilized due to the pins inserted during the operation. The left hand was fixed in a small cast surrounding the two broken fingers and extending down past the wrist. The resulting appendage created a solid club.

The house at 222 Gilbert Street created an eyesore in a block filled with homes built immediately after the Second World War. The homes bore marginal landscaping, peeling facades and crumbling walkways. Billy Don Barrett's home loomed above the tall grass and overgrown bushes near the front of the house. Inside, the house belched of soiled cat litter. Pets, that had not seen a bath since prior to the presidential elections in 1988, left a malodorous trail throughout each room.

Devon had heard Kirsten and Billy arguing earlier in the evening. Billy had been home for nearly three weeks. The level of tension had risen markedly in the past week. Barrett had grown increasingly agitated from the restriction in his mouth. At one point, days earlier, Billy took a wire cutter and split one side of the surgical bonds on his jaw. Exasperated, the attending physician at Douglas County Hospital, had seen enough of Billy Don Barrett. Billy had the wires taken out of his mouth four weeks from the date of the injury and some two weeks sooner than a first year medical student would have recommended.

Devon retreated to her closet as the verbal nightmare grew in the living room. Billy was back to the numbing consumption of anything from grain alcohol to cheap wine. The sedative on this day was Vicodin and the lion's share from a quart bottle of any cheap Kentucky bourbon. A small radio and the confines of the closet reduced the degradation to inaudible levels. Devon felt the pain of each open hand or swinging cast as her mother answered for the lapse in discipline while Billy was incapacitated. At various intervals during the evening, Devon would turn down the radio and pray the heavy-breath laden sobbing and muffled screams of "Stop it, Billy, I'm sorry, Please, please, stop, God, please stop, Billy," had ceased.

Just after ten o'clock, the house grew quiet. Devon curled in the rodeo decorated closet and stared at the magazine in front of her. Billy may have passed out. Devon could hear Kirsten in the bathroom fumbling with an ice bag. The sounds were as recognizable as the bells on an ice cream truck driving slowly down an Oak lined street on a summer afternoon. Devon often fell asleep in the closet, afraid to climb into bed. It was early March and the snow framed every snapshot surrounding Castle Rock and Douglas County. Near midnight and the winds picked up, moving the light snow down the street like a succession of transparent ballerinas.

The covering from Devon's window had been dislodged during Billy's absence. The room was unusually bright as the moon cast a pale glow on fragmented carpet strips. Devon lay curled up in the closet, barely asleep through the catatonic anxiety brought on by nightfall at 222 Gilbert Street.

With nothing more than Billy's scent approaching, Devon opened her eyes. The years of darkness in the closet, the basement confinement, and the duct tape punishment had accentuated Devon's senses much like those of the blind. Acute reactions to silence sent chills up the arms of the young girl. Four weeks brought the mind to the brink of a sanctuary. Barrett entered the room and closed the door. Devon grabbed her knees and buried her face.

"Come out here, girl." Barrett commanded while taking a seat on the bed. The smell of whiskey filled the room.

"Please, daddy." Devon's voice was soft and frightened. "I don't want to do this anymore." The words came but no one heard.

"Come out here." The command was repeated. "I need you out here now. It's what all girls do." Billy fumbled with the belt buckle on his jeans.

Kirsten lay shivering in her bed. The house was quiet, now. Kirsten's head pounded with pain and her eyes closed tightly to the hopeless encounters that came crashing back.

* * *

The twenty-one day session at the Gunner McGarrity Championship Bull-Riding School began promptly at 7:00 a.m. on a Monday morning in February. The school cost one-thousand four-hundred and seventy-five dollars. The current session was full. Fourteen enrollees filled the bunkhouse. There were five sets of bunk-beds and the others rolled sleeping bags out on the floor. Two slept in their trucks. Cody Law found the bunk house to be a mixing bowl dominated by stubborn, tobacco chewing drifters that enjoyed a good fight almost as much as drawing a bull with a zero ride percentage. Cody Law stood out like a neon truck stop in a black and white photo. At thirty-two years old, Cody was the oldest student by six years.

There was Tater Lewis at thirty years old, but Tater was not a student looking for a road to the National Finals Rodeo. Tater was a prison guard at the California State Penal Institute located thirty-one miles northwest of Gunner's ranch. Tater was an ex-Marine and took the course once a year. Tater came to ride Gunner's bulls during one weekend a month. In exchange for the rides, Tater worked on the arena for Gunner, fixing gates, repairing holding pens and generally maintaining the premises. Tater Lewis carried more weight than he did when he was twenty, but he held tough on Gunner's best stock.

The entire group came to Nipomo, California for one reason. Gunner McGarrity was the best bull-riding teacher in the country. They didn't have to like his methods or his philosophical approach. They did like the results. The reputation from Gunner's schools floated somewhere between useful and miraculous. The Gold Buckle on his belt allowed Gunner to command everyone's undivided attention at all times. Without the full attention from each student, they would be asked to leave with a full refund. There were few warnings and fewer departures.

On the first morning, Gunner pounded on the door to the bunkhouse at 7:00 a.m. and then waited outside like a drill sergeant for the detail to fall out. Fourteen, yawning, aspiring bull-riders stood in the red California sun next to the double barns that were used as the classrooms and the home for the mechanical bulls and bull simulators. The student's collective tobacco chewing breath could have killed one of the bulls from fifty yards away. Bud Hale, Kenny Davis, Guy Wood, and Jimmy Hooper came from Red Lodge, Montana, Bandera, Texas, Sheridan, Wyoming, and Midland, Texas respectively. They were young riders under the age of twenty. Kenny and Jimmy had experience on the circuit, but little success. Sonny Moore, 26, from Henryetta, Oklahoma and Olin Martin, 24, from Modesto, California were two former top fifteen riders on the PRCA circuit. During the last year, they had fallen from the top fifty and showed earnings less than ten thousand dollars.

Gunner was the guru. Twenty-one year old, R.D. Rese, from Tucson, Arizona was the 1989 NCAA All-Around Champion from the University of Arizona. R.D. focused on becoming the best in the world. R.D. fully expected to challenge Larry Mahan's record of six all-around titles. R.D. knew that those challenges did not stand a fool's chance until he honed his bull-riding skills.

Harley Haley, 23, from Clovis, New Mexico was the reincarnation of Mason Dayne on a bull. Dayne won the bareback championship in 1976, then went on to become a nationally recognized, country music recording star. Haley wrote songs, played a hypnotic acoustic guitar and possessed the voice of an angel. Harley Haley possessed the devil's temper which landed him in jail more than the songs or the riding had landed him at the cashier's window.

Wheeler Green, 22, was born in New York City. Wheeler grew up in Sioux Falls, South Dakota. Wheeler's parents were killed in a plane crash when Wheeler was three. Brought up by his grandparents in South Dakota, Wheeler never sat on a bull until he was fifteen. Wheeler Green loved to be introduced from New York City. Fresno, Dallas and Missoula filled out the roster of hometowns.

The eclectic mix of cowboys fumbled for the dusty hats and boots scattered about the bunkhouse. Gunner waited outside. The group finally settled into one line. The air was dry and cool. The mountain breezes seemed to catch the flavor of the grapes covering the hillsides around the ranch.

Each morning began with a forty-five minute run. No jogging shorts or running shoes. These boys ran in boots and jeans. Gunner believed in cleaning the pipes every morning. The path followed the property lines up and down the hidden valleys that were home to the hundreds of bulls on the ranch. They looked like sedated cattle when the hacking, struggling students filed by in an ugly image of solidarity.

Once the run was completed, Gunner moved the group into the main classroom barn. Orange juice and apple juice waited on the tables. No coffee or tobacco was permitted before meditation.

Gunner spread the group out. The main barn was large. The troops had regained their breath. Gunner ordered each one of the students to assume a position on the floor, sitting cross-legged.

"Remove your hats, gentlemen." Gunner ordered. "We will be meditating for the next twenty minutes. Meditation will be a regular exercise each morning while you are at the Gunner McGarrity Bull-Riding School. You will get out of the exercises exactly what you lay down. These exercises are not for me. They are for you. If you do not want to improve your riding, improve your rankings, or your income then ignore these opportunities." Gunner scanned thc room and mentally recorded the disenchanted.

"Meditation, boys, is a natural state of consciousness that can occur at many levels. You may miss a stop sign because of a daydream. This is a light form of meditation. Pure consciousness occurs through pure relaxation. Meditation is calm breathing, minimal movement and quiet. Meditation is repeating to yourself that which has become habitually detrimental to your forward progression. Openly confront that which holds you back. If you are intimidated by the top riders, then you must begin to believe that you can duplicate anything they do. Say to yourself, I am confident about my own abilities and it is obvious that I am able to accomplish as much or more than any other man. Daydreams are windows to what you could be doing. How many of you have watched a ride and thought, *if only I could ride like that or if only I had that draw?* End your meditation by repeating a mantra that applies to you alone. Do not be surprised if what you have been repeating comes true." Gunner walked around the room and could feel the negative waves flowing. He smiled and continued.

"We are goal seekers. Bull riders are a breed apart. Our lives are not meaningful unless we have a specific goal on the horizon." The Maxwell Maltz in Gunner barked out like a carnival preacher at a state fair. "You know what you want to be! You know where you want to go! Then why the hell arc you not headed in the right direction? Because, you do not believe it, yet." Gunner was moving through the students. Whether they believed him or not, they listened. The room was dead silent except for the miniature

Moses in blue jeans.

"It's time to determine where you want to go and what you want to be. What is your passion? We know it's related to bull-riding, but where does it end? What is the goal? What is the absolute passionate goal that you would pay someone for the privilege of completing? Be specific. Now, the exercises we practice will eliminate the obstacles now blocking the way to your goals. If you don't have obstacles then you wouldn't be here. If you choose not to explore these avenues then you are aiding the obstacles in your life already. Clear your minds, boys. This is your script. Draw a map to your own success. Quit being a spectator to the pinnacle of where you want to be. Begin, now." Gunner stood at the doorway in a symbolic silhouette, shielding the exit from those thinking about using it.

Cody Law used the twenty minutes to focus on the tasks at hand and the main objective of his new vocation. Cody had always been skeptical of anything associated with hypnosis or meditation. Considering the drastic venue changes surrounding his life, the introduction of Gunner McGarrity's positive mental foundation offered no apparent downside. The mantra chosen by Cody Law consisted of five words, "Devon, I will get there."

The students moved to north barn after meditation. The front half of the north barn was set up like a classroom. The back wall held a huge video screen, whose technology loomed comically out of place in a barn. The right wall held a series of videocassette recorders and a mountain of videotapes. The barn was filled with ropes suspended from the ceiling, a basketball backboard badly in need of paint, promotional posters from the circuit when Gunner was competing, bucking machines and scores of old rodeo equipment. The barn was a playground for boys growing up with an eight-second whistle instead of a referee and a foul line.

Gunner instructed the students to take a seat. Next to each seat was small spittoon. The cowboys settled in and most took out the Copenhagen or Skoal and placed a wad between their cheek and gum. Cody lit a cigarette and was immediately instructed to never smoke in a barn. Gunner McGarrity stood before the fourteen male adolescents.

"We have a unique assortment in the room today." Gunner began. "We have two men that came tantalizingly close to a world championship two years ago and now can't find the upside to eighty points. Most of you have reached a level of talent that will satisfy the local level but will get you buried on the national scene. We will address every aspect of bull-riding to give you the tools to reach any level you want in this sport. You will be the only variable when you leave my school. We have one beginner in the group, who happens to be the elder statesman among you. Cody Law is from Chicago, Illinois. He is thirty-two years old and has never ridden a bull in his life. Cody wants to compete at the professional level this year. I told him that I did not believe that would be likely. I am fairly certain that my bulls are not going to be aware of Mr. Law's fancy boots. The bulls will not weigh Mr. Law's noble motivation. My guess is that Mr. Law will be on a plane back to Chicago, sipping a martini and licking a bruised ego before you guys can remember each other's name. I'm sure all of you can reinforce those thoughts. However, we are not the ones who will determine where Mr. Law ultimately will take himself."

"We are going to spend a day or two in the classroom before we put our asses on any bulls. Some of the basic information may seem redundant to those seasoned riders, but guess what? I haven't seen one your faces on the cover of PRN lately. I suggest that all fundamentally sound bull riders begin with the basics. When the scores come down and the money falls, the most common cause is the dissolution of the rider's fundamental skills."

"We are going to watch some video tape of your rides and the rides of the NFR top five riders from last year. We are going to look at the top ten bulls on the PRCA circuit this past year. Seven of these bulls have gone unridden as we speak today. Why are these bulls so difficult to ride? We will analyze the difference between success and mediocrity in the arena. Outside of the arena is another matter. Bull riding is done between the ears not between the legs. The sooner you all come to grips with that, the sooner you will exceed your own expectations." Gunner pulled a series of tapes from the wall. He held a red laser pointer in his hand. With the flip of a remote control console, the lights in the barn shut off. Gunner stood at the front of the group with a small, dim spotlight on his podium. The screen filled with the logo of the school.

"Gentlemen, how many times does the preparation of your equipment hinder your score or your ability to ride effectively? Experienced bull riders know how to prepare their ropes, their gloves, chaps, boots, and spurs. Bullshit. Some of the most experienced riders that I competed against, didn't know the first fucking thing about preparation. Gentlemen, before we begin to view the tapes, let's review your own preparation to ride bulls." Gunner pulled out the items he spoke of and continued.

"There are unlimited bull ropes to choose from. Spend more than $200 and you are wasting your money. I always rode with two cowbells because the weight helped to pull the rope off the bull quicker than one. Skip the black rosin. It's too gummy. Stay with brown or white rosin and keep it limited to the area where you hold the rope or the hand hold. Spread the rope out in the rigging bag. Don't curl it up in a little ball. The ends can come back to haunt you in a ride if they are all curled up."

"Size your glove and pick the material, but always tie the wrist off."

Gunner demonstrated by pulling a small rawhide tie around his wrist to seal off any loose buckskin at the end of the glove. "Tuck the ends of the string inside your glove, making sure that you don't cut off the blood flow to your hand. I liked buckskin but deerskin or any number of alternative gloves will work. It's personal preference." Gunner reached down and slipped a set of spurs onto his boots.

"I rode with my spurs turned in as much as they could go. Others ride with their toes out more and the spurs don't have to be so pronounced. Check the rowels before each ride. If they are too sharp then they cut the bull and do not hold your leg. If they are too dull they will slip right off and you will see the same result. I used to sharpen the rowels and then I ran them across the concrete to take the edge off. There are many, many other individual nuances that all championship riders attend to. The difference is that they attend to these matters before every ride. Let's get to the videotape."

Gunner hit the recorder and the first rider was Sonny Moore from the NFR Finals in 1987. Sonny rode only three out of ten at the Finals, but he was in top form for the year. Sonny finished twelfth on the money list for the year. Gunner took the three rides from the finals that Sonny completed and then pulled three rides from the past year, where Moore had fallen to below fiftieth on the money list. Gunner critiqued the rides.

"Sonny, your problems are so obvious that I wanted to start with these rides. As you can see in the first three rides, you are up over the bull and continue to climb back to the same spot after every spin and jump from the bull. You start up high in the chutes and stay there. Now, take a look at the rides from this year." Gunner wheeled the laser pointer to the top of the bulls back in the chutes.

"You see where you are starting the ride. You have to be a good six inches back from where you started two years ago. By starting back further, you fall behind that imaginary wall standing up from the bull's shoulder. Once back behind the wall, the rider falls into the house of pain or the area between the flank rope and your rope. Fall back into this area and you will end up in a house of pain. The bull dictates the ride every time from this seat. When the rider falls back on his pockets, the ride is over. Weight on your ass will take the weight off your legs. You will get bucked off every time. If you are lucky enough to pull yourself out of the house of pain then the judges will dock you for falling back there in the first place."

"Everything starts with riding high. Keep that light under your ass. Keep moving forward to regain your free arm position. Sonny, pull that free arm back to the head every time. You have been leaving it out there like a broken branch in the wind. Your free arm is your lead rope. Where your arm goes is where your head goes." Gunner continued to examine the rides of Sonny

Moore, detailing every mistake and holding the undivided attention of Sonny Moore and the entire group.

Gunner started with the most accomplished rider in the group for a reason. Get the most accomplished rider in your corner as soon as possible and the rest fall in like a jigsaw puzzle. The riders were examined one by one, while Gunner charted the mistakes and the areas that each rider would focus on at the arena.

"Olin," Gunner moved onto Olin Martin, a twenty-four year old rider from Modesto, California. Olin had two wins in 1988. In 1989, Olin had no top ten finishes. "Look at your fluidity from '88. Every move spoke of moving with the bull. When the bull turns into your hand, the pivot is smooth. When the bull jumps, your body compensates so your head isn't yanked down when the animal's elevation falls. Olin, you rode the bulls in '88."

"Last year, you fought the bulls. Take a look at your face coming out of the chutes. You are grimacing and hunched over. Gentlemen, when you decide to fight the bulls, you lose, period, end of career. A fucking underweight bull weighs fifteen hundred pounds. The rider weighs less than two hundred pounds. Do the math, Einsteins. Olin, the day you decided to go toe to toe with your rides, was the day you gave up the rankings. When the rider muscles the bull, he pulls the rope with every ounce of his strength. By pulling the rope, you pull your body into a hunched position. The hunched position is one of complete vulnerability. Your ass will slide down the bull's back resulting in the house of pain syndrome or your head will dip too low and the bull's recoiling head will smack into your face. Bulls are always going in a forward motion. When a rider pulls hard on the rope hand, the body moves downward to the point of the force. The body has got to ride high and be continually moving forward with the animal. We ride the bulls, gentlemen. We anticipate the bull's next move and glide to that spot. We do not fight the bulls."

Gunner walked over to Olin Martin, a former two-time student at the ranch, knocked Olin's hat off, shook his head, smiled and concluded. "I've told you that since you were a senior in high school and you are still falling back into old habits. Use your mind, gentlemen. The options are much greater for most of us. Olin, I'm not so sure." The laughter filled the barn. A wad of chew, courtesy of Sonny Moore, came flying in the direction of Olin Martin.

Lunch was an hour break. The dissection of each student filled the first day. At the end of the session, Gunner asked Cody Law to stay.

"There are specific steps we need to complete before I put your ass on a bull. I want to work with you, alone for an hour or so after each session. This may last the first week. It depends on you. Any problems with that?" Gunner asked.

"Not one." Cody replied.

"Good. Let's go down to the arena." Gunner pulled Russell Den aside. Gunner knew that Russell would not be able to pay for the complete course, so beside the obligation to repay Gunner, Russell or any other student in need of financial assistance would be called upon to help on the ranch.

"Russell, pull one of the saddle horses down to the arena. Do not put a saddle on the horse. Cody and I are going to spend some time with the horse."

On the edge of the arena fences, Gunner had erected two mechanical bucking machines and a padded bull simulator that could be manually directed. Gunner placed Cody on the manual apparatus first. The padded seat simulated the bull's back. The height was equal to a competition bull. A long metal rod extended from the front of the simulator, allowing Gunner to raise and lower the apparatus, reflecting the up and down motions of a bull. Gunner instructed Cody on where the free hand should be held and how to arch the back with each lunge from the animal. Cody's left hand was jammed into the hand hold, while Gunner pushed his ass up into the left hand.

"Remember, Cody. Stay up on your hand." Gunner instructed the new rider. Gunner, then pulled the rod down slowly. The simulator jerked down and Cody almost lost his balance. "Stay out over the bull's head." Gunner shouted and pushed the rod back up. Gunner continued the up and down motions until Cody moved into the slide instead of away from the moves. Cody sifted through a series of doubts. Shit, he thought about almost falling off a mechanical bull that was barely moving. Within ten to fifteen minutes, Cody began to catch the drift. Cody began to ride up over the imaginary head, his free arm high and the motion finally became fluid.

"Cody." Gunner announced while Russell finished raking the dirt inside the arena. "I have always found that one way to best introduce new bull riders to the sport is to work on a saddle horse, first. We will work without a saddle and pull a bull rope across the same area as the rope will fall on a bull. The feel and the motion are quite similar." Cody had forgotten or never knew how big horses were. Gunner continued.

"Let's put the horse in the chute first. This is Hank. He is the salt of the earth. This horse would let me put him in a sleep deprivation tank if I ordered him there. Hank will not surprise anyone. For our purposes today and tomorrow, we do not want any surprise moves." Cody couldn't have agreed more. Gunner placed the horse inside one of the chutes. He motioned Cody over.

"Did you bring the rigging bag?" Gunner asked.

"Yes." Cody answered. "I believe that everything on your list is included in the bag."

"Pull out your bull rope." Gunner instructed. He watched Cody slowly kneel down to the bag. Cody pulled the zipper ever so slowly. Gunner looked quizzically at his new student. The zipper continued to come down at a snail's pace. "What the hell are you doing?" Gunner finally yelled.

"I have heard of all the practical jokes played on the new guys. The most common prank seems to be the placement of a snake in the rookie's rigging bag, either in place of the bull rope or in addition to the bull rope. I am simply being cautious." Cody replied smugly, proud of his anticipation regarding the juvenile pranks.

"Cody." Gunner walked over to his new pupil. Gunner's demeanor took on the first condescending overtone. "Cody, there is no snake in your bag." Gunner yanked the bag away from Cody and dumped it upside down. The contents fell into the dirt. A bull rope, two gloves, assorted rawhide ties, a cow bell, some rosin, a shiny new pair of spurs and a slew of boot straps, slid into a pile at Gunner's feet.

"Bull riders will not play practical jokes or pranks on anyone they do not feel is one of them. For now, Cody, you are not one of them. There is an unspoken code of inclusion among all bull riders. Risk is a variable that can only be measured by actuality. There are no fine lines between bull riders. Rodeo is a business like many other businesses. Association to the sport is sought by many. There are unlimited support venues necessary to the successful participation of every sanctioned rider in the PRCA, but there is only one avenue available for the club. If that fucking bull's fury has not crossed your thighs, if the dry mouth before the gate opens has not crossed your lips, then the club is closed. When the rope pulls the circulation in your hand numb and the beast below your ass shivers to explode from the gate, when you can smell the bull's breath from the arena floor, then you have entered a world that you will never be able to explain to anyone. Your brothers will be stretching on the chute platforms and in the staging areas from Calgary to Corpus Christi. Fear is the ultimate divider. One cannot pretend to be a bull rider. The day a snake comes slithering out of your rigging bag is the day these men will welcome you into a very exclusive club. The club maintains a select membership where the dues include small monetary rewards, a brutal travel itinerary based out of a truck, and a broken body. The price is high. Cody, pick up this crap and bring your rope to the chute." Gunner whispered some instructions to Russell Den.

"Come here, Cody." Gunner stood at the chute. "There are a few basics that you need to remember every time you approach a ride. When climbing up into the chute, do not stick your feet inside the bars. An agitated bull could break your foot before you have even climbed into the chute. At the top of the chute drop your rope down like this." Gunner demonstrated with Cody's bull rope, how the rope should fall across the animal's back before the rider enters the chute. "This way, if the rope is going to spook the bull, then you are still on the outside of the chute. Let the rope fall below the bull's torso. The bells will tell you where the rope is. You are going to want to tie the rope off before you get set. Do you know why the rope has a bell attached to it?" Gunner asked.

"The bell helps pull the rope off the bull when the ride is done. Otherwise the rope will continue to get hung up on the bull long after the ride." Cody recalled from the morning session.

"That is only part of the reason." Gunner explained. "Bull riding would look and sound like a silent movie if the riders didn't use the bells." Gunner laughed and went on.

"After you have reached the top of the chute, straddle the chute like this (one foot on the top bar of the opposing rails inside the chute), then dip your knees down to touch the bull's back and let him know you are there. If the bull is going to fuss, then again, you are not in a position to incur any serious injuries. When you drop down on the bull, stay to the right side because you are going to ride left-handed. Again, if the bull pulls up in the chute, then you are not in a position to be slammed headfirst into the chute." Gunner demonstrated both movements. The first, if the rider was seated directly in the middle of the bull. Next, seated to the right side in the chute.

"Place your legs between the back end and the shoulders of the bull. There is more room down the chute at those points. The bull is not as wide between those points. You can see that here on the horse. Warm up your rope and hand-hold with some rosin. Place your hand in the hand hold with the little finger at the exact mid-point on the bull's back, the middle of the backbone. Wait until the rope is pulled to the desired tension. In the beginning you will have to trust me with the tension until you can get a feel for what you like. Once the tension is set, pull the rope across your hand, then behind the wrist and back through the hand again." Gunner demonstrating each movement slowly.

"Pack your hand down hard and lay the rope tail on the bull's neck. Check to see that the bull is flanked (a rear rope tied near the bull's testicles). Move up on your hand and nod. You are gone." Gunner sat on the horse and Russell flung open the gate. The horse did not move.

"Well, you get the picture, Cody" Gunner laughed. "Get up here and go through everything I just did." Cody and Gunner worked on the chute for more than one hour.

The next day after class, Gunner took Cody around the arena on the back of Hank. No saddle, just a bull rope to simulate the feel of a bull. Gunner had Hank cantor along the inside of the arena fences to continue Cody's preliminary drills before actually riding a bull. The first week moved quickly. Evenings were spent in Nipomo, having dinner at a truck stop. The company remained cold. Gunner's assessment held true. The bull riders kept their distance from Cody. Half the students were underage for alcohol and the other half did not drink much.

Cody was somewhat surprised in the beginning at the dead serious manner in which the students approached the school. The baffling focus among the riders would soon become lucidly clear. Cody kept to himself during much of the first week. The nature of the task began to take on realistic expectations. Doubts abounded as to the realistic shot at entering a sanctioned event. Christ, after a week, Cody had not yet ridden a bull. On Saturday night after driving with Gunner to Santa Maria for a "kick-ass" chili dinner and a couple beers, the two men arrived back at the ranch just before midnight. There were no weekdays or weekends at the school. Twenty-one days meant twenty-one consecutive days. Cody pulled the phone outside the bunkhouse, lit a Marlboro and called Cadrell Easley in Colorado Springs.

"Hello, who is this?" Cadrell Easley answered after the phone rang seven times. Cadrell and his wife had been asleep for nearly an hour. Easley's voice was scratchy and hoarse.

"Cadrell, it's me, Cody. I'm sorry to wake you up. Can you talk?" Cody asked, not at all concerned that he woke the man up.

"You are still alive." Easley referenced the bull riding school. "I suppose I can talk to a man who has managed to stay alive when there were those of us, certain that you would give up the mission by now. You didn't quit, did you Cody?" Easley's voice picked up.

"No, I did not quit." Cody shot back, not volunteering the fact that he had not ridden a bull yet.

"What's up. Gunner's a trip, huh?" Cadrell eased up.

"Gunner is a definite trip. This whole school is a fucking trip. I am living in a bunkhouse that has never seen the backside of a vacuum cleaner. There is more tobacco juice on the floor than in the fifteen spittoons scattered around the room. I am taking crap from kids, too young to buy a fucking beer. I own an entertainment conglomerate in the nation's second largest city and I am getting snubbed by high school dropouts and men, who consider riding two-thousand pound, spinning locomotives as a prerequisite to their own interpretation of a divine calling. I lit up a cigarette yesterday and got yelled at like I was eight years old. The other bull riders treat me like a pimple on an elephant's ass, insignificant and barely there. What's going on with Barrett? Have you seen him or Kirsten, lately?" Cody was venting.

The objective had not changed, but an epiphany crept up from Cody's arrival in Nipomo. Cody Law was not welcomed into Gunner McGarrity's Championship Bull Riding School by all. The general consensus centered on the arrogance of a man to announce that he sought to compete with the best riders in the world after a few weeks in training. No one was there to run Cody's declaration up the flagpole.

"I have seen Kirsten and Billy during the past week." Easley answered. "I have not seen Devon, except at the schoolyard. When Billy was in the hospital, Devon walked to the fairgrounds and up town almost every day. Since he has been home. Those trips have stopped. I saw Kirsten walking into a food mart the other day. She was wearing sunglasses but it was obvious that she was also wearing a welt under her right eye. I tried to talk to Kirsten, but she froze up when she saw me. Kirsten put her hand up and told me to stay away, that we were only making matters worse. I'm not sure that the "we" meant the police department or you and I. Barrett has not been out of the house since he went home. The wired jaw has him confined. Even a fuck like Barrett knows the consequences of puking into a wired mouth." Easley spoke as if he were keeping an eye on the family.

"If he is fucking with Kirsten, then we can assume he is messing with Devon, right?" Cody knew the answer.

"With absolute certainty!" Cadrell responded.

"He's going to kill one of them, sooner or later. You know that, Cadrell." Cody spoke ruefully. "Someone should have finished the job a couple weeks ago."

"That would have been you, my friend?" Easley pressed.

"Watch them, Cadrell." Cody asked. "I have a bad feeling about Barrett's ultimate response to the beating."

"I'll watch Barrett, Cody, but I am the reactive end of the spectrum. I cannot prevent the crimes. I can only institute the punishment phase of the equation. If Billy has not learned from the recent engagement behind the Rascal Flats then we have to assume that the problem will only swell." Cadrell was accurate. If the beating did not keep Barrett away from Kirsten and Devon then the logical assumption is to believe that he will hold them responsible for the attack.

"Watch him, Cadrell." Cody insisted.

"I'll watch him, Cody." Cadrell pacified the caller.

"Watch him, follow him, intimidate him, threaten him, handle him!" Cody slammed the phone down gripping the receiver with staggering force. The ear piece end on the phone shattered. The force of the impact dislodged the bell inside the telephone. The faceplate split off like it was launched from an explosion. The noise woke up the students. Dean McKenna opened the door to the bunkhouse and looked down at the broken plastic housing that resembled a telephone. Cody Law was marching across the grounds in search of the answers that appeared to be slipping away. Gunner McGarrity watched from the small bathroom window in his home.

* * *

A battered blue windbreaker barely kept the Colorado chill from Devon's fragile frame. The air was dry, as usual, but the thirty-mile per hour gusts were rare in the protected cocoon of the Douglas County Elementary School. Located at the foot of Castle Rock, the school enjoyed a natural windbreak. Ninety-four students comprised the enrollment. Some grades held less than ten students. South Street Elementary School boasted one hundred forty-four students covering the same years, kindergarten through eighth grade. Castle Rock guarded the weathered brick school, built in 1917, like a broad centurion. Castle Rock had no need for two elementary schools. Traditions die hard west of the Mississippi. Children go to school where their parents went to school. If they want to close a school then let them close the other school. As long as the state funded both schools, both schools would remain open.

Anna Larkin replaced Dana Davenport on the school's faculty. Dana's position was filled from within, but the resulting vacancy on the faculty staff brought Anna Larkin to Castle Rock from a recently completed student teaching assignment in Littleton, Colorado. Anna was young, twenty-two years old, single and pretty. Anna was assigned to teach the sixth grade, a class numbering fourteen students including Devon Barrett.

Anna Larkin watched from the second floor window of her classroom. Devon swung by herself in the cold wind of the winter morning. Most of the students elected to remain inside during the lunch break. As usual, Devon brought no lunch to school. The onset of the second semester had precluded a resilient resurrection within Devon. Anna's first days with Devon coincided with the hospital absence of her stepfather.

During a week of preliminary meetings prior to the start of second semester, Martin Hollis devoted a sizeable share of time to briefing Ms. Larkin on the unusual case surrounding Devon. After typical depictions of the other students, Hollis painted a disturbing backdrop to the plight of Devon Barrett. As Hollis described, Devon Barrett had a history of emotional problems. The best course of action for all concerned would be the placement of Devon in a facility more capable of dealing with problem children. Hollis pulled out reports from social services that categorized Devon Barrett as autistic. Delusions and hallucinations had plagued Devon since infancy.

Devon had never been able to interact socially and the behavior was constant.

Hollis went on to explain that his relationship with Devon's father and his own heartfelt desires to see Devon cope with the delusional demons that poisoned her life had precluded the principal from seeking another scholastic home for Devon. Anna was briefed on the fabricated accusations that led to the dismissal of Dana Davenport. Hollis explained that while the school is concerned with the best interest of every student, any accusations of abuse must be filtered through his office before taking any actions. The teacher's responsibility is to report any pattern of behavior that may lead to the discovery of any improper parental behavior. The teachers will not institute any actions relating to their suspicions. Dana Davenport, not only suspected impropriety regarding Devon's home life, she attempted to take actions consummate with her own well intentioned yet distorted perceptions involving Devon. Children do not always paint the entire picture. Hollis explained that Dana Davenport's inability to separate fact from fiction and her rush to judgement cost her the Assistant Principal's job.

The Castle Rock Police Department and the Department of Children and Family Services were singled out as the entities assigned to make the decisions that Dana Davenport deiced to make on her own. Martin Hollis explained that any actions by the school administration or the teaching staff must be carefully considered within his own office due to the litigious state of the country. Hollis smiled and chuckled as he completed his instructions to Anna Larkin. Instructions, that seemed to be repeated one too many times.

"I know every teacher can relate to the intrusions created over the past ten years by the legal profession. It seems like every time an educator acts within the will of God or the within the walls of morality, the lawyers hide behind the separation of church and state." Martin Hollis stood with his hands behind his back and looked to the ceiling. Hollis was speaking to Anna Larkin. Anna was the only person in the room with Hollis. Martin Hollis never looked at Anna Larkin during his final instructions. Anna recalled the Darwinian ignorance she studied. Anna believed that some men were buried in the notion that life crawled out of the ocean with testicles and anything less was subservient. Martin Hollis scared the young teacher from that moment on.

"We cannot pray in class, but we are expected to encourage homosexuality. We had to stop reciting the Pledge of Allegiance in class because of the reference to God. We might offend an atheist. Every time a child comes crying to a teacher because he or she was disciplined at home, we are supposed to assume child abuse and investigate the parents. I am not an old man. I am forty-six years old. I spent four years in the military. I know the value of discipline and the consequences resulting from the absence of discipline."

"Nowadays, children hide behind the legal wall of emotional abuse when they just don't like being told what to do. Hell, what child likes being told what to do? Education is the standard for nobility when choosing your profession. At Castle Rock Elementary, we will educate our children within the confines of decency and God. The legal edicts may implore the district to hand out condoms and distribute information concerning abortion options in eighth grade, but I will make those judgements. We are educators, Ms. Larkin. Remember that, Ms. Larkin, every time one of your students complains of a runny nose." Martin Hollis completed his induction speech to new teachers. Anna Larkin knew she was in the wrong place even before one student had crossed the threshold of her classroom.

Anna stood with her arms folded and watched the solitary swing move across the sand and snow. Anna had been taught to assume that most autistic children had monumental troubles keeping up in class. Devon Barrett had managed to complete most of her required work well enough to pass. Devon, although alarmingly quiet, had no trouble with language, a trait almost inherent to autistic children. Devon's physical appearance was daunting. Devon's weight, the small scars on her hands, the constant long sleeves and overalls, and the absolute isolation from all classmates painted the most rudimentary case study for a basic child psychology class. Devon was no more autistic than Dr. Suess. In four weeks, Anna opened a slight path of communication with Devon, solely as a result of Devon's fascination with Anna's looks. The older boys talked about the new teacher. The girls pecked and imitated the new teacher.

Anna Larkin stood five feet, three inches tall and weighed less than one-hundred pounds. Long blond hair fell in full Texas style across her shoulders. Anna Larkin could stop traffic from Times Square to the River Walk in San Antonio. Resplendent, dazzling blue eyes planted fantasies in every male student struggling with puberty. Devon saw her mother at a young age. Pictures buried in the garage at 222 Gilbert Street, revealed a stunning young woman lost nearly a decade before.

In school, Devon was lost in a blind cavity that was comparable to the jurisprudence that said the best interests of all supercede the comfort of one. The school board and the principal personified that position simply to keep a "small" problem behind closed doors. Anna stood helpless in so many ways.

Donny Toliver and Marcus Danton were midway through the eighth grade. Both boys had been held back a year because of a stint in a juvenile detention center. The boys were returning to the school building from a lunchtime cigarette break behind the trees on the north side of the schoolyard. They could be seen laughing as they approached the building and the swings.

"Hey, freak." Donny Toliver yelled at Devon Barrett. Both boys roared with laughter. "You may want to think about changing clothes every semester or so."

Donny leaned over Devon's shoulder and pulled the strap on her overalls. Marcus Danton leaned on the metal swing support pole hanging uncomfortably close to Devon's face. Danton smirked and encouraged his friend.

"The farm look is a nice touch but when you get tired of dressing like a hillbilly, give me a call. I'll be happy to show you something that you can't find on the farm." The fifteen year-old boys disappeared, laughing into the school.

Devon Barrett was not unlike other children whose behavior was a learned reaction to repeated encounters. She had learned to fall asleep without crying. The tears never changed anything, so eventually, they dried up. On the playground, as the resident display target for adolescent cruelty, Devon could not stop the tears. The swing slowed in the gusty wind, as her feet scraped the sand. Devon's windbreaker caught the tears falling down her cheeks. The bell rang for the afternoon session. She walked slowly to her locker. Anna Larkin met her in the hallway.

"What did those boys say to you, Devon?" Anna asked protectively.

"Nothing." Devon answered briefly, embarrassed to show the new teacher the frailty that punctuated every aspect of her own life.

"Devon, you are crying. Tell me what the boys said and I will have them report to Mr. Hollis' office." Anna exclaimed, sounding more like the high school staff she had left only five years back.

"They said nothing." Devon repeated while she opened her locker. Devon's eyes never left the floor. Her locker door opened, revealing a myriad of rodeo magazine covers and articles.

"What's all this?" Anna Larkin inquired, genuinely curious. Anna had a crush on Lane Frost in high school. Anna Larkin grew up in Cheyenne, Wyoming. She went to Regis College in Denver. Anna's high school in Cheyenne boasted a highly ranked rodeo team and Lane Frost was more popular than Jon Bon Jovi.

Devon Barrett looked up at Anna Larkin. First reactions led Devon to believe this was another attempt to humiliate the only important aspect of her life. Devon stared at Anna Larkin. Anna read the doubt through the wet, red eyes of her young student.

"God, I used to take so much flack in college because I liked a bareback cowboy named Justin Wheeler. Justin was gone more than two hundred days a year. I'd get calls in the middle of the night from Casper, Wyoming or Weatherford, Texas or wherever the gas money would take them next. Justin traveled in an old Ford truck with at least three other adolescent egomaniacs. They drove all night to the next rodeo, sleeping in the garbage filled back of a pick-up truck and ate most of their meals in gas station diners that featured a food group solely comprised of beans and bread. All of my friends in the dorm told me to give up on a bum like that. Guys like that, they said, were never going to be happy unless they can claim a mobile mailing address." Anna began checking the rankings posted in Devon's locker.

"How long did you wait for him?" Devon asked quietly, not sure if Anna Larkin was a gift from God or a set-up for additional humiliation.

"Hell, I'm still waiting for that demented child to come to his senses." Anna laughed out loud, which brought a smile to Devon's cheeks.

"Justin Wheeler is currently ranked fourth nationally in bareback." Anna pointed to the current unofficial Jack Daniels World Standings posted in Devon's locker. "Justin, Clint Corey, Wayne Herman, Lewis Feild and Ty Murray make up the top five. Justin surprised me at Christmas this past year. He and Ty Murray sent the Wrangler corporate jet to Denver. I met them both at the airport and they wouldn't tell me where we were going. Turns out, we all spent the holidays at Ty Murray's ranch in Texas. I hate the rodeo for the time it robs from me, but rodeo is what Justin Wheeler is. I loved him from the first day we met. There will always be some charm and jealousy to the boundaries a cowboy pays no attention to and the ones we all adhere to." Anna finished and looked down at a twelve-year old girl, frozen in disbelief.

"You spent Christmas with Ty Murray?" The question fell like a brick.

"Well, I prefer to think of the time I spent with Justin at Ty Murray's ranch." Anna sensed a crack. "You bet. Ty Murray is as cute as a button. And polite? I can't believe that Ty rides, whatever, he looks so young and sweet."

"Ty Murray is the 1989 All-Around PRCA Champion." Devon interrupted. "Ty rides bareback and bulls. The All-Around Champion is the cowboy earning the most money in a year while competing in at least two events." The second bell rang. Classes were under way. "May I stay and talk to you after school?" Devon asked while they entered the classroom.

"I'd like that." Anna Larkin replied.

* * *

The beginning of the second week at Gunner McGarrity's Bull-Riding School buried the good intentions. All the "if you want it bad enough" cliches, read easier from the high rise luxury condominium along Chicago's lakefront. The sneering anticipation among a school of seasoned riders vaulted front and center. Cody would ride a bull for the first time on a cold gray California morning.

The first task of the morning after the group run and meditation, was to ready the arena for training. Two students combed the arena floor with the All Terrain Vehicles and a series of rakes attached to the vehicles. Three other students, Cody and Gunner walked down to the lower pastures to secure the bulls and lead them back to the holding pens and chutes. Nine dogs spread out like a well-oiled military formation to round up the bulls. Gunner and his students manned a series of gates along the inner perimeter fences that allowed the men to move the bulls in sections.

The bulls were led through the first series of gates. Then, the gates were secured from the rear and another series of gates were opened to move the bulls closer to the arena. Cody moved with the other students, who knew instinctively where to be and when to move. Cody waited for instructions at each junction. The incredible realization that he would be mounting one of these massive animals in short order, left his intestines on the verge of depositing his breakfast all over the expensive boots that had been the focus of so much attention. The group finally moved the herd into the proper holding pens. Gunner gathered the students on the arena floor. Gunner read off the order of rides for the morning. The last rider would be Cody.

"Gunner." Cody spoke up before the Director finished. "I want to go first."

Gunner McGarrity scanned the students in front of him. Sonny Moore was pulling the spurs tight around his heels. Olin Martin stood erect with his chaps draped over his shoulder. Tater Lewis had his hat pulled so tight on his head that Gunner wondered about the suction created when the hat was pulled off. R.D. Rese looked like an ad for Justin Boots. R.D. wore Justin Boots, a black shirt with Justin logos, and a black Stetson with Justin hat tags above the brim.

"Anybody mind if Cody leads us off?" Gunner asked diplomatically. No one cared. " Let's go. You're up first, Cody."

"Should I bring Manson down to chute one." Tater Lewis asked, referring to Gunner's most docile bull and the bull normally reserved for beginners. Manson rarely bucked or spun a rider. Manson mainly tried to run the rider off his back. Gunner compared the ride to a wide-ass horse with horns. Gunner looked at Lewis for a moment. Cody Law watched the exchange. He had been expecting the bull named Manson, for the first few rides, anyway. Gunner had told Cody that he always starts the rookies on Manson. Gunner pulled his hat back for a second and ran his hands through his hair. "Pull up Bandit, Tater." Gunner ordered.

"Bandit?" Tater Lewis stood frozen. "That mother fucker bucked me off last week!" Lewis was shocked that Gunner would choose Bandit for a man's first ride and somewhat insulted that McGarrity thought so little of the five-year old, red Brahma.

"Shit, Gunner, Bandit spent two years on circuit with an eighty-nine percent ride ratio. Nine out of ten professional rides couldn't stay on him."

"Thank you, Tater for explaining the math. Now I asked you to bring up Bandit. If you cannot handle that, then Russell will bring the bull up here. We have a great deal of work to do with you boys. I do not have time to burp-feed Mr. Law for two more weeks. Put him on Bandit. Mr. Law, do you have any objections? You are free to come to your senses at any time." Gunner McGarrity waited for an answer.

"You will not scare my ass out of here on the first ride. You're the boss, Gunner. You choose the rides." Cody began to collect his gear. Olin Martin and Sonny Moore smiled in tandem at the nervous rookie. Sonny Moore leaned over to Cody Law and squinted his eyes together, while shaking his head and wincing in the imagined pain.

"Fuck, Cody, I don't like riding Bandit. Good luck." Sonny Green smiled at Olin Martin and slapped his hand as they walked toward the chutes in preparation of Cody's ride.

Gunner directed the bulls into the various chutes. There were four chutes in a row. The first chute was the one used by the riders. The next three chutes held the bulls on tap for the upcoming rides. Bandit led the way from the back holding pen to the first chute. Bandit's horns were well over the width of the chute so the bull had to turn his head to fit inside the chute. The animal churned inside the confined space as Cody Law stood on the platform adjacent to the chute holding Bandit.

Now was the time to abandon the plan. Gunner was obviously providing some form of levity for the other riders. Imagine receiving a learner's permit to drive a car and then proceeding, a week later to the pole position at the Daytona 500. Cody Law remembered the release form he was required to sign before any participation in the bull-riding school was allowed. The words came off the page like a snake poised to bite him in the ass. Cody pulled his bull rope off his shoulder and dropped it to the ground. Fuck, he thought, I didn't come here to get killed. Providing a morning amusement break for these boys, at the expense of his own severed spine, was not Cody's plan.

While Tater Lewis secured the gate to chute one, Sonny Moore and Olin Martin checked the slide on the front of the gate and the rope used to pull the gate open. Both men stood on the arena floor, ready to move into position. Tyler McGarrity, Gunner's oldest son, arrived at the arena with his five-year old daughter. Tyler often assisted Gunner at the school and when Gunner was in town, Tyler always observed the classes in session. There had never been a time when Tyler did not learn something from simply watching his father conduct the school. Tyler and his daughter, Megan McGarrity, took a seat in the press box overlooking the arena. Tyler turned on the public address system.

"Hey, Gunner." Tyler called his father Gunner. "Do you want me to tape these rides?" The expectation was that all rides should be taped.

"Absolutely, Tyler." Gunner yelled across the arena. "We may have a slight delay, however." Gunner looked at Cody.

"Cody, it's time to be a man. Drop your rope down the side of the chute and straddle the chute. Don't touch the bull until I tell you to." Gunner stared at Cody. Cody did not move. He looked at Megan McGarrity on the other side of the rodeo floor. A small perch of curls bounced next to her father. "Now!" Gunner McGarrity barked.

Cody Law bent over and picked up the bull rope. He pulled his hat down over his eyes. A rawhide glove hung from his belt. Another glove was wrapped tight around his left hand. Cody bent again to secure the spurs that he had never worn before. Cody moved to the chute and dropped the bull rope down against the side of the animal. The bull's back end was flanked. Tater Lewis grabbed the rope from the chute floor and pulled it back up over the bull. The cowbells rang with the bull's agitation. Cody straddled the chute. At thirty-two years old, Cody suddenly became aware of an urge to urinate. Unfucking believable, Cody thought now, he was going to wet his pants. Gunner McGarrity arrived at the chute.

"You ready?" Gunner asked.

"Bandit?" Cody shot back.

"I'll take that as a yes." Gunner answered. "Cody, drop down on the bull's back. Remember, just touch his back with your knees, to let him know your are there."

Cody Law curled his knees together and skimmed the backbone of the animal below. The bull remained relatively still. Cody put more weight on the bull's back. Suddenly, the bull's head came up with his shoulders, jerking from side to side, crashing the planks with his oversized horns. Cody stood up quickly and jumped off the chute. Now, Cody felt like he would crap in his pants.

"Bandit is just saying hello, Cody. Get back on him. That's nothing." Gunner explained as he jammed his boot down on Bandit's back, sending the bull back to his original position.

"Great, Gunner. See if you can piss him off some more." Cody commented while resuming the straddle position.

"Don't worry, Cody." Gunner helped him get situated. "Wait until I zap his balls just before we open the gate." Cody pulled up and stared at Gunner. Gunner McGarrity winked.

"Pull the rope up, Tater. Cody, drop down now and take your position on the bull. Remember again, stay to the outside with your right arm over the gate. You do not want to be in the middle of the gate. If the bull cranks up again with you on him, keep to the outside and go with him."

Cody Law dropped into position. The experience was beginning to feel like it was not happening to him. Gunner guided Cody's left hand into the hand hold. Gunner called for the rope to be pulled tight.

"It's too tight, Gunner." Cody explained. His stomach churned like sour milk on a hot summer day.

"You're going to have to trust me on this one, Cody. You don't know what too tight is?" Gunner was calm.

"I know this is too tight, Gunner. I'm going to get hung up on my first ride." Cody was scared and they were not playing now.

"You are not going to get hung up." Gunner reassured Cody. "But if you do, don't fall off the side. Do not give up. Stay on your feet and chase the animal until you free your hand. Trust me, I will not pull it too tight."

"Then why did you just explain what to do when I get hung up?" Cody began rambling, stuttering, while delaying the ride.

"I have to Cody. You are not going to get hung up. I promise." Gunner continued, re-evaluating the decision to pull Bandit.

"Stay up on your rope, Cody. Get a hold with your feet." Gunner pounded Cody's gloved hand. "Keep your chin down and stay out over the bull. Keep moving forward." Gunner shoved Cody up as far as he could go on his hand.

"The fucking rope is too tight." Cody was fixated on the rope.

"Cody." Gunner leaned down under Cody's hat and got directly into his face. "That's Devon in the press box. Your daughter is here to see what you can do. Are you going to be another adult that will disappoint that young girl. It's fucking time, Cody. Show me something, GODDAMIT ! " Gunner screamed underneath the hat.

Cody looked up at Gunner for a split second and then nodded to the men at the gate. The wooden gate flew open and an unimaginable explosion of power filled the California sky with churning red Brahma flesh. The earth flailed and swirled in a cyclone of rodeo dust, while Cody's legs whipped up high and lost. The surge of power froze Cody in fear, the way the initial vertical climb in an F-16 will freeze a Blue Angel pilot. Cody felt like he had a Peterbuilt diesel engine pulling his body apart and there were no pedals or steering.

There were no instincts to follow. Cody's rope hand locked down onto the only thing available to cling to. Bandit bucked straight back twice and then jumped to the right, spinning his back end in the air. Cody lost all perspective as to where he was and could only focus on not falling backwards. Cody's hat kicked off his head as Bandit kept spinning in the same direction. Gunner knew that Bandit did not change directions. Bandit was a predictable bull, a consolation for Gunner and meaningless to Cody.

"Stay up there, Cody." Gunner yelled. Bandit hit the ground hard and Cody slipped back too far from his hand. Gunner grimaced as the light closed under Cody's ass. Cody had watched the arena fence spin around his eyes in an uncontrollable frenzy. The bull charged the chute gates and Cody could only envision the end of his life, crushed between a wooden gate and the wayward side of a two-thousand pound, feces laden, spinning mammal with a serious testicle issue.

The moment the bull sensed where Cody was, Bandit flipped his back end up and spun hard again to the inside. Cody was gone at this point. Cody's left hand popped out of the hand hold. Cody's heels were no where near the bull. Cody caught the back-end of the bull sending him airborne. Gunner held his breath.

Olin Martin and Sonny Moore raced to cut off the bull's path to the rider. Cody Law landed on his left shoulder and neck. The force of his fall propelled Cody into a tumble. The rolling action in the soft dirt cushioned any crushing damage to his left shoulder or his neck. Cody Law came to rest face down with a mouthful of California wine country. Cody jumped up with one fist raised high into the air. Following the moment of impact. Cody's kinetic fear turned to triumphant exultation. Sonny Moore corralled Bandit to the holding pen. Olin Martin hung over the holding pen and released the flank rope on Bandit.

Gunner McGarrity sat on the wooden rails of chute two. A wide smile spread across his face. Tater Lewis, R.D. Rese and Wheeler Green erupted in applause and shrieks of triumph. Cody Law had not survived the eight seconds, but he entered a club on that gray California morning that held no openings for the faint hearted. Cody walked over to Gunner, shaking hands with Sonny and Olin along the way. Gunner jumped from his perch to greet Cody.

"You know Bandit finished as a top ten bull during his first year on the circuit." Gunner had forgotten to mention that fact before the ride. "You stayed on him for seven seconds, Cody. If I didn't think you could make it here then you would have been gone by now without me ever putting your ass on a bull." Gunner stated the facts. Gunner McGarrity brushed off the tan Stetson and handed Cody his hat.

"You knew Bandit would throw me." Cody muttered.

"An absolute certainty." Gunner replied.

"Was that supposed to scare me off?" Cody retorted with some sarcasm.

"That was supposed to show you what it is like to ride a bull that has been retired from the circuit for three years because he got too easy to ride. Bandit wouldn't score a fifty-five in competition, today." Gunner was not proselytizing.

"Cody, this is rodeo. The bulls are capable of anything. They can leave you in a wheelchair or a coffin. They will catapult your body into the wooden slats of the chutes. They will pull you around the arena and stomp your insides until you wear them on your shirt. Your hand will get hung up and the bulls will whip you like a rag doll. Your arm will feel like it is being pulled flat off your shoulder."

"Cowboys don't tolerate imposters. They won't take shit from you. You'll sleep in a truck and long for the life you left. You'll trade filets for cold beans and chilled martinis for horse shit coffee that could rot the bottom of a lead pipe. You are going to walk into a world where a couple hundred bucks buys men another month on the road. A couple hundred bucks to you may be dinner and drinks. If you make it far enough, you are going to draw bulls that can't win a dollar. You'll draw bulls that will rip your hand out before the gate is swung open."

"Welcome, my friend. On that rare day, when you capture the "zone", it won't be an accident. The ride will push you to an edge you never knew. The whistle will blow and you'll still be riding high. You will "cowboy up" before a screaming crowd and you will never go back to the life you knew. On that day, you will arrive. It may never come, but you will destroy your body searching for it. Let your brain dominate your blood, Cody. Allow the mind to control the body. Take your manhood from between your legs and place reason and humility before brawn. If you can manage those concepts, then you have the foundation to proceed. Get up on chute one. You will be assisting Rese and Green. We are going to ride until the sun goes down, gentlemen." Gunner announced to the students. "That means a minimum of four rides per man today."

Cody Law stood on the arena floor and reached into the gate to pull the rope for R.D. Rese. Olin Martin patted Cody on the back, releasing a cloud of rodeo dirt.

"Damn, Sonny. It appears that Cody will be askin' for the Dagger before long. What do you think, Son?" Olin Martin was also making a point. The exhilaration of the ride hung on Cody like a sweaty shirt in the Texas sun.

"I expect that is a distinct possibility." Sonny Moore echoed Martin's sarcasm.

"Who is "The Dagger?"" Cody asked ignoring the tease and pacifying the men who have earned the right to doubt newcomers.

"Skoal Dagger." Sonny Moore chimed in. "Skoal Dagger is the most dangerous bull the sport has ever seen. Skoal is a black, nineteen hundred pound white faced bull with a brown line down the middle of his back. Skoal's capable of a one hundred point ride, but no one can stay on him. The mother-fucker has not been ridden in two years. Skoal Dagger is mean, too. The bull goes after the rider once he hits the ground. I've seen bullfighters fucking boycott his rides. Skoal has turned two riders into paraplegics, one quadriplegic and ended the careers of countless other bull-riders." Moore had gotten Cody's attention.

"Skoal is owned by the Hollister Cattle Company." Olin Martin continued on the same subject. "Darwin Hollister is the leading stock contractor for the PRCA when it comes to mean ass bulls. Darwin retired Skoal Dagger after his first year because he was concerned about the safety of the riders. Hollister figured they could turn Dagger out to stud for a time and slow him down a bit. That bull bucks harder at eight seconds than he does at the start of the ride."

"Dagger's signature move is to whip his head back in the split-second the rider drops to the red zone that only Skoal Dagger instinctively senses. The impact into the rider's head and face will cause a pile of grotesque facial damage. Once the rider hits the ground, Skoal isn't done. He likes to stomp your guts right up into your lungs. They took twenty feet of mangled intestines out of Butch Malloy in Albuquerque last year. Troy Hayes lost a liver in Reno after Skoal Dagger literally chased Hayes around the arena, splattering two bullfighters before reaching Troy. Donny Tolbert's mother didn't recognize her son until a month after attempting to ride Skoal Dagger. Tolbert's wife fainted in the hospital when she first went to see her husband."

"What happened to Skoal Dagger?" Cody asked.

"Skoal Dagger is back on the circuit." Sonny Moore replied. "The top one-hundred riders on the PRCA tour last year got together a petition to bring his bad-ass back to competition. The petition explained that the bull-riders did not want Skoal to go out at the top of his game. Cowboys don't like to be told that they lost. Every bull rider on tour wants to be the one to last eight seconds aboard Skoal Dagger. Some refuse. No one holds that against them. Hollister brought him back six months ago. No one has come close to riding him. That fucking bull is undefeated and he knows it."

"Have you ever pulled Skoal Dagger in the draw?" Cody looked at Sonny Moore.

"No." Moore was short.

"Would you want to pull Skoal Dagger?" Cody wanted to know.

"We all do, Cody. We want to ride him for the guys that won't ever get out of a wheel chair and for the guys he mutilated just for fun. It's only a matter of time before someone rides Skoal or he kills somebody. The rider that stays on Skoal Dagger in the Finals walks with the title, simple as that."

"Everyone wants to be the NFR World Champion. That may never happen for me. The fear of failure follows us all, Cody. The fact is, I don't ride as good as Tuff Hedeman or Cody Custer. If I can make a living doing something that I love instead of going to the UPS plant to load trucks, then I can live with that." Moore had lost his teasing tone. There was reverence that hung over the topic of Skoal Dagger.

"Cody." Gunner spoke as he directed Russell Den to close three bulls in behind chute one. Cody turned while assisting Rese to secure his rope.

"Nice ride, today." Gunner chimed. "Don't listen to them, Cody. A bull like Skoal Dagger is so rare that most riders don't consider what to do when they draw him. Immortality or incapacitated? The choice is most often gauged by the heart, not the mind. Bull riders think with their balls." Gunner smiled.

Cody Law completed three more rides on Bandit during the day. Cody never reached seven seconds again on the first day. Each subsequent ride ended almost as soon as the gate was opened. As each ride grew shorter and Bandit seemed to toy with Cody. Cody's determination swelled. Bull riding is an addictive endeavor that rarely justifies the cost. Men travel one-way into a world of broken bodies and broken families. They all believe that if they give it one more year, that elusive pinnacle will be achieved. Few find it, but fewer still, stop trying. The third week at Gunner McGarrity's Bull-Riding School ended with Cody applying for his PRCA permit card. Gunner told Cody that he needed to spend at least two or three sessions at the school before considering a sanctioned rodeo. Cody Law explained that he did not have time for two or three sessions. One would have to suffice.

* * *

Cody had contacted Gary Dietz as his circumstances changed. Desperado Entertainment, Inc. was surviving quite well without Cody Law. Maintaining the current positions had been Cody's instructions to Gary Dietz. Dietz was not surprised when Cody failed to alter the situation in Castle Rock. However, the news that Cody would be spending three weeks at a bull-riding school in Central California, dipped into the psychotic delusions of falling off the deep end. Cody explained to Dietz that the school had something to do with Devon, but that he could not elaborate any further. It was Monday morning in California. Cody placed a call to his corporate offices.

"Desperado Entertainment, Inc., how may I direct your call?" Alexis Mannix managed to slip her sultry voice into a corporate greeting.

"My God, Lex. With that voice, you are going to rouse the libido in every horny man that calls our office. How are they supposed to remember what they called us for?" Cody missed his incredibly hot receptionist, in more ways than he cared to recall.

"Hey, Cody. How's California? By the way, speaking of horny men." Alexis Mannix laughed. Even her laugh heated up the phone. "Do you want to talk to Gary?"

"Yes. Thanks, Lexi."

"When are you coming back, Cody?" Alexis asked before sending the call to Gary Dietz.

"Not for awhile, but I'll know more in a couple weeks." Cody lied to end the exchange. The call was put through to Gary Dietz.

"Cody, how are you? Are you still in California?" Gary Dietz motioned the two people in his office to give him a few minutes. When they realized it was Cody Law, they vanished.

"I am still in Nipomo, California or somewhere relatively close to Nipomo." Cody was glad to hear a familiar voice.

"I am afraid to ask, but how is the school going. Tell me that you have not actually ridden a bull." Gary was shaking his head. Cody knew what he was doing.

"Stop shaking your head, Gary. We have completed more than two weeks, now. I have ridden fourteen times. The last two rides, I completed."

"Completed? What do you mean?" Gary asked. "You rode a bull and didn't get killed?"

"No. Completion means eight seconds on the bull. I stayed on the bull for eight seconds or until the whistle blows."

"Cody, you have lost your mind. I have stumbled onto TNN a couple of times while channel surfing. You are not telling me that you planted your ass on one of those fucking bulls. The bulls all seem to enjoy stomping into the ground, whoever is dumb enough to get on their back. If you wanted to go to a dude ranch and play cowboy, I could understand that. You told me this has something to do with Devon, but for the life of me, I cannot imagine what a bull-riding school has to do with a daughter you do not know?" Gary Dietz imagined the tale could not get any stranger.

"Gary, Devon's predicament in Castle Rock is much worse than I envisioned. Kirsten will not allow me to get anywhere near the girl. Kirsten is scared to death. Mr. Billy Don Barrett has not only been using my daughter for much more than a punching bag, he has Kirsten believing, and rightfully so, that Barrett may react with lethal consequences upon the discovery of Devon's real father. Kirsten asked me to go and leave them alone. I told you that three weeks ago."

"What I did not tell you was that I was able to walk around Kirsten's home before she arrived home on the day that I saw her. Devon lives in a prison. Her room is covered with strips of carpeting from floor to ceiling. There is one light bulb hanging from the ceiling. A stark metal bed frame and a beat-up dresser comprise the room. Devon's world is inside her closet. Scores of rodeo pictures hang from every inch of the closet. The pictures chronicle the current and past professional bull-riders. The only place where Devon feels comfortable is with her rodeo bull-riders. She follows the rankings of the PRCA. Devon could recite an in-depth biography of all top twenty bull-riders. She knows the intricacies of the sport from why each rider is successful or why certain riders have slumps. The only thing in Devon's world that doesn't hurt her is the rodeo. Devon can go there without fear. The same cannot be said for anywhere else in her life. I have decided that the only way into Devon's life is to become a bull-rider." Cody paused for the anticipated rebuff.

"Cody, at thirty-two years old, you are a baby in business. Our company has established a standard in Chicago that has bred imitators from the smallest club owners to the jealous icons infatuated with their own success. Listen, most men, correct that, all men would never consider the route you are taking. I'll give you meritorious, chivalrous and noble. Roll them all up and we'll find you, but you cannot ride bulls. Fuck, you cannot ride a fucking horse that pulls little kids around for twelve hours a day. I've been down that road with you. We were on vacation together when you passed on horseback riding because the fucking barns smelled like a sewer. What chance does a thirty-two year old Chicago saloonkeeper have in re-writing the western rule books. Cody, aren't you supposed to grow up on a ranch or leave home in Texas at the age of six to live with your grandfather in order to be a rodeo star? I am trying not to take this lightly because of Devon, but are you fucking crazy? " Gary Dietz was beginning to think something was seriously wrong with his boss.

"Next time, Gary, try to remember when or if I asked for your advice." Cody rolled his eyes and felt more comfort in his relatively new surroundings.

"I am going to run this course. I received a permit card for the Professional Rodeo Cowboy Association, yesterday. I will be entered in a sanctioned PRCA Rodeo within a few weeks. I might get knocked into another state, but count on one thing, I will be pursuing the only certain opening in Devon's life."

"How is Devon going to get the connection between you and Kirsten? How, for that matter, is Devon going to hear about you? It sounds like Devon follows the stars on the rodeo circuit. Tell me you are not planning to crack the top ten in your first month?" Gary Dietz inquired facetiously.

"I will contact Devon at the right time." Cody answered briefly.

"Cody, you belong here. Have you thought about that? The business is here. The things important to you are here in Chicago." Dietz began to search.

"You're right, Gary." Cody stood up in the bunkhouse at Gunner McGarrity's ranch and continued. "I have done nothing else except think about where I am and where I am going. I don't belong in Chicago, Gary. I don't belong anywhere. My parents moved to Savannah, Georgia five years ago. I am not married. I have no significant other. My business is in Chicago, but have you ever analyzed what we do?"

"What do you mean?" Dietz asked.

"Have you ever broken down the business we are involved with every day? We hold seminars to teach our employees how to serve the public more alcohol. We teach young people how to pad the "per check average" with expensive upgrades in wine and liquor. We put revealing apparel on beautiful women and prance them around our clubs with trays of shots called blow jobs, brain hemorrhages, sex on the beach and B-52's. We encourage men to purchase as many of these drinks as they can afford and only deem them unfit when they cause a disturbance."

"Quiet drunks can go all night. How many customers during your days behind the bar, did you send out at closing that drank enough to fill a small tanker truck. As long as those patrons exhibited no offensive or abusive actions, they were allowed to consume unlimited alcohol. Shit, Gary we joked about these guys. They would come back to the bar the next day and we would all laugh about how blind drunk they got the night before. How many times has a customer humorously wondered how he ever made it home the night before. It was all a big joke, while the same patron was sipping a beer at noon the next day. We send drunks into their cars every night and pass the responsibility off as compliance with local statutes."

"The reality is our profits occur after midnight when the alcohol sales escalate. We charge people eight dollars to park their car for an hour. We pay our servers $1.90 per hour. The corporation retains a law firm to litigate everything from dram shop lawsuits to neighborhood petitions advocating a dry district. We pay lawyers to argue that our clubs should be allowed to operate within so many feet of a school or a church. Desperado Entertainment, Inc. sent money through the Illinois Restaurant Association to help fund a lobby at the state capital in Springfield. The lobbyists were hired by a consortium of major liquor companies. Their goals were simple, to fight any legislation aimed at lowering the legal alcohol limit for DUI arrests. We spent money to make it easier to drive drunk."

"The goals of Desperado surround the inebriation of our patrons and we celebrate the successful completion of those ideals. The problem is that we have no ideals. With time to reflect on my own life, I never imagined that my success would be gauged by our own ability to lubricate and sedate anyone with a dollar. I want to reach my daughter. If I do not, then I feel the time and the people I have come to know in Colorado and California will show me something that almost slipped right through my life."

"What's that, Cody?" Gary was listening intently.

"Core." Cody replied.

"What is core?" Gary followed.

"Core is what a twelve-year old girl from Castle Rock and a fifty-two year old, tobacco chewing philosopher have in common. Core is when someone puts at risk, that which they cannot lose. I know I sound like an esoteric fool. Time to think is a dangerous commodity. I have lived and prospered over the past decade quite well and without an ounce of integrity. I have a daughter, whether she knows me or not, who is being sexually molested by her fucking stepfather. Devon is twelve years old, Gary. She doesn't worry about sixth grade issues. She worries about a man presented from day one as her father, slipping into her room at night, drunk, smelling like stale bourbon and forcing Devon to perform sexual acts she shouldn't even know about. Where is my integrity when I fall asleep in comfort each night and my daughter cannot find a safe place within her home to sleep at night? Devon has shown more courage during each day than I have thought about during thirty-two years. Does my profession make anyone's life better? Fuck, no! I cannot afford to spend one minute wallowing in guilt. What is different now, is that I will embrace the trail I laid and not ignore it. Core is not something to lie in wait for, it has to be achieved." Cody Law was changing fast.

"Achievement is relative, boss. Your daughter's plight is not a platform for you." Gary wondered.

"It's a thin line, Gary. I respect your concerns."

"I wish you the best. You know that?" Gary meant what he said, although the subject was uncomfortable. Gary Dietz did not care to psychoanalyze the merits of his life. Men and women in the hospitality industry are generally leery of exposing the many unspoken practices in their businesses that exploit or contribute to alcohol addiction.

"I know that. How does Alexis look today?"

"Hotter than a sweltering July afternoon in Atlanta." Gary sighed.

"Damn! Run the show, Gary." Cody hung up the phone.

* * *

~CHAPTER IV~

Three months later, late May, 1990

The semester in Douglas County had gone by fast. The children were anticipating the summer break. Anna Larkin had guided her sixth graders through the tedious curriculum of mathematics, history and science. In March, Anna sent each child home with a letter detailing the eight week curriculum guide covering the unit on Human Sexuality that would commence on March 18 and finish in mid-May. Each child was encouraged to bring back a signed awareness statement from their parents prior to the start of the Human Sexuality Unit. It was not uncommon for three or four students to fail to bring the signed statements back. The statements were an accommodation precipitated by the conservative objections in the community to the subject matter covered during the sexuality classes. The statements were not mandatory for the children to attend the classes. The Human Sexuality Unit was a Colorado State requirement.

The program was designed to encourage a healthy awareness of one's self and others who have many feelings, sexual and otherwise, and to understand these feelings and probable changes as they evolve throughout one's life. Among the many facets of the sexuality unit, students are taught to recognize conflicting messages about appropriate and inappropriate sexual behavior when presented in contemporary society.

Devon Barrett was one of the students that did not return the awareness statement. When the classes began in March, Devon had trouble with the subject matter and excused herself to the nurse on many occasions, claiming the flu or severe headaches to avoid the class.

Anna Larkin had called Kirsten Barrett for the purpose of a meeting to discuss Devon's aversion to the sexuality unit. The suspicions surrounding the Barrett's floated through the faculty since Dana Davenport's dismissal. Anna felt the proper channel to address the issue would be through Devon's mother. After all, Anna envisioned the meeting as an opportunity for Kirsten Barrett to purge herself of the sins perpetrated by her husband.

Devon's troubles continued throughout the unit and Anna's attempts to meet with Kirsten proved futile. As the unit wound into the final phase, Devon refused to attend. This time she claimed that her parents objected to the material on religious grounds. The final phase of the Human Sexuality Unit covered Society and Culture, examining issues including sexual abuse, rape and incest.

Anna Larkin had been preparing for this day for nearly eight weeks. Today was the third meeting that Anna had requested with Kirsten Barrett. Before each of the first two meetings, Kirsten called to cancel. Reasons were vague, but the intent was obvious to Anna Larkin. No cancellation calls or messages were received on the third scheduled meeting day. Anna had suggested on the third request that they meet at Kirsten's home if the school was a problem. The school would be fine, Kirsten had responded. The meeting was set for the third week in May, merely two weeks until the end of school. Anna Larkin prepared her classroom not unlike a nervous teenager before a first date. Anna's palms began to feel clammy Anna looked at her watch and noticed that Kirsten was due to arrive in fifteen minutes. The first year, sixth grade teacher began to review her notes again.

Devon's physical condition was a billboard for abuse. State law in Colorado obligates all teachers to report child abuse, suspicion of neglect, or merely the presence of any unusual behavior or marks leading to the belief that a caretaker is placing the child in imminent risk of serious harm. Devon's demeanor from day one could have easily been construed as behavior far outside the province of her peers. Anna Larkin's numerous written reports were all noted by the principal's office, but dismissed unilaterally. Martin Hollis' responses detailed the repetitive nature of the allegations and the extensive investigations into the charges. All charges were found to be unfounded and the girl exhibited all the signs pointing to autism in addition to the realization that some children are simply not healthy by nature.

Anna Larkin was dumbfounded by the explanations. Devon Barrett was not autistic. Secondly, a principal in the Douglas County School District or any school district could not possibly justify Devon's appearance as a result of poor health.

Anna Larkin had taken the liberty to research the case of Devon Barrett. Before she risked her job, which had been the result of previous actions concerning Devon Barrett. Anna Larkin sought to learn everything she could about Devon and her family. Anna was able to obtain copies of the Douglas County Hospital records relating to Devon and her family. Anna appealed to the maternal instincts of the woman in records at the hospital. The in-bred female bond with all children and two-hundred dollars produced the files.

The sheets on Devon were predictable. No charges were ever filed. No one pressed charges. The injuries sustained were explained by some inane justifications provided by Devon's father. The visits were few over the years but these records failed to divulge the other emergency room visits spread out over the greater Denver area and as far away as Colorado Springs.

Anna had contacted Dana Davenport and received a copy of her letter to Martin Hollis. Dana Davenport's dismissal left many faculty members bewildered and troubled by the actions of Martin Hollis. Within closed ranks, Anna Larkin heard of Dana Davenport's efforts on behalf of Devon Barrett. Dana's efforts continued in the fall through DCFS in Denver, but by Thanksgiving, the inquiries had stopped. The Douglas County Hospital files on Kirsten were more extensive than the files on Devon. The injuries to Kirsten included a wide variety of maladies. Kirsten had been treated in the emergency room for numerous lacerations, blunt trauma injuries, burns and an automobile accident, where Kirsten was actually run over by a vehicle. The incident resulted in a fractured leg. The report explained the incident as patient related. Apparently, Kirsten Barrett had forgotten to place the vehicle in Park. In her scramble to rectify the moving vehicle, Kirsten slipped under the driver's door and had the front tires run over her leg while the vehicle was sliding backwards. The witness to the accident was Billy Don Barrett.

The most unusual discoveries in the hospital charts centered on the birth certificates. Devon's biological father was not Billy Don Barrett. The natural father was a man named Cody Law.

Also unusual, was the presence of another birth certificate dated 1981. Kirsten and Billy Don Barrett had a baby boy in October, 1981. The father, this time, was Billy Don Barrett. Present in the file, was a death certificate for William Don Barrett, Jr. The baby died on January 7, 1982. William Don Barrett died before he was four months old. The baby drowned accidentally in the bathtub at home. A paramedics call on the afternoon of January 7, 1982, resulted in a DOA arrival at Douglas County Hospital. The police investigated and no charges were filed. The first officer on the scene was Officer Cadrell Easley. Now the framework began to piece together.

Anna Larkin could now assume that Kirsten Barrett had become obsessed with losing Devon. After losing the baby, whether Billy had some responsibility there or not, Kirsten would now protect Devon at all costs. The veil of that protection could allow Kirsten to cover Billy's abuse under the absolute fear that Billy would kill Devon if she had him prosecuted. As Devon grew older, Billy's abuse escalated as did Kirsten's helplessness. Billy's threats combined with the high school hero syndrome prevalent in Castle Rock regarding Billy Don Barrett, could only serve to verify Kirsten Barrett's position as a prisoner.

Anna Larkin and Kirsten Barrett were to meet after school. Devon walked home from school. Devon was expected at a certain time and any deviation from that time was not allowed. On the day of Kirsten's meeting with Anna Larkin, Devon arrived home on time. Kirsten was not at home when her daughter arrived. Anna Larkin replayed the meeting in her mind many times. The evidence was overwhelming that something was wrong with Billy Don Barrett. Anna did not know what the right approach would entail. The school board was not behind her. They did not know about the meeting. Anna had asked Kirsten for a private meeting. The police had turned a blind eye. The Department of Children and Family Services would not release any of their reports on the Barrett family. In fact, they would not confirm that they had a file on the family. What, In God's name, were they protecting, Anna thought?

"The files for any ongoing or past cases are not public record, Ms. Larkin." A clerk at the county office of the Department of Children and Family Services had declared.

"I am not the public." Anna Larkin announced. "I am the girl's teacher."

"We can notify the Superintendent's office. They can formally issue a request for a file." The clerk replied.

"Are you a mother?" Anna asked the clerk.

"Yes, two girls." The annoyed clerk responded.

"Are they healthy? Do they have a good relationship with their father?" Anna asked condescendingly.

"Excuse me?"

"Never mind." Anna left.

One woman at DCFS told Anna, in confidence, that a police officer named Cadrell Easley may be able to provide some of the information that she was looking for. Officer Easley would not confirm anything over the phone. When he met with Anna Larkin, both individuals were apprehensive about the motivations of the other. Cadrell was concerned that the Police Department was setting him up for dismissal. Anna Larkin was concerned that Easley would report to Principal Hollis. Cadrell Easley agreed to meet with Anna Larkin at the Castle Rock Police Station two days before Anna was to meet with Kirsten Barrett. They met in the sterile lobby of the main police station. Definitive dissertations of justice adorned the walls inside the station. Anna and Cadrell shook hands mechanically, careful to appear professional.

"Officer Easley." Anna began. "Devon Barrett is losing the battle. I need to know whom she is fighting. At every turn, the help set up to aid this child is the very entity that is perpetuating the problem. When I meet with Devon's mother, I want to give her the tools and the support necessary to move Devon away from whatever is destroying that little girl."

"It won't happen." Cadrell Easley flatly announced.

"Why not, Officer?" Anna stood tall and arched her back. "Is it impossible for this town to believe that an old football star is systematically killing his daughter and we can all have a front row seat?"

"No, ma'am." Cadrell politely answered. "I'm not certain anymore as to what this town is or is not capable of. What I am certain of is, Kirsten Barrett has not and will not follow through with anything remotely connected to prosecuting Billy Don Barrett."

"Why won't she leave him?" Anna continued. "Surely, there are means of protecting them from his threats?"

"It does sound simple, doesn't it?" Cadrell asked.

"The man is beating you and molesting your daughter. What can be clearer than to get the hell out of the relationship as fast as possible?" Anna placed logic into the equation.

"It won't happen, ma'am." Cadrell repeated, still somewhat convinced that Anna Larkin may be a versatile actress.

"There is a file on a baby that drowned accidentally in 1982. Do you have any reason to believe that Billy Don Barrett had something to do with the baby's demise?" Anna reached for something.

"Billy Don Barrett was not in town when the baby drowned." Cadrell replied.

"Obviously, his claims were confirmed?" Anna followed.

"Barrett was driving a truck in California at the time. The employment records confirmed his location. Excuse me, ma'am. The total sum of what you assume is logical, but untrue. The baby drowned in a bathtub while under the care of his mother. Kirsten Barrett was bathing her new son while Devon watched from a seat next to her mother on the bathroom floor. Kirsten left the room to answer the door. According to the boy's mother, Kirsten asked Devon to watch her brother while she answered the door. William Don Barrett slid under the water while Devon was playing with a bathtub toy. A four-year old girl does not have the capacity to care for an infant. The baby died during Kirsten's absence." Cadrell despised the inference to Devon's culpability.

"Are you telling me that Devon's parent's have held her responsible for her brother's death?" Anna asked.

"I am not a psychologist, Ms. Larkin. I do know, Ms. Larkin, that one does not need an engineering degree to construct a reasonable assumption." Cadrell Easley opened the door. "Retribution can mask anything. Construct another set of circumstances where a parent may allow another parent to ravage a child in the home."

"Do you believe that Kirsten is allowing the abuse to go on because she is punishing Devon for Billy Jr's death?" Anna Larkin could not fathom the possibility.

"Ms. Larkin, I have lost count of the rational explanations that I have considered as plausible explanations to the Barrett family. Kirsten is not functioning on all cylinders. Through the beatings and intimidation, Billy Don Barrett may have succeeded in more than his own insulation." Cadrell struggled with his own ineffectiveness.

"Do you know a man named Cody Law?" Anna Larkin switched gears and startled Cadrell Easley.

"How do you know Cody Law?" Cadrell turned the interrogation around.

"What is the connection between Cody Law and Kirsten Barrett?" Anna threw it right back.

"I am not going to play this game anymore, Ms. Larkin." Cadrell spoke sternly. "I have been working to make something happen for Devon and Kirsten for years. There are statutes and laws we must adhere to. Many more than I would care to explain or justify. Do not play games with me concerning Devon Barrett. She does not have a better friend in Castle Rock."

"Cody Law is Devon's real father." Anna blurted out, while not happy about being scolded." The Douglas County Hospital records show a man named Cody Law listed as Devon's father. Devon knows nothing about Cody Law. Do you?"

"Cody Law is Devon's biological father." Easley confirmed. "He and Kirsten had a brief relationship twelve years ago. Devon was the result. Apparently, they each went their separate ways before the baby was born. Devon has always believed that Billy was her natural father. I guess that is the way Kirsten wanted it." Cadrell explained. "What does this have to do with your meeting, anyway?"

"If Kirsten wanted Devon to believe that Billy was her father, then why did she list Cody Law as the father on the birth certificate?" Anna asked.

"I do not have a clue, Ms. Larkin." Easley answered and was becoming irritated by the dialogue.

"Kirsten Barrett must have believed that Cody Law would have some role in Devon's life. Otherwise, why list him as the father?" Anna reasoned, although she knew none of the individuals.

"You are wrong, Ms. Larkin. Mr. Law was in town recently and Kirsten Barrett made it abundantly clear that she wanted nothing to do with him. She also made it clear that he was to have no contact with Devon." Easley muttered.

"Then why list him as the father, if you want nothing to do with him?" Anna kept coming back to the same point. "Does that make sense to you, Officer?"

"No, ma'am. Nothing in Kirsten's files makes a bit of horse sense to me. Fear can make a person crazy, ma'am." Cadrell began connecting with Anna Larkin.

"I have a letter from Cody Law to Devon." Anna revealed. "Mr. Law sent it to me, through the school district. There is a letter for Devon and a cover letter for me. Mr. Law explained a simple search to identify the sixth grade teacher at Castle Rock Elementary School. Mr. Law, obviously wanted to reach Devon without going through Kirsten or Billy. The cover letter to me is short. Mr. Law is careful not to reveal to me that he is Devon's father.

He explains that he is an old friend of Kirsten's. Mr. Law asks that I pass his letter on to Devon without giving it to anyone else. He specifically asks that the letter not be shown to Kirsten, Billy, the police, or the principal. If I choose not to give the letter to Devon, then he asks that I please dispose of the letter. Mr. Law describes his request as unusual and inappropriate on the outside. He invited me to read the letter to Devon before I gave it to her. Mr. Law assured me that any apprehension to pass the letter to Devon would dissipate after reading the letter."

"Did you?" Cadrell asked.

"No, not yet." Anna answered coyly.

"Abide by his wishes, Ms. Larkin." Cadrell requested. "Do not give that letter to anyone except Devon."

"Do you know, Mr. Law?"

"Yes. Will you abide by Cody's wishes?"

"How well do you know Cody Law?" Anna probed.

"Do what he asks, Ms. Larkin. Trust me on that one." Easley beseeched. The meeting ended abruptly. Cadrell Easley had to go on duty.

Kirsten Barrett was due any minute. The bright sunshine flecked through the windows into the deserted classroom and painted warm, bright yellow boxes underneath the empty desks. The afternoon history lesson loomed high and bold on an extended map attached to the blackboard behind Anna Larkin's desk. A smattering of children remained in the hallways. Anna Larkin fussed with her make-up, although she never used much. Anna resembled a younger version of Lauren Hutton. Both possessed a profile that could fill out an expensive evening dress or turn heads in a sweatshirt on a windy summer afternoon. The other female teachers at Castle Rock Elementary did not care for the attractive blond. Overly concerned with her appearance, Anna heard a faint knock on the door.

"It's open. Come in, please." Anna Larkin shouted. Kirsten Barrett walked slowly into the small classroom. Kirsten Barrett wore a Denver Bronco's jersey and blue jeans. The immaculate figure from high school had put on a few pounds. Kirsten was not heavy, but neglected. Kirsten's hair hung long over her shoulders, long overdue for a visit to a beauty parlor. Kirsten swung the keys to the car in her hand. There were no plans to stay long.

"Thank you for coming, Mrs. Barrett." Anna began. "May I call you Kirsten?"

"Suit yourself, Ms. Larkin. Is that what we are supposed to call you? Ms. Larkin?" Kirsten was not happy to attend the meeting.

"Anna is fine. I'm sorry we got our signals crossed for the last two times we tried to get together." Anna coddled her guest.

"Ms. Larkin, we have not tried to get together at all. You have asked me to come meet with you and I have declined because I have heard what you are going to tell me before. You seem to be more persistent than most, so I have agreed to meet with you for one purpose. You are concerned with Devon's behavior and appearance, correct? Am I on the right track, Ms. Larkin?" Kirsten Barrett had not trusted another human being in over a decade.

"Yes, but..." Anna was cut off.

"Devon does not eat well, Ms. Larkin." Kirsten recited her lines like a scene from a play given over and over again. "I believe that Mr. Hollis has explained the autism and it's implications. Devon is a loner, Ms. Larkin. I'm sure, that since you are a teacher, you are aware of the differences in children. Some are gregarious and outgoing. Many have to be disciplined or they will bounce off the walls all day long. My Devon is quiet and prefers to stay away from the crowd. This is not always a bad thing, Ms. Larkin." The sarcasm cut the room with veracity and venom. The body language in Kirsten Barrett left little doubt that Kirsten would be leaving shortly.

"Devon is not autistic!" Anna snapped. "Let's get off that road. Devon is bright and does not exhibit any pathological delusions or hallucinations. Devon has no peculiar speech impediments, does not rock back and forth in any hypnotic chants, and learns faster than most of the kids a year ahead of her. Devon is being abused by her father and you know it."

"I knew I would get this shit again." Kirsten shot back. "Have you met Devon's father?"

"No."

"Did Devon come to you for help?" Kirsten knew the answer.

"He is killing your daughter, Mrs. Barrett. How can you not see that?" Anna had few options.

"Did my daughter ask for your help? Answer me!" Kirsten demanded.

"No, Mrs. Barrett, they never do." Anna replied.

"You have been in Castle Rock for less than a year. You have never met my husband and we just met two minutes ago. The school has worked with Devon for seven years. Yet somehow, you are more qualified to know my family than the people we have lived and worked with for years. Have you discussed this with Martin Hollis?" Kirsten turned and headed for the door.

"No, I wanted to meet with you first. I will help you in any way that I can." Anna knew the futility of these arguments. No one will receive help or seek help without acknowledging the crime.

"I do not want your help, Ms. Larkin. I do not need your help and neither does Devon. Do not request any more meetings with me. I would take Devon out of your class, but the end of the school year is less than two weeks away so there is no point to that. Bring this up again and I will file a formal complaint against you with the school board. The Douglas County School Board has little patience for unfounded accusations from any of their employees in the district."

"I have never met your husband and I have never met Devon's father." Anna blurted out. Kirsten stopped and turned around to face Anna Larkin. "Maybe someday, I can meet them both?"

"Your tenure in Castle Rock, Ms. Larkin, will be brief." Kirsten stared at Anna Larkin.

"Speaking of Castle Rock, Mrs. Barrett. Is it customary in Castle Rock to send a four-year old to trial for killing an infant?" Anna Larkin began to lose control. Kirsten turned again and left the room.

"Don't you walk away from me!" Anna Larkin demanded. "We are not finished, here!"

Kirsten Barrett never looked back. Anna Larkin was sobbing in an empty classroom.

* * *

The last day of school fell into the royalty vault of a child's life like birthdays and Christmas. Children remember the anticipation of the last June morning in a classroom, no longer burdened by books and rules. Thoughts of freedom and discovery for the next three months raced about the bulging clock on the wall above Ms. Larkin's desk. The fears of September were light years away. No one could recall or cared why the school board required attendance on this day. Maybe the state required a certain number of school days in session to render public funding. It did not matter.

The children ate cookies and took turns talking about what they had planned for the summer. Anna Larkin was careful not to call on Devon Barrett. The summer was an unwelcome interruption to the only sanctuary in her life with a schedule. School was the safety net. Summer signified chaos at home. Billy stayed out later and drank more. The late night visits were more frequent and more unpredictable. The fairgrounds often brought solace, but the windows to slip away were rare and Devon never knew what the time would cost.

On the light side, Barrett may designate a missed evening meal with a few hours tied, taped and blindfolded in the closet. In his most inebriated state, Billy Don Barrett discovered sodomy. The liquor overrode any fear of discovery. Failing to reach an erection, Billy found other objects to complete the task. Closet brooms and plunger handles often found their mark. The winds of summer did not blow kindly on Gilbert Street.

Devon appeared more sallow on the last day of school than usual. The bright mountain sunshine brushed a blazing yellow blanket against the infamous formation known as Castle Rock. Anna Larkin released the hounds at high noon. The yelps and whistles followed a thundering herd to the play-grounds and streets outside. A reticent girl slowly gathered a few items from her desk and clutched them close to her chest.

"I noticed that your boyfriend moved from tenth to eighth in the rankings. He's a lock for the Finals, huh?" Devon asked Ms. Larkin.

"Nothings a lock in rodeo. You know that." Anna replied. "Come here, sweetheart." Anna held her hand out to Devon. Those three simple words produced the unfamiliar sincerity Devon craved. "Justin always tells me that a rider's ranking is an illusion until the final stop of the year. One rank bronc can send the best rider home for good."

"Yeah, he's right." Devon beamed, ecstatic to expound on the one subject close to her heart. "Skyler Yates led the bull riders rankings a couple years ago. Yates held a sizable lead before the Pendleton Round-Up in Oregon. At Pendleton in the short-go, he pulled a Red Rock clone named Diamondback. Diamondback threw Skyler Yates against the back post in the gate before the gate was pulled. Yates snapped three vertebra in his back and hasn't made it out of a wheelchair, yet."

"Great, now I feel relieved." Anna sighed sarcastically.

"Oh, I'm sorry, Ms. Larkin." Devon bumbled. "You know what I mean..."

"I know, Devon." Anna Larkin reassured her soon-to-be ex-student. "You know more about rodeo and bull riders than most of the guys in it! Come here, I want to talk to you about something."

Anna Larkin had been devastated by her meeting with Devon's mother. The meeting was never mentioned to Devon, but Anna took more than a week to consider what to do with Cody Law's letter. Anna Larkin assumed that the letter would become another avenue to harm the girl. After the first week following the meeting with Kirsten, Anna read Cody Law's letter. The next day, Anna brought the letter back to school. It was the last day of school.

"I am going to give you a letter, Devon." Anna began. "The letter is from a man named Cody Law."

"Cody Law!" Devon interrupted. "He's the thirty-two year old rookie bull rider that just scored a seventy-nine for a first place tie with Larry Tatum in Redding, California at the Redding Rodeo. I read about him last week in PSN. He's traveling with Gunner McGarrity. I guess he's some business guy from the Midwest that is on one lucky run. They say he earned his PRCA card in three weeks. They also say that he has drawn some easy bulls and the judges are jacking the score because it's a good story."

"I don't know much about that, but I want you to read this letter before you leave. I'll wait out in the hall and come back in here when you are finished. O.K., Devon?" Anna reached for her purse.

"O.K., Ms. Larkin." Devon spoke clearly, yet a bit confused. Anna Larkin handed Devon the letter. Devon walked back to one of the empty desks. The joyful sounds of the children freed for the summer began to diminish as the marauding horde made their way into the neighborhood. Anna walked out into the hallway and stood against the wall with her arms folded. She remembered when the end of school was such a happy day. Devon Barrett opened the handwritten letter...

Dear Devon,

I have written this letter in my head a thousand times. It has come out different a thousand times. We met Devon, a few months ago at the Douglas County Fairgrounds. You were standing on the fence and watching the bull riders from a nearby college. I asked you a couple questions about what they were doing. Boy, you answered like an encyclopedia on rodeo.

My name is Cody Law. I was in Castle Rock to see your mother. I knew Kirsten a long time ago. We met in Hawaii. Your mother was there on a vacation with three of her friends from Denver. I only spent a couple days with Kirsten in Honolulu. They were the most special days that I have ever shared with another person. Your mother was a spirit from the sun, blessed with sparkling eyes filled with playful romance that found a companion in the stormy ocean surf. I let a gift from God slip through my fingers before I knew what had happened.

Kirsten left because her vacation was over and the short relationship we enjoyed could not continue. I did not hear from Kirsten for nearly a year. In the only letter she wrote to me, Kirsten explained that she had a baby. She had just married a man named Billy Don Barrett. The letter explained how successful Billy was going to be and that while she enjoyed her stay in Hawaii, her life was in Colorado with Mr. Barrett. I believed, in my heart, that Kirsten was saying good-bye forever. It was not my place to interfere with her plans to seek the kind of life she always wanted. After all, I was a vagabond bartender with little to offer.

Circumstances and apologies are not going to fill the years that I assumed Kirsten and her family had been thriving in Colorado. Your mother told me that Billy was heir to a successful family trucking business. For myself, I moved back to my home in Chicago and opened a small restaurant. Fortunately, one restaurant turned into many and I built a very successful string of restaurants in Chicago.

I met a man recently in one of those Chicago restaurants. The man was visiting Chicago from Colorado. He was a police officer from Castle Rock. The unique connection sparked a conversation about Castle Rock. I described an old acquaintance from Castle Rock and he described his duties as a police officer in Castle Rock. I told him that my friend in Castle Rock was a girl named Kirsten Myers, but she may be married and I did not remember her married name. The police officer knew Kirsten and your family. He described your house and your family. He told me that Kirsten had a twelve-year old daughter named Devon. My heart fell to my socks. He told me how pretty you were. After I met you, I knew he fell way short in describing the stunning girl on the fairground fence. The police officer and I talked in Chicago for hours. I wanted to know as much about you as he could tell me.

I came to Castle Rock as soon as I could. When I met with your mother, she was surprised to see me, to say the least. After twelve years, your mother was nervous and scared to see me. Devon, your mother wants to protect you more than anything in the world. She was afraid that Billy would become angry if he knew about me. Kirsten told me to leave Castle Rock. She told me not to contact you in any way. If I did, then I would be placing you in danger. I had to honor your mother's wishes at that time.

Before I left, I saw your room and your closet, Devon. I wouldn't punish a dog in a room like that. Tucked away in your closet, were the clues to our destiny. I knew a bond or a kinship between us had to be more than just a coincidence. When I was a little boy, I dreamed of riding bulls in a big arena with my family and everyone I knew cheering for me. My father gave me cowboy boots and a hat when I was three. I rode an imaginary horse through the city streets. Damned if Billy The Kid didn't make it home every night. I met Jesse James and the Texas Rangers, pearl handle pistols and silver lawman stars. My heroes chased eight-second dreams and I grew up to chase a dollar.

After my stay in Castle Rock, whether Kirsten and I connected or not, I was enrolled at Gunner McGarrity's Bull Riding School in California. Everyone told me that I was too old to start riding bulls. Everyone, except Gunner. We are only defeated Devon when we stop believing.

A lost relationship has taught me more about courage than climbing onto any stomach turning, one ton mean-ass Brahma bull can require. I know your mother wished things could be different but she is scared. I left the day after I spoke to Kirsten, but one task remained before I left for California. I had to meet you, so I followed you one day from school to the fairground. Someone once told me that my eyes looked like an empty forest with pretty trees but nobody around. I saw those pretty trees in your eyes and nobody was there, either.

A few months ago, I started riding bulls and working with Gunner McGarrity. I am certain that you are well aware of Gunner McGarrity and his rodeo career. Gunner is traveling with me now. I have been pretty lucky in the first few rodeos that I have entered. What I am doing has everything to do with you, Devon. I'll explain more later. I am going to backdoor my way into your mother's life. There are some specific goals to achieve this season. Once there, Devon, I'm coming for you and Kirsten. I know what has gone on for years. I know that any adult pledge to you will fall on deaf ears.

Gunner has helped me envision where I will be by the end of the year. He is a man like no other. Where I will be, Devon, is with you and your mother. Everything will change for you, Devon. I am just outside of Santa Maria, California. Gunner and I stopped at Gunner's ranch after Redding. I have taken a week off to work on some specific problems with my bull riding that Gunner wanted to address now. I think about you every day. On good days, I get my butt tossed around like a discarded can of Spam. I've got traveling companions that call me grandpa. On most nights, I question the sanity of what I want to accomplish. I think about you every night when I try to sleep. The past twelve years come stumbling back into my eyes and I think about what you have been through. I am writing this letter atop a bluff overlooking Pismo Beach on the coast of Central California. I took one of Gunner's ATV's and rode to the eastern edge of the ranch. I would have taken a horse but I still can't ride the damn animals. I am riding competitive bulls, but horses are a different story. I am hoping someday that you and I can ride this trail together. The view is spectacular. If you think California is a congested mess of traffic and Hollywood types, then I cannot wait to show you this little slice of paradise. There's a stiff California wind pushing the stars around tonight and I can see the one with your name on it. It's real, Devon.

Devon, stay with me on this for now. Contact Officer Cadrell Easley with the Castle Rock Police Department if you need anything or you want to talk to someone. You can trust Officer Easley. I don't say that about many people, but there are no finer men than Cadrell Easley and Gunner McGarrity. My own father would have a horse race on his hands with these guys. I hope things have been better recently for you. I tried to arrange some changes for you. Your surroundings will change dramatically before the end of the year. Do not show this letter to anyone, including your mother and Billy Don Barrett. You can contact me through Anna Larkin or Gunner McGarrity's ranch in Nipomo, California. Keep this letter and hold it to your heart. Know that I am coming for you and every time you begin to doubt, read it again. There is a secret you and I share, now.

Your loving father,
Cody

Devon Barrett read the letter twice. She folded the letter carefully and placed the envelope in her pocket. Devon gathered her things and walked into the hallway. Anna Larkin was waiting. Devon kissed Anna on the cheek and thanked her for the year. In the nine months that Anna Larkin had known Devon Barrett, Anna had never witnessed bright eyes, mischief or hope in Devon's face. Cody Law changed that in one letter on a June day in Castle Rock.

* * *

Two months later...

Rodeo in America is a closed society. More than half of the U.S. population does not know the scope of rodeo's popularity. There is the occasional channel surfing that leads to sliding by a rodeo telecast, which disappears as fast as the picture can change. The Eastern perception of slow drawls and bad jeans in rodeo is no more insightful than the perception of country music as a twang'y steel guitar behind the whining lyrics of prisons, good old dogs and whiskey. Some slow drawls do exist, as do whining lyrics and Hank Williams memories.

The reality is that rodeo, like any growing sport is big business. While the faithful enjoy the predictable ballads of George Strait over the thunderous pyrotechnics surrounding Garth Brooks, rodeo ticket sales in America exceed twenty million tickets per year. Anheiser Busch, Ford Motor Company, Dodge, and Caesars Palace are all major sponsors of the Professional Rodeo Cowboys Association. Related sponsors include Justin Boots, Wrangler, Jack Daniels, Tony Lama Boots, Copenhagen Tobacco Company and hundreds of U.S. companies sponsoring the regional rodeos leading to Calgary, Cheyenne and the National Finals Rodeo in Las Vegas every December.

While the Eastern half of the country is adverse to any outward affiliation or association with rodeo, the contestants live within a cocoon of camaraderie. Contestants are rarely pitted against each other. The cowboys compete against the animals and therefore, share a rare bond among athletes competing for the same thing. The rodeo cowboys share the climb from junior events to high school competition, through some college and on to the professional venues. The solidarity within hard times binds them closer. The lonely months on the road, driving from one rodeo to the next with little more than gas money to get by, become cathartic initiations endured by all combatants.

The fraternity hazes rookies, but will shut out an outsider. Cody Law began traveling with Gunner McGarrity, Sonny Moore and Olin Martin. Sonny and Olin went along because Gunner decided to tag along and see how long it took Cody to bee-line back to Chicago. The early drift was the show. The boys would enjoy the break in the road routine. Cody's failures would be fun to watch. What the show didn't plan for, was any degree of success. Cody Law, in spite of the improbable nature of his task, had an uncanny knack for riding bulls. Gunner began to say that Cody looked like an ostrich with a squirrel in his shorts, but the son of a bitch stays on the damn bulls.

Bull-Riding Champion Glen "Pee Wee" Mercer said the adrenaline is so great when you first start riding bulls that you black out. He went on to say that while you are still outwardly conscious, one cannot remember anything about the ride. This happens, according to Mercer, for the first thirty or forty rides. Gunner laughed about Cody being hit hard one day and the blow from the bull will knock him into consciousness.

In professional rodeo, entry fees are divided. Half goes into the pot for the whole rodeo prize money. The other half goes into the day-money pot, which is split between the guys that make qualified rides that day. If only one guy makes a qualified ride, he gets it all. If more than one rider qualifies, the money is split equally. It takes $2500 to fill a permit and then be eligible to buy your PRCA card. Then you are a member. Until then, a permit only allows you to enter PRCA rodeos, if the slots are available. With the bigger rodeos, permit slots are almost impossible to find. Cody filled his permit after the fourth rodeo he entered.

Cody's first rodeo check was the Laughlin River Stampede in Nevada. Prior to Laughlin, Cody first entered a rodeo in Lubbock, Texas. Cody pulled a short predictable bull named Bad River, a much rougher surname than the bull's reputation. Cody's stomach churned like a diesel engine gone berserk. The restless spectators settled in for the bull-riding. Gunner began warming up the tail of the rope. Cody slid his gloved hand up and down the rope. The friction heated the rosin while Cody continued the motion. The rope and glove began to heat up and become very sticky. Gunner grabbed Cody's arm and told him to stop. The rope was warm enough. He told Cody that if he rubbed it any harder, the goddamn rope would burst into flames. Gunner placed his hand across Cody's chest, in case the bull lurched in the chute.

"Tell me when it's too tight." Gunner said as he pulled the rope.

"Good, man, good." Cody barked back, not sure of anything at this point, except that he wished he could make himself instantly disappear. Gunner laid the tail of the rope across the bull's back.

"Arena's clear. Slide and ride cowboy." Gunner yelled. With his free hand, Cody pushed his hat down hard and nodded for the gate to be opened.

Bad River is a bit hard to get out of the chute on. At times, he will buck in the chute. Other times, he will lay down. Gunner told Cody that if he times it right, the ride could last only seven seconds because it takes Bad River a second to get right when the chute opens. The advice could have been in Japanese. Cody didn't have a clue what Gunner was talking about. The gate opened and the last thing Bad River had on his mind was lying down. Bad River jumped and spun in the air so fast that Gunner thought he looked like a bull waiting to buck somebody into yesterday. Cody came off the bull's neck on the first jump and hit the arena floor before the gate had stopped swinging. Cody got up and fully expected everyone to be laughing at him. Cody scurried back to the chutes and looked up at Gunner.

"Nobody is laughing at you, boy." Gunner spoke as he helped pull Cody back over the rails. "Back here, these boys have earned the right to smile. Those folks in the seats can't say a thing. They know it, too."

From that day on, when the arena director called, "Pull 'em up boys. We're ready to rodeo," Cody Law placed in the money in fifteen of twenty three rodeos. The circuit took Cody to Austin and Huntsville, Texas. Stops in Duncan, Oklahoma and back to Stephenville, Texas led Cody and Gunner into May. June kicked into gear with a second place in Flagstaff, Arizona at the Pine County Pro Rodeo. Cody kept quiet at all times behind the chutes. The other competitors left him alone, for the most part. An occasional slap of encouragement from a fellow bull-rider felt great. The more frequent comments about how the luck would run out soon, did little to further the isolation he carried with him at all times.

Cody's success surprised no one more than Gunner McGarrity. Gunner had been a bull-rider, lived with bull-riders, trained bull-riders and never witnessed the accomplishments he had orchestrated with Cody Law. Gunner believed in Cody's motivation or the project never would have gotten off the ground, but Gunner never thought Cody could learn to ride a bull at a competitive level in such a short time.

When Cody first came to Gunner's ranch and began the first days of the school, Gunner found Cody watching tapes late at night in the barn. Cody has amassed Gunner's complete collection of National Finals bull riding tapes beginning in 1970, the year Gunner won the World Championship. Cody studied the tapes for a minimum of four hours per day. Cody studied the great rides in each round, but he focused on the unsuccessful rides. Meticulously, Cody dissected each fall. The slow motion was run to chart each move before the fall. Every rider had certain inborn characteristics. Cody charted every move that precipitated a rider being thrown. In the most scientific manner, Cody evaluated the percentages and likelihood of an unsuccessful ride, given the trends of each rider. Gunner used to tell Cody that he could not recapture the years to develop an instinct. His only hope was to imitate the best and avoid their mistakes. Cody would spend hours in the hotel rooms, staring at videotapes. There were tapes for each of the ten rounds that make up every Finals competition. From 1970-1990, that would total two-hundred videotapes or three-thousand rides.

In Flagstaff, Cody pulled a placid brown and white purebred Bradford bull named Harley. Cody stayed on through the whistle, but Cody felt the seventy-two points were a gift to the city-boy. Any Texas ranch brat would have pulled a fifty something on that same bull. In the short go, Cody drew an 1800-pound motley faced Simental-Brahma cross with short horns and an impressive resume, named Rising Star. Rising Star had been around and had been exposed to many world-class riders. A bull like that does not trick anyone.

Rising Star bucked like he drank nitroglycerin for breakfast. Cody hung on to Rising Star like a frozen deer caught in the headlights of an oncoming vehicle. Cody was simply too inexperienced to ride Rising Star, but the bull could not shake him. The other bull-riders were glued to the top of their chutes for the end of Cody's ride. They knew something very special was beginning in Flagstaff that night. Nobody rides a bull like Rising Star with three months experience. Cody's score was an eighty-eight. Only a sensational ride by the Bud Lite standings leader Corey Bluff, on an up and coming bull named Red Wolf, pushed Cody to second place. The explanations were non-existent. What every bull-rider knew however, was that Cody Law could not fake it.

Cody finally gave in to one avenue of his own wealth after earning his PRCA card. Cody bought a brand new Chevrolet Suburban for the foursome to shuttle across the western states. Struggling nomads protest little when an eight-speaker stereo rings with Mason Dayne and all the gas bills are picked up by Santa Claus.

The story grew across the circuit. From Reno to Flagstaff, from Greeley and Calgary to Cheyenne, Cody Law became the most unlikely story to hit America's Sport since the death of Lane Frost. Amidst rodeo's marquee events and the nearly 700 grassroots rodeos across the country, Cody Law took a foothold in something the nation craved. People Magazine ran a follow-up story on Cody Law to the story they ran nearly one year ago featuring the young nightclub entrepreneur from Chicago.

People ran the story in mid-August. The three-page spread was entitled, "A Chicago Law Moves West." Cody Law was attracting attention at every stop on the PRCA Tour. His traveling companions enjoyed the notoriety while the predictable jealousy among the veterans never materialized. The sport became news in parts of the country where people couldn't tell you three of the seven events at a rodeo.

Gunner chuckled as he summed up the new phenomenon. "We're the lost souls of this country. Until they can relate to one of their own, we're just uneducated back page costumes for the annual country and western night at the Catholic school benefit. I swear, God is the only one who can explain how Cody is staying on those bulls, but he is pulling out the fantasies of every man fighting to make the mortgage payment. Cody's tapped the silent masses, those who laugh at cowboy hats and wished to God that they had the freedom and the gristle to pull one tight over their eyes. We do what they can't. They can live through Cody. Hell boys, its blue jeans, chaps and bulls. Don't get no better than that."

Autumn took the tour to Phoenix, Arizona for the Rodeo Showdown at the America West Arena. Cody, Gunner, Sonny and Olin arrived in Phoenix from a moderately funded rodeo at the New Mexico State Fair in Albuquerque. Gunner loved going to Phoenix or Cave Creek, especially in the fall. Situated behind a service station at the corner of Scottsdale Road and Shea Boulevard in Scottsdale was a honky-tonk relic called Handlebar J's. Every self-respecting rodeo cowboy while in Phoenix or Cave Creek for a rodeo, had been carried out of Handlebar J's at one time or another. Handlebar J's was an old red brick tavern behind a gated patio, complete with a wrought iron canopy entrance framed by a battered brick wall surrounding the outdoor seating. The one story structure reeked from the forty-year old rib smoker in the back kitchen. The simmering slabs filled the air with a redolent distinction that wore the name Handlebar J's. The Herndon Brothers Band played six nights a week. The ceiling was home to thousands of old boots and cowboy hats. The menu was barbecue anything and the two-steppin' was real. The biggest, degenerate desperadoes dragged their soiled, yoked back MoBetta shirts out on the dance floor every night. You went home alone if you didn't dance at Handlebar J's.

The one constant at Handlebar J's was the owner, Gwen Herndon. Gwen worked the tavern like an old friend for decades since her husband passed away. Approaching seventy, she was not ready to say good-bye any time soon. Gwen's doormen, bartenders and wait staff showed respect for the hard working widow and nothing less was expected of the clientele. Gwen Herndon's son, Ty Herndon was the lead singer in the Nashville recording group called McBride and the Ride. Ty would go on, in later years, to record national hit after hit as a solo artist. Another son headed up the featured band on premise every night.

Gunner McGarrity knew Gwen well. Gunner's winning ride at Phoenix in 1970 was highlighted by a four by six-foot poster along the back wall behind the stage. During every break by the band, a video screen dropped from the ceiling and played rodeo bloopers and spectacular wipeouts from the PRCA Tour archives. Gunner's arrival was grand. Nothing lights up a cowboy bar like the rodeo boys. Rodeo contestants and past champions were royalty at the bar. Cody Law, Sonny and Olin were all introduced by the band. A special welcome was reserved for Gunner. World Championship Gold Buckles were respected from Arizona to Wyoming, from California to Texas and every beer joint, barroom, and diner in between.

As the new arrivals enjoyed the fruits of attention, such as free libations, a few autograph seeking tourists, and a voluminous supply of buckle bunnies, the evening took a rancid turn into the inevitable path of confrontation. While the Herndon Brothers fielded request after request, the building rumbled slightly from the arrival of twenty or thirty Harley Davidson motorcycles. A Wyoming chapter of the Warriors Motorcycle Club roared into Scottsdale and parked outside the patio of Handlebar J's.

The Warriors are the third largest "outlaw" motorcycle club in the United States. The Hell's Angels, The Outlaws and the Pagan Motorcycle Club comprise what the government calls the "Big Four". The Warriors originated in northern California in 1960. They operate chapters in Texas, Mississippi, New Mexico, North and South Dakota, Wyoming and the state of Washington. The Warriors hold chapters in Denmark, Australia, France and look to expand to many other Eastern European locations during the nineties.

Outside the bar, the club members mingled and stretched from a long ride. Gunner was holding court at the bar with a bevy of young women, smitten with the man perched atop the vertical bull in the poster that characterized Handlebar J's. Cody, Sonny and Olin chased a few Coors beers with some Jack. Cody curled a Marlboro in his fingers. Sonny and Olin pushed some Copenhagen in place. Cody excused himself to the men's room.

As the band broke for a twenty-minute hiatus, the Warriors entered the bar. Walking in a line along the main bar, the Warriors inside the tavern numbered a dozen or more. The road worn group looked like they had spent the last month in solitary confinement without the benefit of a shower. The long standing Cheyenne, Wyoming chapter of the Warriors were led by a large man with shoulder length hair and a barbed wire bush that hung under his chin like a bedraggled pelican refuse. His name was Sal Miller. Miller was a short stocky, barrel-armed man in his mid-thirties. The lead club member wore a denim cut-off club jacket and no shirt. The denim jacket featured the Warriors logo, the chapter affiliation and a decimated American flag patch rendered nearly unrecognizable from the grease. The doormen explained to the new guests that shirts were required but the ensuing trouble loomed unworthy of the general rules. The outnumbered bouncers relented.

Inside the men's room, Cody stood at one of the four urinals against the wall. In walked the nearest living relative to Attila the Hun. The Warrior denim vest was filthy. The motorcycle club member approached the urinal next to Cody. The man appeared to be in his late-thirties with a horrendous complexion hangover. A stringy black beard barely covered his pock marked face. Cody's bathroom companion stood five feet ten and weighed well over two hundred and fifty pounds. Cody did his best to avoid any eye contact. The war stories from Fat Boys brought Cody a wealth of knowledge pertaining to the Hell's Angels and their marauding behavior. Cody continued his business and hoped to slide back to the bar momentarily.

The man next to Cody pulled up to the urinal and fumbled with his pants. He honked up a grotesque wad of phlegm, which he proceeded to spit somewhere on the floor. The man finally found his mark and the proceeding stream sounded like a faucet filling a bathtub. While Cody drained the final traces of a couple Coors beers, the man next to him released a volcanic belch accompanied by another exploding orifice below the waist. The malodorous combination hit the air like a constipated camel's breath or an Illinois Department of Transportation outhouse on Interstate 294 in mid-July. Cody closed his eyes and shook his head in silence. The fetid breath had a voice.

"Something wrong, Tex?" Came the visceral inquiry, obviously in reference to Cody's black Resistol hat or maybe the man was simply referring to the general atmosphere of the establishment they occupied. An intelligent exchange would not be forthcoming. Cody zipped his jeans and turned to the source of the hovering pollution.

"Well, if you want to know pal, I have never understood why some men feel that clearing every body cavity and aperture in the presence of another man is somehow NOT offensive or is NOT a disgusting habit that is only excused for infants and puppies." Cody spoke with a lance of condescending sarcasm, fully aware of the path to follow.

"I always questioned the necessity in most men to share certain bodily functions with perfect strangers. I suppose the question becomes moot for an oversized sow like you Pigpen. Tell me something, do you guys eat bacon or is there some kind of family thing going on there?"

The response did not disappoint Cody. The startled boar turned instantly and lunged for Cody. The man did not have his appendage back under cover and the off balance lunge proved the perfect fodder for Cody's quick reply. Cody took one step back and slammed his right foot and shin against the back of the man's calves. The floor, soaked in chewing tobacco residue, urine and beer, proved thoroughly unstable to a fat man with his dick hanging out. The legs gave out in the close quarters and the frazzled mass of filthy hair and denim fell awkwardly to the floor. Cody pushed his heel into the man's cheek and drove it home with authority.

"Go run and tell your friends fat man, that someone was mean to you in the bathroom." The man on the floor tried unsuccessfully to right himself under the pressure of Cody's boot. "I'll be at the bar. Maybe, I'll see you there?" Cody left the bathroom and walked rather briskly to Gunner, seated at the bar.

"Maybe we should think about leaving soon?" Cody commented as he watched his bathroom buddy rejoin the pack near the front entrance. "I believe that I may have irritated the new arrivals."

"Looks like that option is not available at the moment." Gunner replied. The group had the main entrance closed and began moving. The entourage reached Gunner at the bar. The man with flecks of gray in his temples looked rather inviting to the Warriors' leader. Miller approached Gunner and stopped. The man eyed the young women next to Gunner. He reached up and knocked Gunner's hat to the floor.

"Hey." The large man belched. "If it isn't Roy fucking Rodgers. There is only one thing worse than a fucking cowboy. It's an old fucking cowboy that doesn't know when to leave the ladies alone."

The procession of motorcycle club members stopped where Gunner sat. Gunner McGarrity reached down and picked up his hat. Cody and his group watched from the adjacent stools. Sonny pulled on Cody's arm. Olin knew the drill. Gunner placed his hat back on his head and stood up next to the Warriors' leader. At five feet, six inches tall, Gunner hardly presented an imposing figure. The dark bar hid well Gunner's chiseled arms and leather hands. The music almost dropped off on cue. The piped in break music faded as the tapes prepared to switch. Gunner's eyes caught Sonny and Cody, then shifted back to Sal Miller.

"I will excuse the fact that you insult my intelligence by opening your mouth." Gunner's light banter and meaning took a minute to discern. Gunner pulled on twenty years of tavern brawls and the adrenaline awoke in the old veins.

"I will excuse the fact that you insult my patriotism by wearing an American flag on your jacket that is covered with more grease than the floor at the Tri-Stop Garage back in Abilene. I will even excuse the fact that you fight in a pack like chicken-shit parasites."

"You got balls, Tex." Sal Miller laughed. "Anything else bothering you before we clear the bar of all this cowboy crap?"

"Well," Gunner sighed. "While we're on the subject, I have to take issue with an insult to Roy Rodgers. My daddy and I loved Roy Rodgers. "Before he finished the sentence, Gunner slammed his Justin two inch heal onto the top of the Sal Miller's instep. Gunner's boot caved in the five metatarsal bones and the tarsal bones that meet at the instep. They snapped like cold branches on a winter afternoon. The excruciating pain froze the stunned biker for a split second. At the same time, Gunner flipped his own hat off and slammed his forehead against Miller's temple, sending him to the floor quicker than Bad River gave Cody a mouthful of rodeo dirt in Lubbock.

The mantra in the world of outlaw motorcycle clubs is one man fights, they all fight. The remaining Warriors went after Gunner with the fervor of a wolf pack at a deer carcass in Yosemite. The lead bartender yelled fight and rang a massive cow bell hung over the center cash register! The bell rang through the bar in the audio image of the dive call in a Navy submarine. Sonny Moore and Olin Martin took out four of the Warriors with roll blocks that sent the group sprawling across the bar tables at Handlebar J's. Cody came out with a forearm elbow, exploding the face of one club member and spinning full circle, Cody connected with a back fist landing flush against the nose of another. Gunner stayed on Sal Miller, following him to the floor and slamming his club-like fist into Miller's face again and again.

Wanna-be cowboys scattered in fear, while the women close at hand became human mattresses for the brawling participants. Three bartenders jumped the bar, while one floor walker and three doormen converged on the melee. The police arrived within minutes due to the astute call made by the lead doorman after the motorcycle club made clear their intentions at the door. Three Warriors fled during the chaos. Nine others were arrested. Gunner, Cody, Sonny and Olin Martin cleaned a myriad of cuts caused more by the close quarters of the fight than the accuracy and talent of their adversaries. Handlebar J's resembled a John Wayne movie set after the scene had wrapped. Remarkably, the time was early. The fight occurred at ten o'clock. Even a few families on vacation in Phoenix were finishing dinner when the incident began.

Taverns are built to withstand fights. Within minutes after the fight, the bar tables were placed upright, the instigators removed and the Herndon Brothers Band announced the fight ranking in the bar's history. Gunner was singled out as the one adhesive factor to a genuine cowboy bar fight. Larry Herndon mimicked the signature quote of one Michael Buffer from the stage, while turning a spotlight on Gunner and his group.

"Please welcome back, again." Herndon feigned the legendary fight announcer." The undisputed Heavyweight Champion of the Woooooooooooooooorld........Gunner McGarrity!"

The Handlebar J's faithful exploded in a thunderous ovation. Gunner waved his hat high above his head and put his arms around Cody, Sonny and

Olin. The music resumed with a stirring rendition of an early Garth Brooks hit called "Rodeo." Handlebar J's stood tall and preserved the vanishing icon of the saloon. Cody and Gunner toasted battle scars and compared knuckles.

The evening broke soon after because the bulls don't ask about hangovers. Cody, Sonny and Olin made some promises that they would not keep while Gunner gave Gwen a kiss on the cheek and flashed the mischievous smile that hadn't changed in something short of two decades.

The Suburban was parked near the Jack-In-The-Box adjacent to the service station on Shea Boulevard. Sonny Moore and Olin Martin climbed in the back and waited for Gunner to catch up. Cody leaned against the vehicle and lit a cigarette. Gunner left the bar and crossed the parking lot. While waiting for Gunner to make his way to the Suburban, Cody turned to the commotion in the Jack-In-The-Box parking lot. Cody pulled on the Marlboro as a Hispanic man chastised what appeared to be his daughter in the fast-food parking lot.

"Get in the car." The perturbed father ordered. He pushed a little girl into the vehicle and she slipped under strength of her father's girth. The little girl, maybe seven or eight years old, hit her head against the car and incurred another command to get in the car.

"I said, get in the car!"

Another shove shook the small child and she fell again. The fear in her face was palpable to everyone but her father. The man reached down and pulled the girl up with no more compassion than a mule pulling a plow. The orders resumed, "Let's go, I said."

Cody dropped his cigarette and walked toward the lot.

"Where are you going?" Gunner asked as he reached the Suburban. Cody did not answer. "Cody, where are you going?"

The question echoed. There was no answer.

Cody Law approached the Hispanic family and their vehicle. The father pulled away from his daughter when he noticed Cody approaching.

"Can I help you?" The man asked in an obvious south of the border dialect.

"Manny!" Cody enthusiastically answered at the same time he reached the father.

"Who?" The father inquired.

"Manny, you son of a bitch. Manny, I haven't seen you in years." Cody embellished. "Don't you remember me. We worked together some five years ago."

Cody rushed toward the man, who dropped the hold on his daughter. Cody wore a black Resistol hat, a tight black tee shirt that stressed the definition in Cody's upper body, blue jeans and a Montana Silversmith buckle, a gift from Gunner after Laughlin. Cody reached the confused man in seconds.

"Manny." Cody repeated while putting his arm around a long lost friend. "Walk over here, buddy. I'll scare your family by the way I look. My buddies and I got into one hell of a barroom brawl just a few minutes ago over at Handlebar J's. My shirt and jeans are covered with beer and blood, most of it is not mine, if you know what I mean?"

Cody slapped his new friend on the back. The two men had moved down the lot behind a panel van. The bewildered man did not want to offend an old friend, but he could not place Cody's face, nor could he remember working with Cody. He finally spoke up.

"Hey, pal." The voice was laden with a heavy Hispanic accent. "I do not know who you are. I must look like someone you once knew. Maybe you just had too many beers or someone clocked you harder than you think?" The man began to walk away, giving Cody a pathetic, condescending farewell glance.

"Wait." Cody's voice was short. The man turned back to Cody and looked angry. Cody Law sent the toe of his Tony Lama right boot into the groin of the man standing in front of him. The kick landed with remarkable accuracy and buckled the victim instantly. Cody then slammed the side of the same boot into the man's kneecap, collapsing the man completely. His right patella had fractured. Cody always sent the first blows to a man's right side. The chances were better than average that a foe would be right handed and would lead with a right kick. Cody snapped up the man's right hand and twisted it backwards causing the wrist to teeter on the edge of another fracture. No resistance followed. The wallowing groans of pain alerted his family, yet they were out of any sight lines.

" Now, I want you to get up and come after me. Nothing would make me happier than to continue with this encounter but I can sense that our meeting will be brief. This doesn't make sense to you, does it?" Cody pulled his prey closer and did not wait for an answer. There was little response from the injured man.

"From today..." Cody stopped until he was certain that someone's undivided attention would not fade. "I walked you away from your family because I did not want them to see what I was going to do to you. Incredibly, I have more respect for your family than you have for your own daughter. If she is not your daughter than I should break your neck in front of her. Is that your daughter?" Cody pushed more weight on the wrist.

"Yes" The pained response was barely audible.

"From today, you will not treat that little girl like she is your personal pinata. Every time you get the urge to slap her around or slam your fat ass into her, remember our little lesson today in manners. Your one job is to protect your children. Can you fucking remember that?" Cody pulled to within an inch of the man's face. "Can you remember that?" Cody screamed again.

The loud voice brought the other family members. Cody picked up his hat and glanced at the young girl and her mother, now frightened by what they saw. Cody walked briskly past the pair as they backed away in fear that Cody may harm them as well. Gunner, Sonny and Olin had made their way to the commotion. Gunner looked at the man clutching his knee and grimacing in pain.

"Are you fucking crazy, Cody? What did this guy do to you?" Gunner inquired while they scurried back to the Suburban.

"Nothing." Cody answered.

"The guy did nothing to you, so you ran across the parking lot and kicked the shit out of him?" Gunner wondered out loud.

"Something like that. Now, let's get the fuck out of here. Where are we staying tonight?" Cody asked Gunner.

"We always stay at the Holiday Inn about a mile from here. Go left at Scottsdale Road. Rooms are cheap and they always discount the rodeo boys." Gunner recalled.

It had been years since he made the stops. The Suburban rolled out of the lot onto Shea, approaching Scottsdale Road. From the fast food parking lot, Gunner noticed the little girl staring at Cody's Suburban as they pulled away. A heavyset woman helped her husband into a maroon, 1978 Lincoln Continental. The police were not summoned. The little girl continued to eye the Suburban until Cody pulled out of view. Gunner signaled for Cody to turn. The Holiday Inn was at the next corner. The Suburban slowed to pull into the Holiday Inn lot. Trouble was, the Holiday Inn was gone. Turns out that the hotel was torn down ten years ago. Cody looked at Gunner in the passenger's seat. Cody turned the vehicle around and headed back into Phoenix.

"Nice call, Gunner." Cody proudly announced to the snickers in the back seat.

"It's been awhile. Where are you going?" Gunner asked.

"I'm treating my traveling companions to a night at the Phoenecian. Anybody have a problem with that?" Cody inquired.

"Not me, Cody. It sounds like a brothel." Sonny Moore chimed in.

"What is the Phoenecian?" Olin Martin asked.

"The Phoenecian Hotel is the finest hotel in Maricopa County. Hell, it is the finest hotel in the state." Gunner proclaimed. "They've got more fountains at the Phoenecian Hotel than at Caesar's Palace in Las Vegas. They must have sixty-four pools and a concierge for every guest. They're gonna think we are there to clean some of those pools."

"I met a girl at Handlebar's one night after a particularly good ride in a rodeo up in Cave Creek, maybe fifteen years ago. Some girls get the biggest kick out of taking a cowboy home to roost. When a man says yes ma'am, they smile. When a man kicks up the dance floor as well as he handles a one-ton spinning Brahma, there is no stronger aphrodisiac. Cowboys are like rare Cuban cigars. You may not want to smoke them all the time, but you have to try one sometime. Women get tired of men with manicured nails and hands softer than their own. There is something about a worn out pair of Justin boots next to the bed that drives a New York City girl a little bit crazy. The young lady that I met years ago, was a stewardess for United and her crew was staying at the Phoenecian. I spent two days combing every inch of the grounds at that hotel. I made love to that girl in every pool and bathhouse on the grounds. She had an uncanny desire to have sex in the most unusual places. Far be it from me to deprive my host of those simple wishes. The Phoenecian Hotel is one hell of a hotel."

There were two separations from Jacquie during Gunner's two decade long marriage. Gunner seemed to recall that the relationship in Phoenix occurred during one of the separations, although a separation never qualified as a prerequisite for any extra curricular activities.

The hotel staff took the Suburban when the quartet arrived somewhere around eleven o'clock. Cody approached the front desk while Sonny and Olin walked around the main lobby as if they had been dropped into the Palace of Versailles. The Phoenecian lobby is series of marble football fields dressed in opulent chandeliers and oversized designer furniture. A mammoth Baldwin grand piano stood before the entire glass expanse overlooking the manicured grounds and the three acres of pools. The three-hundred foot water slide wound like a serpent through the concrete caverns and the private cabanas. A solo pianist played to the half dozen patrons of the lobby lounge. The few were expense account suits, sipping Grand Marnier and smoking Cuban cigars that they loathed.

Cody signed for two rooms at the rate of four hundred ninety five dollars per room. Sonny and Olin agreed they would sleep in and headed for the bar. Cody told them to sign for the drinks. Cody and Gunner went to their room. The night had been eventful enough. The rodeo would fill the America West Arena at six o'clock the next day. Cody wanted to arrive before three. The draws would be posted at that time. The local Phoenix newspaper had requested a few minutes with Cody before the competition began. The luggage consisted of three dusty rodeo bags and Gunner's duffel bag. The bellhops handled the bags as if they were contaminated.

Sonny and Olin had disappeared. Gunner and Cody met the bellhop at their room. Cody tipped the man and closed the door. The dust from the bags resonated in the room like a small cloud hopelessly out of place. Gunner called his wife at the ranch in California. Through the years, Jacquie had stuck by the wandering bull-rider and never asked the questions she knew the answers to. Rodeo wives learn early on, that changing the men they chose to marry is not an option. Infidelity, while inexcusable, is not often broached because true cowboys don't lie. The hypocrisy is wearing a bright orange fluorescent coat, yet nevertheless, cowboy logic never claimed to make a whole bushel of sense. Gunner spoke to his wife for a few minutes. Cody pulled a beer from the small refrigerator in the room. He tossed one to Gunner.

"Cadrell Easley has been trying to reach you." Gunner relayed before cracking the beer.

"Did he leave a number or a message?" Cody asked, somewhat alarmed.

"Devon was not enrolled in class for the September start of school. Easley said her mother informed the school that she and Billy would be home schooling their daughter for the upcoming year. He thought you should know." Gunner spoke regretfully. Gunner looked at Cody and anticipated the response.

"He told my wife that the parents have the right to make that decision, but Easley is concerned that the decision does not bode well for Devon."

"What time will the bull-riders finish tomorrow night?" Cody asked.

"The last gate will pull before nine-thirty." Gunner replied.

"We'll be on a plane to Denver by midnight. Will you go with me?" Cody knew the answer.

"Absolutely." Gunner pulled on his beer.

"I want Sonny and Olin to come as well."

"You know they will, Cody. What do you think is happening with your daughter?" Gunner despised the speculation because the answers were all too obvious.

"I have to do what I should have done when I first arrived in Castle Rock. We are not leaving without Devon. Can she stay at the ranch?"

"We already have a room set up for her. I asked my wife when you first came to the ranch, if she thought I was wasting my time. Jacquie told me to be prepared to bring the girl back to the ranch. I told her that I meant wasting my time with teaching a city boy to ride bulls. Jacquie's answer had nothing to do with riding bulls." Gunner laid back on the bed and closed his eyes.

"Make the reservations, Cody. Why do you think I am traveling with you? Are we going to pay a visit to Mr. Barrett, as well?"

"We will have to find out if Cadrell has any more information for me. Easley has made some progress with the local District Attorney. We are not going through channels, Gunner. We are taking Devon and Kirsten, if she wants to go, away from Barrett. I'm Devon's father legally and I can press charges against Barrett without the mother's consent. I never wanted to do that. The entire prosecution would then fall onto Devon. We may not have a choice. I cannot wait much longer for Kirsten to allow the access. I believe Devon may trust me now. I've been able to get four letters to Devon through Anna Larkin, Devon's sixth grade teacher. If the trust is there, then we can go in there and pull her right out. If Devon folds, then we may lose the window forever. You, Sonny and Olin may face a variety of legal problems. Barrett will come after me with more charges and a host of civil litigation actions."

Cody Law stood up and walked to the window. The floods lit up the mountainside with a sea of white lights. The Phoenecian guestroom buildings were long sprawling cream colored structures meandering through two championship caliber golf courses. The mountains rose up from the base of the resort with divine images unparalleled in the ruddy, rugged flavor of the Southwest.

"To answer your question about Billy Don Barrett, I'm not bringing Sonny and Olin to Colorado so they can feather out any potential winter ski sites. Our first stop in Castle Rock will be a dirty little gin mill called The Rascal Flats."

*   *   *

The Rodeo Showdown in Phoenix attracted a near capacity crowd at the America West Arena in downtown Phoenix. Sonny and Olin didn't make the short-go, while Cody entered the final round in a tie for first place. The fairy tale continued with Cody's first round draw, a black and white spinner named Bull Sheet. Bull Sheet was fast and light at slightly less than sixteen hundred pounds. Cody continued to look like he had to be glued to the bulls. His unorthodox hand and arm movements came from inexperience, but he somehow stayed on the bulls. The judges, who normally deduct points for a flailing rider, seemed to reward points for the growing story surrounding Cody Law.

Cody rode to an eighty-four to land in a tie for first place going into the evening round. Nationally, Cody stood at the seventeenth position in the national rankings, an absolutely phenomenal accomplishment with no experience coming into the season and missing the first three months of competition. Presently, Cody stood two spots away from the National Finals. The top fifteen nationally in each event make the NFR Finals in Las Vegas. Ranking is determined by the amount of prize money won during the year.

In the final round at the Rodeo Showdown in Phoenix, Cody hung on again aboard a big-ass purebred Brahma bull named Shorty. This time, the judges did not reward the awkward ride. At the halfway point in the ride, Cody slid back and down into his riding hand. Cody's left leg fell well under the bull's belly and recovery appeared to be lost. The shaved spurs did nothing to prevent the slide. Cody dug in, but the spurs either cut the bull or slid off his belly like he was covered with the black grease from an automobile lubrication gun. Somehow, Cody used the bull's spinning jump to the left to right himself and complete the eight second ride. The horn blew and Cody was taken off-guard by the bull's reversal in direction. The resulting jump sent Cody backwards and caught the bull's back end as it was catapulting skyward. Cody's left hand popped out of the hold and Cody did a complete somersault over the bull's head resulting in a spectacular tumble of chaps, boots and hair. Cody's hair was quite a bit longer than most contestants and made the illusion of slow motion perceptible. A competent boxing trainer would never allow his fighter to go into the ring with long hair. The effects of an opponent's punches are accentuated by the flailing hair and the sweat flying in every direction.

In bull riding, many believed that Cody's hair enhanced the perception of ferocity in the bull's movements and thereby boosted the scores. The last ride in Phoenix, however, did not present that case. Cody's most spectacular gyrations occurred after the horn had sounded. Cody popped up and played to the hysteria from the crowd. The near disaster during the ride cost Cody valuable points. Cody's final score was seventy-one, which pulled him down to fifth place. Cody Law remained in the seventeenth position nationally with one more planned stop on the tour before the National Finals in Las Vegas. Gunner marveled at the consistency exhibited by Cody Law. Cody had finished in the top five for the past five weeks. Sonny and Olin had failed to place in the last five stops. Gunner mentioned to Cody that he ought to pay more attention to the bullfighters and the bull than the crowd when he gets thrown.

"O.K., boss." Cody smiled at Gunner. "I haven't done a somersault like that since I took a high school gymnastics class my junior year."

Two PRCA rodeos would be held on the last weekend before the finals. One would take place in Grand Rapids, Michigan. The other would kick off in Steamboat Springs, Colorado. Gunner, Cody and the group had planned to enter the Colorado Springs event as their last stop for the season, excluding the Finals if anyone made the top fifteen. The unexpected trip to Castle Rock may ultimately cost Cody a shot at the Finals, a possibility no one entertained in March, and a consequence that Cody considered meaningless without Devon.

Cody and his friends could not get a flight out of Phoenix to Denver until the next afternoon. The flight put them into Denver at 6 p.m. After collecting the gear, renting a vehicle and the subsequent drive to Castle Rock, Cody, Gunner, Sonny and Olin arrived in town at 7:30 p.m. Cody pulled up to the Castle Rock Hotel. It was Sunday night and any actions would have to wait until Monday morning. Cody and Gunner discussed the arrival options during the trip and both decided that visiting Anna Larkin should be the first priority.

The group could arrive at the Castle Rock Elementary School before classes began. Gunner implored Cody to forego his desires to race into the Barrett home and snatch Devon. Gunner reasoned with Cody to discuss the current circumstances with Anna Larkin and Cadrell Easley before reacting in a manner that may aid Billy Don Barrett. Cody knew his actions over the next twenty-four hours may very well determine what role he would play in Devon's future.

Cody put a call through to Cadrell Easley after the quartet settled into the hotel. Easley was not at home. His wife said he was working a second job during the basketball season. Cadrell worked a security detail at the McNichols Arena in Denver. Off-duty police officers were hired to handle the security for the food and beverage concessions. All cash collections at the Denver Nuggets home games were logged in and transported to the night depository by the off-duty police officers. The officers made thirty dollars per hour for their time. A partner in the Denver Nuggets organization was also the Executive Director for the Professional Rodeo Cowboys Association. Cadrell Easley was the only officer from outside the Denver Police Department to be offered the job. Cody left a message that he would be meeting with Anna Larkin before classes began at the Castle Rock Elementary School.

The Monday morning air brought an unusual cold autumn downpour to the Rocky Mountain region south of Denver. Denver and Colorado Springs were buried in a series of uncharacteristically potent thunderstorms. The mountains to the west usually knock the violence down from any eastward moving storms. On this Monday, the black clouds swirled like an expedited video image. Sheets of rain cut off the view to the mountains in sporadic intervals. The deep cloud cover belayed the sunlight. Cody and three cowboy friends rode to the Castle Rock Elementary School in a driving rainstorm. Castle Rock stood in the center of the storm which drifted in during the night and played havoc with the early morning skies. Most of the children had not arrived at the school when Cody pulled the rented Chevrolet Blazer up to the front entrance.

All four men walked into the school. Dripping in the main lobby, four men in jeans and cowboy hats stood waiting for someone to ask them why they looked like lost children attending their first day of school? Cody and his friends stood among the first arriving children. Gunner asked for help in locating Anna Larkin. The children paid no attention to Gunner. Gunner stood with his mouth open and his arms held outright. Cody spotted the school offices.

"Wait here." Cody suggested. "The school office will know where the teachers are. I'll find out where we can find Ms. Larkin."

Cody walked to the office door and disappeared behind it. The students numbers continued to grow. They ran in from the rain in packs. Most gave the wet strangers a passive glance and then moved on. Gunner shook his hat. The water sprayed Sonny and Olin.

"You know my daddy used to soak a new hat in water right after he bought one. Then he would leave it on his head until it dried. That way he claimed, the hat would fit perfect." Gunner recalled and smiled at his own hat.

"Did it work?" Olin asked, an innocent simple man who fell for everything.

"Fuck, who knows?" Gunner laughed. "I just told him to buy a goddamn hat that fits before you have to soak the thing. You'll never catch me walking around for two days wearing a dripping wet hat. Hell, I loved that man, but when he wore that wet hat, he looked like a lost mule who'd been thumped on the head with a shovel."

Cody Law walked out of the school office and closed the door behind him. The black Resistol covered his eyes. Cody shook his yellow slicker and pulled it up over his shoulders. The coat was still very wet from the rain.

"Anna Larkin is no longer employed at Castle Rock Elementary School. According to the school secretary, Anna took an extended leave of absence. She has been gone for two weeks. The woman believed that Anna had returned to Durango for some unspecified family business." Cody mimicked the secretary's dialogue.

"Like a death in the family?" Gunner asked.

"If it was a death in the family then why not say it is a death in the family? Anyway, a death in the family does not normally create a loss of employment." Cody reasoned.

"You do not believe the woman, do you?" Gunner knew the answer.

"Of course not." Cody explained. "Remember the pattern that I detailed for you when I first read the letter written by Devon's former teacher. I think her name was Davenport. The non-response by the principal was mind-boggling. Easley told me that the principal was a former classmate of Barretts. Maybe Anna's concerns about Devon produced the same results encountered by Davenport?"

"Did you ask to see the principal?" Gunner followed.

"Yes, but I was told that he is not in." Cody replied.

"And you believe that?" Gunner prodded.

"Absolutely not." Cody announced. "Let's go visit, Mr. Martin Hollis."

Cody squinted as he read the name on the office doorway. The four men re-entered the school office and startled the elderly secretary behind the main desk.

"We would like to speak to Mr. Hollis, please." Cody repeated an earlier request.

"I'm sorry. Mr. Hollis is not in, as I already explained once to you. I can take your name and he will get back to you when he arrives." The response was rehearsed.

"When will that be?" Cody asked.

"I'm not sure. Mr. Hollis has meetings scheduled off the school grounds for the better part of the day." The woman was unusually agitated.

"Is the storm making you nervous, ma'am?" Cody inquired. "It's kicking up one hell of a ruckus."

"Please." The woman had not been coached well. "You will have to call back at another time."

"I thought you just told me that Mr. Hollis would call me back?" Cody badgered the woman. Before the woman could respond, Cody walked past her desk and into the office marked for Principal Martin Hollis. Cody opened the door abruptly, only to find an unhappy overweight man seated behind a very large mahogany desk.

"I do not know who you think you are, sir?" Martin Hollis addressed Cody Law peevishly. "Mrs. Haverson, call the police." Hollis hollered into the front office.

"Tell them, the Castle Rock Elementary School has some unauthorized guests trespassing on school property. You men are free to leave right now. Otherwise, you can explain the intrusion to the Castle Rock Police Department." Hollis' chin was shaking slightly.

"My name is Cody Law. I am Devon Barrett's father. I am here in Castle Rock to see my daughter." Cody moved closer to the desk. "We came to your school to speak to Anna Larkin, one of Devon's former teachers."

"Billy Don Barrett is Devon's father. Ms. Larkin is no longer on our faculty. I believe that Ms. Larkin has returned to her home in Durango." Hollis stuttered a bit.

"I am Devon's biological father, which is recorded on her birth certificate." Cody stared at the man impeding his morning.

"Your concerns are moot, Mr. Law. Devon Barrett is no longer a student at Castle Rock Elementary School and Ms. Larkin has moved on. Either you leave now or we will press charges on trespassing and breaking into my office." Hollis seemed to be gaining confidence.

"Let's go, Cody" Gunner insisted. "Anna Larkin is not here and the fat pillow with hair behind the desk can't see the freight train barreling down the tracks right at him. He's Billy Don Barrett's pal."

Gunner reached out and pulled Cody's arm. Sonny and Olin had left the office. Gunner headed out the door. Cody began to follow but stopped. Cody turned back to Martin Hollis and walked back to the front of the desk. The two men stood face to face. Martin Hollis rose in triumph when the four cowboys began to leave the office. Now that Cody had returned briefly, Hollis appeared pallid and disoriented. Martin Hollis glanced out of his windows hoping to catch the squad cars pulling up. They had not arrived yet. The space between the credenza and the desk began to close. Hollis couldn't decide to sit or remain standing. The short silence became excruciating.

In one abrupt swipe, Cody reached up and grabbed the tie Martin Hollis wore around his neck. Cody grabbed it high by the throat and yanked Hollis across the desk. Martin Hollis' feet left the floor and his body hung precariously out over his neatly attuned desk. Hollis placed his hands out to prevent himself from falling flat on the desk.

"Cody." Gunner yelled and reached out for his friend. "Leave him be. Remember what we talked about. Devon has got to be the priority."

Gunner pulled on Cody's free arm. The other arm remained locked in a vice-like hold on Martin's tie. Cody's right hand had also grabbed a handful of fleshy white skin hanging loosely under the chin of Martin Hollis. Cody pulled Hollis closer, close enough to see the turbulence in Cody's eyes.

"Put your fat hands together when I leave, Mr. Hollis." Cody spoke close enough to smell the breath that was now frozen in fear. " Put them together and pray that I find Devon safe. Pray that you can find a way to justify the harm that you have brought to my daughter. Pray that I can find a way to justify the harm that you have brought to my daughter. You better pray awfully hard, Mr. Hollis." Gunner pulled Cody off Martin Hollis.

"Tell me, Mr. Hollis." Gunner almost had Cody out the door. "Do you believe that when I find Devon, she will be all right?"

There was no answer. Hollis' squatty fingers fumbled awkwardly with the tie and his staggered breath struggled to regain the air that Cody had squelched with his grip. Hollis struggled to hold up. Martin Hollis gasped for air through his nose. His teeth were locked shut. The seething remnants of two glazed donuts began to climb up his throat. Martin Hollis was about to vomit in fear. Some men compensate academically for an adolescent fear of isolation. Fat children inevitably fall under similar variables. The fear of a physical confrontation can be carried from adolescence and cause the body to begin to shut down in the wake of such fear. Hollis tried to answer, but his chest began heaving with problematic irregularity and refused to allow any sentences to form. Hollis knew the actions concerning Devon Barrett would eventually come back to plague his soul. Judgement Day had arrived and the maker was wearing a cowboy hat.

"Have you ever seen Devon's bedroom, Mr. Hollis?" Cody's voice rose.

No answer.

"Have you ever bothered to find out why Devon weighed forty pounds in the sixth grade?"

No answer.

"Do you believe in God, Mr. Hollis?" Cody looked outside to see a squad car pull into the school drive. Martin Hollis turned to view the police car. "Do you believe in God, Mr. Hollis?" Cody repeated. Gunner and Cody were out the door.

"Yes, I believe in God." Martin Hollis began to find some air again in light of the police car's arrival.

"That is a good thing, Mr. Hollis. Devon believes in God, Mr. Hollis. You had six years to help my daughter and you refused. Do you think God helped Devon?" Cody pulled away from Gunner to continue the confrontation. "Do you think God is going to help you when we come back?"

"Where were you for those six years, Mr. Law?" Hollis blurted out.

Cody spun around faster than a goalie in the crease watching a three-on-one fast break carve up the ice with a passing clinic. Cody Law took two running steps and jumped on the desk where Martin Hollis stood motionless. Straddling the open day-timer, Cody stood high above the trembling school administrator. Hollis looked up at the black, wide-brimmed hat pulled low over Cody's eyes. The tight black tee-shirt was tucked neatly into a pair of faded Lee blue jeans. Wet cowboys boots marred the top of the desk and the yellow slicker hung like the hangman's cloak during the days of the Salem witch hunts.

"Repeat what you just asked me, Mr. Hollis." Cody ordered.

No answer. Hollis didn't know where to look. If he looked up, he would look into Cody's eyes. If he looked straight ahead, he would look into Cody's crotch. Hollis tried to look down.

"I want you to ask me again, Mr. Hollis, where I've been for the last six years?" Cody voice level rose dramatically.

No answer, again.

"Cody." Gunner yelled. "Forget it. Don't lose it now, pal. You are three blocks from your daughter. If you take him out, you may never see Devon. Hollis is not worth it. Let's go." Cody jumped back down to the floor. He turned and joined Gunner at the door.

"Look, Cody." Gunner pointed to the floor near the desk. A slow stream began to meander the floor from the back of the desk.

Cody and Gunner left the inner offices. With Sonny and Olin, they made their way out the front door. Gunner ran up to the arriving officer.

"Mr. Hollis is waiting inside for you. He will be so happy to see you. I think he said the guy is now walking around the second floor somewhere. I'm not sure, but Hollis knows exactly where the guy is."

Gunner patted the officer on the shoulder and pointed to the second floor with a sweeping motion. The Castle Rock officer thanked Gunner while running into the office. The rain continued and the officer was not in a hurry to remain outside. Cody, Gunner, Sonny and Olin piled into the Blazer. 222 Gilbert Street was only blocks away

The Blazer pulled up in front of 222 Gilbert Street. The neglected landscape showed the effects of the dry summer. The October rains barely covered the overgrown, dried out grass surrounding the house. Weeds fell limp and long in between the cracks across the sidewalk. The battered cars were gone. The shades were still closed tight. Cody sat in the Blazer. The wipers resonated across the windshield, screeching as the rain let up. Gunner, Sonny and Olin waited for Cody. Now, it was his call.

"We have to let Barrett know we are here." Cody changed the plan. "If we try to burst in and take Devon and Kirsten out of there, then he'll have the ammunition he needs to take out a warrant on us. If he doesn't know that I am Devon's father by now, then it is time to tell him, whether Kirsten agrees or not."

"Cody, Barrett is not going to stand for any deviation in his routine." Gunner answered. "Billy Don Barrett will not let you see Devon. You go in there and ask for an audience, you'll get a baseball bat in the head."

"Then we don't ask for an audience. We give Devon and Kirsten a choice. Any problem restraining Barrett when we go in?" Cody turned and looked in the back seat.

"Not from back here, boss." Sonny replied. Olin nodded.

"Gunner?"

"Let's go find your daughter, Cody. It's about time." Gunner pulled the door open and stepped outside. The others followed. The four cowboys walked to the front door. Sonny pulled his hat tight. The rain had slowed to a light drizzle. Cody knocked on the door. The tension filled four men, accustomed to fear but the rodeo chutes never held the unknown like the door at 222 Gilbert Street. Cody knocked again and yelled for Devon. No answer. Cody pounded on the door.

"Barrett! Open the fucking door, now." Cody slammed his fist against the door. "Shit, I know he's in there."

"Cody, bust it open!" Gunner yelled.

"Don't do it, Cody." Cadrell Easley yelled from the street. The Castle Rock officer climbed out of the squad car. Newly elected Douglas County District Attorney Shana McDonough accompanied Cadrell Easley.

"We'll go in." Shana McDonough announced. Three cars pulled up with six officers in protective vests and helmets. Easley approached the men at the door. Cadrell Easley came face to face with Cody Law. Shana McDonough stood next to Cody Law, as well. Shana McDonough was tall and Irish, the daughter of a New York City Detective. Shana wore a manicured beige business suit from Christian Dior, kept dry under a small Ralph Lauren umbrella. Her red hair startled strangers at first. The hair, a windblown look more at home on the cover of Outdoor Adventure Magazine, was styled short and hugged her ashen, white skin. Shana was very pretty, naturally, without the abundance of any extensive make-up. Four years in the Bronx at the D.A.'s office and a messy divorce brought a search for the simpler life. The mother of one daughter, Shana McDonough brought style and professionalism to an office in need of a bureaucratic enema. Shana's ex-husband was a prominent Manhattan defense attorney. They met in New York as Assistant District Attorneys. The divorce had taken a toll as Shana sacrificed great monetary gain to secure sole custody.

"Officer Easley dropped Devon Barrett's file on my desk. He asked me if I could read? Officer Easley told me that many men when they reach my position, apparently lose the ability to read and reason. The revelation of the decision to home school Devon caused Officer Easley to bring the matter before my office, again." Shana McDonough continued.

"The Douglas County District Attorney's office agreed to convene a custody hearing based on Devon's original birth certificate and Devon's testimony, given to a police representative and a DCFS social worker. My office has now made a judgment that should have been clear six years ago. Colorado State law under the Children's Code, Section 19-10-104 clearly requires anyone with reasonable cause to report child abuse. The statute specifically includes hospital personnel, school officials and social workers, among many others, as being directly responsible for reporting any activity that may result in the abuse or neglect of a child."

"At first, I thought the file dropped on my desk was a test. It had to be the *Child Abuse for Dummies* version. There could be no more egregious examples of parental misconduct in the national record annals of the DCFS and the FBI combined. A biological father retains parental rights over a minor unless or until those rights are terminated by a court. Officer Easley informed my office that the natural father was en route to Castle Rock and would be seeking custody of his daughter. In accordance with Section 19-10-104 and Colorado Statute, Section 19-10-109, my office will act based on the receipt of the report by Officer Easley. In the opinion of the District Attorney's office, the assistance of local law enforcement is required for the immediate removal of the child from her home, to be placed in protective custody. An immediate investigation will follow. The investigation will not only focus on Billy Don Barrett and his actions over the past six years, but the investigation will look into the failure of social services, the hospitals and the schools in reporting suspected child abuse and, in my opinion, blatant child abuse. "

"We have a search warrant, Mr. Law. Please step back." The District Attorney pulled the documents from a briefcase. Shana McDonough did not play football with Billy Don Barrett. She did not see Barrett play football, and the newly elected District Attorney didn't care if Billy Don Barrett was the second-coming of Floyd Little.

Cody Law pulled back from the door, as did the men he arrived with. The police officers knocked on the door and identified themselves. Cadrell Easley led the onslaught. Still, no one came to the door. The demand to open the door was repeated several times. Easley waited. No answer.

"Knock it down." Shana McDonough ordered. Two representatives from the Department of Children and Family Services waited in a squad car. McDonough would take no more chances with Devon Barrett. The state was prepared to take custody of the child pending an investigation. One more demand was called.

"In the name of the Douglas County District Attorney's office and the Castle Rock Police Department, open the door."

There was no response. Two officers levied a battering rod against the door. The door to 222 Gilbert Street blew open with a splintering explosion. The police entered the home of Billy Don Barrett. Shana McDonough followed. Cody Law, Gunner, Sonny Moore and Olin Martin tailed the vests and the blue uniforms. The house was empty. There was no furniture, no occupants and no sign of the family that had lived there for six years. Easley moved from room to room. The police practiced the maneuvers they had rehearsed at the police academy. Cody Law ran into Devon's bedroom. The scrap carpet strips hung from the walls and ceiling. Some strips had been dislodged, but the job was abandoned long before completion. There were small remnants of paper taped to the walls of the closet. The rodeo collage had been torn down abruptly. Otherwise, the room was empty. Billy Don Barrett and his family were gone.

Two officers ran out the back door. Questions arose concerning the basement. In the frenzied four or five minutes since entering the home at 222

Gilbert Street, no one found anything. McDonough, Easley and the remaining officers convened in the empty living room. Cody Law stood in the hallway that led back to Devon's bedroom. Gunner, Sonny and Olin stood by the front door.

"Where are they?" Cody Law demanded. "Where, the fuck, are they?"

"I don't know." Cadrell Easley answered.

"Didn't you tell me, Cadrell, that you would keep an eye on Devon?" Cody asked.

"We did, Cody. I had three other officers working with me to watch for anything unusual occurring with Barrett and his family." Easley explained.

"Moving doesn't constitute something unusual?" Cody tried to slide past sarcasm. Easley had been diligent enough to bring the file to the first female District Attorney in Douglas County.

"Cody, no one saw them moving. They must have pulled out in the middle of the night over the weekend. I followed Barrett home Friday night at 1:30 a.m. They still lived here, then." Easley recalled.

"Where is Devon, now, Cadrell? Where she was on Friday night doesn't help us much, this morning." Cody walked to the front door. "This is a tiny goddamn town with one fucking child abuser! How can anyone lose the whole fucking family? Shit!"

Cody turned and ripped down the fragmented curtains hanging in the front windows. The entire rod came crashing to the floor. Cody stood and stared at the imbecilic result of his tantrum.

"Unfortunately, Mr. Law." Shana McDonough spoke up. "Trashing this house any further, if that's possible, is not going to find your daughter. My office will issue a warrant for the arrest of Billy Don Barrett. We will find him, Mr. Law. As you pointed out rather emphatically, this is a tiny goddamn town."

Cody Law walked up to Cadrell Easley. Cody lifted his hat and scratched his head. The long hair fell into his eyes.

"Do you have any idea where Barrett is, Cadrell?" Cody was mired in a vanquished no man's land. Alienating the one man who had fought for Devon was not Cody's intent.

"No, Cody. I have no idea, but I can tell you, he's around. Billy Don Barrett won't go far. He's too stupid." Easley responded with certainty.

"If he's so stupid, then why are we standing here trying to figure out where he is?" Cody looked to Shana McDonough.

"If he's so stupid, then why has Mr. Barrett never spent a day in jail for the goddamn misery he has put on Devon and Kirsten. Stupidity has to begin in the eyes of the beholder, doesn't it? How stupid do we look in Billy Don Barrett's eyes? Put out your warrant, Cadrell. Call the Castle Rock Hotel when you find him. I'm staying there." Cody Law left the empty house on Gilbert Street. Gunner, Sonny and Olin followed to the Blazer.

"Are we going to the hotel, Cody?" Gunner asked as a break in the cloud cover tried to brighten the wet autumn morning.

"Are you hungry, Gunner?" Cody asked.

"No."

"Good, we're going out for breakfast." Cody picked up the pace to the Blazer. "I know a great place in the center of town called The Rascal Flats. It's mostly a piss-drunk tavern, but they manage to serve some eggs to the early morning alkees. You hungry now, Gunner?" Cody asked.

"Famished." Gunner climbed into the front seat.

The Rascal Flats Tavern doubled as a Castle Rock breakfast stop. The Flats catered to the blue-collar workers coming off the third shift in the brick yards surrounding Castle Rock. Marla Wemple opened the establishment seven mornings a week. Ronny Fields was a sixty-two year old black cook, who manned the antiquated flat grill behind the bar. The smell of bacon slabs and burnt ham slid through a mountain of scrambled eggs on most mornings.

Marla was pushing seventy, but no one ever asked. She looked like twelve miles of bad country roads with a chewed up pencil behind her ear and a small order pad tucked into her ample waist apron. Marla always kept a bulky supply of Kleenex stuffed down the front of her server's uniform that resembled a cross between what the I.H.O.P. girls down the interstate wore and an oversized tunic. Marla's sassy tongue delivered every order when it got there and not a minute sooner. Marla loathed Curly King, the alcoholic owner of the Flats, but she set her own rules and Curly went along, provided they rarely woke him up for the breakfast call.

On this Monday morning, there were a few patrons eating breakfast. Two beer bellies at the bar were sucking down hardboiled eggs and Budweiser for the morning fare. Seven men comprised the clientele and no women, except for Marla. The Rascal Flats could have doubled as a Rocky Mountain ZZ Top convention. The men were bedraggled alcoholics, lost for a shave since Jimmy Carter was President.

Cody Law parked the Blazer in front of the Rascal Flats. Gunner got out and rummaged through a couple bags in the back of the vehicle.

"What are you doing?" Asked Cody, as Sonny and Olin waited on the sidewalk.

"I'll meet you inside. I forgot something." Gunner remarked. "Order me the raspberry crepes with a side of fresh fruit, fresh coffee with honey and a toasted croissant."

"No salmon omelet?" Cody and his friends headed for the door.

Cody and the boys entered The Rascal Flats and approached the bar. The scattered men looked up from their greasy plates. Marla Wemple stood at the end of the bar near the grill. The overdone eggs sizzled and a thin haze mixed with the stale odor of the ancient wood floor soaked with twenty-seven years of beer. Marla looked over the bifocals secured on one end with a safety pin.

"You boys lost?" Marla inquired.

"No ma'am." Cody spoke up. "We are looking for a friend. Seems like he moved recently. We used to hang together years ago. Do you know where we can find Billy Don Barrett?"

"How do you know Billy?" The question came with the exhaled cigarette smoke from the large patron seated next to Cody at the bar. The man curled the cigarette in his mouth and turned to face Cody. A pungent breath hit Cody like a cold Nebraska wind.

"I don't remember asking you anything, Sasquatch." Cody calmly replied. He turned back to Marla Wemple. "Could you help us locate Billy Barrett?" Cody repeated.

"Call Curly, Marla. I think he would want to know about this." The smoke muffled the response.

"Call him yourself, Boxcar." Marla snapped. "I never cared for his kind. I have no idea where he lives. I know he used to live a few blocks from here. More than a couple mornings, I found him passed out in a booth here, when I came to open up."

"Boxcar?" Cody remarked. "That's an odd name for a mother to give her son. Maybe you can give us an address to find Billy Don Barrett?"

"Maybe you should count the bodies in this place and decide to look elsewhere. We don't like people nosin' around here, boy." The man called Boxcar pushed his barstool back and stood up, a movement not without a considerable effort due to the massive girth hanging over a helpless belt. Another physical malady at the bar mimicked the move by Boxcar.

"You a cop?" The question came from a table in the room. "We don't see no badges, so if you ain't no cop, then you best be on your way."

The three other men at the table pushed their chairs back, as if the show of solidarity was intimidating. Cody grimaced as he caught a glimpse of the heart attacks in waiting filling the plates on the tables. In force, the plates must have held four dozen scrambled eggs and week's worth of bacon.

"I see you already made friends, Cody." Gunner spoke up as he entered the room.

"Gentlemen, please excuse my friend's manners. It appears that these rodeo sloths like to stir the pot, if you know what I mean." Gunner fell into that lazy Texas drawl that calmed a room faster than a Lone Star preacher on an Abilene Sunday morning.

"Come here, pal. Let me show you a magic trick. We're not here to start any trouble. You got a few tired cowboys lookin' for something to eat and a friend we haven't seen for a couple years."

Gunner pushed his way between Boxcar and Cody. He cleared the bar in front of him. Gunner reached into his front pocket and pulled out a can of lighter fluid. He sprayed the top of the bar, creating a small puddle of the fluid. Gunner took an old Zippo lighter that he pulled from Cody's bag. The lighter was a gift from the Chicago Chapter of the Hell's Angels when Cody opened Fat Boys. Gunner had seen Cody pull the lighter from his bag many times. The lighter was too bulky to carry in a pocket. Gunner displayed the antique lighter complete the engraved logo of Harley Davidson. Gunner flipped the top and the thick wick filled with flame. Gunner lit the puddle on the bar. A bright blue flame roared up from the bar and burned stationary near the man called Boxcar. Cody and Boxcar pulled back from the flame. Gunner laughed and held up his hand.

"Cool, isn't it?" Gunner smiled at his pyrotechnics. Boxcar stared at the diminishing flames. Marla Wemple shook her head and lit a cigarette.

"Big fucking deal." Boxcar barked. "You're a fucking Houdini. Now take a walk, boys."

Gunner reached up and grabbed Boxcar by the hair and slammed his face into the bar. Boxcar's nose exploded with blood. The brave patrons froze. Gunner took the can of lighter fluid and doused the foot-long beard on Boxcar's face. The beard was dripping from the fluid. Holding the back of Boxcar's head, Gunner lit the big Zippo lighter and brought the lighter to Boxcar's beard.

"Now, we would like to know where to find Billy Don Barrett. If you can't remember where he lives, I will set your head on fire and you will never recognize the scarred mess that used to be your face. Can anybody tell us where to find Billy Don Barrett? I'll count to three and then we can watch ol' Boxcar fry. " Gunner held tight with a grip Boxcar never felt in his sorry twenty-seven years.

"Billy Don took a mobile home, off Franktown Road, about ten miles west of here." The psychotic display took a toll on the man called Boxcar.

"Where in Franktown?" Gunner slid the lighter to the man's chin. The lighter made a hissing noise amidst the blue flames.

"There's only one mobile park on Franktown Road. It's called Sunset Park. Billy's got the last unit on the right. There's only one street." Boxcar caved faster than the fashion skiers run for cover when the real snow hits Vail.

"Thank you. Gentlemen, we'll stop back if we get a chance." Gunner tossed the lighter back to Cody. "Be careful with that thing. It's fucking dangerous." Gunner turned to move toward the door and Cadrell Easley filled the doorway.

"Cody, you are predictable, if not the most persistent mother fucker I ever met." Easley shook his head.

"Did you see what this mother fucker did?" Boxcar pointed to Gunner McGarrity. The lighter fluid masked the usual stench that filled the room.

"We all saw what happened, Easley." A suddenly brave patron from the egg mountain table spoke up. The others nodded like those little dolls that ride on the back dashboards of Tijuana.

"You see what happened, Marla?" Cadrell stopped and asked Marla Wemple.

"See what?" Marla looked up over the bifocals. "A couple cowboys walked in and Boxcar, here, asked one of 'em for a light. That's all I saw. Oh, wait. I did see Gavin, here. "Marla pointed to the green jacket at the second table, singling out another societal malcontent sipping Jack on a Monday morning. "I saw Gavin doing the horizontal mambo with Curly's sister in the parking lot two nights ago. Gavin's car was a rockin' like it was possessed and the windows were steamed over like the honeymoon suite at the Broadmoor Hotel down at the Springs."

"You're full of shit, Marla." Gavin's startled response shifted the abbreviated attention span within the room.

"Any criminal activity, I mean?" Cadrell loved Marla Wemple. Marla was one of the few people that spoke without the fear of reprisal in any form. Candor not only came from within the soul, but it evolved from a manifestation of one's own liabilities. When liabilities became nonexistent, the words flowed freely. Marla Wemple always spoke her mind.

"Nothin' criminal, Cadrell, aside from some of these deadbeats cashing unemployment checks and buying liquor." Marla lit another cigarette.

"Arrest, this mother fucker." Boxcar demanded pointing to Gunner McGarrity.

"Absolutely." Easley patronized the man running napkins through his beard. Cadrell, Cody, Gunner and their friends left the Rascal Flats. They gathered around the rented Chevrolet Blazer.

"Your friend named Boxcar, turned out to be a wealth of information." Gunner looked at Cadrell Easley. "Are you going to arrest me?"

"No case, Gunner. By the way, you almost torched Billy Don Barrett's baby brother. Boxcar is Barrett's brother." Cadrell walked to the police car. "I'm going to call this in. Any chance that you boys will stay here and wait for us to arrest Barrett?"

There was no answer.

"I didn't think so." Easley pulled the blue and white squad car onto Wilcox Street. The Blazer followed.

* * *

The trailer park was not difficult to find. Three additional uniformed patrol cars and one unmarked car met at the entrance to Sunset Park. Riding in the unmarked car were two Castle Rock detectives, a DCFS representative and Shana McDonough. The group discussed the entrance procedures and various alternative plans in the event Billy Don Barrett objected to being placed under arrest. Cody waited patiently against the Blazer while the police outlined their plans.

"Cadrell." Cody shouted in a loud whisper. "Can we get to the trailer. That fuck will get wind of this and bolt. The longer you stay here and plan the second-coming of D-Day, the more chance we have of Barrett splitting." Cody was agitated.

"Mr. Law." Shana McDonough intervened. "You and your friends will wait here at the entrance to the trailer park. Under no circumstances will any of you enter the grounds or the premises until we have Barrett under arrest and Devon and her mother are safe. We have charged Billy Don Barrett under the general criminal code, not the child abuse statute. Mr. Barrett will be charged with assault, battery, sexual misconduct, sexual assault on a child and possibly attempted murder. By using the general criminal code, the court has the option of running the sentences consecutively. Child abuse is a Class 3 felony if the child sustains serious bodily harm. Otherwise, child abuse is a misdemeanor."

"Child abuse is a misdemeanor?" Cody interrupted.

"The criminal code, Mr. Law, is not an equal opportunity destroyer. I did not write it, nor do I endorse all of it." Shana McDonough rose above the fray.

"Excuse me, Ms. McDonough, what does a Class 3 felony mean? I'm not an attorney or a cop." Cody continued, careful where he stepped.

"A Class 3 felony under the general criminal code is any crime punishable by not less than two years in jail and not more than five years in jail." Shana McDonough clarified.

"Under the state's criminal justice system, an individual charged with child abuse causing serious bodily harm can receive a maximum of five years in prison?" Cody waited for an answer.

"Well, Mr. Law, you can..." Shana McDonough stuttered.

"You can beat a child into a brain dead coma, but as long as the child doesn't die, you can only get five years in jail? Do I have that part correct,

Ms. McDonough?" Cody jumped all over this. "And you can continue to beat the child until you get caught and again, as long as the child is alive...five years is it?"

"If an individual is charged under the current child abuse statutes involving Class 3 felonies, those are the penalties. That is why, Mr. Law, that we choose to pursue general criminal charges whenever possible. Now is not the time to debate the merits of the Colorado criminal and juvenile statutes."

"It took six years of text book, blatant child abuse against Devon for a D.A. to bring charges against Barrett. How long do you think it will take a Douglas County judge to hang criminal charges on their boy when a misdemeanor will cover the legal bases, Ms. McDonough?" Cody waited, again, for an answer

"You don't move from this spot, Mr. Law. Are we clear on that, Mr. Law?" Shana McDonough had no problem wielding power. The other police officers waited for her signal. Cody nodded. The police cars moved into the trailer park. Cody got back into the Blazer and watched the procession disappear on the first turn.

"Cody?" Gunner asked quietly.

"What." Cody stared straight ahead.

"Did she tell you not to follow them and to wait here until the police had everything under control?" Gunner scratched his nose and picked up his hat. Gunner's sinewy hand brushed the gray streaked hair back from his forehead.

"Did you know that child abuse is a misdemeanor in this state unless you cause serious bodily harm to the child? Then it becomes a Class 3 felony." Cody asked Gunner and the boys in the back.

"Maximum five years, right?" Gunner popped back. Cody's eyes opened wider than the headlamps on a Burlington Northern locomotive. "Hey, I've been around a few jails. The subject has come up from time to time."

"There's no guarantee that any judge around here will let the criminal charges stick. All this could result in Billy Don Barrett walking out of a Castle Rock courthouse with a misdemeanor conviction for torturing my daughter for the better part of six years." Cody imagined the possibility was much higher than a good chance.

"Did the lady D.A. tell us to stay put?" Gunner repeated.

"Yes." Cody slammed his foot down and the Blazer jerked forward into the gravel and dirt cloud churned up by the police cars. Gunner pulled his hat back on, tight. No one spoke. There would be no waiting at the entrance.

The ride took less than three minutes down a road with no name. Sunset Park was the only designation for the trailer enclave, so the road had come to be known as Sunset Park Road. Mailing addresses simply were assigned a number. The units resembled an unkempt array of frustration. Tattered clotheslines hung in front of most units. The park was made up of double and single units. Small wooden staircases fronted each home. The police car procession brought out many of the residents. The road became lined with women holding small children and men wishing that someone else's luck was worse than their own.

Cody pulled up before the last unit. The police vehicles would prevent any further progress. Barrett's unit was engulfed with uniformed officers. Cadrell Easley stood at the door with the two juvenile detectives. Three Castle Rock police officers took positions on the backside of the trailer. Three other officers stood before the stairs to Unit 1201. All officers released the strap on their revolvers. The officers at the door had their guns drawn. Shana McDonough stood next to the car she arrived in and glanced back to Cody's group. There were no more reactions from Ms. McDonough.

Cody and his group stood outside the Blazer and waited. They were twenty yards from Unit 1201. The unit begged from neglect. A screen door hung open on one hinge. The front and back windows were closed off with heavy black curtains or canvas. The isolating effect was achieved whatever the material. Billy Don Barrett's car was parked next to the unit. The morning air was silent. The rain had subsided and the low thick cloud cover hung past the mountains, barely visible to the west. The wind was calm. Cadrell Easley knocked on the door.

"Billy Don Barrett, this is the Castle Rock Police Department. Open the door." Easley stepped back.

The surrounding officers pulled their weapons. Easley repeated the order. There was no answer. Cadrell Easley could hear music through the closed door. A baby began to cry amidst the eerie silence. For a moment, all heads turned to the infant down the street. Easley looked to the District Attorney, with the representative from DCFS standing next her. Shana McDonough nodded. Cadrell Easley stepped back to the wooden railing at the top of the stairs. He braced himself against the railing and kicked the door. The door burst open and Cadrell and two officers moved into Unit 1201. Cody, Gunner, Sonny and Olin raced to the side of Shana McDonough.

"Mr. Law, let us do our job." Shana McDonough whipped around to front Cody's group. Cody and the men with him stopped in their tracks. Everyone froze for the next thirty seconds, an interminable interval for all.

Easley stuck his head out the door and yelled," Call for an ambulance! Barrett is in custody and we have a situation here. "

"What does that mean?" Cody turned to the District Attorney. His heart dropped to the pit of his stomach.

"I don't know, Mr. Law. You are to remain here. We dispatched a paramedics unit to the entrance of the complex before we arrived. Do not impede anything at this moment or I will have you removed from the scene." Shana McDonough had not bargained for the brutality on the outskirts of Castle Rock when she left Manhattan. The District Attorney ran to the stairway leading into Unit 1201.

The ambulance arrived in seconds. The bright red and white vehicle pulled up to the front of the trailer. Two paramedics entered the trailer. They carried a stretcher. Cody squirmed and paced in place.

"Gunner, I can't sit here and wait any longer." Cody pleaded to Gunner for some nod of approval.

"Cody, you have to evaluate the circumstances from a neutral perspective. Anger will serve no one at this point, especially Devon." Gunner pulled from the bowels of Psycho-Cybernetics and at the same time questioned his own logic in spewing the reflective commentary that would be best served at another time and in another place. Cody Law was begging for something more than esoteric rhetoric.

"Get the fuck in there, Cody. Devon's your daughter." Gunner yelled.

Cody raced up the stairs to Unit 1201. The front room was a dark, small area containing two beat-up, vinyl kitchen chairs, and a 1972 RCA black and white television hooked up to an old set of rabbit ears. A filthy area rug, the obsolete variety with the circular knotty rings of alternating colors covered the front floor. The colors were indiscernible. The mobile home was owned by Michael Barrett, alias Boxcar, Billy Don Barrett's younger brother. Two police officers stood in front of a six foot, plaid sofa filled with duct tape patches and cigarette burns. Unattended tears on the arms of the sofa revealed the soiled remnants of the padding and small glimpses of the wooden frame.

Billy Don Barrett sat awkwardly on the sofa. His hands were cuffed behind his back. Billy was wearing jeans that were open at the waist, no shoes and no shirt. Billy's sat restless on the sofa with squalid, matted hair. The growth on Barrett's face fell somewhere in between growing a beard and not shaving for more than a week. Billy Don Barrett was not heavy. There was an abundance of body hair, curling up Billy's stomach and chest, while winding over his shoulders and back. A tight abdomen was heaving up and down from anger. Billy Don Barrett's face reflected the years of alcohol abuse. His eyes sat well back from his cheeks. His eyes were abstruse and hollow, filled with rancor. Barrett stared at Cody Law. Barrett looked like a malnourished wolf, cowering in the woods. Cornered, the wolf would eventually strike out at someone or something. Cody stared back. Cody could smell the Jack Daniels oozing out of Billy's pores. Noon had not yet arrived.

"Who, the fuck, are you?" Barrett lashed out at the stranger in a black

Resistol hat. Barrett's body twisted in the sofa, as if he wanted to bite Cody Law.

Seated next to Barrett on the couch was Kirsten Myers Barrett. Her hands were cuffed behind her back. Kirsten's head was down. Kirsten made no attempt to make eye contact with anyone in the room.. Kirsten was wearing a Denver Broncos sweatshirt over baggy blue jeans. She wore no shoes. Kirsten's hair hung down and helped to hide her face. Kirsten appeared to be talking to herself. Cody could hear the incoherent dialogue, but he could not clearly identify the woman. For a moment, Cody began to approach the woman. The woman on the couch could not be Devon's mother? Why would Kirsten be handcuffed next to Billy Don Barrett, Cody wondered?

The room was filled with confusion and commotion from the back of the trailer. Cody turned and moved to the back room of the trailer. Cadrell Easley and two detectives stood with Shana McDonough. The paramedics were huddled over the bed against the far wall in the small bedroom. A tripod stood in the other corner with an elaborate video camera perched atop the three legs. Cody looked at the bed, where the paramedics were working feverishly. Towards the end of the bed, Cody saw two small legs moving rather aimlessly. At the top of the bed, Cody could now see the paramedics working to free a set of handcuffs, secured to the bed frame. Inside one end of the handcuffs was Devon's bruised wrist. A blanket covered Devon's naked body.

"Devon!" Cody lunged for the bed. Cadrell Easley grabbed Cody around the neck and pulled him back. The abrupt severity of the movement and the strength of Cadrell Easley knocked the wind out of Cody's lungs. Cody was oblivious to the grip on his neck. He gazed through the movements of the paramedics at his daughter. The unfolding scene could not be true. Before, Cody had read letters and visited the empty bedrooms. Cody thought kids were supposed to be afraid of the dark or scared by Halloween movies about babysitters. The little girl struggled to see who just yelled her name.

"Cody, back off. I don't know how you got in here, but you have to leave, now." Cadrell had released his hold on Cody's neck. "We are going to bring Devon out, but you have to wait outside of the trailer. Cody, you are going to trash some aspect of this arrest and that is all Barrett's attorneys will need to spring their client. Now back off, Cody." Easley raised his voice and released his lock on Cody's neck.

"Cody?" A small voice asked. "I got your letters."

The paramedics had released the handcuffs attached to the bed. They moved away and Devon lay flat on a soiled mattress with just a blanket to cover her. The handcuffs swung against the bed frame. The clanging metal bracelets slowed to a gentle tap. A frightened young girl looked up to Cody.

"Devon, I'm here, baby."

"Cody, back off." Cadrell Easley repeated.

"Officer Easley, please take Mr. Law outside." One detective requested. "We need to secure the trailer and that task is impossible with visitors. Mr. Law, the paramedics are going to bring the child to the hospital and that will be the best place for you to spend time with your daughter. The mother and father have been arrested. No further harm will come to Devon."

"Mother and father?" Cody was confused. Cody flashed back to the woman on the sofa. "Why is Kirsten under arrest?"

"Mr. Law, I am not going to make the same request twelve times. You are to leave the trailer, immediately." The detective repeated. "The videotape on the camera shows Mr. Barrett raping your daughter, Mr. Law. The child's mother was filming the act. There is a box of videotapes in the closet that if I were a betting man, would hold more of the same. It's your time to go, Mr. Law. We need to do our jobs and the paramedics need to bring Devon to the hospital. The DCFS representative will ride with the ambulance. Meet Devon at the hospital, Mr. Law. The tests and questions tend to get rough."

The detective had been talking to a black hole." Officer Easley, for the last time, escort Mr. Law to the door and make sure he stays outside. We will brief you later today, Mr. Law. For now, keep out of the way."

The detective turned to speak with Shana McDonough. She had remained unusually quiet inside the trailer. The grim reality of what they found, brought Shana McDonough back to the streets of New York. Shana McDonough had begun her career exposed to the unimaginable cruelty of nine million people living on the head of a pin.

Cadrell Easley led the detectives and the District Attorney to the rear bedroom after he found the front living area deserted. Shana had followed the detectives into the only bedroom of Barrett's mobile home. In smaller communities, the District Attorney often accompanied the police on arrests that had the potential to be kicked back out of the system. The Barrett's did not hear the police and Cadrell Easley because, as it would be learned later, they always played loud music during the sessions with Devon. Screams were muffled and hidden behind the music. The first thing Shana McDonough saw upon entering the room was Kirsten Barrett, frozen and startled behind the video camera. Billy Don Barrett was perched atop Devon, naked and fresh from three fingers of whiskey. Barrett was kneeling between Devon's legs and pulling a gorged erection. Devon's hands were cuffed to the front bed frame and Billy had her legs spread apart with his knees. Kirsten helped to secure Devon's legs to each side of the bed with duct tape, twine or torn towel strips tied around each ankle. Billy would check the camera while Kirsten undressed Devon for her stepfather. Kirsten operated the camera with precision.

Upon reviewing the tapes, the camera hung onto the fear and the panic in the eyes of the child. Although Devon had been accustomed to the severe retribution of Billy Don Barrett, the videotaped rapes were uncharted waters. The camera funneled Devon's excruciating pain that would accompany Barrett's penetration into the sadistic pleasure of the devil. Possession could be the only plausible excuse to manifest so much unspeakable pain. Devon was twelve years old. The District Attorney and the detectives viewed the videotape through the camera. The police secured the bedroom, while Shana stood silent.

Cadrell Easley walked Cody Law to the door of Unit 1201. Billy Don Barrett was ranting about the illegality of the intrusion and how he would beat the charges like he beat all the charges to date. Cody's heart stared at Cadrell Easley's department issued 357 Smith and Wesson pistol lodged in the black leather holster of the standard Castle Rock police uniform code. The strap over the revolver remained unsecured and the pistol begged to be seized. Putting a bullet in Barrett's forehead, Cody rationalized, should have been done the day he read Dana Davenport's letter to Martin Hollis.

Cody's seldom heard inner voice of reason must have prevented the impulse to command the vigilante justice that may have worked to relieve his own guilt, but would have done little to aid Devon.

"Cody, wait outside for Devon. Talk to Devon before she leaves in the ambulance and tell her that you will be waiting at the hospital when she arrives." Cadrell, too, had waited for this day. "Cody, tell her that we have ended the bad chapters in her life." Before Cody could respond or thank Cadrell Easley, another voice came from the sofa. Kirsten lifted her head slightly and looked at Cody.

"Cody." Kirsten called out coldly.

"Shut up, Kirsten." Billy demanded. "Don't say a fucking thing."

"Cody." Kirsten ignored the command. Barrett repeated the demand, screaming to his wife.

"Get him the fuck out of here." Easley requested from one of the uniformed officers guarding Barrett. Take him out and put him in the back of my unit. Give Kirsten a minute, here." Billy Don Barrett was removed from the trailer.

Cody turned to face Kirsten. She had trouble looking at Cody. "I want you to take Devon, Cody. I will not oppose your custody." Kirsten's words came across muffled and weak.

"I'm not sure that you are in much of a position to oppose anything, Kirsten. Is it true what the officers told me back there? You allowed Barrett? Wait, you participated in raping our child? Devon is a child! Christ, she is your child?" Cody broke off the questions.

"Billy made me do things, Cody. It's time to take Devon and share the responsibility. It's your time, now. I suppose we call it split duty." Kirsten's voice trailed off. The words became bizarre declarations, as if things had followed a natural progression. Kirsten looked to the window, away from Cody.

"Look at me, Kirsten." Cody demanded as he knelt in front of her. Kirsten turned her head and looked to the officer remaining in the room.

"Where's Billy?" Kirsten mumbled. The tide had gone. Cody would try again, but logic would prove as elusive as Kirsten's hold on the events of the morning.

"Look at me, Kirsten." Cody's demand quickly became an outright order.

Kirsten stared ahead, blankly. Cody placed his right hand under Kirsten's chin and physically turned her head slowly, so they could look eye to eye. Kirsten stared through him. Cody kept his voice low.

"You want us to share custody, Kirsten? The only thing we will ever share, other than the time it took to make Devon, is the self-deception that we somehow control the things that happen in our lives." Cody realized that Barrett had killed Kirsten long ago. A reincarnated corpse sat before him.

Cody got up and left the dilapidated trailer. Kirsten followed with the other uniformed officer. She was placed in a separate police car from her husband. Cody waited for the paramedics to bring Devon out. Gunner came over and stayed silent. The arrests spoke volumes and all of Gunner's questions would be answered in due time. The biggest question was answered at that moment. The paramedics carried Devon out of Unit 1201. The little girl was alive, not well, but alive. Shana McDonough walked out of the trailer shaken, visibly. She stopped before Cody Law.

"May I follow you to the hospital. It's your place now, Mr. Law. I do not want to be intrusive. I can obtain the legal reports from the hospital at another time. I know it is my office that gave Barrett a free reign. I would like to go for Devon." Shana McDonough waited for Cody to answer.

"Devon may very well need a woman during the next few hours. Can you help if the circumstances arise, Ms. McDonough?" Cody looked up.

"If you let me, Mr. Law."

* * *

The ride to Douglas County Hospital took ten minutes. Cody's group followed the ambulance with Devon and the DCFS representative. Shana McDonough followed with the detectives. Billy Don Barrett and Kirsten

Myers Barrett were taken to the police station to be formally charged. The arraignment would come the next morning under the jurisdiction of Douglas County Circuit Court Judge Miles Forkin. The emergency room crews were ready when the ambulance arrived. Devon was taken to the empty Intensive Care Unit space. The room was well equipped, private and empty at the time. The emergency room held three separate bays that were marked by curtains. The staff opted for the privacy of the ICU.

The gurney wheeled past Cody in a hurry. Cody stopped the progress for a moment. He looked down at his daughter for the first time as her father. Devon was bundled on the gurney, frightened and extremely vulnerable.

"The doctors are going to make sure you're O.K., Devon." Cody began awkwardly. "We need to talk when the doctors are finished with their check-up. You'll be going with me, Devon. I swear to you, no one will hurt you ever again. I've got some pretty big cowboys with me that are going to make sure no one lays a finger on you again." Gunner, Sonny and Olin tipped their hats to the little girl they had heard so much about. The paramedics pushed the cart forward.

"We should get the examination started." The attending physician stated. "Time, sometimes works against the victim in similar cases."

The physician was careful to keep the statements between Cody, himself and no one else. The entourage moved into the ICU. Cody and the others stood silent and helpless, again.

The police were kept out of the examination. Initially, the emergency room personnel were alone with Devon. After no more than ten minutes, the assembled staff grew considerably. The attending physician called in a pediatrician, a gynecologist, an anesthesiologist, and a general surgeon. Present at all times, was the representative from the Department of Children and Family Services. The attending physician came out to speak to Cody, the police and the District Attorney. Dr. David Normal was forty-three years old. Prematurely gray and thinning hair did well to nurture the traditional values of knowledge and wisdom, the values most laymen expect from any physician. Dr. Normal had been head of the trauma unit at Douglas County Hospital for seven years. Dr. Normal would complete the examination.

"Ms. McDonough, is there a legal guardian present?" Dr. Normal asked.

"Yes. Mr. Cody Law is the girl's biological and legal father. Devon's birth certificate will reflect those facts. The stepfather has been taken into custody with the girl's mother. They have been charged under the adult criminal code and will be arraigned tomorrow." Shana McDonough informed the doctor. Cody stepped forward.

"Mr. Law, I am Dr. David Normal. I am the head of the trauma unit at Douglas County. I have completed an initial exam on Devon. It is my opinion that Devon be given a complete exam under anesthesia. We will need your permission to proceed." Dr. Normal waited holding a clipboard and a form to sign.

"Could you be more specific? I would like to know what I am giving you permission to do to Devon. Is that an unreasonable request, Dr. Normal?" Cody was scared.

"Not at all, Mr. Law. My apologies. Some family members prefer to remain under general terms in the case of sexual abuse. The details are sometimes difficult to hear." Dr. Normal spoke candidly.

"Just tell me what's going on with Devon, please." Cody fell short of where he could have gone.

"Mr. Law, there is evidence of damage to the vaginal and anal lining. The hymen has been broken, which confirms vaginal penetration on at least one occasion. The initial exam revealed tears in the rectal lining. The immediate danger is unknown. I have called in a pediatrician and a gynecologist to assist. We need to take Devon to the operating room and conduct a thorough examination under anesthesia. Devon will have a breathing tube during the procedures. A general surgeon will conduct the procedure that should take no more than thirty minutes. If everything goes well, Devon will be up and awake within the hour. We have pulled blood for HIV and Hepatitis tests. These are required tests in rape cases regardless of the age of the victim. The general surgeon will take samples of hair and fluids from the victim. The anal procedure necessary is called an anoscopy. The surgeon will search for anal tears and bleeding using an anoscope. A vaginal examination will follow using an instrument called a vaginal speculum. These instruments are necessary for a thorough exam and they are administered under anesthesia. If the surgeon determines the injuries are of an acute nature and require immediate attention, the he will surgically repair the bleeding. Devon will feel nothing during the examination. Mr. Law, your daughter has been traumatized sexually in her vagina. She has also sustained anal trauma. We need to access when the trauma occurred and if there is an immediate threat to Devon's health. The operating room is the most comprehensive avenue we have. Will you sign the permission form?" Dr. Normal held little back.

"You'll let me know something as soon as you have some answers?" Cody signed the form.

"Absolutely, Mr. Law." Dr. Normal checked the form. "Thank you." He returned to the ICU and through the glass, Cody could see a bevy of movement. Devon's bed disappeared into an elevator. Cody could barely see his daughter through the I. V. tubes and the huddled professional group that accompanied her to the operating room.

"Did you listen to all that?" Cody turned to Gunner and Shana

McDonough. They both looked up and nodded. "Ms. McDonough, promise me something?"

"If I can, Mr. Law."

"Tell me that the next time Devon will have a chance to see Billy Don Barrett or Kirsten, will be when she is watching her own children graduate college. Can you assure me that the court will charge Billy Don Barrett with multiple crimes and if convicted, the sentences will run consecutively?" Cody paused and put his hands to his mouth. "Let me rephrase the question. Is there any chance in the world for Billy Don Barrett to walk on these charges?"

"No!" Shana McDonough did not hesitate.

"When this file found your desk, there had to be so many second thoughts about the way Devon's case was handled? In other words, were you absolutely certain that Barrett was given a pass, year after year?"

Cody rubbed his mouth along the clenched hands below his chin. Shana McDonough began to answer. Cody sat up in his chair. The waiting area in the Douglas County Hospital filled with uniformed police officers and plain clothes detectives. The local paper had just received word from the police scanner. The State Police arrived because the Sunset Park Mobile Home location was technically outside the city limit of Castle Rock. The Denver papers had already dispatched reporters to Castle Rock. Sonny Moore and Olin Martin waited with Gunner McGarrity, alongside Cody. Shana McDonough spoke up.

"Mr. Law, you know the answer to that question."

" You're right." Cody stood up.

Dr. David Normal walked out of the elevator less than thirty minutes from the time they brought Devon to the operating room. The entourage had dwindled to one. The trauma unit director walked up to Cody Law.

"The examination is complete, Mr. Law. Devon will not require surgery. We discovered damage to the rectal lining and the vaginal walls. The damage was not sustained recently. By recently, I mean during the past twenty-four hours. There was no semen present. Devon was not raped today. The damage to the rectal lining is particularly disturbing. While there is no bleeding, the wounds were substantial indicating foreign objects had been used to cause the type of damage we discovered."

"Foreign objects?" Cody asked in fear of the answer.

"Devon has been penetrated by broom handles, plunger arms or any number of household items."

"That son of a bitch!"

"Physically, Devon will recover completely. Since no acute tears were present, Devon can be released later this afternoon. We will give the medical clearance, but DCFS and the District Attorney will have the final say on where Devon is allowed to go." Dr. David Normal continued.

"Devon is in recovery at this moment. The recovery time is short for the brief time she was out. You can go and see her in about fifteen minutes. If you have any other questions, I will be here until 7:00 p.m. Please feel free to have someone page me at any time. I'm sorry we had to meet under these circumstances. Your daughter will recover physically in a short period of time. There was some minor trauma to her wrists and ankles, mostly bruises. Devon is a stoic young girl. She was not hysterical. Our examination and intrusion into her body may be no more than an extension of the abuse in her mind. Trust will be a hard commodity to come by, Mr. Law. Begin slowly and expect little." The two men shook hands. "Protect that little girl, Mr. Law. Somebody messed her up pretty good."

DCFS and the police huddled in the waiting room. Shana McDonough was called into the huddle, briefly. Cody spoke to the nurse's station about where to see Devon when the recovery time had elapsed. The District Attorney called Cody to meet with the police.

"Mr. Law, the police would like to take a statement from Devon as soon as possible. They would like you to be present. The DCFS and the police will record the statement and I will make every effort to keep Devon's testimony at any trial limited to these recorded statements. The judge, in any case, has the final word on whether a child must testify, but the evidence seems overwhelming, considering what the police found upon entering the mobile home today. I feel it is very unlikely that any judge would require the testimony in person if we complete a recorded statement today."

"The need to complete the statement as close to the time of Barrett's arrest as is possible, will limit the defense options to challenge the content and accuracy of the statement. I will bring in a court stenographer and we will videotape the statement. A videotaped statement usually will carry the same weight as an in-person witness. Mr. Law, I know the timing is awful, but the statement is crucial to the case and to keeping Devon from testifying in front of Barrett. Many child abuse cases fall apart when the child is face to face with the parent in court. Incredibly, many children retain the need to please the abusive parent even when given the opportunity to send the abusive parent to prison." Shana McDonough believed herself to be on solid ground and kept in mind, the delicate nature of the request.

"You wanted to come to the hospital for Devon, Ms. McDonough?" Cody was angry.

"Is this what you meant by coming to the hospital for Devon? If I remember correctly, Ms. McDonough, you told me that you did not want to be intrusive. You told me that it was your office that allowed Barrett to operate without consequence for so long. Congratulations, the ride-a-long speech got to me. After what you witnessed inside the mobile home this morning, you are now telling me that you want to put a video camera in front of Devon, again? Are you fucking crazy? I think your compassion here can only be gauged by a conviction. If there is not enough evidence on this matter without Devon's testimony to convict Barrett, then you best look elsewhere to find more. Kirsten is another issue, but do not come to me with the bullshit lines, that the whole case will rest on Devon." Cody glared at Shana McDonough.

"Mr. Law, I believe that you have to know how these cases work, up front." The District Attorney tried to rationalize an emotional response.

"I will tell you, Ms. McDonough, how this case will not work." Cody interrupted. "Devon will not have a video camera stuck in her face today or next month without her consent and mine. Now, if you'll excuse me. I am going to see if Devon is awake."

"Mr. Law, we need to get a statement from Devon as soon as possible. If that fact does not make you happy, then I am sorry. It does not change the rule of law, however insensitive the system is perceived. Prepare for this now and you will make Devon's life easier down the road. Go see your daughter, Mr. Law. I hope she is well." Shana McDonough turned and walked back to the detectives. Collectively, they would ask the questions for any statement given by Devon Barrett.

* * *

Devon was sleeping when Cody walked into the private room on the second floor. The female representative from the Department of Children and Family Services sat in a leather chair by the window. The woman was white, young, overdressed and reading the Wall Street Journal. The dress was uptown Manhattan and the make-up was meticulous. She looked up when the door opened, but knew Cody from the morning events. The young woman returned to the paper. Cody moved quietly to the edge of the bed.

"How long has she been sleeping." Cody asked in a whisper.

"Not long." The young lady responded. Cody looked up and then looked back at Devon, sleeping so frail and delicate. The Journal did not move and Cody leered at the unconcerned woman. Finally, in a sanctuary where no one could touch Devon, another indignity is thrust upon the young girl. Cody fought every fiber of common sense that told him to let it be and wait for Devon to wake up. Men rarely change and they certainly do not change when it matters most. Cody reached over to the paper and pulled the Wall Street Journal down, revealing the DCFS representative.

"Go get yourself some coffee, ma'am." Cody suggested.

"I'm fine, thank you. The District Attorney has ordered DCFS to stay with the child at all times. " The young woman returned to the paper. Cody reached up and pulled the paper down, again.

"Humor me, then." Cody quietly requested. The young woman looked puzzled. Cody continued, careful to speak softly. "Reach down inside yourself and pull up a performance that at least gives the general impression that you give a fuck about what has happened to my daughter. The Department of Children and Family Services failed this child more times than Barney nailed Betty behind the Bedrock Bowl. So whenever you're around me, pretend that you fucking care about Devon or I'll make sure that the District Attorney, who used to date the Governor, has your assignment moved to changing bedpans at an orphanage in Commerce City." The paper was folded instantly following Cody's fabrication regarding the District Attorney's dating exploits.

"I apologize for any disrespect, sir. That was never my intent." The answer surprised Cody. The point was made. Cody was mad and looked to placc blamc anywhere.

Cody removed his hat and ignored the woman from that point on. The room was generic hospital tundra. Devon's bed was a mechanical twister machine hooked up to a Jeopardy clicker and a few beeping monitors. The bright afternoon sun rattled through the venetian blinds and painted the floor in yellow stripes. The Rocky Mountains loomed in the distance through the window as if an artist drew an oasis of respite. Devon's flaxen hair fell soft across her shoulders. Sleep proved to be the haven so elusive for so long. Cody watched his daughter and wished her peace for an eternity. The desire to speak to Devon and tell her how things would be different took a backseat to the slumber she now enjoyed. Cody took a seat next to the bed. Cody's friends waited downstairs. Gunner told Cody that they would not be leaving without them.

Exactly one hour after the operating room examination, Devon woke up. Her eyes blinked repeatedly. She gazed at the tube in her arm. She was not afraid. The very medical mechanisms and sterile surroundings that tend to frighten most young patients, proved to be tranquil for the small girl in Room 202. Cody watched his daughter and groped for something to say. Devon's hand pulled the hair from her cheek. Cody reached up and placed his hand in hers.

"Hello, Devon." Cody uttered, disgusted with waiting months to be grand and coming up with the profound words of ...hello Devon.

"You're Cody?" A small voice asked.

"That's right. My name is Cody Law. I am a tongue-tied imbecile at this moment. I've got volumes of speeches that I planned to rattle off when we spoke, but I can't seem to form the sentences that I rehearsed a thousand times." Cody lowered the railing and sat on the edge of the bed.

"I hope you're not disappointed that I'm not the prince of wisdom. It's kinda' nice to just be here." Cody smiled. The sunlight breaking through the venetian blinds bathed the simplicity of the moment.

"Anna told me that your are my father. I knew that when I read your letters." Devon filled the room with the connection that Cody craved.

"Anna was right. She gave me the only avenue to find you. I never knew about your life. Your mother and I knew each other for a brief time. Kirsten told me she had a baby, but she married another man, a man she said she loved. I know now, that she tried to protect me from bearing my own responsibility. Your mother didn't want to force me to do anything. Like a young fool, I believed the lies. To stay away was easier for me. Your mother told me that everything was fine. Although we shared something special, that time was over. I will go to my grave Devon, regretting my decision to let her be. I can't change the past, but if you'll let me, I promise things will be very different." Cody welled up, struggled to swallow and stumbled in the words he had not rehearsed enough.

"I'm glad you're here, now." Devon squeezed Cody's hand. "Can I stay with you?"

"Absolutely, Devon. If you can understand one thing in all of this, and most of it is beyond me, understand that God has a timetable for all of us. My time with you, Devon, can start today. Deal?" Cody stared down at the girl he never knew.

"Deal!" Devon beamed. The aspirations of a child fell into a father's arms.

Time fell through the afternoon like a rolling snow squall on the north face of Pikes Peak. Devon and Cody talked for an hour, mostly about rodeos and bull riders. When Cody left to grab some cokes, he came back with friends. Sonny Moore and Olin Martin came into Room 202 with the formal introduction provided by Cody, but sounding like the PRCA Announcer of the Year. Cody rattled off Sonny's hometown, his current ranking, past career highs and then pushed the hospital room door open to provide the entrance for Sonny Moore. Devon's eyes lit up brighter than the North Star on a crystal clear Western night. Next up, the hometown and the highlights came again. Enter, Olin Martin. Devon tried to clap, but the IV line made it too difficult. Olin and Sonny met Devon and crowded the end of her bed. They pushed each other for a closer spot on the bed, as if they were brothers arguing about anything and everything before mom and dad got home. Devon laughed out loud at the hi-jinx, when Olin actually slipped to the floor from a Sonny Moore shove that caught him off-guard. Cody saved the best for last.

"I've got one more person for you to meet, Devon." Cody held the imaginary microphone to his mouth. Devon sat up and delighted in the mechanical mattress beneath her.

"You're probably not going to know this guy, Devon." Olin Martin slid in. "He's really, really old."

"Yeah, Devon." Sonny added. "This guy rode broncs and bulls when they had to use 'em for transportation to get each rodeo." Cody stood by the door. He opened it slightly and whispered something through the door. Cody cleared his throat.

"Without further delay," Cody erupted into the imaginary microphone. "We are pleased to welcome today, a four-time winner at the Calgary Stampede. We welcome the two-time winner at Cheyenne Days, a nine-time member of the PRCA top-ten money list, and winner of the 1970 PRCA World Bull Riding Championship. Please welcome..."

"Pssst." Devon pulled at Sonny's arm.

"Wait, Brother Cody." Sonny commanded. Cody stopped short of the final introduction. Devon whispered something to Sonny. Sonny Moore got up and walked over to Cody to relay the information.

"I have been corrected." Cody resumed, feigning disgust at the interruption. Cody's chin rose up and he looked over his nose at the source of the interruption. "The announcer does not like to be corrected, but there are those rare occasions where the announcer has been less than correct, not incorrect, less than correct. Continuing, the THREE time winner at Cheyenne Days and the current record holder for the highest score in a PRCA sanctioned event, a ninety-six aboard Hell Bent in 1971 is here tonight. Born in Texas, now residing in Nipomo, California, please give a warm Colorado welcome to...Gunner McGarrity!" Cody held the imaginary microphone in the air. Cody threw open the door and in walked the biggest Texas smile since John Travolta asked Mickey Gilley if they could make a little movie in his bar.

"Damn, this child is smarter than the combined IQ of the top ten bull-riders in any given year and a hell of a lot prettier. Thank you, darlin', for the correct introduction. "

Gunner pulled his hat off and held it against his chest. Gunner looked like Sam Elliott without the thick white mustache. The two distinct voices had to be cloned from similar gene pools. A mop of thick gray hair fell onto Gunner's forehead. Gunner approached the bed, leaned down and kissed Devon on the cheek. Devon looked at Cody.

"That was probably the coolest thing that ever happened to me. I never met anybody famous. I read about all the rodeo legends and past champions.

I even memorized all the bull riders, but I never thought I'd get to know one." Devon left the morning events long ago. Cody thought, for a moment, how sad if that kiss was actually the coolest thing that had ever happened to Devon. Cody managed a smiled, from watching Devon follow Gunner around the room with her eyes.

"Be careful, Devon." Gunner warned. "Aren't most legends supposed to be, how do I say, pushin' up daisies from six feet under?"

"Don't believe all that legend crap, Gunner." Sonny broke in. "It's hard enough fittin' that big ol' head in the car as it is."

"Jealousy, boys." Gunner began to strut. "Jealousy is the surest form of flattery. Not only, am I wearing this Gold Buckle, but I am standing next to the President of the Gunner McGarrity Fan Club."

"There is no Gunner McGarrity Fan Club." Olin Martin recalled. "Most of the members would be on Social Security by now." Sonny snickered at his traveling partner.

"To the contrary, my uninformed brothers, there is a whole new breed of rodeo fan that enjoys watching riders STAY on their animals. It's so tough to develop a following when the fans only know you by the circle in your back pocket and they keep calling you Wrangler. Hey, Sonny, you ever thought about changin' your name to Wrangler? That way, every time you get your ass tossed in the first round, the crowd won't have any trouble knowin' your name." Gunner put up his hand and high-fived his new young friend. She slapped him back and soaked in that Texas mischief from a big, old country kid.

"Hey, how mad would they get if we smuggled in some French fries and chocolate shakes?" Cody wondered out loud.

"I'll bet we could make it to that McDonalds down the road, grab some treats and be back in this room before anyone knew we were gone." Gunner announced.

"Devon, you up for the Golden Arches?" Cody asked.

"The what?" Devon looked confused having been kept from the onslaught of the fast food invasion.

"McDonalds, Devon. Cody, she's too young to know what the golden arches mean. Hell, they don't even have golden arches anymore." Gunner scolded Cody. The room was crammed with the intangibles that made a little girl forget about where she had been only hours before.

"Come on, boys." Gunner directed. "Leave Cody with Devon. We'll be back in a few minutes. I know I saw a McDonalds around here somewhere. Let's go." Three cowboys argued down the hall about who would ride in the front seat.

"You have nice friends, Cody." Devon told her father. "What should I call you?" The question followed bluntly. Children have the remarkable talent to avoid small talk.

"What do you want to call me?" Cody countered.

"I like Cody." Devon smiled again.

"Then Cody it is." The matter was settled.

"When will I be able to change my last name to yours?" Devon stayed on the point. Cody paused and had often thought about how long it would take to reach the point of changing names.

"Today, if the fit is right." Cody said the right thing.

"I think the fit is perfect, Cody. Devon Law, what do you think?" Devon propped up proud in bed. Cody leaned over and put his arms around his daughter. One small arm squeezed back. He whispered in her ear.

"It's perfect."

The carry out posse returned in thirty minutes. The hospital room took on the look of a teenager's car after homecoming. Empty French fry containers and half-empty chocolate shakes spilled out over the wastebasket. Gunner held court, keeping Olin Martin and Sonny Moore as mesmerized as Cody's daughter. Gunner filled the room with the true tales of rodeo life. Gunner recalled many of the more colorful experiences of his leathery past. The story of Galveston County in 1969 was never far from Gunner's mind.

"Devon, can I tell you a story that scared me so much, I'm sure I wet my pants, but I couldn't tell?" Gunner pulled up a chair next to Devon.

"Sure." Devon answered shyly.

"We were outside of Houston in Galveston County for a rodeo just off Galveston Island. It was late fall in 1969. I could taste the finals. I was sick of reading about everyone in the Finals. I was that close. A driving rainstorm filled the arena on the last night of the rodeo. I trailed two top ranked bull riders by a total of three points. The weather whipped up a ground swell that spooked the animals. A chaotic scramble broke out in the back pens. Six saddle-bronc riders pulled out at the gate. Not one bareback rider made the horn. Devon, they slid right off the horse. The steer wrestlers hit the ground to plant and set off a rooster tail of mud that left them black from head to foot." Gunner remembered the late summer monsoon.

"Hell, with all the damn steer wrestlers, it looked like Miss Budweiser was pulling three-sixties on the arena floor." Gunner lit up with the story. "Rodeos don't get canceled. You don't get bathrooms to clean up in. The barrel racers never made it to the third barrel. The horses gave up in the mud. Two of the first three girls got thrown."

"The rodeo wallowed through the scheduled events. The bleachers and back holding fences wavered in the gale force winds. The final three bull-riders prepared to ride in the storm. The platforms shook behind the chutes. The rain fell in sheets of medieval arrows, causing the entire structure to creak and whine like a New England shrimp boat caught too far off the Gloucester coast. Each wave of rain hit the gates with drenching ferocity and caused the first two bulls, pulled for the final round, to thrash uncontrollably inside the gates. Judges ruled for re-rides before the gates had been opened."

"I never saw two consecutive re-rides before the gates had been opened." Gunner shook his head.

"Jesus, I've seen riders nearly killed in the chute before a ride and the judges didn't call a re-ride. At the Finals in 1973, Billy Scovill broke his back in the chutes. Billy nodded and the gate opened. The bull's front end spun out, stopped and then pulled back into the chute. The bull's back end bucked up hard and fast enough to send Billy headfirst into the rails. The force of the bull's body, which was nearly vertical, rear end in the air, slammed Billy forward snapping three vertebrae. No re-ride. The judges ruled that Billy called for the gate and the bull came out and then backed in again. Billy never rode again." Gunner slowed down and remembered Billy Scovill. Billy kissed the front end of a twelve-gauge five years later from a wheelchair. Gunner left that part out.

"Tater Scanlon rode first and bucked off as soon as the gate opened." Gunner tipped his hat back and continued.

"Hats blew throughout the stands like confetti at a New Year's party. Clay Mathews was the next to ride. He led the short-go by two points with two riders to go. Clay pulled Slack Jack for his final ride. Clay rode Slack Jack to the horn, only the rain fell so hard that the judges didn't see the end of the ride and called it for no points. Protests in rodeo do not exist. If a cowboy does not like the call of the judges, he never slides into the mode of professional athletes in other sports. There are no tantrums or fines for bumping an official. No one spits in the judge's face or confronts the judges face to face. Cowboys are never seen screaming their displeasure to the delight of the crowd. Cowboys accept the calls and prove their mallet by riding again and again. Bad calls in rodeo are no more than bad draws."

Gunner continued. "I knew at that point, that I had to stay on the bull for a victory. Any ride for the eight seconds would constitute a win in Galveston County. The Galveston County Livestock Show and Rodeo was not Cheyenne, but the payday was comfortable and anything in Texas was worth the buckle. That night was all about the rank and the prize money. I pulled a bull that threw me two weeks prior. The bull was a fast, light, mixed breed named Brown Sugar."

"The temperature had dropped to forty-one degrees. It was early September in Texas. Man, it felt like the Cowboy Downhill in Steamboat in

January. " Gunner wrapped his arms around Devon and pulled her close.

"The wind howled and raced across the arena like the yellow mustangs running wild in the Black Hills. The gulf roared up just off Galveston Island. The Dickinson, Texas arena shook from the sixty year-old bleachers to the four light towers. The off-season storm had arrived, full tilt. Brown Sugar slammed against the gate as I climbed onto the chute. I tried to straddle the boards, but Brown Sugar was spooked. I remember his horns. They were long and Brown Sugar had to turn awkwardly to fit into the chute."

Devon's eyes never left Gunner. Sonny and Olin sat in silence, sipping the remnants of warm chocolate shakes. Gunner relayed the difficulty of pulling the rope tight. The cascading curtains of water would make the effort almost futile.

"The deerskin gloves were soaked." Gunner rubbed his hands together. "The rosin was useless. Bobby Chesney and the other saddle-bronc riders gathered around the gate. Chesney told me that I wouldn't last four seconds. Chesney and the saddle-bronc riders were always jealous of the bull riders. The girls always waited for us. At the moment I was ready, I lost my hat to the wind. I should have known then. I called out to the arena for someone to pull the gate. No one could see a nod on this night and I didn't have a hat to tip. When the gate pulled open, my handhold slipped down. The rope was never secure. The rain was torrential. My gloved hand slid out of the grip. Lightning struck the scorer's tower at the same moment the gate flew open and the lights in the arena went black."

Devon held her breath. Gunner sat on the bed next to Devon. Cody watched Devon with Gunner. Gunner surged ahead.

"I was bare-ass on a bull without a grip and with no lights. The bull charged out of the gate in complete darkness. The huddled spectators remaining fell silent. I remembered how the force of the bull had never been more acute than that ride. Rodeos are all about controllable power. Uncontrollable power as a contestant is failure. I felt like I was a moth on the back of a freight train." Gunner paused.

"Brown Sugar didn't like the darkness any more than I did. That little bull sprung up higher than a jackrabbit on a frying pan. I was a ping-pong ball in a hurricane. The saddle-bronc riders should have put money down. I hit pay dirt in record time. The mud filled my mouth in the blackness and the only clue to the bull's position was his snorting breath that creased my cheeks. Somehow, the flailing animal kept missing me. I spun around in the mud like a wounded blind prey. The sky exploded in a firestorm of lightning and deafening thunder. For a second, I saw Brown Sugar at eye level. The light flash sketched a silhouette of Taurus charging for the fear he sensed in me. I could feel the earth rumble beneath my knees. I hit the mud and stretched out flat. That bull ran right over me. One hoof scratched my ear as it barely missed my head. Another grazed the instep on my boot. I lay below the surface of the mud. My instinct was to rise up and scat to the nearest gate, but I had no clue where Brown Sugar was. The storm noise buried any noise from the bull. Brown Sugar careened about the arena for what seemed to be an eternity."

"The bullfighters ran for cover. The flank rope remained intact. Brown Sugar remained a time bomb. The sky unloaded on the silent arena with more sheets of rain. Trees snapped in the background and you could hear the crackling sounds of downed wires. A ballistic bull searched for something that was not there. I crawled around like an infant in chaps. I swear, I almost cried when I reached up and felt a slat on the gate. I know I wet my pants, but I was soaked and covered with mud, so no one ever knew. I climbed over that fence and knew that I had just survived the dumbest decision of my career. Clay Matthews won the round. I cashed the second place check for the happiest payday of my life." Devon flashed a gap toothed smile from ear to ear. A cowboy's tale ended.

Shana McDonough entered the room. Accompanied by the DCFS representative, who Shana agreed to pull for Cody and his friends, the District Attorney asked to speak to Cody outside the room. Shana and Cody walked into the hallway.

"Cody, can we speak to Devon, now?" Ms. McDonough asked.

"Just you?" Cody inquired.

"No." The answer came expectedly. "We would like to record a statement. The detectives, myself and the Department of Children and Family Services will be present. We want you to stay, as well."

"I will go in alone. I will talk to Devon and if she does not want to do this now, then it's over. I'm her father and I can stop it. Are we clear on that?" Cody demanded.

"You can call it, Mr. Law." Ms. McDonough agreed. "If we do not take a statement today, then we will be giving Barrett's attorneys, whoever they are, the gap they need. I'm not here to persecute a child, Mr. Law. I'm here to put this piece of shit away. Go talk to your daughter."

Cody walked back into the room. Devon was hounding Gunner to talk about Lane Frost. Gunner made the mistake of telling Devon that he knew Lane, well. Gunner promised to spill everything he knew about Lane Frost at another time. Cody eyed Gunner and the message was clear. Gunner pulled Sonny and Olin out of the room. They agreed to wait for Cody and Devon for as long as was necessary.

"Devon, I need to ask you something, now." Cody began. They were alone in the room. "The police need to ask you about what happened with your stepfather. Billy Don Barrett is under arrest and they plan to keep him for a very long time. Your mother is under arrest, as well. They may each have a trial or they may put them on trial together. Regardless of how they are tried, the District Attorney does not want to bring you in to testify. If you can tell them about Billy, you won't have to do it in court. Do you follow me, so far?" Cody went slow.

"Are you going to stay with me?" Devon looked down, somewhat ashamed.

"I am not leaving your side, Devon." Cody assured his daughter. "The police want to record a statement from you so that they can use the statement in court. That way, you don't have to talk about this in front of anyone else. Do you want to do this, now. If not, Devon, I'll tell them to leave."

"What should I do, Cody?" Devon asked with the purity of dependence Cody never contemplated. The decision was his. It had been easy to lay the call on Devon, when protesting to the District Attorney. Devon laid the call back on Cody.

"Talk to them, Devon." Cody spoke without the slightest hesitation. "I am not going to lie to you, Devon. I never thought that the first day I got to be your father, I would have to tell you what to do. They are going to ask about the bad things that Billy did to you. They want to record everything you say. Trust me, Devon. If there were another way, I would tell these people to take a walk. They are here to help us, but they have to have your words to make that possible. If you want to leave it be, then I'll tell them to go. You and I will leave the hospital together. If I have to pack you in my jacket, I'm not leaving here without you."

"I want to talk to them, Cody." Devon curled the words emphatically. Cody must have misunderstood.

"Are you sure, Devon?" Cody came back, somewhat shocked.

"I used to sneak into the library at school and read the bible. I didn't understand much of it, but everyone seemed to quote the bible. Mr. Hollis quoted the bible when I had to see him. My stepfather used to quote the bible all the time. My mother used to tell me what the bible said I should do. Every time I got a quote from the "Good Book," something terrible was about to happen or had already happened. I know they were wrong, Cody. Can I tell them that?" Devon queried her new father

In that precise moment, Cody looked at Devon and thought about what twelve year-old girls should be asking their fathers. The merits of honesty and candor with an investigative team from the District Attorneys office did not come to mind.

"I want you to tell them that!" Cody concurred. "Devon, when they ask you a question, don't look down. Look straight ahead and hold your chin up high. Let Billy know who you are. He is going to see the tape of your testimony. Let him know that he has lost."

The deposition took twenty minutes to set up properly and test the equipment. Devon's testimony was set to begin. Shana McDonough sat with a note pad, presumably to jot down certain passages to return to or poignant remarks to be used later at trial. The juvenile detective conducted the actual questions. Two other detectives sat by. Cody asked for Cadrell Easley to be present. Before long, the room took on a stadium atmosphere. Devon sat quietly next to Cody, holding his hand. During the set-up, Cody looked down at Devon and asked.

"You O.K.?"

"I'm O.K." Devon returned the look and forced a smile. Cody had no clue as to what would unfold during the testimony. Devon knew it all.

"For the record." The questioning began. The Juvenile Detective rolled through some formalities with date, name and location. There was some confusion with Devon's last name. Devon stated her name as Devon Law. After some early clarifications, Devon was convinced for the purpose of the testimony, that using the name Devon Barrett, would be less confusing.

"Devon." The detective began. "We want you to tell us about your family. Take us from the beginning or from where you can first remember something being wrong at home. We will have specific questions to ask later, but now is the time to tell the truth about what happened in your home."

The shuffling had stopped. The busy hospital traffic outside Room 202 fell quiet. A window, cracked halfway for the fresh air, caught a distant car horn that faded quickly. Devon held her chin high. A video camera flashed an LED red light just below the lens. A faint humming noise could be heard as the tape rolled in the camera. Cody wanted to end the process before it began.

"My earliest memories from being a little girl stem from my baby brother. I think I was four years old at the time. I don't think my mother wanted to have a baby when she had me. I'm not sure, but my mother never talked much to me. I always followed her around from room to room. She took care of me, I guess, but I never got to do the things that the other kids were doing with their mothers. Mommy fed me and made sure that I had shoes and clothes, but we never did stuff together." Devon glanced over at Cody. Cody nodded his approval.

"Mommy seemed so happy, when she had Billy Jr." Devon continued. "I'm not sure what I did to make mommy so mad, but Billy came along and mommy got much happier. I remember that because I always liked to watch my mother smile and laugh at Billy Jr. She used to pick him up over her head and wiggle him around. He laughed and she laughed. Billy Jr. always drooled from way up high like that, but he loved it, too." Devon paused. She had not spoken about much for years. Her life was one of silence. Devon found it odd to talk so much. The words came staggered at times, but they had been rehearsed in her mind over and over. Someday, Devon imagined, the bad days would end.

"Do you remember the day when Billy Jr. died?"

"Yes sir." Devon looked at Cody again. "Mommy was giving Billy Jr. a bath. I sat on the floor next to them and watched. I think the doorbell rang or the phone rang. I don't remember which one. Mommy got up after the bell kept ringing. She looked down at me and said she would be back in a minute or less. The rest of the day is hard to remember. I know there were police cars and ambulances in front of the house. Mommy was crying and yelling at the policemen. My mother locked me in my room while all the fire trucks and police cars were at my house. She was yelling at everyone. I sat in my closet and tried to hold my ears closed. I couldn't listen to what they were saying."

"What were they saying, Devon?"

"My mommy said that I killed Billy Jr. She said it was my fault. Mommy came into my room and yelled at me. She was crying. She said that all she did was ask me to watch Billy Jr. for a minute or two. The police said he slid under the water, but I don't remember my mommy asking me to watch Billy Jr. I'm not sure about much from that day, except that I never meant to kill my brother. My dad kept telling my mother that we both killed Billy Jr." Devon started to drift.

"Can you remember when your father first hit you?"

"My parents became really strict as each year went by. I think it was because of what I did to Billy Jr. I had all these rules in the house and out of the house. I was timed to get home from school by a certain time. If I was late, I couldn't eat dinner. If I didn't finish certain chores like the laundry and the dishes by a certain time then I didn't get any food. They locked me up in a closet for hours at a time. They told me that they had to put me in the closet or they would have beaten me."

"Did you tell anybody about this?"

"The first time I told anybody about what went on in our house, I was at school and I told one of my teachers. She paddled me and told me never to lie about things like that again. My father kept drinking more. I could tell by the way he smelled. He used to hit mommy and if I was watching, then he'd hit me too. I kinda expected my daddy to hit me and punish me when I did bad stuff. I didn't think my mommy would do that stuff, too. I wanted her to protect me, but as I got older, she helped him more and she did stuff, too. I couldn't get away from being bad. I remember always being hungry. I used to stay after school to look for garbage that I could eat. I knew that when I went home, I would do something bad and I wouldn't get anything to eat for dinner that night. Sometimes, I went three days without dinner or lunch."

"I got in trouble at school for stealing food. Then I just stuck to the garbage. School used to be the best of my world. It wasn't all good, but there wasn't as much bad stuff at school as there was at home. I told Ms. Davenport stuff, but I made her promise not to tell anyone else. I think she did, because all of a sudden, Ms. Davenport wasn't there anymore. I felt safest in the classroom. No one could hurt me there. My father couldn't do bad things to me in school. I would have slept at school if I could have. The other kids didn't make fun of me in class. When we were on the play-grounds, I tried to hide most of the time. I didn't have any friends. I used to have some friends, but when they came over, my mother would send them home. I wasn't allowed to bring kids home. I was told that I spent enough time with these kids during the day. I knew that wasn't the reason."

"After awhile, the other kids stayed away from me. They all said I looked really weird. I was pretty skinny, I guess. They made fun of my dress and my shoes, 'cause I wore the same dresses almost every day. I only had three. I missed a lot of school days, but Mr. Hollis said he understood. School got better with Ms. Larkin. She helped me get in touch with my real father, but then she went away. My mother didn't like Ms. Larkin. She said Ms. Larkin was out to hurt her. Mommy said Ms. Larkin was like a lot of women, who aren't married and don't have kids. I told my mother about Ms. Larkin's boyfriend, how he's a rodeo bareback rider. Maybe he's a saddle-bronc rider, I forget. Anyway, Mommy tells me that rodeo guys never come back to get married and Ms. Larkin gets all crazy when she thinks about that. According to my parents, if it isn't Ms. Larkin, then the school will keep trying to hurt Billy Don and my mother. They will find ways to hurt other parents, so that was why they didn't let me go back to school this year. Mommy said she would teach me everything at home. I missed school this year. The other kids don't mean to be the way they are. Anyway, I still missed it. Can I have some water?" Devon asked the detective.

"Of course." The detective reached over and gave Devon a glass of water. Cody gave Devon a reassuring nod. Cody was asked not sit next to Devon for the purposes of the camera. The testimony would be more effective and scrutinized less if there were not an adult in the tape with Devon, especially her biological father who would be seeking custody. The defense attorney for Barrett would jump all over that for coercion and rehearsed testimony. They would almost certainly require Devon to repeat the testimony on her own. Devon drank the water. The purging was well fed. Devon went on.

"Daddy was hurting me all the time by the time I was nine or ten years old. I remember riding to hospitals so far away. I hurt so much and my parents drove so far away. They kept telling me to keep quiet when we got to each hospital. They made me practice a story before we got to each hospital. I got pretty good at telling doctors what my parents told me to say. My father always told me that if I told the truth about how I got hurt, only bad things could happen. Adults wouldn't believe me and they would punish me further for lying to them. My father kept drinking more and the battles with my mother happened almost every night. They always talked about me in their fights. None of it was very nice. I thought they could be much happier if I ran away. I tried that once. The police found me a couple hours later. I didn't hide good. My punishment was back to the closet, but Billy made me drink something really bad and that caused another trip to a hospital. Most of the time, after that, my father made me drink Tobasco sauce in the closet. It would make me throw up and cough a lot, but we didn't have to go to the hospital. I was happy we didn't have to go to the hospital."

"You are doing great, Devon. If you want to break, just tell us. I know how hard it is to talk about this." Shana McDonough leaned down and talked to Devon.

"Oh." Devon's eyes lit up. "Did your parents do bad things to you?" She asked the District Attorney innocently.

"No...no, I meant I...I can imagine how you must feel." The D.A. stumbled at midfield. Shana tried again. "Do you want to break, Devon?" Shana asked, fully embarrassed.

"No, ma'am. I'm O.K." Devon missed the blunder. "When I was eleven, I think, my father made me start doing things to him that made me sick. I was so hungry most of the time and he would come into my room at night with big pieces of cake or sandwiches. I had to put my mouth around him for a few minutes and then I would get the cake or sandwich. He told me that all the other girls had to do the same thing for their fathers, but I never asked anyone else. I didn't think he was right. My mother came in to the room once and ran out. They fought about what he was doing that night, but he kept coming to my room at night and my mother never came back." Devon froze the adults present in Room 202. At every turn in the details unfolding, the group expected Devon to cry from the depths of her toes. They all wanted her to, because they could then join her. Devon didn't cry. The recollections came from somewhere no one could find.

"After I turned twelve, my father raped me. I know what that is. He got hurt bad that year. Somebody beat him up pretty bad. Things got easy for a few months when he couldn't do anything. Slowly, the visits began again at night. He made me swallow him all the time. When he got his strength back and most of his wounds healed, he changed for the worse. I knew he blamed my mother and me for the beating. He was convinced that I told somebody about the things he did. He screamed at my mother all the time about that. The first night he came at me, I thought he was there to have me do the other thing. He climbed onto the bed and told me that I was old enough to fulfill all my obligations as a daughter. He pulled my underpants off and spread my legs. He was so strong and he said I had to do these things. I know it hurt, but the other stuff was worse. Sometimes, he brought the dog piles in the house just 'cause he was drunk and smeared them all over my face. If he thought I sassed him, I got dragged outside and he mashed the dog piles in my face. When he pushed himself inside me, it didn't last long and he was gone for the rest of the night. He used to push his fingers in there and sometimes he put other things in there." Devon stopped.

"What other things, Devon?"

"I remember a plunger handle one time. He sometimes got so drunk that his stuff didn't work for him. My father would climb up on me and start swearing. He told me that it was my fault and he pushed other stuff into me. I know what he was doing was wrong, but he left me alone after we did the sex stuff. I knew that I didn't have to go in the closet or starve if I did the sex stuff." Devon watched the stunned group. The twelve year-old girl was driving the boat.

"Where was Kirsten during the "sex stuff?" The detective had lost his highly polished game plan.

"My mother seemed to ignore the room. When I would rest in my own closet, my mother often opened the door to bark some orders at me. The room had nothing but a bed. I made my closet my room because I could keep my rodeo magazines in there and I could get used to being in a closet so that when I got locked in another closet, it wasn't as bad. My mother always had bruises."

"About six months ago, my father came into my room and told me that we were going to make a movie. He handcuffed my hands to the top of the bed frame. Then he put a bandana or headband around my eyes. I couldn't see anything. I never thought about death, except all the times I wanted to kill myself. I was convinced that my parents would be happier if I wasn't around. The blindfold scared me. I thought that my father was going to kill me. He didn't. He took off my clothes and then I heard the door to the room open. Someone else was in the room. It had to be my mother because no one ever came to our house. I heard someone in the room, but that person didn't speak. I heard something that sounded like a video recorder or camera. They had those at school so the sounds were pretty familiar. I knew we didn't have a camera like that, 'cause I never saw one in our house. We never took any pictures. We didn't have a family album. There were some pictures of Billy Jr. around for a few years, but they disappeared after awhile."

"My father never spoke to the person in my room. He started to run his hands up and down my arms and front. He never did that before. He was making more noise than I could remember. During the sex stuff, I used to think about anything else, so I thought a lot about Anna at school. She was my friend. Sometimes I would bleed a lot when my father did stuff to me. The blindfold was making me sick. I got so scared. I tried to tell him that, but he kept doing things. When he finished, I felt something else go up into me. I tried to tell him again. He told me to be quiet again. Then I threw up all over myself. He swore at me and told me that we would do this all over again because I ruined it."

"The one person left the room. I knew it was my mother because I knew her smell. My father left me handcuffed to my bed with vomit covering my stomach and chest. I didn't have any clothes on. I was able to slide the blindfold off by moving my head up and down across the mattress. Then, I saw the video camera standing next to the bed. A little red light was flashing. I didn't know if it was on. My father came back later and the same stuff started. The blindfold was put back up on my face. Two people were in the room again. Someone wiped off the vomit. My father got on top of me again. Then it was over." Devon took some water.

No one in the room moved. The investigative team could barely breathe. Cody Law tried to find Cadrell Easley, but everyone steered clear of eye contact with anyone. Devon's testimony induced the individuals in the room to place their own children in Devon's seat. The testimony brought every case that was tossed aside for reasons of convenience or difficulty back to the fold. Police thought about how many standard answers or trivial calls they may have dismissed with something like Devon's nightmare occurring behind the grateful farewells of a marital misunderstanding or a nuisance domestic call. The DCFS representative wanted nothing more to do with fieldwork. Shana McDonough started to plan the first meeting with the Chief of Police in Castle Rock. Those thoughts were brief. Shana had to excuse herself. The graphic nature of the testimony had physical effects on the District Attorney.

The case against Billy Don Barrett was locked. Devon's testimony would seal it. The District Attorney's office even had the videotapes. The professional side of Shana McDonough couldn't help from salivating at the devastating testimony about to drop directly on Billy Don Barrett. Shana couldn't keep the professional focus. Her own father's image raced across her mind. She was reminded of the days they spent sailing and sipping red and blue snow cones at the Fourth of July parade. The unique bond that linked a daughter to her father was like no other bond. Shana wanted to call her father just to make sure he was still there. Devon was just a child...Shana tried to reach back into the professional mode. It wasn't there anymore. She excused herself, expeditiously. There were no explanations. Everyone knew.

"Devon." The silence had left everyone to private thoughts, which proved worse than the testimony, itself. "What was Billy doing this morning when the police arrived?" The detective moved ahead. The tape was more telling than anyone from the D.A.'s office had hoped for, from a legal perspective. The chilling testimony embodied a cataclysmic image of the anti-Christ. The haunting, calm details were unnerving, almost metaphysical on a Satanic level.

"Billy Don was going to make me do the sex with him, this morning. Most of the time, he only came at night. But, since they started with that camera and I'm at home all the time, Billy just comes in when he feels like it and starts doing the sex thing with me. Sometimes, Mommy runs the camera and sometimes, she doesn't." Devon stopped and looked back at the detective.

"Did Billy Don rape you this morning, Devon?" The policeman asked.

"You mean, the stuff you'all came in on this morning?" Devon knew they caught Billy with his pants down. She looked a bit confused.

"Did Billy Don Barrett complete penetration this morning?"

"What is your problem?" Cody shot up. The sudden movement jolted the group.

"You've got a tape for Christ's sake. You broke in on the act. The doctors can confirm everything Devon said and you ask her about penetration? Are you enjoying this detective?" The bitter question hung. Cody didn't back off. The detective stood up with Cody's remark. The two men stood inches from the other.

"I've got two daughters of my own." The detective stated under a heavy chest, pumping with anger.

"Then act like it." Cody barked. The grown-ups were falling apart.

"Mr. Law." Shana McDonough intervened. "The records need to establish exactly what happened on the day of the arrest. There was no intent to prolong the details that your daughter has so courageously provided."

Shana McDonough turned to the detective, a man in his mid-forties and unaware of the lines crossed. Detective Robert Wright had been raised in a bible-belt community north of Des Moines, Iowa. The product of a strict religious background, Wright found himself questioning Devon's culpability to her own environment. The graphic details were given so sedately and collectedly, the jaded detective was trained to question the source.

"Detective Wright." Shana continued. "If you cannot complete the interview in short order, then I will replace you, now. We have ample testimony to hang Billy Don Barrett. If Devon's testimony has made you uncomfortable, look to your own failures from the beginning. Otherwise, excuse yourself now. I have never been privy to such a display of strength from someone so young. My office officially stopped working for Billy Don Barrett when I took office. I suspect the police department may do well to follow suit. I believe that you have a choice, Detective. Are there any reasons to protect Mr. Barrett, any further? Any hesitation will be an answer, not acceptable. Detective?"

The District Attorney would not back away, now. Shana knew the process of reconciliation had to begin in earnest without judicial or moral delays. They all owed Devon much more than that. Shana thought again about the stupidity of claiming to be in a position to know how Devon felt.

"My apologies to Mr. Law, Devon and the District Attorney. I have no agenda, Ms. McDonough. I am sorry for my insensitivity. Do you accept my apology, Mr. Law?" Detective Wright almost sounded convincing.

"Ask my daughter, Detective." Cody replied back.

"Devon?" Detective Wright turned to Cody's daughter.

"What?" Devon asked. The adults had not held her attention. Devon wanted to find Gunner and talk about Lane Frost.

"I am sorry for the last question. It was kind of harsh. Will you forgive me?" The Detective asked.

"Does that mean we're done?" Devon countered.

"Almost."

"Then I forgive you." Devon just wanted to leave.

"I have no more questions." Detective Wright declared, although he had planned on others. "Does anyone have any questions for Devon at this point?" Most shook their head. There would be no more questions. Shana McDonough had one.

"My wish is to get Devon away from the deposition as fast as possible. The testimony will be heard in court and I can confidently assure you, the tape will not be challenged. The one remaining variable in the case is Kirsten." The District Attorney sat down next to Devon.

"Is there anything else you can tell us about your mother and her involvement in what Billy Don did? I guess what I am looking for is something definitive or concrete that triggered her to snap. Do you think Devon, the constant fear of violence from Billy Don brought your mother to a point where she couldn't do anything? It is not uncommon for men to literally brainwash their spouse by physical intimidation. These women lose all self-respect and give up. They become puppets for the men they fear. Was that your mother, Devon?" Shana McDonough waited for the anticipated answer.

The District Attorney wanted the answer on tape from Devon. Shana pulled back and lingered. Cody waited and watched. Devon stared at both for a prolonged, unsettling period of time.

"My mother was supposed to protect me." Devon's eyes filled for the first time during the entire deposition.

"She didn't protect me. I saw the way she looked at Billy Jr. Maybe I did kill him. Maybe I pushed his head under the water and held him there." Devon began to sob. Tears rolled off her cheeks like a broken damn. Devon's breath became hysterical, a labored sequence of hyperventilation. Devon's words came from a broken heart.

"Mommy let Billy slap me all the time. She didn't care if I had any food. She never talked to me. I wanted someone to talk to so bad and it was supposed to be my mother. She was supposed to hold me when I cried. No one held me when I cried. I cried in the closets. I cried on the way to school. I cried underneath my father. Mommy was supposed to help me. She wasn't there. She was my MOTHER!" Devon screamed at Shana McDonough. Shana couldn't move or speak. "She was my mother." Devon's voice tailed off and fell into the strained sorrow that had now been exhumed. Devon buried her eyes in a blanket for a moment. She couldn't regain control. Devon looked up to find Cody.

"I wish you had been there, Cody." Devon cried so loud. The words were not meant to hurt Cody.

"We're done here, Ms. McDonough." Cody cradled his daughter while she let out the years of wondering whether anyone would come. Her crying became more pronounced. Cadrell Easley kissed Devon on her head, which was buried in Cody's chest. Cody looked up and Cadrell was crying. Shana McDonough and the detectives packed up the gear and put their papers away. DCFS, the District Attorney and the police left the room and moved down the hospital hallway. They could hear Devon until the elevator doors closed. Shana pulled her fingers away from her ears inside the elevator. She could hardly swallow.

Thirty minutes after the deposition team had pulled out of Room 202, Devon and Cody walked out of the north elevator to the main lobby. Devon ran over to Gunner, who was waiting with Sonny and Olin near the nurse's station fronting the Emergency Room entrance bays. Devon pulled on Gunner's arm and asked about Lane Frost. Gunner saw the bloodshot eyes and the red cheeks.

"Come on, Gunner. You said that you would tell me about Lane Frost. You said you knew him real good." Devon tried to jar his memory.

"Lane, who?" Gunner curled his eyelids and winked at Devon.

"Gunnerrrrrr..." Devon begged. Gunner scooped her up and skipped out the front entrance. The afternoon had turned sunny and the Colorado pine trees filled the air with a magic scent. Cody watched Devon run after Gunner and tackle him by the manicured gardens just inside the main drive. Devon was attempting to pound Gunner into submission by repeated little fists on his back. She kept repeating...

"You promised, Gunner. You promised." In a couple minutes, they were sitting on the grass on a cool fall day. Gunner was full into a Lane Frost story. Devon sat Indian style, mesmerized by the accounts from the old cowboy. Sonny Moore walked over to Cody and asked.

"How'd it go upstairs?"

"Rough, man. Thanks for asking. Where's Martin?" Cody looked around.

"I think he found his future wife in a nurse's uniform. She keeps telling him that she is engaged, but he remains unfazed. He tells her that engagements are designed to be broken or else they wouldn't exist." Sonny enjoyed the put-downs directed at Olin.

"What does that mean?" Cody watched his daughter.

"Who knows, Cody? That D.A. was looking for you." Sonny pointed to the lobby.

Cody Law walked into the main lobby from the courtyards outside. The sunshine felt great. Shana McDonough wanted to say thank you.

"Your daughter was magnificent, Mr. Law." Shana beamed.

"People describe a theatrical performance as magnificent, Ms. McDonough." Cody remarked.

"You know what I mean, Mr. Law. Devon was extremely brave. You should be very proud, Mr. Law."

"I am very proud. Thank you." Cody accepted.

"Billy Don Barrett and Kirsten will be arraigned tomorrow morning, ten o'clock, at the Douglas County Municipal building in the main courtroom, first floor." The District Attorney reached out for Cody's hand. They shook hands. Shana squeezed hard.

"I'll be there alone, Ms. McDonough."

"There will be a custody hearing in the same courtroom at one o'clock. Devon does not need to be present for the hearing. My office will begin a Dependency and Neglect action against the Barretts. The state will file a motion for termination of parental rights for Kirsten. Billy Don Barrett has no legal rights to Devon based on the birth certificate. Parental rights are not born from time. If the probability is high for the parents or custodians of the child to be judged incapable to be a fit and proper parent for the next five years, then the judge will grant the motion for termination of the parental rights. The probability is not high in this case, it is certain. The motion will attest to the fact that you are the biological father, so the judge may simply claim the mother's rights are terminated. The real father's rights override all others. Adoption is not an issue. Billy never adopted Devon because he thought he was the father all along. You can address permanent termination of the mother's rights at a later date. After tomorrow, you will have five years to figure it out. I'm sorry it was so rough upstairs today." Shana smiled at Cody Law.

"Thank you, Ms. McDonough. Call me Cody." Cody went to meet his daughter outside.

"Cody." Shana tried before they parted. Cody stopped and turned around. "Judges like women in the picture. If you can somehow show the judge that a woman is in the picture, that will help your cause."

"I didn't know that I had a cause?" Cody commented.

"You never know in a courtroom, especially given the track record from this town. Just something, for your information." Shana McDonough walked out with Cody Law.

* * *

~CHAPTER V~

Devon stayed with Cody at the Castle Rock Hotel. Devon had never stayed in a hotel before. Cody ordered cheeseburgers, fries, and ice cream sundaes with extra chocolate sauce. Devon watched two movies with all the cowboys and they almost cleaned out the Coke machine down the hall. Devon fell asleep near the end of the second movie. Cody covered his daughter with blankets and tucked her in next to him. The day to beat all others ended in peace. Sonny and Olin retired to another room. Gunner called Jacquie after midnight in Colorado. Gunner thought it might be wise to expect a couple houseguests very soon.

The municipal building in Castle Rock began the day buzzing with local reporters, media contingents from Denver, national morning shows, the endless complement of pseudo news and entertainment reporters, and representatives from the PRCA and Pro Rodeo Sports News. Devon stayed with Sonny and Olin for the morning. Cody told Devon that he had to go to court and would be back in time for lunch. The whole group would travel to Steamboat Springs late in the afternoon, as soon as the second court proceedings were concluded.

The weekend rodeo in Steamboat would be Cody's last chance to qualify for the NFR Finals. Cody stood in sixteenth position going into the final weekend before the rankings were certified. The short-go was a must and a top five finish would likely put him over the top. Three bull riders holding totals ahead of Cody were injured. The finish would be very close. Cody had to compete in Steamboat Springs. Devon trembled with excitement when Cody announced their itinerary.

Gunner and Cody drove to the arraignment. Interviews with the rookie bull riding sensation combined with the egregious nature of the crimes became the focal point of the media on the courthouse grounds. Child abuse cases garner abnormal media attention. Cases that fall through the cracks for so long elicit a feeding frenzy for zealous reporters looking to uncover the road to notoriety. Cody refused to talk about anything related to the arraignment. Gunner paved the way through many of the reporters and asked for some space. Shana McDonough had two Assistant District Attorneys rescue Cody and Gunner from the reporters. Most of the reporters followed the group into the courtroom. Castle Rock justice was not accustomed to a full house. The courtroom hummed with the capacity crowd.

Cody and Gunner were given front row seats, courtesy of the District Attorney. Billy Don Barrett and Kirsten Barrett were led into the courtroom in shackles and orange county jail scrubs. The courthouse security deputies were armed and stood guard at the exits. All other persons allowed inside the courtroom were unarmed, including uniformed officers from the Castle Rock

Police Department. None too happy about participating in trials where the Castle Rock officers viewed themselves as sitting uniformed targets, the police department turnout proved substantial. Many Castle Rock officers, like Cadrell Easley, had been asked to back away from the 222 Gilbert Street domestic disturbance calls. Kirsten and Billy Don sat down next to their court-appointed attorneys. The defense table was no more than eight feet from Cody Law. Neither defendant feigned any emotion. Kirsten kept her head down at all times. Kirsten's body language spoke clearly, as in a woman drowning in terminal languor. Billy Don scanned the room and seemed to marvel at the newly anointed notoriety the pair had garnered. Gunner never took his eyes from Cody Law.

"Hear ye, hear ye." The court bailiff called out. "The State District Court for Douglas County and all surrounding counties is now in session. Judge William Sharpe presiding."

The bailiff stood erect and slammed the gavel. Judge William Sharpe was young in terms of receiving a judicial appointment. Sharpe made a name for himself in Denver as a prosecutor and ran for the state senate at the age of thirty-eight. He lost a close election, but landed on the bench with a new Governor and a new administration in 1988. Sharpe was white, forty-one years old and educated locally. Sharpe graduated from the University of Colorado in Boulder and went to law school in Greeley at Northern Colorado. The judge grew up in Fort Collins. Judge William Sharpe had three children under the age of ten. Shana McDonough had hoped for a judge with children, young children.

The bailiff read the charges against the two defendants. The charges were identical for each defendant. Billy Don Barrett and Kirsten Barrett were charged with one count each of assault, sexual assault and sexual assault on a child. The charges were Class-3 felonies that carried a maximum of five years for each count. Complicity sealed the direction for the District Attorney concerning Kirsten. The state would be seeking concurrent sentences or the maximum of fifteen years cumulative for each defendant. The judge asked the defendants if they understood the charges. They did. They were asked how they would plead. Not guilty on each charge was announced by the defendants.

The court appointed attorneys for Kirsten and Billy Don conferred at the defense table. Edward Steinway, the young public defender assigned to Billy Don Barrett rose and asked the court for the bond to remain at $10,000 each.

"The bail, you honor, set by the arresting officers at the time of the arrest was $10,000. In Douglas County, we do not stack bonds. Class-3 felony bond is commensurate with $10,000. The defense contends that each defendant is a long time resident of Castle Rock. They have families and relatives living in the area, and both defendants represent non-flight risks." The defense attorney read from a file he pulled from his briefcase.

"Kirsten Barrett has no prior criminal record and Billy's minor misdemeanor offenses do not personify the profile implied by unattainable bond. Neither defendant resisted arrest. The bond was set at $10,000 and should remain at $10,000." Edward Steinway returned to his seat. Shana McDonough took the floor.

"Your honor, the defendant's flight risk, while certainly questionable considering Kirsten and Billy Don Barrett pulled up stakes and left their home in an effort to avoid detection prior to their incarceration, is not the issue. The grievous nature of the charges and the sanctity of the laws we embrace preclude anything but the maximum bond in this case. Child abuse cases stand alone in the criminal justice system. They do not provide for anything less than a fair trial for the defendants, but they warrant special consideration in the bond process."

"The state believes that the case before this court cannot be filtered with the double talk of flight risk and community standing. The evidence will produce a pattern of ignored red flags and a system that failed one young child over and over again. Allowing Kirsten and Billy Don Barrett to walk on a " slap me on the wrist " bond is another way of telling Devon that her case is insignificant, a message the system has told her all along."

"The state asks the court for the bond to be set at one million dollars each. Anything less insults the children we are prevailed upon to protect. Our children do not ask to come into the world. As adults, we bring them here and by doing so accept the responsibility of making their lives secure and promising. When that trust is violated, consequences must follow. The consequence we address today is bond. Please send a message reinforcing parental responsibility and the consequences associated with anything less."

"Of course, here we are not simply addressing the dereliction of parenting skills. The defendants are accused of brutally violating a child. I have one young daughter. I think about what I will tell her when the case before us is concluded. I hope I can look her in the eye when that time comes. Thank you, your honor." Shana McDonough concluded.

"Your, Honor." The defense attorney for Billy Don Barrett stood up. The judge nodded. "The District Attorney is an eloquent speaker, but the facts remain unchanged. These are Class-3 felony charges for first offenders and the bond should be set accordingly. Our system is not dictated by grand-standing, however polished the oration may be. "

"Thank you, council." Judge William Sharpe remarked. "I do not require a lesson on how the bond process is admonished. Each case is reviewed separately and I have been to the mat more times than you care to count. The bond set at the time of the arrest is often temporary. They used to teach that to first year law students." Judge Sharpe was not happy about being lectured by junior PD's. "Bond is set at $500,000 for each defendant. The trial date will be three weeks from today. We are adjourned."

The onslaught of media attention to child abuse cases and high profile custody cases is intrusive and painful, often subjective and gratuitous. In Douglas County, the press found both. Judges come up for re-election and do not want to address a front-page case with leniency. Courtroom cameras place judicial decisions in the court of public opinion. Child abuse cases grab headlines and every judge is aware of the ramifications associated with soft bonds and flight. Countless organizations, such as The National Council on Child Abuse and Family Violence, Prevent Child Abuse America and the Court Appointed Special Advocate (CASA), monitor pending high profile cases. These and other organizations address liberal rulings by sitting judges and provide a myriad of support mechanisms aimed at unseating the same liberal judges at election time.

Judicial rulings have much to do with perception and fallout. During the election process, judges do not want to explain any specific leniency on bond hearings, only to have the released defendant commit the same crimes while free on bail. Analogous to the child abuse bond issues would be the drunk driver standing before the court. A lenient approach to the drunk driver may find the same driver back in court before the same judge, only days later. This time, however, the charges include drunk driving again and vehicular homicide. The victim's family will be seeking answers. The case against Billy Don Barrett and Kirsten was no exception.

The arraignment took less than fifteen minutes. Kirsten was led out first. She looked at her parents, seated near the front of the courtroom. A stranger now occupied the shell of what their daughter had been. Kirsten did not cry. Estranged from her parents years before, Carl and Vicky Myers felt more like they were attending a wake than a hearing. Cody watched and waited for some recognition or some validation from the girl he knew so long ago. Cody found neither. As he waited in vain, a graveled voice summoned.

"Hey, Cody Law." Cody turned quickly, surprised and alarmed. "Now that I know Devon is your daughter, I don't feel so bad. In fact, the whole thing was kinda' cool." Billy Don Barrett glared back across the front row. "Devon was a pain in the ass and some kids just don't much care for discipline. Course, you wouldn't know about that, would you?"

Barrett pulled away from the court security to elicit the response intended. Cody Law did not wait to evaluate his response. Cody leapt over the meticulously stained partition and lunged for Billy Don Barrett. The courtroom became a seedy West Side alley on a cold Chicago night. Every drop of adrenaline raced to Cody's heart and the man in the orange jumpsuit was going to die by Cody's hand. The sudden explosion of activity triggered a logistical circus. Armed court security guards and Castle Rock Police officers wrestled Barrett away from the defense table. Cody pushed forward, undaunted by the chairs and tables impeding his progress. Gunner shadowed Cody's thrust, and tackled his friend before a vigilante confrontation could evolve. McGarrity's savvy premonitions proved frightfully accurate. Barrett was shuttled out of the courtroom laughing. Gunner held Cody down for the time it took to remove Barrett from the courtroom. Judge William Sharpe was pounding his gavel so hard the stem broke from the mallet. Gunner pinned Cody to the floor like a wrestler looking for the takedown points.

"You have Devon. Don't give her up before she has a father." Gunner pulled Cody back by the hair. They lay on the floor beneath the defense table.

"You were looking for Barrett to do this. I saw it in your eyes when we got here. Settle down, Cody. This is over. You did just what Barrett wanted you to do. Now, deal with the judge and hope he doesn't pull Devon right out from under you." Gunner released Cody.

Two police officers secured Cody as he stood up. Cody held his hands up to signify there would be nothing more. Barrett was ushered out instantly. The judge was vehement.

"Bailiff, remind the participants. My courtroom does not tolerate an outburst of this magnitude!" Cody was jostling to compose himself.

"Your honor." Shana McDonough took charge. "The defendant, Billy Don Barrett incited the response. Mr. Law reacted instinctively and the matter was defused. The State will move to gag Mr. Barrett in future proceedings if the behavior is repeated. The State will also be more cognizant to the delicate nature of the charges and the individuals related to those charges. My office will accept full responsibility for any further repercussions from Mr. Law and the family members in attendance. We will fully concur with the court's efforts to ban the family members from the proceedings in the event of any repeated attempts to disrupt the court regardless of the defendant and the content of his incantations." Shana McDonough stood before Judges William Sharpe with respect and humility.

"This court will not accept anything less, Ms. McDonough." The judge ordered.

"Understood, your honor." McDonough responded.

"We are adjourned until the trial date." Judge William Sharpe relented. "Mr. Law, control your emotions, sir. This may be a difficult trial to attend. Check the anger at the door and let us do our jobs. Is that clear, Mr. Law?"

"Very clear, your honor." Cody humbly replied. The judge stood up and left the room. Shana McDonough closed her eyes and released the air in her lings that stood her up like a new Marine recruit on the first day of basic training. Cody left the courtroom.

* * *

The custody hearing began promptly at 2:00 p.m. Judge William Sharpe returned as the presiding judge. The state began by filing a motion for the termination of parental rights against Devon Barrett. Cody Law filed a petition alleging and proving Kirsten to be an unfit mother (Sec 19-11-105 CRS), thus terminating Kirsten's parental rights.

No motion was required to address Billy Don Barrett's parental rights. There were no parental rights. Billy Don was not the biological father. Blood tests and the birth certificate confirmed those facts. Billy never adopted Devon because he was told that Devon was his natural child. In his marriage, Billy had no reason to raise a paternity issue concerning Devon. If a wife lies to her husband concerning the accuracy of the birth father, a surrogate father who believes that he is the real father, has no parental rights under the law regardless of the time spent raising the child. The biological father retains all parental rights over a minor unless or until those rights are terminated by a court. Among those rights is the right to custody.

Without a contest from Kirsten, and the pending case against Kirsten would preclude any effective contest, the court has full authority to waive the mother's consent or co-operation in deciding what is in the best interest of the child. Cody Law's appointment as Devon's legal custodian seemed certain. The proceedings and resulting court orders would eliminate the stepfather from the mix, permanently. Judge William Sharpe spoke after the formal motions were filed and there were no objections from any relatives or agencies.

"Mr. Law, this case is a no-brainer. You are the natural father. The blood tests and the written evidence confirm that. Kirsten Barrett, as the child's mother, failed at the most assumptive level. The argument could not be made to claim that Kirsten is a fit mother. It is apparent that you have the financial means to support the child. The Department of Children and Family Services does not object to appointing you as Devon's legal guardian. Devon has given a statement approving the appointment. We have all the ingredients for a slam-dunk, Mr. Law. However, I have some issues to sort out." Judge Sharpe turned the pages on his desk. Cody Law felt the floor begin to give way. This could not be happening, Cody thought. They could not invent another way to hurt Devon. Cody had believed they had found them all.

"We work in soft science, Mr. Law, when it revolves around children and custody." Judge Sharpe continued. "There is an element of abandonment here that bothers me. There is a question as to whether you legally abandoned the child? How many times during the years, Mr. Law, did you make any attempts to keep track of the child or contribute financially to the child's well being?"Judge Sharpe took off his glasses and rubbed his eyes waiting for an answer.

"The information given to me by Kirsten following her pregnancy was very explicit." Cody turned to Shana McDonough in disgust. The District Attorney did not return the glance. Cody addressed the judge.

"I was told to stay away, your honor. Kirsten married the man she wanted to be with. Kirsten told me that they were doing well. Kirsten's life was falling out the way she wanted it to fall. She wrote to me after Devon was born and told me to stay away from her forever. Any attempts to contact her would jeopardize her marriage. She told me not to worry. They would be terrific. Her last line was to have a nice life. I respected Kirsten's wishes. I saved the letter if you would like to see it. I would have to instruct my attorney in Chicago to retrieve the letter at my residence." Cody continued.

"I did not make any attempts to contact Kirsten or the child because I was asked not to. Kirsten knew where to contact me and I heard nothing. At the first sign of trouble, Kirsten could have reached me and I would have been there immediately. If there are questions as to the importance of my relationship with Devon, then I submit my resume from the last six months. I abandoned no one! I was asked to back-off and I respected those wishes." Cody rode a fine line between antagonizing the judge and making his point.

"Mr. Law, how can I not consider the actions in the courtroom this morning when granting custody of Devon. You are a single man and have never raised a child. My first introduction to you is an explosion of anger. Mr. Law, you disregarded every rule of the courtroom and physically went after another man. I am only assuming that your intent was to hurt Mr. Barrett? However valiant and self-gratifying the attack may have been, how am I not to question your ability to rationally handle raising a child? Can you give me some direction here, Mr. Law?" Judge Sharpe waited again. Shana McDonough was flabbergasted at the direction of the questions.

"Your honor." The District Attorney interrupted. "Is this line of questioning necessary or appropriate considering the extenuating circumstances at the close of the arraignment this morning and the abominable, degrading climate provided by the child's mother and stepfather?"

"The question was directed to Mr. Law, Ms. McDonough. However, the abominable past home life for Devon is all the more reason to do everything possible to avoid more of the same. The question still stands, Mr. Law." Judge Sharpe was sincere, not condescending.

"The question doesn't stand very well, you honor." Cody began to answer.

"You ask me how you can not consider my actions this morning as relevant in determining Devon's legal custodian. Consider them all, your honor. I am Devon's father. I have come to know Devon over the past few months. I have come to know the nightmare of her life. I have seen her bedroom on Gilbert Street. There are prison cells more appealing."

"I was present when the police arrested Billy Don Barrett and Kirsten. They were raping my daughter while she was handcuffed to a bed frame. Devon's mother was filming Billy Don Barrett mount her twelve-year old daughter. Judge, a twelve-year old girl. The mother and stepfather had stripped and bound a seventh grader. While Billy Don Barrett struggled to stick his penis into my child, Devon's mother filmed every horrific moment. Billy could watch the rapes whenever he desired."

"I sat through Devon's deposition to the District Attorney's office for the upcoming trial. Devon spoke of Billy making her drink urine and smearing dog feces in her face for arriving home two minutes late from school. Barrett used to starve Devon and then bring food into her room at night. If she provided oral sex, she got to eat. She was ten at the time." Cody stopped to compose his voice. His hands were visibly shaking and his voice was cracking.

"This is the man who turns to me in court this morning, and tells me that now that he knows Devon was not his daughter, the things he did to her were fun, kind of cool are the exact words Barrett used. Your honor, I want you to consider what I did in court this morning. I want you to consider every word and action that fell out in front of you this morning. The worst he's going to get is fifteen years for what he did to Devon. Sit next to your child tonight and then question what I did. Re-read Devon's deposition and then sit next to your child tonight. Fifteen years and he was laughing at us. I'm not certain about what I would have done to Barrett, had I been able to reach him. I will stand up for my daughter. I can promise you that. I hope you damn well consider what a father will do when his child is brutalized, degraded and humiliated. No one in this town has ever stood up to Billy Don Barrett. Devon asked for help and everyone told Devon to stop lying. They all kissed Barrett's tail and talked about football in high school. Well, he stopped playing years ago and Devon paid the price." Cody sat down. Judge William Sharpe looked across the courtroom at Cody Law.

"Mr. Law, do not attack Mr. Barrett in the future. You are giving him exactly what he wants. Do not put me in a position again to give Mr. Barrett what he wants. According to these documents, the child will be raised in California on the ranch of Mr. Gunner McGarrity. Mr. Law will establish immediate residency in California on the grounds of Mr. McGarrity's ranch.

Are these facts correct?" The judge asked Shana McDonough.

"Yes, your honor."

"Mr. Law, we have what is called Interstate Compact. Here in Colorado, we will conduct an investigation as to the competency and safety of Devon's new environment. Sometimes, these investigations take a year to complete. Nothing is final until I receive a favorable finding concerning Devon and her new home. I am granting the motion for you to become Devon Barrett's legal custodian, as of today. The motion has been given priority on this docket to protect the child and expedite the matter. I am satisfied that Mr. Law will have the best interest of the child in mind at all times. May I suggest Mr. Law, that you designate in writing, a successor as legal guardian should you become incapacitated. Given your present occupation, my suggestion may be wise to heed. Have your attorney execute a superabundance of prudence. Ask him what that is. Are we through with this matter for today counselor?"

"Yes, your honor." Shana replied.

"My father was a steer wrestler out of Wyoming when he was younger. The name of Gunner McGarrity is very familiar to me, PRCA World Champion bull-rider in 1971, I believe." The judge recalled.

"1970, your honor." Gunner chimed in. A big smile rode his face from ear to ear. "Was your father Walter Sharpe?"

"Yes he was. My dad died a couple years ago. He always told us that next to his family, his only other true love was rodeo." Judge Sharpe thought of his father.

"You are lucky his love for rodeo came after the family. Most times, your honor, it's the other way around. Cowboys aren't very good at placing priorities in moral order. I knew your father. Walter Sharpe was a good man, a tough man, too. What would Walter Sharpe have done in the courtroom this morning?" Gunner asked.

"You and I both know the answer to that question." Judge Sharpe responded. "Next case."

Gunner took Cody by the arm and they left the courtroom. Judge William Sharpe moved on to the next matter.

Cody, Gunner and Shana McDonough stood on the courthouse steps following the hearing. Shana made a statement to the reporters present and announced that Cody Law would have nothing to say regarding the hearing. Shana told the reporters that Cody had been granted legal custody of his daughter. She explained that Cody wished to spend some time with his daughter and there would be no comments on the upcoming trial. Shana thanked the reporters for their concern and the matter was closed. Shana walked to the parking garage with Cody and Gunner.

"What are your plans for the immediate future?" Shana asked Cody.

"We are going to Steamboat Springs this afternoon. I believe Devon will enjoy her first PRCA rodeo as part of a bull-riding team." Cody smiled.

"The judge and the DCFS are under the impression that you all are taking Devon back to California." Shana remarked.

"We are." Cody agreed. "But, there is the matter of a slight detour. I promised Devon that I would take her to the NFR Finals in Las Vegas in December. I would prefer to bring Devon as the daughter of a contestant."

"Good luck, Mr. Law."

"Can I send you and your family a ticket to the Finals if I qualify?" Cody asked.

"I will expect them." Shana McDonough stepped up and gave a Cody a kiss on the cheek.

"I have no words to thank you." Cody shook his head and held Shana's hands.

"I know, Mr. Law. There are times when my job actually means something. The only sobering factor is that for my job to mean something, your daughter had to endure hell. Feeling good comes with a high price. Cherish your daughter, Mr. Law. They only come by once." Shana McDonough squeezed Cody's hands.

Cody and Gunner drove back to the Castle Rock Hotel. Three rodeo contestants and one former bull-riding champ have little to pack. The early afternoon gave Colorado a good name. Castle Rock was bathed in fading sunlight and the light cloud cover burned a bright orange sky over the western Rocky Mountains. Cody took Devon for a ride, out to the Douglas County fairgrounds. The big vehicle pulled up to the deserted fairgrounds. A couple of deer scurried past the fences, badly in need of some repair. The wind was strong. Cody left his hat in the truck. Devon sat on the hood of the Suburban. Her long curls blew wildly in the wind. Devon put her hands on Cody's shoulders. Cody thought she might blow away.

"Devon, your life is going to change dramatically after today." Cody began. "The one thing that I never really asked, was what you wanted. Everything has been about what I wanted for you. I never asked."

"What are you asking me, Cody?" The voice was still small.

"Is there something I'm missing? Devon, I'm new at this. I just want you to be sure." Cody brushed Devon's hair away from her face. The wind threw it back.

"There has never been anything in my life that I could possibly miss." Devon answered back. Cody could feel the tears in his own eyes. There were no tears in Devon's eyes.

"That's it." Cody smiled. Devon hugged her father. Devon and Cody shared the wind for another ten minutes. It was time to return to the hotel and get ready to head up to Steamboat. Cody made a short stop at the District Attorney's office. Devon and Cody gave an envelope to Shana McDonough's secretary.

"Please have Ms. McDonough give this note to Billy Don Barrett. It is very important." Cody instructed the District Attorney's secretary. Cody and Devon were back at the Castle Rock Hotel in minutes.

"Let's get out of here." Gunner was waiting none too patiently. "We have a draw to catch."

The ride took the entourage up Interstate 25, through Denver, catching Interstate 70 West. The mountains grew with breathtaking beauty as the Suburban passed through Dillon, approaching Winter Park, Breckenridge, Keystone and Vail. Cody remembered Kirsten talking about concerts at Red Rocks, the nearby natural rock formations used for decades as a venue for many big-name concerts. An exit sign directing traffic to Red Rocks brought back the night Kirsten and Cody drank red wine and listened to the Eagles inside Diamond Head.

Devon rode in the front seat with the window down most of the way. The cold rushing wind blew color into Devon's sallow cheeks. Devon stared at Cody more than the Rocky Mountain postcard winding across her eyes. Cody took Highway 131 North at the Wolcott exit. Steamboat Springs was ninety minutes north. Gunner and Olin sat in the back seat yapping about bulls and draws. Sonny Moore tried to spit the Copenhagen in his mouth out the back window and found most of it back on his lap. The group arrived in Steamboat as the sun disappeared behind the western slopes.

Steamboat Springs holds special meaning to cowboys. First settled in 1876, the town was named for a pulsating geyser that shot hot mineral water in the air every few minutes. The first ski runs were cut in 1958 on Storm Mountain, later renamed Mt. Werner following the tragic death of local Olympian Buddy Werner who died in an avalanche in Switzerland.

In January, the eighteenth annual Cowboy Downhill convened in Steamboat Springs. Rodeo stars past and present compete for charity from the slopes of Sunshine Peak to Rendezvous Saddle. The Bear River Bar and Grill is ground zero to soothing the bruised bodies and bruised egos of the annual visiting cowboys. Romick Rodeo Arena just past the Yampa River in Steamboat Springs played host to dozens of local and sanctioned rodeos throughout the year. Cody Law was interested in one rodeo only.

The upcoming three-day rodeo included Friday and Saturday night preliminary rounds and the finals on Sunday evening. The Steamboat event was often the final chance for many cowboys to reach the NFR finals. Devon sat quietly as Cody pulled up to Steamboat Grand Hotel. Cody opted for the finest hotel in Steamboat Springs. Devon would be treated to the best. Of course, Gunner, Sonny and Olin agreed unilaterally to support Cody's decision to spoil Devon on her first rodeo trip and her first trip anywhere, for that matter

* * *

.

Billy Don Barrett sat in the Douglas County Justice Center for the second night. Prisoners were rare for any extended stays at the Douglas County Justice Center. The Justice Way complex held the capacity to house more than two hundred inmates. The jail cells could be described as luxurious for a jail. The cells were built in an atrium spectrum surrounding the day room. There were separate facilities for men and women. Each cell contained built-in beds, not bed frames extended from the walls with chains. Windows kept the cells bright.

The day room consisted of televisions, card tables and a snack table. Accessibility to the day room was based on the classification of each inmate. Inmates that were not judged as a threat to officers, other inmates or the facility were given access to the day room. Drunk drivers found themselves in jail for the night. Misdemeanor fights often landed bruised egos in jail for the evening until an angry spouse posted bail. Felony inmates were scarce.

Barrett sat alone in the sterile cell. A toilet and two bunks comprised the five-foot by eight-foot cell. Meals were brought in plentiful and surprisingly well prepared. Barrett ate better in jail than he ever did at home. Remorse was absent in Billy. Barrett was convinced his actions warranted nothing more than the loss of custody. At half past nine on the second night in jail for Billy Don Barrett, the Douglas County Justice Center Deputy on duty approached Barrett's cell. Barrett sat up from the sound of the approaching guard.

"A message from the District Attorney, lowlife." The guard had followed the charges and the drift of gossip throughout the Justice Center. The climate was not one of compassion for Billy Don Barrett. The guard handed Billy a note through the bars of the cell. Barrett took the note without reaction.

"What's this?" Barrett asked.

"It's sealed. How the fuck am I supposed to know? I was instructed to deliver the envelope. Maybe it's a bedtime story." The guard walked away.

"Aren't you supposed to open everything first?" Barrett became guarded and suspicious.

"Not when the District Attorney hand delivers it. Flush it down the toilet for all I care. I was told to bring it to you. I brought it to you." The deputy went back to his desk.

Billy Don Barrett ripped open the envelope and pulled out the paper inside. The paper contained a poem. There was no signature. The small typed poem read:

Twas two months before Christmas and all through the county,
not a citizen was fretting the end of your bounty.
The signs had been clear through the whiskey and beers,
the child had awakened despite all those years.
Recall, if you will, the half year that has passed,
and the night that we met, our first and our last.
The Flats after closing, you cradled a binge,
kissing my Louisville slugger whose force made you cringe.
A jaw that was shattered, both hands fared no better,
with heartfelt comeuppance, I write you this letter.
A wounded esteem, she carried to school,
from the callous accounts you deemed kinda' cool.
Remember the Flats, you worthless sick fuck,
Daddy is back, it's the end of your luck!

Billy Don Barrett wadded up the note and threw it against the wall.

"Guard, someone get in here! Guard, guard!" Barrett yelled.

"What is it?" The deputy called out rather annoyed.

"Hey, man I need to talk to Judge Sharpe. I'm getting threats from this guy, Cody Law. He can't fucking do that." Barrett demanded.

"Nobody threatened you. What are you talking about?" The deputy approached the cell.

"This letter, man." Barrett picked up the crumpled note and showed it to the deputy.

"Let me see that." The deputy asked. Billy Don Barrett handed the note through the bars. The deputy stuffed the note in his pocket and walked away.

"Hey, you son of a bitch. Give me that note, back." Barrett was holding the bars and jumping up exasperated.

"What note?" The deputy calmly remarked.

* * *

Friday afternoon, the draws were announced for the first round in Steamboat Springs. Cody, Devon and Gunner walked from the parking lot to the arena for the draw. Devon marveled at the ease of access they enjoyed to the back bowels of the rodeo arena. Devon's only experience with rodeos came at the Douglas County Fairgrounds and even there, most back areas were reserved for contestants and chute laborers, while strictly off-limits to spectators. Devon looked at those men with numbers on their backs as special people. Even the horsemen, the gatekeepers and the stock contractors wore badges that signified they must be special, too. Cody reached down and placed the laminated card around Devon's neck. The fourth of July popped into her eyes. Devon held the card in her hand and stared down. The white card read Cody Law, PRCA Full member, #256400.

Behind Romick Arena, the draw was posted next to the first aid tent. Cody would ride Scatman in the first round. Gunner shrugged his shoulders when Cody told him the bull's name.

"Have you been on this bull before?" Devon asked.

"No, I know that." Cody tried to remember. "I think I saw him down in Texas. It's not like I have so many to remember. Christ, I'm drawing a blank on Scatman. We've entered more than twenty rodeos over the past five or six months. I know I've heard that name before. I just can't remember where."

"It doesn't make any difference, Cody. You know that and I'll bet Devon knows that. If you had ridden the bull before then you could use the experience. Second hand opinions are not what you want. Most of the time, they're dead wrong anyway. With you, the advice may be deliberately misleading. The rookie sensation thing is wearing off. Some of these guys are pissed off because you're doing so well. Some of them think the judges are paving your way to the finals." Gunner had been hearing rumbles.

"That's crap. I can't get a score if I don't stay on." Cody shot back.

"It doesn't matter what they say. The only ones complaining don't have the stones to say it in front of you. They couldn't move up in the rankings if they were glued to the goddamn bulls. It all comes from within, Cody. The bull is a vehicle but the obstacle is your mind. They will never read it in the papers before they see it in your eyes." Gunner had a way to silence a group. "You guys, hungry?" Devon jumped off the fence and grabbed Gunner's hand.

Gunner liked to have his group arrive early. The evening rodeo began at 7:00 p.m. The Suburban pulled into the parking lot at 5:10 p.m. Devon soaked up each step of the day. The gate guards at the parking lot bug-eyed the truck when they read Cody's PRCA Membership Card. The contestant parking lot was close to the arena. Half of the lot was up on grass. Miles of rickety fences rolled over the hills surrounding Romick Arena. Campers and pick-ups jostled with gear. The sound of leather was all around. Devon watched Cody and the others unload everything necessary for the evening. Gunner carried a spare rigging bag with extra ropes, brown and white rosin, gloves, chaps, boots, shirts, jeans and dozens of wraps, Ace bandages, elastic supports, knee braces, wrist braces, elbow pads and the like.

The wind kicked up a bit of dust. The evening shadows fell across Cody,

Sonny and Olin. The view captivated Devon. They were silhouettes against Howelsen Hill, timeless images that beckoned a forgotten era. Each cowboy held a rigging bag over his shoulder. Hats were pulled down tight. It was time to go to work. Cody carried a pair of colorful, embroidered chaps on one shoulder. Sonny and Olin wrapped new bull ropes around their bags. Noisy spurs foretold each step. Cowbells clanged from bull ropes while the swirling dust trailed the convoy. They walked in harmony, almost choreographed by the precise formation they appeared to follow. Each step kicked up more dust. Cody pulled Devon under his arm.

They walked to the covered canopy leading to the arena. The wind told of the exact location of the animals. Cody's long hair hung from the back of his hat. Sonny spit with the wind and the Cope flew ten feet. Crowded pens of bucking horses rumbled with sporadic activity. The horses seemed to know they were first. Everyone knew Gunner and most people knew Cody by now. Devon could stay with Cody until the competition began. The volatility of the animals superceded any reason to allow children behind the gates.

The activity began behind the chutes. Rigging bags stacked against the fences. Ropes hung from the top fence poles and cowboys pulled them with rosin. The cowbells rang through the commotion. Devon sat up high on the platforms adjacent to the chutes as Gunner and Cody introduced her around. Everyone welcomed the young girl they had read so much about. The crossfire of chewing tobacco never fazed the young visitor. Keep your feet moving and your hands to your side when you walk through the back, Gunner told Devon.

"These guys never look where they spit. They turn and spit. It's just rodeo. My daddy always told me to handle it or sit in the stands."

Gunner winked at Devon. Suddenly, Gunner almost jumped out of his boots. Jason and Tyler McGarrity walked through the arena and headed for their father. Gunner jumped off his perch and reunited with his sons. Three men hugged in the arena. After everything that had happened with Cody and Devon, Gunner had missed his boys. They missed their father.

"Are you riding?" Gunner asked Jason. "I didn't see your name on the draw list."

"No, pop." Gunner loved that reference. "I rode in Salt Lake City last weekend. Won a thousand bucks, but you know where I'm at in the standings. My back needs three months rest, so here I am. We read about all the crap in Castle Rock and mom told us what was going on. Hell, every cowboy from Kansas to California is talking about Cody. Tyler met me in Salt Lake City and we drove in last night." Jason stood as an exact replica of Gunner minus the gray hair.

"Cody's been shaking up the old establishment pretty good. We thought you guys could use some moral support." Tyler smiled at his father.

"Cody." Gunner yelled. "Look who's here. Devon, get over here."

Cody and Devon joined Gunner and his sons in the arena. After introductory hugs and handshakes, it was time to get ready. Gunner took Devon over to the P.A. announcer's booth. An old friend called the rodeo. Scully Ryan had been calling rodeos for thirty years. Scully called Gunner's winning ride at the Finals in 1970 and called his last ride when Gunner retired. Scully was thrilled to entertain Devon. Jason and Tyler offered to sit with Devon, but she told them to go help her dad.

The rodeo wound through the events without incident. No major injuries and no major delays were unusual. The bull-riders were up. Spectators hustled back to their seats. The events waited for no one. The most popular and the most dangerous event in rodeo began at 8:40 p.m. Thirty-eight bull riders were on tap for the opening round. The twelve highest scores would move on to the next round. Cody was slated to ride in the tenth spot. A fall tonight would end any hope of making the NFR Finals in Las Vegas.

Cody paced around the back contestant area. He hooked on his spurs and tied off his jeans near the boot. Cody pulled on his chaps and tied them tight. A clean black button down Wrangler shirt came out of the rigging bag. A special pair of lizard boots held the sharpened spurs. The boots weren't expensive, just lucky. Cody rolled up his sleeves, high above the elbow. He tied off the glove using his teeth to attain the right strength. The eighth rider got bucked off in six seconds. Sonny and Olin rode second and fourth. Both failed to reach the horn. One rider had made the horn thus far and the score was marginal. Cody paid no attention to any of the falls or the posted scores. Gunner paid attention to all of it.

Jason and Tyler readied the bull. Scatman weighed nineteen hundred pounds. Jason knew him from Dallas. The bull was unpredictable. Scatman rode to a ninety in Dallas last year, but kicked out of the chute twice last month. The six-year old, black and white menace shook up the riders so bad on both occasions, they didn't last three seconds when they finally put the rides together. Scatman was scary, but Cody didn't know that. A bull can be no more frightening than the knowledge within the rider. Cody climbed up over the bull's back. He straddled the bull but had not touched him yet. Scatman stood up on his back legs. The huge bull's head knocked Cody back onto the platform while Jason, Tyler and Gunner struggled to push the bull back down to all fours. The chute shook with the tremors of a small earthquake. Cody could feel the thunder in the anchored beams of the arena.

Three thousand spectators shot back in their seats from reflex observation. Scatman settled back down. Devon sat on the Public Address table and messed up the papers of Scully Ryan. Ryan pushed the papers on the floor and motioned Devon to move up higher for a better view. Even Scully Ryan couldn't shake the jitters. Something extraordinary was happening in Chute #3.

Gunner took over the rope pull. He laid the handhold across Scatman's back. Gunner motioned for Cody to take his place. Scatman shuffled in the chute. Jason McGarrity held onto Cody's chest. The bull settled. Gunner pulled the handhold into place. Cody straddled the bull. Scatman stood still. Cody lowered his backend onto the bull. His legs curled around Scatman's girth. Cody's legs could feel the tension beneath him, waiting to detonate. Gunner pulled the rope tight. Cody slid his hand into the small opening and began to wrap the rope. Gunner spoke next to Cody's face.

"Everyone knows what you did to find your daughter. There isn't a spectator in the stands tonight that could find fault with skipping this ride, Cody. No one with an ounce of common sense, given what you've been through, could focus on riding this two-ton freight train. Devon's here and you don't have to ride tonight. Every bull rider in this draw would take their daughter and get lost. Give me the word now Cody and you can hold your head up forever."

Gunner worked the wrap and the gate stood still. Cody looked up when uncertainty could kill him. The massive animal shook the chute. Gunner focused on Cody's eyes. There was no more time. A bull rider cannot afford the smallest gap of indecision. Gunner grabbed Cody by the shirt.

"Fuck 'em all, Cody!" Gunner was in Cody's face and under his hat. "I never had an ounce of common sense from the get go. Devon didn't come here to watch you get bucked off some second rate, small town bull. Ride this mother-fucker for ten seconds. Throw in some extra time for your daughter. Finish this, Cody. Half this country goes through life never finishing a thing. They think what we do is fucking nuts. We beg to differ. I'd never trade one eight second ride for any goddamn pension plan. I thought 401K was a fucking cereal. You're not one of them, Cody. You never were. They push keyboards and cell phones because they can't do this! We can't explain this moment, but you can define it. Time to howl, baby, you're daughter is watching! Nod your head and do something no one has ever done before. Do it, now! " Gunner screamed into Cody's ear. The rope was locked and Gunner backed away. Cody tipped his hat and the gate pulled open.

Scatman exploded from the gate. The nineteen-hundred pound, black and white, motley-faced Simental-Brahma cross with big horns set no pattern. A big bull isn't supposed to leave the ground with such an athletic spin. He spun left, jumped twice and kicked in a big circle. Cody stayed high, while the crowd sensed something special. The rookie was out of his element. Scatman spun twice more left and then reversed his spin. Gunner almost fell off the platform, yelling at Cody to stay high. Scatman gained speed and Cody remained high. Scatman bucked vertical and the bull's airborne position seemed to defy the laws of physics. Scatman churned up the arena floor to no avail.

The horn sounded and Cody raised his left hand in a clenched fist. He freed his right hand three seconds later and tumbled off the bull for a twelve-second ride. Scatman careened off the back gates until the flank rope was released. Cody ran to the chutes and watched Scatman disappear behind the closing gate. Jason and Tyler McGarrity jumped off the platform in triumphant exultation. Cody hung on to the gate and searched for Devon.

Perched atop the Public Address table, Cody waved to the mass of bouncing hair. The score flashed above. Eighty-nine points sealed the first round. Gunner McGarrity stuffed a wad of chew deep into his lip. Cody Law climbed over the stands to reach his daughter. Devon buried her face in her father's chest. A smattering of dirt covered her cheek and the breathless rhythm of Cody's chest carried Devon to a place that her dreams never conceived.

Cody Law took first place in Steamboat on Sunday afternoon. Cody rode three consecutive bulls for the title. The win moved Cody into fourteenth place on the national money list. Cody Law had made the National Rodeo Finals in Las Vegas, Nevada, beginning December 3-11.

Cody set PRCA records in 1990 for rookie points in six months, money won by a rookie in six months and the Romick Arena highest score for a rookie in a PRCA sanctioned event, eighty-nine on Scatman. Cody still couldn't ride a horse very well, but the bulls had mainlined into his blood to the point where only another bull rider could explain the addiction. Cody and Devon had six weeks to settle on the California ranch of Gunner McGarrity. Cody had long ago, transferred power of attorney to Gary Dietz in Chicago for the purpose of running the corporation. Cody would address selling Desperado, Inc. after the NFR Finals.

* * *

Sonny Moore went back to Oklahoma from Steamboat, Springs. Sonny grabbed a Greyhound Bus ticket and assured Cody and Gunner that he would meet them in Las Vegas for the Finals. Sonny told Cody that he would be proud to work on the rodeo team for the finals and help look after Devon in Las Vegas. Rodeo teams have more to do with support away from the arena than in the arena. At the NFR Finals, access to the chutes was very strict. Fellow contestants assisted with the preparation for each ride. Saddle bronc riders and bareback riders may have provided support to the bull riders. Settling the animals, pulling the ropes and securing the flanks were all tasks, provided by NFR personnel and contestants.

At the National Finals Rodeo, coaches, mentors, trainers and the like, were not given access to the main floor chutes. Gunner knew the last week before the Finals would be extremely important. The chemistry between the four men held tight. The physical training and regimen that Gunner had laid out for Cody during the weeks before the Finals, did not necessitate partners. The intangibles had to be addressed.

"Hell, Sonny, you don't think we would break up this winning combination now, do you?" Gunner smiled.

"I can't tell you how much you and Olin have helped me the last seven months. Promise me that I'll see you in Las Vegas." Cody hugged Sonny Moore.

"Sonny, be at the ranch by Thanksgiving. I don't want you to meet us in Las Vegas. We need to spend a week together before Vegas. Can you make it?" Gunner asked.

"Count on it." Sonny grabbed his gear and disappeared into the bus terminal. Olin Martin accompanied Cody, Devon and Gunner for the trip back to California. Olin came from Modesto, so Cody agreed to take the long way in, by heading north to Interstate 80. Cody and Gunner would head across southern Wyoming, Utah and Nevada.

Devon got a chance to see some of the most beautiful serene stretches of the American West. They drove through Reno and dropped off Olin in Modesto, eventually skirting down the California coast on Highway 1 to Santa Maria and Nipomo. Olin agreed to the same conditions as Sonny Moore. Thanksgiving dinner on the ranch, then one week of work and off to the Finals.

Devon came from an area surrounded by the mountains. By the time Cody reached the Pacific Ocean, Devon was beside herself. The ocean had been a geographical mirage in her mind for twelve years. Devon had read about the waves and the beaches. Now, with the Suburban windows rolled down and Cody searching for a radio station through an avalanche of static, Devon laid her eyes on the endless cobalt blue water and the white-capped waves slamming into the sand. Devon hung out the window like a sedated Golden Retriever hypnotized by the wind and salt in the air.

The coastline appeared desolate and undisturbed for long stretches. Limpid sanctuaries where Mother Nature clearly meant for man to pass on by. Other stretches along the same highway flipped the landscape diametrically. Vehicles parked one by one along miles of the coastline. Communities crammed into thin coastal beaches, straddled precariously above the tumultuous water. The highway then came back to miles of unbroken tranquility and one wondered whether the populated commerce of California had slipped into the Pacific Ocean.

Devon asked more questions than Cody and Gunner had answers. Cody stopped in Monterey for root beer floats, toured San Simeon for a history lesson on narcissistic extravagance and buzzed into Pismo Beach to buy a Los Angeles Dodgers cap for Devon.

The drive took them past Pismo Beach and then inland to the ranch. A central coast California sunset laid the long shadows across the vineyards and pastures leading to Gunner's ranch. The upper road near the ranch passed gated monuments and stonewalled pastures belonging to the Silicone Valley and Southern California baby millionaires. Sprawling ranchlands owned by non-ranching neophytes. Soft suits with manicured nails and foreign cars were turning the rural communities surrounding the coastal ranches into expensive playgrounds for men with no penchant to outdoor life.

Private golf courses sprung up at the foothills of the Sierra Madre Mountains. Gunner saw the new influx of wealth as the invasion of a neutered society. Men went to hair salons and sported earrings. Italian leather loafers were replacing snakeskin boots. The point simply eluded Gunner.

"Sweaters? Have you ever seen a cowboy wear a sweater? Stay in the fucking city." Gunner used to say. "Don't bring it out here."

They passed a small well-maintained spread near the upcoming entrance to Gunner's ranch. Cody remembered driving past the spread for the first time with Gunner, just after he had arrived from Castle Rock in late January or early February. The three-bedroom house came with a small barn and maybe fifteen or twenty acres. On the south end of the house, separated by a row of low hanging Cottonwood trees, the new tenants had cultivated a text-book garden, the type of garden that yuppies plant from In-Style Magazine.

A couple from Los Angeles had brought their five year-old son to the Central Coast region to find a better way of life. After no more than a month on the small spread next to Gunner's ranch, one of Gunner's rank bucking bulls got loose and somehow wound up tangled and stuck in the new neighbor's garden. Rather than destroy the garden, Gunner first tried to lure the bull out. By bringing down a docile bull, Gunner thought that the docile bull would naturally bring the rank bull out of the garden with a minimum of damage and commotion. Gunner had not disturbed the neighbor, who remained unaware of the bull in his garden.

After failing to lure the bull out of the garden with the docile bull, Gunner gave up and started screaming at the bull. "Get your mother-fucking ass out of there...you cock-sucking son-of-a-bitch...I'm going to end your miserable fucking life if you don't get out of there, right now!"

Gunner was screaming at the bull, but the new neighbor couldn't see the bull and thought Gunner was screaming at him and his family. The man kept the family inside until Gunner gave up and left. Two days later, the new neighbors had packed up and moved back to Los Angeles.

Gunner McGarrity had driven Upper Los Berros Canyon Road for twenty-three years. Gunner taught his sons to drive up the same dirt road. Nine miles took nearly thirty minutes. A bad break in the road slowed the Suburban to a crawl. Devon remained fixed outside the passenger's window. The entrance to Gunner's ranch was a simple open gate. The fence lines bordered the roads and the feed bins appeared from nowhere. Devon sat up in the truck as they bounced onto Gunner's property. To her left, Devon marveled at the bulls dotting the grounds. Eighty or ninety animals were sprawled on the rolling slopes of the lower acres. Two red Brahmas blocked the road, some thirty yards from the entrance gate.

"Stop the truck, Cody." Gunner barked. "We've got a couple martyrs that want some attention. Devon, come with me." Devon jumped up without hesitation and followed Gunner to the front of the truck. Gunner took off his hat and slammed his right foot into one of the two-ton mammals resting on the road. They scurried off like scared puppies and Devon ran after them in simulated assistance. Gunner scooped up Devon and carried her back to the truck. Cody waited for them to hop in and then proceeded to the main residence.

The truck drove past the arena and Devon wheeled inside the vehicle to take a good look at the wooden sign hanging over the entrance to the rodeo arena. Gunner McGarrity's Championship Bull Riding School stood out like a wart on a silk blanket in the middle of wine country. Cody pulled the truck up to the open dirt, parking expanse between the structures comprising Gunner's ranch. Jacquie McGarrity waited on the deck of Gunner's main home. A small white banner had been stenciled in magic marker. Welcome Home Devon, spilled into the eyes of a tired young traveler.

The beef patties crackled on the stone barbecue pit behind the main house. The deck overlooked a steep grade covering two-hundred acres of inner coastal property, representing the north pastures of Gunner's ranch. Maybe, fifty or sixty bulls watched Devon and her friends arrive. A wooden table spread with plates, bowls of potato salad, chips, condiments and pitchers of lemonade were places Devon found for the first time.

One of the nine dogs on Gunner's ranch hopped into Devon's lap, mid-bite into a cheeseburger. The dog was no bigger than an oversized chipmunk. Big brown eyes almost drowned the tiny black nose. The dog sat perfectly still on Devon's lap. He was a terrier mix, a mutt, Gunner found roaming the grounds. That was how all the dogs wound up at Gunner's. They were strays, lost and most of them were emaciated from starvation. Dogs do not fare well in the wild or on their own. A tiny tail brushed Devon's knee feverishly. The miniature mutt looked as if he were smiling.

"He's precious, Gunner." Devon beamed.

"Say hello to Atilla." Gunner announced.

Cody burst out laughing, hysterically. Devon held the little dog and Cody laughed so hard that he had to stand up and walk around. Cody kept laughing while looking back at the dog and repeating his name.

"Atilla, as in Hun, a warlike Asiatic invasion." Cody grabbed a bottle of beer from the table and pulled a drink. With a mouthful of beer, Cody tried not to look at Atilla, but to no avail. The beer exploded from Cody's mouth in a white stream shooting over the railing surrounding the deck. Cody stood against the rail with beer dripping from his mouth. He was shaking his head and laughing.

Cody and Devon took the small house where Jason had been living. Jason moved down to Los Angeles at the start of the rodeo season last January. Although Jason spent more time on the ranch than he did in Los Angeles, the home was clear. Cody and Devon's temporary new home was built ninety feet from the main house. Tyler and his wife had occupied another home on the property located some one-hundred yards from the main house. The accommodations were adequate and available. The two-bedroom ranch home was small and dusty.

Cody and Devon spent the better part of the first night cleaning. Gunner and Jacquie came by with chocolate chip cookies and milk. Jacquie took Devon inside and helped her set up the bedrooms. Devon's room was tiered in brightly colored Aztecan wallpaper. Devon cleaned the white lampshades on either side of the bed. The simple white lampshades defined the sanctuary. Devon walked to the door and pulled it open all the way. She stood there and made certain that the door remained opened. Cody and Gunner sat outside on the porch. Cody smoked a small cigar. Gunner rarely chewed at home.

"Cody, we get started in three days." Gunner remarked. "You ready to clear your mind and focus on one thing for six weeks?"

"I've already won, Gunner." Cody mused. "No one expected me to do anything on tour. Hell, I don't think you thought I could fill my card."

"Cody, I'll help you prepare for Las Vegas if you're in it to win!" Gunner stared straight ahead and continued. "If you're going for the experience, then skip it. Buy a ticket and watch. It's safer. There are merits to giving your best efforts, but those are post-party consolation prizes. The Finals are about finishing first. You haven't won anything, yet. "

"I'll be there." Cody dropped three steps to the dirt and snuffed out the stale cigar. "For now, I'm going to spend a few days with Devon. It's time we tried out our new digs."

To Cody, the digs were the Four Seasons Hotel off Michigan Avenue in Chicago. The accommodations came with one young daughter. Cody put Devon to bed. Jacquie had purchased pajamas, new sheets and new blankets. Devon looked reborn in the starched white cocoon of her new bed. Cody left the light on and kissed Devon good night. Devon turned and snuggled as if she were born in the same bed. Cody was staring. Cody wondered how Devon's life would have been different if he had lived up to his responsibilities and not hidden behind the self-serving excuses justified by Kirsten's one letter twelve years ago. Cody stood silent. Finally, he smiled and went to bed.

Before the sun completed the outlines on the eastern horizon, Cody woke as usual. The nightclub and restaurant business was one of late nights. The mornings were Cody's favorite time during the past eight months. Everything moved slower in the early morning. Cody liked that pace to begin each day. The pace was new and addicting. The cigar had left an awful dry taste in his mouth. Cody wondered if they had remembered toothpaste. Cody crawled out of bed and nearly stumbled on his first step. At the bottom of his bed and curled up on the floor, Devon lay sleeping.

Gunner didn't waste any time setting the routine. Three days off to rest, recuperate and get to know Devon. Uninterrupted, the seventy-two hours flew past. Cody was up early for a five mile run before breakfast each morning. Gunner rode the ATV alongside Cody while he ran the trails on Gunners property and the surrounding lands. Devon and Atilla came for the ride on the second day of training. They never missed a training run after that day. The physical aspect of the next five weeks would be crucial. Gunner felt that the body had to maintain the conditioning aspect to bull riding and performance. Gunner believed that bull riding was all about timing, rhythm and balance. Cody would ride bulls four times a week. There would be four rides on each of those days. Gunner did not place Cody on rank bulls. He focused on medium jumpers, but minimized the injury risk by avoiding the most difficult bulls on the ranch.

Bull riding and boxing are comparable. Rest for any boxer is imperative, but rest alone will destroy a man's timing. A boxer must continue to spar in between fights. The boxer must continue to train and keep his body in the best physical condition possible. Timing and balance are crucial to the success of any fighter. Sparring partners must be agile and evasive, but rarely will they threaten the meal ticket. Sparring partners are middle of the road boxers. Bull riders must prepare the same way. By staying sharp and continuing to ride up to the Finals, a bull rider does not lose his rhythm or his timing. The adrenaline of the finals will take the rider to another level.

The days Cody did not ride were spent running and lifting. The weight room was the main barn and also the classroom. Dozens of videotapes were reviewed every night. The ghosts of another era gathered cobwebs in the corners. Gunner's mechanical bulls made money a decade before at the county fairs, but they were useless as a training tool. Timing on a mechanical bull was nothing like the animal. Gunner had used the mechanical bulls some in class for beginners, but the vast majority of his students were not beginners and therefore the Urban Cowboy toys had been retired.

Two weeks after Cody and Devon arrived at Gunner's ranch, Shana McDonough called to tell Cody that Billy Don Barrett's trial had been continued. Barrett had fired the court appointed attorneys and enlisted the services of Taylor Bennett, a prominent defense attorney from Denver. Bennett and Barrett were high school classmates and teammates on the football team. The new defense team requested a month long continuance based on the attorney change. The judge granted the time requested. Shana assured Cody that despite the upscale legal infusion, the evidence was irrefutable and F. Lee Bailey couldn't spring Barrett. Shana reminded Cody that steering an airtight child abuse case into a legal scrum was the equivalent to judicial suicide. Shana assured Cody that Judge Sharpe would allow very little room for the defense to manipulate or delay any of the trial proceedings.

Cody shared the information with Gunner, but no one else. Cody was concerned, if not demoralized. Cody had tried to ignore the premonitions. Pessimism is one man's perception of experience. Optimism is the absence of experience. The call did not create the doubt, albeit the doubt was already in place.

Meditation became more important as the Finals grew closer. At first, Cody followed like a sheep, mimicking the physical movements and daydreaming for the most part. During the first weeks at the ranch, Cody stumbled into sporadic squalls of peaceful concentration, but there was no rhythm or consistency with the exercises. Cody never knew if he was meditating properly, but during meditation one day, those thoughts vanished. Cody's mind focused on where he wanted to be and how he would arrive there. Visually, Cody saw Devon years from now. He saw Devon with him at the Finals. Cody watched them build a house together overlooking the ocean from the highest point on Gunner's property.

On Monday afternoon, four days before the Finals would begin, Shana McDonough called again. Cody picked up the call.

"Shana, this is Cody Law. Tell me that you're calling for more tickets to the Finals."

"I wish I could tell you that, Cody." Shana's voice staggered.

Cody closed his eyes. Cody held Gunner's cell phone and leaned against the Suburban. Cody was sweating from a morning workout. He waited silently for Shana to continue.

"Cody, Taylor Bennett got Barrett's brother, you remember Boxcar, and six other losers from Rascal Flats to testify that Gunner assaulted him on the morning of Barrett's arrest. The information gathered as a result of the assault led to the search warrant of Barrett's trailer home. The waitress, Marla Wemple, backed up their story. Curly King, the owner of Rascal Flats, filed the complaint. "

"The mother fucker wasn't even there." Cody interrupted.

"Mr. King claims to have witnessed the entire incident. Cadrell Easley is on suspension." Cody felt the nausea crawl up his throat. Shana went on.

"Judge Sharpe threw out the warrant attained from the information gathered at Rascal Flats. Therefore, any evidence found in the trailer is inadmissible. Cody, the eyewitness accounts from that day are gone. The cuffs and mattress are gone. The videotapes are gone. The cameras are gone. The case falls back to Devon's word against Billy's. Judge Sharpe also threw out the $500,000 bond and reduced the bond to the original $10,000. Billy and Kirsten are out of jail." Cody slid to the ground and buried his face between his knees. He tried to compose himself.

"They still have Devon's deposition, right?" Cody groped.

"Since the case is now down to Devon's word against theirs, Judge Sharpe has granted another defense request. Devon will be required to testify in person. Since her testimony is the only thing that can convict Billy and Kirsten, then the defense contends that they must be able to question the child in court. Judge Sharpe had to agree. You and your friends gave him no choice." Shana had to deal the blame.

"Shana!" Cody shouted into the phone. "Six Castle Rock police officers saw Barrett naked on top of my daughter! Her hands were cuffed to the bed. Kirsten was filming the whole thing. They all saw it!"

"Cody, it doesn't matter. None of it can be used in court. The warrant was obtained illegally, therefore anything found as a result of the warrant is tossed. Devon has to testify in person." Shana McDonough was adamant.

"Devon will never step foot in a courtroom to face Billy Don Barrett again. I will not put her through that again." Cody curled up against the vehicle. "I will not do that to Devon. Do you hear me!"

"I heard you, Mr. Law." The tone became formal. "My hands were tied here. There are rules of evidence and there is the matter of the constitution, Mr. Law. Citizens are not allowed to torture people to obtain information. Did you think that by withholding those facts, they would go away? "

"Citizens are not allowed to torture people, but they are apparently allowed to torture children, Ms. McDonough. What about the custody order?" Cody assumed the worst.

"The custody order remains valid. They are separate issues at this point. Barrett has no rights regarding Devon. He is not the father, nor the adoptive father. Kirsten can make an issue of custody if she remains free. An acquittal brings the custody case back before Judge Sharpe if Kirsten seeks custody of Devon. Judge Sharpe will weigh the actions at Rascal Flats in subsequent hearings pertaining to Devon's best interests. The court will find Mr. McGarrity's actions unacceptable. You were present during the assault on Mr. Barrett's brother. Complacency will be viewed as unacceptable behavior by the court." The District Attorney paused.

"My behavior was unacceptable?" Cody mocked sarcastically

"They'll walk, Cody."

"Devon will not testify. You had enough evidence to market a theatrical release nationwide on both of them. Do your goddamn job, Ms. McDonough. Devon's appearance is not negotiable!" Cody was up now and shouting into the phone.

"Watch your tone, Mr. Law. My office has worked very hard to make this case while you and your friend may have damaged the case and the judge irreparably. We are working to put Billy Don Barrett away, so I would suggest to you that we would accomplish much more showing respect as opposed to launching into accusatory tantrums." The District Attorney preached.

"Why did I think the patterns of the past twelve years in Douglas County would change?" Cody was pacing. The dry California ground kicked up the dirt as Cody's boots scraped the parking area. "Devon doesn't testify."

"They'll walk, Cody." Shana McDonough repeated.

"They already have, Ms. McDonough." Cody ended the call. The information would be passed on to Gunner later that afternoon. Gunner and Cody agreed not to tell Devon.

The National Rodeo Finals were to begin on a Friday night and would stretch ten rounds. Cody and Devon talked about school. Cody would enroll Devon for the second semester, beginning in mid-January, 1992. Devon would attend school in Santa Maria, California. Cody would begin building a house during the spring.

* * *

Two days before the Finals began Cody, Gunner, Devon, Sonny and Olin arrived in Las Vegas, Nevada. Cody insisted on financing the group. Caesar's Palace would be home for the next twelve days.

By the holidays in 1990, Las Vegas remained the barometer for hypocrisy. Las Vegas is commercialism on steroids, voyeurism on parade and the nocturnal home to a population that had simply missed the boat. Caesar's Palace may have possibly been the last place Cody envisioned bringing Devon, but the Finals threw a slight detour into any stabilization plans.

Checking into the hotel, Cody enjoyed watching his daughter soak up the outrageous extravagance that was routine in Las Vegas. Cowboy hats and suede jackets filled the hotels in Las Vegas during the National Rodeo Finals. The marquee acts were geared toward country music. Headline signs that normally held the names of Lisa Minelli, Rodney Dangerfield and Tony Bennett, now held the names of Reba McEntire, Alabama and Alan Jackson.

The most difficult ticket to obtain in Las Vegas during the course of any year is the NFR Finals ticket. Rod Stewart, Billy Joel, Wayne Newton and other top names brought outrageous ticket prices from city ticket brokers. On any given weekend or weeknight throughout the city, brokers retain scores of tickets to every venue. But nothing compares to the demand for NFR Finals tickets.

In 1990, there were more than twenty million tickets sold to rodeos in the United States. Those rodeos were limited to certain states and certain geographic areas. Projected ticket sales to fifty states and the attendance for rodeos would have exceeded most major sports. They all came together to view the best during ten days in December.

Devon was frightened by the vast casinos in Caesar's Palace. The slot machine bells and chaotic movement pushed Devon under Cody's arm as they made their way to the front desk. Cocktail waitresses in Roman metallic skirts looked ridiculous. Pathetic puffy men filled the five-dollar black jack tables and dreamed of Baccarat.

The guestrooms smelled like perfumed antiques. Years of mediocre housekeeping had begun to expose the consequences. Smoke hung on every inch of the rooms. Cody carefully removed the bedspreads. The sheets were a much safer bet. Cody and Devon would share a room with two king-sized beds.

Cody, Gunner and Devon would take a cab to the Thomas and Mack Center, the home of the NFR Finals, to take a look at the draw for Friday and Saturday nights. Sonny and Olin put on their best ostrich boots and slapped on a tidal wave of after-shave lotion. They smelled like the cosmetic counters at Bloomingdales. Sonny and Olin stumbled into the elevator in fine cowboy style. The single male nitwit syndrome invaded the casinos in

Stetsons and pressed Wrangler jeans. Cody and Gunner grabbed Devon and headed for the inflatable cowboy standing twenty feet tall on the steps of the Thomas and Mack Center. Since the National Rodeo Finals moved to Las Vegas in 1985, the 15, 001 seats have been some of the toughest tickets in professional sports. The Grand Opening of the Thomas and Mack Center was held on December 16, 1983 and featured Frank Sinatra, Dean Martin and Diana Ross.

The rodeo contestant draws for the first two rounds were pulled on Wednesday. The PRCA office at the Mack Center posted the draws in the afternoon. On Wednesday night at the Riviera Hotel, the back numbers were handed out to the contestants in the Finals. The back numbers were determined by the money ranking of each contestant during the year. All events were combined for the back numbers. The rankings were determined by to the total amount of money won by each contestant regardless of the event. The numbers would range from one to one hundred twenty.

The bull rider's draw was posted outside the PRCA office behind the Thomas and Mack Center. There were dozens of trailers set up for offices of the governing rodeo bodies and the sponsors. Dozens of other television trucks and satellite trucks readied their equipment for the cable broadcasts of ESPN, TNT and TNN. Gunner led the way to the rear staging area behind the Mack Center.

Gunner won his 1970 Bull Riding Championship in Oklahoma City, but had learned the layout in Las Vegas over the years. The bull riders were drawn in the order of their national money ranking for the first two nights. Cody finished in fourteenth position, so Cody Law would ride second on Friday and Saturday night. The top ranked rider would ride last. After the first two rounds, riding orders for rounds three through ten were determined by the Finals ranking. Gunner reached the PRCA office. He stood and read the draw. Cody walked up with Devon, seconds later.

"Did you find the bull riders draw list?" Cody asked, not bothering to look. Cody was watching Devon marvel at the television trucks and the massive white satellites. Gunner didn't answer. Cody stopped and turned to Gunner. He repeated the question.

"Did you find my draw, Gunner? Who am I riding?"

"Skoal Dagger in the first round." Gunner replied and stared at the draw sheet hoping there was a mistake.

* * *

Cody and Gunner took Devon all over the Las Vegas strip on Wednesday night. They explored every neon carpet within walking distance from Caesar's Palace. The trio filled up on cotton candy and junk food for hours. Cody and Gunner bought Devon more Las Vegas trinkets than Bugsy Malone ever dreamed about. By the time they arrived back at Caesar's Palace, Devon looked like Charo in the late show at the Stardust. Devon fell asleep watching the gaming channel and learning about the finer points of bacarat. Gunner pulled two beers out and handed one to Cody.

"What time do you think Sonny and Olin will roll in?" Cody asked after downing nearly half the beer.

"They had to find some women by now." Gunner reasoned. "The money between them had to be gone in an hour. I'm sure they were entertaining two of Nevada's finest on your tab."

"That's fine. I owe them much more than they could ever imagine." Cody killed his beer. "You ready?" He looked at Gunner. Gunner stared at Cody for a few seconds, surprised at the empty beer.

"Sure, pull out one of those little bottles of Jack Daniels will you?" Gunner pointed to the in-house bar. Cody pulled out two bottles. They cracked another beer and toasted the miniature liquor bottles.

"You're worried about the draw?" Cody broached the subject they had both been avoiding.

"Cody, you have to buck off Skoal Dagger on purpose." Gunner said it.

"What?" Cody sat up.

"Let Devon sleep. Let's go out on the lanai. I love that word. It reminds me of Hawaii." Gunner grabbed his beer.

"What do you know about Hawaii?" Cody mused and followed Gunner outside on the small deck ten stories above the sleepless city.

"Pepsi Cola brought me to Hawaii, maybe six or seven times to work on commercials for one of their campaigns. They hired me to work with incredibly beautiful women and teach them to ride horses for the commercials. The gig of a lifetime fell into my lap. My job was to coddle young models and teach them to stay up on a horse long enough to film the spots." Gunner laughed thinking about the months in Hawaii.

"Isn't that like sending a Doberman into a meat factory to protect the merchandise?" Cody inquired.

"Maybe, but the spots came out perfect." Gunner replied.

"How bad were you?" Cody knew the answer.

"Let's just say, that I knew how the Publisher's Clearing House winners felt." Gunner shook his head and put a wad of Copenhagen in his mouth. "Cody, you need to get past Skoal Dagger any way you can on Friday night."

"What do you mean, buck-off on purpose?" Cody followed.

"When the gate opens on Friday night for your ride, let the bull clear the gate and fall off immediately on your own terms. You cannot pass on a draw or they will disqualify the contestant. Cody, you can win here with seven or eight rides out of ten. Skoal Dagger is not for you. Buck off him from the gate and concentrate on the other nine rides. You have no other choice." Gunner spoke from the heart and knew what he was doing.

"You're telling me to throw the ride?" Cody asked innocently. "They throw fights in Vegas, not rodeos."

"Cody, have you ever seen Skoal in person?" Gunner asked.

"No."

"He's like no other bull I've ever seen. The riders that have ridden Skoal compare him to the lions called the Ghost and the Darkness. In Kenya, the lions killed twenty-eight Indian workers in Africa and some say the lions killed more than one hundred forty Africans. The lions' methods became so uncanny, the stalking so well-timed and so certain of success, many believed that they were not real animals, but devils sent to extract atonement. Skoal stalks the riders after they fall. Skoal has an agenda. Bulls don't have agendas. Cody, arguing that Skoal Dagger may be the reincarnation of the Ghost and the Darkness is not an indefensible position." Gunner leaned over the rail and shot a wad of tobacco juice into the wind.

"I'm from Chicago. Those lions are at the Museum of Natural History in Chicago. We went there as kids. That's a fable, Gunner. Folklore grows from fascination and exaggeration. I thought everyone wanted to draw Skoal Dagger. I think you told me once that Skoal was the ticket to a gold buckle." Cody lit a cheap cigar from the lobby.

"You have shown remarkable talent for a rookie, but you have been luckier than a Jack Russell Terrier with two dicks at the Westminster Kennel Club Dog Show. Your rides score higher because you are a phenomenon. I love you like a son, but you can't ride Skoal Dagger. No one can. I never thought that I would ever see a bull that no one could ride, but I have. I couldn't ride that mother fucker on my best day thirty years ago. The riders are bigger, stronger and more talented now than when I won. They can't ride him, either."

"I've seen riders fall off bulls on purpose, for various reasons. In Calgary once, Tommy Cole broke his jaw, three ribs, and an ankle. Tommy was one ride from a title. We carried him to the chutes and placed him on top of the bull. If he didn't ride the last round, he would have been disqualified. Tommy held such a big lead that all he needed to do was finish the competition. The gate opened and Tommy fell off the bull as it left the gate. Case closed. Tommy took first and spent the next week in the hospital."

"He was injured, Gunner. He didn't throw the ride." Cody argued.

"Reasons vary, Cody. Tommy threw the ride and everyone knew why.

This is no different." Gunner reasoned.

"This is completely different and everyone knows that. I'm not going to throw the ride. If I can't ride Skoal, then like you said I have nine other rounds to make it up. Hell, you told me that Devon didn't come all this way to see me get bucked off some small town, second-rate bull." Cody came back.

"That WAS a small town, second rate bull. This is Skoal Dagger. No one has ever ridden Skoal and you are not about to be the first. It isn't over when you get bucked off. That son-of-a-bitch comes after the rider. Buck off near the gate and he won't have the time to come at you. It's one round, Cody. Do it!"

"What if I stay on him?" Cody came back.

"You won't, Cody. This bull is different. Please, trust me on the call. Promise me you won't try to ride him." Gunner pleaded.

" It's your call, Gunner."

" It's my call all the way, agreed?" Gunner pushed for the assurance.

" Agreed." The two men went to bed. Gunner left for his room. Cody pulled the new chaps from his rigging bag and laid them on the bed next to Devon. The whiskey kicked in and Cody fell asleep moments later.

* * *

Gunner McGarrity picked up the phone in his room on Thursday morning. Gunner was up, but always sounded as if the call woke him.

"Gunner McGarrity?" A female voice inquired.

"Well, that depends darling. Who wants to know?" Gunner responded.

"This is District Attorney Shana McDonough from Castle Rock."

"Remind me to enlist your help, should I ever need to find someone." Gunner mused.

"You wife told me where I could reach you, Mr. McGarrity." Shana answered.

"What can I do for you, Ms. McDonough?" Gunner asked, although he knew why she was calling.

"Mr. McGarrity, has Cody explained the turn of events here in Castle Rock regarding Billy Don Barrett and Kirsten Barrett?" Shana began.

"I will assume you are talking about Barrett and his wife leaving jail? Cody explained the overturned warrant caused by my unorthodox interrogation of the man called Boxcar. I suppose now, that Mr. Boxcar has filed assault charges against me and you want me to give myself up, maybe even plead guilty? Hey, could I work out a deal with the court. I hear you can nearly kill a child in Castle Rock, videotape the crime and walk the next day. Doesn't sound like I have much to worry about because I just threatened to trim a guy's beard." Gunner could have kept going.

"Your actions have potentially ruined the case against Billy Don Barrett and Kirsten Barrett, if Devon does not testify in person. Sarcasm doesn't erase what you did Mr. McGarrity. I am calling you to ask for your help in convincing Mr. Law to bring Devon in to testify. This is complicated now, Mr. McGarrity. We need Devon to make the case. Will you help us?" Shana McDonough waited.

"Complicated?" Gunner pulled from his Texas roots. "Cowboys are simple, Ms. McDonough. If it's mine, I'll protect it. If it's got four legs, I'll ride it. If it stinks, I'll smell it. You don't have to explain it, ma'am. Like I said, if it stinks, I'll smell it. Ya'll can't look straight ahead because you're too busy fighting about who has the best view. Cody Law goes his own way and my job is to back him up. Can you guarantee that Barrett's new fancy lawyer won't carve up Devon like a holiday turkey when he takes a run at a frightened twelve year old girl? "

"Of course, I can't give that guarantee. All Devon has to do is tell the truth." Shana responded.

"That's what she's been doing for years and no one seemed to care." Gunner shot back.

"The trial is to begin in January." Shana continued to try.

"You have my answer, ma'am."

"You're going to let Billy Don Barrett go free?" The District Attorney hammered home.

"No ma'am. I believe that is on your plate, Ms. McDonough. Cody will take care of Devon, now. I know how important Devon's best interests have always been to the courts. I am going to tell Cody that you called. If any plans change, he will contact you. Good-bye, Ms. McDonough." Gunner placed the receiver back on the telephone.

Cody took a long run on the Friday morning of the Finals. Sonny and Olin had marginally stayed away from the subject of Skoal Dagger. They took Devon to breakfast while Cody went for a run. The buzz among the contestants centered on Cody Law, again. The rookie pulled Skoal Dagger. The other riders almost seemed jealous and relieved at the same time. Many mumbled about the possibility of rigging the draw to give Cody, Skoal Dagger. They knew that didn't make much sense. If Skoal knocked everyone out of competition, then why would the PRCA put the new meal ticket on Dagger right out of the gate? There were no pre-arranged draws. The draw was a computerized roulette wheel. Everyone knew that. Skoal Dagger would bring more attention to Cody during the first round. Attention became the one thing that many contestants felt, however unintentionally, fell Cody's way too easily.

Cody thought little about the petty references to his notoriety. The sidewalks of Las Vegas were filled with chain smoking gangs of polyester. Sweatshirts with big pictures and trite sayings splattered the bellies of the wandering masses. Cody dodged the slow moving tourists as he picked up speed towards the Thomas and Mack Center. Dreams varied among the triple deck ice cream cones and teased hair. Some dreamed of the winning slot payoff from anything with a bell and a handle attached to it. Others fantasized about the free buffet inside the Golden Nugget Casino. Either end, daydreams danced all along the sidewalk.

Cody's run crossed Paradise Road and brought him through the miles and miles of iron fencing set up outside the Mack Center to house the animals for the NFR Finals. Tranquillity in the afternoon filtered through the smell of manure. Cody pulled up winded and stopped near the Animal Care Center, a large white tent near the top of the ramp leading to the arena floor. The concrete walls rose up from the arena entrance and stretched fifty or sixty yards back up the ramp. The ramp was lined with segregated small pens. The pens were filled with the animals necessary according to the order of events.

Bareback riding was the first event of the Finals. Fifteen horses filled the first pen, closest to the arena entrance. The contestant numbers for each animal were tied to the horse's neck. Seventeen steers filled the second pen for the second event, steer wrestling. The contestant numbers were stapled to the animal's ear. The horses were docile and magnificent until flanked. A flank rope is tied near the animal's testicles to induce bucking. Cody watched a bored concession worker manning a popcorn machine in a tent filled with thousands of popcorn bags.

Cody walked down the concrete ramp leading into the Thomas and Mack Center. He pulled the door at the bottom of the ramp and entered the bowels of the arena. The first staging area was filled with a series of wooden pens, animal walkways and gates. Cody walked past the empty animal runs and filed down the hallways past the contestant locker rooms and medical rooms. UNLV athletic offices had been transformed into make shift command centers for the PRCA. Cody walked the last ramp to the main arena floor. He stood against the chutes on the south end of the arena. Sixteen thousand empty seats greeted Cody as he climbed up on the platform he would use in eight hours. The lights were on full tilt and the arena floor was combed and raked clean. The laser messages from the rafters above sporadically flashed the logos of the PRCA and main sponsors like Justin Boots, Wrangler and Dodge on the arena floor.

The Grand Entry director was barking orders to his staff. The empty private boxes wrapped around the second level of seating that was plastered with the advertisements associated with the University of Las Vegas basketball program. The public address system bellowed the testing patterns of the set-up crews. Cody stood silent in Nike nylon running pants, a yellow nylon windbreaker and a white headband. He felt the beads of sweat running down his chest and his heart beat fast with anticipation of the evening to come.

Standing on the chute platform, Cody wondered if the NFR Finals officials would let Gunner work his ride. In that instant, Cody remembered what Gunner had told him about Skoal Dagger. Suddenly, the stands were full and Cody imagined thousands of people watching him throw the ride. The arena hummed with the thunder of Skoal Dagger. Every spectator would be seated for one ride during the opening round of the Finals. At the start of the bull-riding event, no one would be filling Budweiser cups or buying jackets at the PRCA merchandise stands. The stadium would freeze in silence for that one ride during the opening round on Friday night.

"You look lost, buddy." A voice startled Cody and he turned to acknowledge the source.

"I wish I was, man." Cody replied. A lanky cowboy smiled at Cody Law.

"You workin' chutes or gates tonight?" The cowboy asked assuming Cody was part of the crew.

"No, I'm a contestant. First time jitters, you know that sort of thing." Cody commented.

"What event?" The man inquired. He stood erect in tight blue jeans. An expensive Resistol hung low over his eyes. The black shirt was pressed clean. The gold buckle seemed bigger than the tiny waist could handle. The inquisitive stranger appeared to be a well-defined contestant looking much more at home than Cody felt.

"Bulls." Cody kept his answers short.

"Whew, I thought for a minute that you looked too smart for those beasts. No wonder you're nervous. Bull riders must have some inherent self-destructive genetic disorder. I never understood why men get on animals that seem to enjoy a stomping party." The stranger took off his hat. The chiseled face seemed so familiar.

"How encouraging." Cody acknowledged. "I haven't seen you around the circuit, although you look like the poster-boy for Wrangler or Roper. Are you riding tonight?"

"No, I'm just helping out tonight." The elusive cowboy replied. "What's your name?"

"Cody Law." Cody jumped off the platform and turned to walk back up the ramp. It was time to head back to the hotel and catch a nap if he could.

"Fill in the mystery my friend. That buckle didn't come from the

Shepler's catalog and we're not friendly enough for me stare down there and read it."

"I'm here to do some promotional work for the PRCA and TNN." The voice clicked in immediately. "The Nashville Network is putting together a National Finals Rodeo special and they are filming it to the backdrop of my songs."

Reality dropped in like a blacksmith's hammer. Cody couldn't believe that he hadn't recognized Mason Dayne.

"You're Cody Law? They are talking about you from here to Reno. You got Skoal Dagger tonight, right?" Cody ignored the question.

"Man, you shoulda' looked me up when you went into this business. I woulda' put your ass on bareback. Mustangs are much prettier than Brahmas, plus they don't crap all over their ass. I've seen Skoal Dagger, once. That bull tossed Cody Custer, who was ranked eighth in the world at the time, before the rodeo announcer was done with the introduction. As soon as Custer turned the bull outside, he lost control. In fact, he never had control. Skoal Dagger hadn't been ridden in more than five-hundred attempts. Cody knew it and Skoal Dagger knew it. When Cody Custer hit the ground, Dagger was on him like a body crab. Bull riders are lunatics and Skoal Dagger is a goddamn predator."

Cody listened to the man. The lyrics came to life with every word. Cody stared, mesmerized for a moment and pulled off his headband. Cody's hair hung all over his face.

"You're Mason Dayne?" Cody marveled at the icon of rodeo songs.

"Pleased to meet you, Mr. Cody Law." The former 1976 World Champion Bareback Rider stuck out his hand. "Tell me something, Mr. Cody Law. I have been reading about you in everything from People Magazine to Sports Illustrated. As a father, I can imagine your rage. As a father, I admire your convictions. As a rodeo rat for the better part of forty years, I can tell you that you have shaken the pot. PRCA rookies in the Finals are rare, but those rookies have been on bucking animals or roping steers for the better part of their recently ended childhood. What you did to get here was a miracle! I've read that your daughter is now safe with you?"

"Devon is with me. I have legal custody as we speak, but the way the courts work, the custody order may be in jeopardy. Devon's stepfather is free now after a mountain of indisputable evidence against him was tossed. A search warrant uncovered a child pornography torture chamber. The same warrant allowed police to witness Devon's stepfather in the act of raping my twelve-year old daughter. The police found Devon's mother filming the act. The warrant was thrown out because Gunner McGarrity and I didn't say please when asking about the family's whereabouts." Cody paused.

"Gunner and I go way back." Dayne mentioned.

"The D.A. will only proceed now with the case if Devon testifies in-person and that is not going to happen. I've got her now and she's not going anywhere." Cody explained.

"Why continue the risk here?" Mason Dayne reasoned. "What you did was altruistic and pure. Jumping into rodeo at thirty-two years old, having zero experience, to reach your daughter was only slightly more gallant than foolish. Bull-riding is a choice we can discuss at another time. You've got Devon now, Cody. Why get on Skoal Dagger? That animal gives me the creeps. You can walk now with your daughter. Every cowboy in this field will salute you."

"You sound like Gunner McGarrity, now." Cody recounted.

"There's a first." Mason smiled. "I love Gunner. He's the best."

"I'm staying to compete, here." Cody announced. "I never claimed to be a Rhodes Scholar. Do you have a daughter?"

"Sure do." Dayne replied.

"I'm a new parent. I wasn't around to teach Devon how to ride a bicycle or watch her go to school for the first time. I wasn't able to take her picture in a new dress standing on the school steps crying because she didn't want me to leave. Devon's life was unspeakable pain and all I could do was watch. Rodeo gave Devon an escape and it gave me a chance." Cody stopped for a moment. Mason stood silent.

"Walk through the hotel with Devon and watch her look at the cowboys. She holds my hand with the grip of an ox. She introduces me to everyone as Cody, her father and bull-riding finalist at the NFR. Devon dresses like me, from the jeans to my hat."

"The world is not about Devon to Devon. When the majority of adults that I know walk through life feeling like the world owes them something more, I am astounded by the wisdom of Devon's innocence. The one person having a justifiable claim to the world's debt, expects nothing and demands less."

"Devon is completely fulfilled watching me practice and helping Gunner ready the rigging bags. Gunner gave Devon a chestnut quarter horse named Tulip. After four weeks at Gunner's ranch, Devon taught me how to ride a horse. Devon doesn't want fancy tours or amusement centers in Las Vegas. Devon wants to hang with the cowboys and tell everyone about Cody. I am not about to take that from her. Skoal Dagger can throw me to Albuquerque, but I'm not walking out on Devon. That trend is over, for good." Cody didn't mean to make a speech, but made no apologies. Dayne wasn't looking for one.

"Cody, rodeo is all about the challenge. You can ride anything on the ground that you can conquer in your mind. The only intimidating animals are those that beat you before you mount." They shook hands and Cody hustled back up the ramp. He wanted to spend some time with Devon before the Finals. Cody stopped suddenly, turned back around and yelled down the ramp.

"Mason!" Cody shouted and scurried back to the arena floor when he caught the attention of Mason Dayne. "Can I talk to you for a couple minutes?"

"Absolutely, Mr. Cody Law. What can I do for you?" Dayne replied.

The former Wyoming State High School Bareback Champion had recorded more than twenty albums spanning his rodeo years and the years since his retirement from the circuit. Newly signed to his first major label, Capital Records in 1989, all twenty-two albums were now licensed by a major Nashville recording company. Dayne was poised to burst onto the national music scene after a two-decade apprenticeship riding wild yellow mustangs and playing music in every honky-tonk bar along the way. A cowboy singer/songwriter not only found an audience, Dayne captured a Western attitude. Cody Law approached the former World Champion one more time.

"I've got a small problem and I wonder if you could bail me out tonight?" Cody began as he reached the bottom of the ramp.

The two men talked briefly, shook hands again and Cody ran back up the ramp to catch a cab on Paradise Road. Cody's parents were due in town at any time, now. Gary Dietz had brought a contingent from Chicago. They arrived last night and had breakfast with Devon, Gunner and Cody in the morning. Dietz brought Desperado's two Vice President/General Managers, Brian Helton, Restaurant and Catering and Alexandra Warring, Nightclub Division. Accompanying Gary Dietz from Chicago was Tolbert Lawerence, Cody's personal attorney and a very close friend. Cody arranged for rooms at Caesar's Palace for everyone. Since the Finals covered ten days, there was no rush to organize an official reunion.

Cody, Devon and Cody's parents took a long walk down the Las Vegas strip before Cody had to get ready for the first round of the Finals. Rusty and Jenny Law missed Chicago. Cody had been unusually vague when the move west began nearly twelve months ago. Cody had told his parents about having a daughter in Colorado. Beyond that, the details were sketchy and rare. Before the final arrests were made, Cody detailed the entire year for his mother and father. Subsequently, they were kept up to date as the arrests, arraignment and custody hearings concluded.

Jenny Law never quite connected with the rodeo and the role her son was about to play. Rusty Law was as proud as any father watching his son put on a Little League uniform for the first time.

The Opening Ceremonies would begin promptly at 6:30 p.m. Cody would not ride Skoal Dagger until approximately 8:45 p.m. Bull riding was the last event, but Cody would ride second of fifteen riders on the first two nights.

Cody and Devon talked about the ranch in California. Devon talked about Gunner McGarrity and the five-hundred acre rodeo training ground where she and Cody would build a home. Cody's mother followed along and cherished every moment with Devon. Devon missed Tulip and she wondered if the horse would forget her. Cody expounded to his parents about Devon's horseback riding prowess and about how proud he was of the way she took to riding. Cody revealed under strict confidence, that he was more nervous about the Grand Entry than he was about riding his first bull.

"What's the Grand Entry, Cody?" Rusty asked. Cody's father was remarkably well informed as to the structure of the PRCA. Since Cody's involvement in the sport, Rusty started from ground zero. Six months later, Rusty followed the rankings religiously.

"Before the National Finals and at many major events, the contestants are introduced as a group before the National Anthem is played. The rodeo announcer calls out the home states of each contestant in alphabetical order. One rider with his own state flag, precedes the entrants from that state. The contestants ride one by one on horseback into the arena. The mounted contestants form a horseshoe inside the arena. When all the contestants are introduced and assembled like a unit from the United States Calvary, the announcer will welcome them all as one. The horses will scatter and bolt the arena at full speed."

"Devon, I have more trouble riding a damn horse than I do riding a bull." Cody picked up his hat and scratched his head. He looked down at Devon quizzically. "Got any suggestions?"

"Don't hold the reins too low and whatever you do, don't plant your butt in the saddle. Ride up on your thighs, just like a bull. But Cody, above anything else..." Devon paused, looked back up and roller her eyes at Cody.

"What, Devon? Above anything else, don't what?" Cody pleaded.

"Don't fall off your horse during the introductions. I don't think I could bear the humiliation." Devon folded her arms. Rusty and Jenny giggled.

"Thanks for the support. There's going to be nearly twenty thousand people in the stands and millions watching on television. You'd be nervous too, if you rode a horse like me." Cody rationalized. Devon looked up and rolled her eyes again.

"You got that right, Cody." Devon scurried off down the sidewalk.

"Why you little...." Cody gave chase.

~CHAPTER VI~

The Thomas and Mack Center was ablaze with activity. Rows of limousines paraded down the main drive to drop off the faithful. Parking lot attendants flashed foot-long flashlights to direct the streaming cars. Hundreds of cabs sped down the back entryway, past the cheap motels and kicking up the dust from the access roads to the Mack Center. Scores of fans were jumping out of cabs lined up in terminal traffic tie-ups.

An inflatable cowboy stood twenty-two feet tall at the top of the escalator leading to the main entrance. Semi-trailers were parked back to back along the perimeter of the Mack Center. The PRCA sponsor trucks spread tables across the pavement, displaying their products from power tools to fertilizer. PRCA merchandise trailers opened like sardine cans with over-priced shirts, jackets, hatpins, coffee mugs, backpacks, and a myriad of products splattered with the PRCA logo. The concession attendants scrambled to reach the lines of buying customers. The National Finals Rodeo had arrived.

The myth that America had forgotten the Old West could never have been more erroneous then on opening night of the NFR Finals. Tight jeans, cowboy boots and big hair bucked the impoverished perception that America was immersed in the Smashing Pumpkins and the explosion of inner city ethnic rhyme. Las Vegas for ten days gave up the silk shirts and gold chains, while ushering in the suede and leather. No other weekend on the planet brought together as many enthusiastic followers as the World Series of Professional Rodeo.

Cody and Gunner had left an hour before Cody's entourage would leave Caesar's Palace for the Thomas and Mack Center. Gary Dietz, Brian Helton, Alexandra Warring, Sonny Moore, Olin Martin, Tolbert Lawerence, Cody's parents and Devon arrived in a private stretch limousine. Devon stayed close to Sonny and Olin in the limousine. Devon wore the official PRCA Contestant jacket of her father.

Cody's entourage took their seats seven rows from the arena floor directly behind the bucking chutes. Jason and Tyler McGarrity were waiting for the others. The video screen above the Thomas and Mack Center scoreboard rolled a PRCA Rodeo highlight film of the past twelve months. Devon stared at the screen and erupted each time Cody flashed across the screen. The stadium was filling fast. The Opening Ceremonies would begin on time. Very large men were wedging themselves into tiny seats. Every fan had some connection to rodeo.

The spectators came from every state in the union and every walk of life. The box seats have been traditionally reserved for contestant relatives, stock contractors, potential stock contractors, wealthy ranch rats, and the growing legion of associated businesses finding profit within America's first extreme sport.

From underneath the stadium seating, Cody was more nervous than at any other time in his life. The trepidation did not go unnoticed.

"Boy, you got over two hours before you get out there tonight. You think Skoal Dagger is pacing around the pen sweating and wondering whether anyone would notice if he took off and skipped the whole affair?" Gunner McGarrity made light.

"Hell, Gunner, I can't decide whether I'm nervous about the damn Grand Entry or that bull's got me spooked. I know what we talked about..." Cody started to say.

"Hold it, Cody." Gunner interrupted. "I know you are going to ride Skoal Dagger tonight. I gave it a shot, but honestly, I wouldn't have given anyone a nickel to the dollar that you would have bucked off that bull. Fuck, I wouldn't."

"Then what was all that shit about me not being able to ride Skoal?" Cody demanded.

"That wasn't shit, Cody. No one has ridden that animal. What do you want me to do? Do you want me to fill you up with some mindless, you're the one, garbage?" Gunner inquired.

"It couldn't hurt." Cody smiled. "It sure beats, you got no chance."

"Horse-shit." Gunner delicately continued. "Give this fucking two ton assassin, the ride of his life, Cody. Remember, it's eight fucking seconds. Don't think about the horn. It'll find you. Think about nothing. Don't get ahead of yourself in the ride. If he throws you, get the fuck out of the way. Know where you are going before you hit the ground. Trust me, he does."

"What about the Grand Entry?" Cody shook his head and looked at the chaps he held in his hands.

"Cody, I'm telling you. If you fall off that horse in the Grand Entry, my family and I will personally jump into the arena and beat the crap out of you. Then you will have nothing to fear from Skoal Dagger." Gunner nodded.

"You and Devon should start your own motivational support group. The opening ceremonies have started. They are going to boot your ass pretty soon." Cody reminded Gunner.

"In fact, they are clearing the hallways now" Cody pointed to the PRCA staff removing press and family from the back chutes and the inner hallways to the medical rooms and the locker rooms. The chute boss was giving last minute instructions to the chute laborers, flank men and pickup men. Gunner hopped up and walked down the hallway. Cody watched Gunner talk to the PRCA chute boss. They shook hands and slapped each other on the back. Gunner walked back to Cody.

"What happened?" Cody asked.

"You never tell a former World Champion where to go at the NFR

Finals. Would you tell Joe Namath to get off the sidelines at the Super Bowl?" Gunner replied. "When your hand gets wrapped on Skoal Dagger, the last eyes in your face are going to be mine."

Cody walked back up the entrance ramp to the staging area for the Grand Entry. One hundred twenty contestant riders gathered in the staging tent behind the arena. The procession began with Arizona followed by California. One lead flag rider from each state that was represented raced into the main arena. The contestants from that state rode in behind the lead rider.

The Thomas and Mack Center thundered with the beginning of the National Finals Rodeo. The Fourth of July exploded in a symmetrical firestorm falling from the rafters of the Mack Center. Some of the horses were spooked and the well-trained riders pulled the agitated horses back into place. Gunner, watching from behind the bucking chutes, winced in anticipation of Cody's entrance. Christ, he imagined, all Cody needs is a high-strung quarter horse to get in touch with his ancestral instincts. All the states represented were from west of the Mississippi River, with one exception. Illinois produced one contestant. The rodeo announcer rocked the public address system:

*From the great state of Illinois...*the stands erupted in an earthquake squall of delight.

The NFR welcomes rookie, Cody Law...

The lead rider from Illinois carried the flag high and fast into the arena. Devon, Cody's parents and the entire Law contingent stood up. A twelve-year nightmare evaporated on the tear-stained cheeks of Cody's daughter. Gunner braced himself up on the catwalk behind the chutes. The dirt kicked up from the entrance gates and Cody Law raced into the arena like a barrel racer with a Gold Buckle on the line. Cody's hat was pulled down tight and he guided the horse to the expanding horseshoe of contestants. The horse pulled up perfectly still in the exact spot desired. Cody pulled back on the reins and the horse reared up and stood tall on his hind legs. Cody spun the horse around, front legs flailing, to the stirring ovation and led him back to a stationary position. Finally, Cody's horse dipped on one front leg in a short bow. Cody kept his head down and the crowd roared a vociferous approval.

Gunner grabbed an ear to ear grin from his vantage point. Devon watched Cody with sheer awestruck adoration. The Grand Entry proceeded. Texas and Wyoming led the numbers charge with forty-one and thirty-six respectively. When the Grand Entry concluded, the riders traced the same entry lanes in a military styled retreat. The bareback riders gathered at the bucking chutes. The first event was about to begin.

The staging tent rumbled with the entire contestant ranks dismounting their rides. Cody Law stood outside the chaos. A well-dressed cowboy approached Cody. The man smiled and winked at Cody Law. Cody and the cowboy exchanged hats. The man unbuttoned his shirt and returned it to Cody.

"How'd it go?" Cody asked.

"Perfect, like you were born on a horse. The commissioner of the PRCA may drop you a note about showboating during the Grand Entry." Mason Dayne smiled slyly.

"What did I do?" Cody did not want to know.

"You stood up your horse and took a bow." Dayne laughed.

"I didn't?" Cody shook his head.

"Just like the Lone Ranger and Silver." Dayne laughed out loud. Cody and Mason shook hands and hugged. "Good luck tonight, my friend."

"Thanks for everything." Cody nodded and stuck his own hat back on his head. Cody walked away with his rigging bag over his shoulder. Mason Dayne brushed off his jeans and boots.

The National Finals Rodeo spun through the first round flawlessly. The events began with bareback riding, followed by steer-wrestling, team roping, saddle-bronc riding, calf roping, barrel racing and finally, bull-riding. The 1990 roster of bull riders at the NFR read like a segregated hall of fame. Names like Hedeman, Dunn, Murray, Custer, Lambert, Branger, Gaffney, Branger and Nuce filled the air around Cody Law with stagnant intimidation. The bull riding began at 8:35 p.m. Cody Lambert, from Henrietta, Texas rode first.

Skoal Dagger jostled in the chute waiting for Cody Law to mount. Lambert bucked off his mount at five seconds. No score. The Thomas and Mack Center fell silent. Gunner and Cody were taking a great deal of time. No one would question the wait. Skoal Dagger was a purebred Bradford bull, the stock ideal for breeding. Skoal caused so much havoc in the early days, the original contractor gave up on bringing him to market as a breeding bull. He was too mean.

Skoal Dagger was a cull and on the market at an early age. Hollister picked up Skoal Dagger for fifteen hundred dollars at the age of two. At Hollister, they knew Dagger had bucking potential. The first year out, Dagger barely allowed riders out of the gate. The fury was eerie. Most great bulls were gamey and did their jobs. Great bucking bulls possess huge hearts and buck hard on every ride. Great bulls surrender nothing, but they do not stalk and measure the rider. Skoal Dagger was that mean.

At six years old, Skoal Dagger was a careening oversized projectile, an unraveling upheaval of power and a physics package of muscle and blood that no rider had held for eight seconds. Skoal sat on four sawed-off, Civil

War cannons. His back was strung so tight that riding high provided little advantage. Slide down slightly and Skoal could feel it instantaneously. The bull bucked the riders forward as he whipped his head back. Stay up high and Skoal will go vertical and force the rider to slide. Great bulls buck the riders off. Skoal Dagger worked like an outfield coach, tossing up riders and whacking them off.

Cody straddled Skoal's back without touching the bull. The flank rope was secured. With that, Skoal blasted up on two back legs and spread thin the cowboys above the top planks of the chute. Spectators, twenty feet away, dove for cover. Gunner pulled Cody off the chute and threw him to the runner plank. Thousands sucked the air out of the Mack Center. Skoal Dagger nearly shattered the gate. The bull began to literally climb the gate. Nineteen hundred pounds were off the ground. The bull settled after fifteen terrifying seconds. Cody looked at Gunner as they both scrambled to stand up. Skoal dropped down in the chute and left an icy glare hanging over the arena floor.

The bullfighters huddled one last time. Spectators close enough and old enough, knew they had seen those eyes before. It was from the leader of a California cult during the "Helter Skelter" summer of 1969.

"That's his way of introducing himself, Cody." Gunner explained. "He'll settle down now because he won't risk a re-ride."

Cody Law climbed back aboard the top planks of the chute. The thought flashed in Cody's mind, that if a bull could actually push the envelope within the rules and stop on the edge, what could he do outside of the rules? And how could a fucking bull know the rules? Cody cleared his thoughts. Eight seconds, eight seconds, he repeated in his mind.

The constant blather from the public address system had ceased. Cody's family held hands. Devon closed her eyes. Gunner lowered the rope and pulled it into place. Gunner pounded the rope around Cody's hand. Cody slid up high on the bull's back.

"Get out of the way when you're off, Cody. Arena's clear, man. Slide and ride, cowboy." Gunner yelled under Cody's hat.

The fans inside the stadium had begun a climbing crescendo of cheers, not unlike the momentary anticipation of two heavyweight prizefighters staring at each other before the opening bell.

"Kick his ass!" Gunner yelled louder and released the hold on Cody's chest. Cody nodded to the arena floor and the gate flew open.

Twenty thousand people stood up and erupted in noise. Most bulls buck either in the right lead or the left lead for the fist few seconds. That will determine which side the owners load them on. With Skoal Dagger, there was no preference. He spun either way out of the chute with no set pattern. Skoal Dagger reared in the air higher than most veteran bull riders had ever seen a bull jump. When he reached his peak, Skoal broke over and kicked his back end ten feet high. That was the first jump! Two more equally spectacular jumps spun Cody's hat airborne.

The bull churned like a high-speed oil drill. The earth buckled with each thunderous change of direction. Somehow, Cody stayed above the fray. Skoal took a vertical jaunt and then started spinning to the left, doing what is known as drifting. While Skoal was spinning, he kept sliding backwards with his front legs while his back-end rose almost vertical to the ground. The sliding motion forced Cody's upper body toward Skoal Dagger's head, his signature move. Cody dug in with his spurs and kept pushing back with his riding arm.

Four seconds, five seconds, six seconds, the time seeped by like thick molasses in breathless animation. One more swipe of the mighty bull's head narrowly missed the teetering rider. The horn sounded, barely audible over the screaming stadium. Cody Law had ridden Skoal Dagger! Cody pulled his hand out of the handhold and caught Skoal's back end kicking up. The force of Skoal's thrust sent Cody head over heels some six feet in the air. Miraculously, Cody landed on his feet and stuck the dismount like a gymnast leaping from the high bar. Instinct took over in jubilation. Cody, with his arms raised high in the air, fists clenched, searched for Gunner amidst the raucous arena.

At that split second, Cody found Gunner waving his arms and screaming frantically from atop the chute. The pandemonium saw Gunner leap from the top of the chute into the arena. Instantly, Cody spun around to find Skoal. The bull was now inches from Cody. Skoal Dagger gored the frozen rider at full speed. The impact of Skoal Dagger's left horn punctured Cody's sternum and threw him up over the bull's back. In one horrific sequence, Cody Law's lifeless body fell limp at the feet of the paralyzed bullfighters. The bull had ignored the distractions of the colorful firing line between the bull and the rider. Gunner was too late. Skoal Dagger trotted back through the exit gate. The bull was immediately isolated from the other animals.

Medical assistance raced into the arena. Gunner moved aside and waited on his knees in the dirt. The Thomas and Mack Center fell into stunned silence, ripped from the heights of implausible triumph to the depths of unthinkable tragedy in the blink of an eye. Scores of well-organized medical personnel surrounded the fallen rider. Trained paramedics began shouting instructions immediately. Skoal Dagger had crushed Cody's sternum or breastplate between the rib cages. The horn lacerated the right ventricle of the heart. The paramedics ripped open Cody's shirt or what was left of the shirt. The wound was bleeding, but not outwardly gushing. The paramedics knew the damage and bleeding was occurring inside of Cody's chest. The heart was in ventricular fibrillation or fatal arrhythmia, where the heart was pumping but the blood pressure was zero.

In a young man, the heart muscle would continue to beat in a fatal or near fatal cardiac injury. The heart had been ripped open so the blood was flowing into the chest and the body's blood pressure would instantaneously drop to zero.

The severity of the silence sent the contestants rushing to the gates. Most had been present to watch Skoal Dagger. Those who were not watching will remember forever, where they were when the truculent gasp of the Mack Center froze the event. Pressure was applied to the external wound. The paramedics placed a breathing tube down Cody's throat to the trachea. A normal saline IV drip was started. Cody was placed on a long backboard with a cervical collar. The paramedics had no way of determining if the spinal cord had sustained any trauma. The patient was unconscious. The paramedics knew that there was little they could do for cardiac trauma on the scene. Cody's only hope, at this point, was to get to the hospital as soon as possible. A surgeon would have to open Cody's chest to assess the damage and repair the lacerations to the heart.

Cody was transferred to the ambulance, which had been backed into the arena from the entrance next to the roping event gates. The vehicle moved as if it were in slow motion The unfamiliar kaleidoscope of swirling emergency lights hovered next to where Cody lie. Gunner was allowed inside the ambulance.

Gunner had sent security personnel to reach Cody's family. Cody's family was told to accompany the UNLV Police to the University Medical Center, a nationally recognized trauma center, located minutes from the Thomas and Mack Center. The family and friends in the seventh row seats had been emotionally remanded in shock. Cody's mother fainted. Sonny and Olin jumped the seating barriers and rushed to join Gunner. Gunner told Sonny and Olin to accompany the family to the University Medical Center.

Gary Dietz and the contingent from Chicago stood like statues in front of their seats, hoping through their lack of rodeo knowledge that what they had witnessed was somewhat routine and Cody would be fine. Cody's father tried to attend to his wife and discern the activity in the arena. All of it was not good. Where only a minute before, Rusty Law stood welled with pride. Rusty Law basked in the adoration for his son as if the crowd's approval channeled through him. His ankles swelled with pride. Lost in the sudden chaotic venue, Devon stared ahead and waited for instructions.

The ambulance pulled out of the Thomas and Mack Center with a screaming entourage of police cars. EKG leads were attached to Cody and the information was immediately forwarded to the hospital. The activity was chaotic and the blood pressure remained at zero. The paramedics administered CPR during transport. The internal wound caused the blood to flow outside of the vascular tree and the blood vessels. Cody's chest cavity was filling fast with blood. The CPR was worthless and potentially could have caused more damage, but the rules dictate the procedure. The ambulance arrived at the University Medical Center in seven minutes. Cody had been down nearly fifteen minutes. He showed no signs of waking up.

The University Medical Center in Las Vegas employed ten, full-time trauma surgeons. The University Medical Center has been treating an average of nine thousand trauma admissions per year in Las Vegas. A separate resuscitation operating room or trauma operating room was available twenty-four hours per day in the emergency room. The arrival of Cody's ambulance to the emergency room triggered a choreographed army of precise flow. Cody Law was wheeled into an operating room within seconds of his arrival. An eight-person team manned the operating room for the procedure. Three nurses, an emergency room technician, a respiratory therapist, the trauma team leader and two surgical residents began the life saving procedures necessary to give Cody a chance.

An oxygen tank was hooked up directly to the trachea tube in Cody's throat. The tank pumped pure oxygen into Cody's lungs with each manual squeeze of the breathing bag. Normal room oxygen is twenty-one percent. The bag pumped one-hundred percent pure oxygen. Bags of o-negative blood were hung and immediately pumped into the patient. There was no time to cross-reference the blood and find a match. O-negative is the universal blood for emergency surgeries.

The new blood was pumped through a rapid infuser. The old blood filling the chest cavity was collected in a cell saver, mixed with an anti-coagulant and prepared for reinsertion into the patient when necessary.

The nurse opened a bottle of Betadine and poured it all over Cody's chest. The experienced surgical team knew they had little time. The surgery was not a delicate exploration. The patient was in cardiac arrest. The surgeon had no time to carefully cut through each layer of skin and muscle while closing off lacerated blood vessels along the way. Life saving open-heart surgery on an arrested patient translated into an invasive assault on the patient. The surgeon told everyone to back away and be careful while calling for a twenty-two blade. The large knife began mid-chest and cut laterally from the patient's left side, all the way around the chest to the table. The incision line came between the fifth and sixth rib. A rib-spreader was set in place, holding the rib cage open. One surgical resident turned a mechanical arm attached to the stainless steel posts anchoring the spreader. The emergency room technician secured the suction and cleared the blood from the chest cavity. The opening grew wider.

The lead surgeon opened the pericardium or the covering around the heart. Once the heart was delivered from the pericardium, the attending surgeon immediately knew that the injury was not amenable to repair. The laceration to the right ventricle was shredded and torn, impossible to suture. The bull's horn coupled with the massive power behind the two-ton animal annihilated the heart. Cody had been down more than twenty minutes. The frenzied activity in the operating room ceased. The surgeon slowly peeled off the gloves and threw them onto the floor.

"Shit!" The frustrated surgeon screamed louder than the staff anticipated. "Call it."

The few spectators in the concession walkways of the Mack Center stood motionless, staring at the television monitors throughout the hallways. The frenzied activity on the arena floor cast a veil of sadness that permeated throughout the stadium. Sonny Moore and Olin Martin raced to the family box in the seventh row. They led a hurried procession through the stunned crowd. Sonny picked up Devon and carried her down into the tunnel used for the contestants and PRCA staff to enter and exit the Thomas and Mack Center. Chute laborers took off their hats and said prayers. Cody's father relented and insisted that the group proceed to the hospital without them. Cody's mother needed medical attention. They would follow as soon as possible.

Three UNLV security vehicles transported the family and friends to the University Medical Center across town. Devon rode with Sonny and Olin in the first car. The others followed in two separate cars. The cars arrived in minutes and the group was led to the waiting area, where Gunner had been pacing for ten or fifteen minutes. Gunner ran to Devon and grabbed her from Sonny's arms.

"Where's Cody, Gunner?" Devon asked, not certain that she wanted to know the answer.

"Cody is in the operating room, Devon. He was hurt bad. The doctors are doing everything they can to help your father. He's as strong as the goddamn bull that hit him. If anyone can pull through this, your father will."

Gunner had both arms around Devon and could not stop the tears running down his cheeks. Devon remained emotionless. The group surrounding Devon, consisted of Gary Dietz, Brian Helton, Alexandra Warring and Tolbert Lawerence. Sonny and Olin showed little resilience from previous accidents they had witnessed inside the rodeo arena. The seven faces reflected nothing but the gravity of the moment.

"Can I sit, Gunner?" Devon asked, now the placid centurion among the group. Gunner placed Devon on one of the semi-padded row seats inside the waiting area.

"If Cody dies Gunner, you can take me back to Castle Rock." Devon hung her head and sat motionless.

Gunner stared down at Devon, incapable of understanding anything at this point. Gunner gathered a semblance of coherent thought and reached over to Devon's cheek. Gunner's rough hand mangled from years of bull riding and ranching scraped the silk skin of Devon's chin. Gunner pulled the girl's face to look him in the eye.

"You're with us now." The message was short and interrupted. The lead surgeon approached the waiting area. Men resonated language implicitly from posture more directly than from speech. Gunner stood up to accept the inevitable news.

"Can we speak privately?" The surgeon inquired. Gunner followed the doctor after telling Devon to wait with Sonny. Devon stood up and followed the pair like a shadow. The doctor paused when the little girl began to follow them.

"I am Cody's daughter." Devon declared defiantly.

"Is there someone you can sit with for a few minutes, young lady? I need to speak to Mr. McGarrity, briefly." The doctor performed his duty reluctantly.

"She's with me." Gunner responded for Devon.

"I would rather speak to you directly, Mr. McGarrity."

"You will speak to us directly. Cody's daughter has more right to know the condition of her father than anyone in this room." Gunner was direct. The surgeon complied immediately.

"Cody was struck in the sternum. The bull's horn punctured the chest and lacerated the heart. At the moment of impact, Cody was in cardiac arrest or complete heart failure. The paramedics were virtually helpless on the arena floor. The rodeo paramedic team knew that the only chance to save your father was to get him here as soon as possible."

"When Cody arrived, his heart was not working. We had to engage emergency surgery on Cody and attempt to sew the heart back together. We did everything humanly possible, but the force of the contact destroyed the heart. I could not mend the damage. We were unable to successfully close any of the wounds inflicted by the animal. Cody died on the arena floor and we could not repair the damage inflicted. I have never seen a surgical team work so feverishly and so hard to save a patient, but we could not bring him back. I'm so sorry. Your father did not suffer. He died on impact." The doctor knelt down to speak directly to Devon.

"Be proud of your father. I've been the Director of the Trauma Unit here for four years and a surgeon for nineteen years, but I grew up in Oklahoma. I was raised on rodeo. Championships had nothing to do with teams or uniforms. They were all about buckles. They were all about courage. I am very sorry for your loss, Devon. There is nothing I can say to bring Cody back, but there is true honor in the way Cody lived and the way he died. Remember that for the rest of your life." The surgeon stood up.

Devon remained stoic, understandably despondent, but almost phlegmatic. "I watched you ride, Mr. McGarrity, many years ago. I was a big fan. I wish we could have met under a different set of circumstances." Gunner shook hands with the exasperated physician.

"Me too, doctor." Gunner had few words. Gunner pulled Devon close to his side. Devon was rigid and cold.

"Mr. McGarrity?" The Trauma Unit Director had a question. Gunner looked up. "The paramedics said Cody rode Skoal Dagger for the full eight seconds before the accident."

"It was no accident." Gunner glared back.

"The rodeo paramedic team said the judges gave Cody a ninety-eight when the score was posted. I know it doesn't matter now, but I wish I could have seen Cody ride." The Sooner native commented.

"You're wrong, doctor." Gunner grabbed Devon's hand. "It matters more than ever now. Cody kicked Skoal's ass and the bull knew it." Gunner and Devon returned to the group and confirmed what they already knew. Cody's parents had arrived minutes earlier, while Cody and Devon were talking to the surgeon.

Everyone stared ahead in silence. Shock is a strangling emotion that no one can anticipate or prepare for. Devon looked up at Gunner.

"I'd like to see Cody" Devon requested calmly and quietly. Some were sobbing. Others were frightened and nervous. Devon grabbed Gunner's hand and repeated the startling request. I'd like to see Cody before we leave."

"Wait here Devon." Gunner answered. He walked back to the surgeon. Gunner and the surgeon disappeared for a brief time. Gunner returned and took Devon's hand. "Are you sure, Devon?"

Gunner and Devon walked to the surgical operating room. They paused at the door. Cody's clothing had been gathered up. A white sheet covered the body on the table. Devon and Gunner entered the room. Gunner waited near the door and let go of Devon's hand. Devon walked to the table. Cody's face was uncovered. The color was gone from Cody's cheeks. Devon stared at the ashen figure, lying so still. Devon reached across Cody's chest and laid her head on his shoulder.

"I'm so sorry, Cody." Devon whispered and began to cry. "I thought the bad things would stop, Cody. I'm sorry. I can't stop them. I'm so sorry. You tried so hard."

Devon's words became muffled and she wanted, so bad, just to wake him up. Gunner allowed the final farewell to play out. The terms were not his call. Devon finally backed away and turned to Gunner. The tears ran down her cheeks.

"They didn't have to take Cody, Gunner. He didn't do anything." Her eyes were clouded almonds. Devon's shoulders dropped in market surrender. The final plea hung over the room like a cold summer rain. Devon ran out of the room. Gunner let her go.

"Rest in peace, my friend. You earned it." Gunner made the sign of the cross and kissed Cody's forehead.

The ninety-eight point ride awarded Cody Law aboard Skoal Dagger at the 1990 NFR Finals would stand as the highest point total for a single ride in the history of Professional Rodeo. No one would ever ride Skoal Dagger, again. A funeral would be held in Chicago on the following Tuesday. Thousands would pay their respects during the memorial services at Holy Name Cathedral in Chicago.

Gunner took Devon back to the ranch in California on the morning after Cody died. They chose not to attend the funeral in Chicago because that part of Cody's life was foreign to them. Gunner meant no disrespect to any member of Cody's family or inner circle of friends and business associates, but Gunner did not want to bring Devon across the country to be poked and prodded by strangers who knew Cody for years and never understood anything about him.

Tolbert Lawerence met with Gunner and Devon in their hotel room before they left for California. Tolbert carried some papers for Gunner to keep. Cody had appointed Gunner and Jacquie McGarrity as Devon's legal guardian in the event Cody could not continue in that capacity for any reason.

"You knew about the guardian appointment, right?" Tolbert asked Gunner. "Cody told me that he discussed it with you."

"We discussed it." Gunner answered, not particularly happy about discussing it under the present circumstances.

"Mr. McGarrity, Cody Law was a wealthy man." Tolbert Lawerence declared.

"I'm not certain that this is the best time to discuss Cody's estate?" Gunner responded quizzically, if not slightly offended.

"We will formally announce the conditions of Cody's will during the next week. Forgive any inference that these matters are relevant tonight. My office will contact you at the California address. Suffice it to say Mr. McGarrity, Devon will be receiving nearly four million dollars. You will be receiving more than two million dollars. Cody's parents are well taken care of. The remainder of Cody's assets comprise real estate holdings, both personal and commercial. Cody is the majority interest in the corporation that owns a sizeable portion of Chicago's nightlife. Provisions in the will address the sale and assignment of those assets. By this time next year Mr. McGarrity, you and Devon will have received somewhere in the neighborhood of ten million dollars each. "

"Cody was my friend as well, Mr. McGarrity. He asked me to handle these details should anything ever happen to him. As executor, I will be in touch. As Cody's friend, I knew that Cody thought the world rotated under your heels, Mr. McGarrity." The formal attorney's voice began to flutter. "We all envied the trust and admiration that Cody held for you, Mr. McGarrity. Cody confided in me quite a bit."

"A lot of good that did him." Gunner spoke humbly. The dollars never registered.

" More than you know, Mr. McGarrity. I'll say good night, now." Tolbert Lawerence shook hands with Gunner and they agreed to speak during the week.

Devon had not broken down since the hospital. She was quiet and sad, but the emotional disintegration was absent.

"Devon." Gunner began after Tolbert left the hotel room. "Cody made sure that if anything happened to him, Jacquie and I would become your legal guardians."

Gunner had noticed that Devon could not look anyone in the eye since Cody's ride. Devon and Gunner had been back in the room for a couple hours. Gunner asked the hotel security to make sure that no one disturbed the room. The hospital had done an excellent job in keeping the press away from Devon and Gunner. Gunner anticipated the same dilemma at the hotel. The staff at Caesar's eliminated those concerns. Devon was wearing the same clothes that her father had worn.

"Gunner, you can still take me back to Castle Rock." Devon mumbled and continued to stare straight ahead. " It's where I belong. "

The statement was not a martyred plea to stay. There were no self-effacing, Machiavellian motives. Devon believed for years that there had to be something wrong with her. Although the things Billy Don Barrett did to her were criminal, degrading and tortuous at the very least, Devon continued to imagine that there had to be some reason for the cruelty. There had to be a reason why the cruelty continued for years. The reason had to come from within her.

Cody cleared Devon's demons briefly. When Cody died, Devon's rationalizations reverted to the long-standing inner belief that she was evil in some way. Devon preferred to risk going back to Castle Rock over watching something nefarious happen to Gunner and his family.

"You are never going back to Castle Rock." Gunner stated emphatically.

"When Cody found out about you Devon, his entire life changed. Trust me, Devon. Cody was never happier than during his time with you. He would have never traded that time, however short, for a lifetime of wealth without you. When Cody chose rodeo to help him find you, he found so much more. Rodeo defined men and who they were, not what they do. That's why Cody didn't give up bull riding when he found you. Cody wanted his daughter to know where he stood and who he was. It was the first time in your life to see what a parent could accomplish through the love of a child. I am going to do what Cody asked me to do. I am going to take care of you, Devon because I promised Cody."

"If God's testing you, then he has to know by now that he's overmatched. Cody never would have left if he knew different. You got his soul, Devon. You'll never walk one step further without Cody's strength. Cody had to wait twelve years to instill the safety and strength in his heart. It's obvious now that Cody came into your life to tell you that his presence had always been there." Gunner paused and Devon's eyes followed him across the room.

"I could cash in my pity tickets and wallow in a bathtub of guilt." Gunner turned to look back at Devon. Devon never blinked. "Did I teach Cody just enough to get him killed? I won't insult Cody with weak sorrow. I respected Cody as a man and I will not denigrate him by questioning the decisions we made and those we cannot change. Everything he did put you and I exactly where we are. You got him now, Devon. This is a train ride we are taking together! It may shake a little, but nobody is hopping off. Got it?"

"Got it." Devon felt safe again. She got up and threw her arms around Gunner's waist and cried like a baby.

* * *

A week had passed since Cody's death. The ranch in California gave Devon another chance to reconstruct a fleeting childhood. Gunner and Jacquie made breakfast every morning with Devon. Jason and Tyler spent much of the week on the ranch. Devon rode Tulip from early in the morning until the boys brought her back to the house as the sun cast an orange glow across the ranch.

It was Friday morning on the West Coast. Gunner was stumbling through a disastrous skillet of scrambled eggs. Devon had taken Tulip up to the access road leading to the rodeo arena. Gunner's Bull Riding School did not start up until one month after the NFR Finals each year. The telephone rang and startled Gunner. It was early.

"Hello." Gunner grabbed the phone thinking Jacquie might still be asleep.

"Gunner, is that you?" A familiar voice came through. "It's Junior Mayer."

"Hello, my friend. It is always good to hear from you." Gunner was genuinely glad to pick up the phone and hear an old friend on the line. Junior Mayer was an old bull riding traveling partner. They drove together across the country from rodeo to rodeo, more times than Gunner could remember. Junior was the Contestant Director for the PRCA, now. "What's up, Junior?"

"I never got a chance to talk to you after Cody's accident. We're all sorry about what happened to Cody. We know that was as much you aboard Skoal Dagger as Cody. You know Barker, Cahill and some of the other boys felt like maybe we let you down. Skoal should have never been in the mix." Junior had rehearsed the call. He was nervous.

"You know that's crap, Junior. The riders wanted Skoal in the mix. It wasn't you, but hearing from you is good, man. Big weekend comin' up. I haven't followed the Finals. Who's got the best string?" Gunner asked, but didn't care.

"Hedeman has six out of seven. A couple others got five." Junior knew Gunner didn't care. "How's the girl, Gunner?"

"Better than me." Gunner admitted. "Devon has had so much to handle, but she has kept this ranch together during the past week. I don't want to let her out of my sight."

"We all followed this thing, Gunner. What you and Cody did was remarkable."

"What Cody did was remarkable." Gunner interrupted. "What Devon has been through at twelve years old and the strength in that little girl is remarkable."

"Gunner." Junior hesitated for a second. "We want you and Devon to attend the last night of the Finals, if you can."

"We?" Gunner balked.

"The PRCA Board of Directors, the contestants, all your friends, Gunner. We want to pay our respects properly, our way." Junior was sincere.

"Three or four guys have offered to send their planes to get you and Devon and your entire family. It's been an empty week, here. I know it's probably more for us, but there's a page missin' here, partner. Can I tell one of these big-ass contractors to send a plane to Santa Maria?"

"I don't know, Junior. Devon is just settling in here at the ranch. I don't know if bringing her back to the Mack Center is such a good idea? I don't know if it's such a good idea for me?" Gunner hesitated to tell Junior that he thought it could be a disaster.

"It's your call, Gunner." Junior agreed.

"No, it's Devon's call. I'll get back to you later today." Gunner said good-bye and hung up. The scrambled eggs looked like a skillet of black marbles.

Gunner walked out to the main barn, no more than twenty yards from the house. Jason and Tyler were helping the permanent ranch workers load some fence posts destined for the north ridge. The boys had stayed around all week. Gunner knew they had put their lives on hold to make Devon feel like a sister.

"Where's Devon?" Gunner asked as he grabbed a handful of metal.

"She took Tulip down to the arena. I told her not to go any further." Jason answered. "Attila went along with her."

"Oh, now I'm relieved." Gunner smiled and rolled his eyes.

Gunner walked outside behind the original barn to the new ten-stall open-air barn. The new thoroughbred complex at the ranch was part of Gunner's dream. A sixteen-stall stallion barn was planned for next year. Two foaling stalls would be complete in the spring. A fifty-foot sand based round pen was under construction. The main mare pasture utilized a forty-acre lake. Ten separate paddocks were planned for next year, as well. Gunner envisioned a facility that could continue to train bull-riders, but expand into the thoroughbred racing market. If bulls were Gunner's passion, horses were his love. The thoroughbreds had not arrived and the time line remained sketchy. Financial considerations always dictated the project.

Gunner pulled out his own horse, Brave. Brave was an athletic quarter horse, a thoroughbred/mustang cross. Brave was unusual because he was black. At sixteen hands, Brave stood calm and elegant for his breed. Gunner took off from the barn at full stride. The boys still enjoyed the showmanship and natural ability that Gunner possessed on a horse. Gunner didn't ride bulls anymore, but he continued to brush a canvas of western royalty atop any high-stepping stallion. Gunner McGarrity was born with spurs on his heels.

Gunner rode Brave down to the rodeo arena near the bottom of the main drive. Tulip was tied correctly to the front gate. Gunner pulled up and wrapped his reins around the front gate. The horse wouldn't go anywhere, but it was a good example. The arena was empty. The complex resembled a deserted relic from an old movie set. Devon was sitting on top of one of the chutes. The stalls were empty, but the aroma lingered. Attila sat patiently behind Devon. The dog was accustomed to the mammoth creatures inside the chutes, so he opted on the side of caution and stayed back. Attila figured out that a bull could come barreling down those runways at any time. The dog sniffed a little and then backed off. Gunner laughed at the delusional mutt.

"Makes you kinda wonder how many times that little dog has been kicked in the head." Gunner wondered out loud. Devon had heard the horse ride up. "Whatcha' doin out here?" Gunner asked.

"Just thinking. I like this place." Devon replied.

"Thinking about anything special?" Gunner played the fool.

"Gunner..." Devon gave him a look.

"O.K., O.K. I got a phone call this morning from a friend." Gunner began. "This guy was an old rodeo partner of mine. We used to travel across the country together and try to make enough money at each rodeo to eat three squares and make the entrance fees at the next rodeo. He works for the PRCA as one of the contestant directors. I have no idea what he does, but I know him and he is a close friend. His name is Junior Mayer. Junior asked me if you and I would go back to the Finals for the last night. Junior says that there are a whole lot of people that thought what Cody did was something very special. They want to be able to tell you that in-person. They'll fly us into Las Vegas on a private plane. They will also bring in Jacquie, Jason, and Tyler. If I push, I know they will pick up Sonny and Olin, wherever they are."

"What do you want to do, Gunner?" Devon predictably asked.

"I don't want to do anything that could make things harder for you, Devon."

"What would Cody want, Gunner?" Devon was watching Attila join Gunner's canine contingent. The dogs followed Gunner everywhere like long shadows on a summer afternoon.

"Cody would still be laughing at poor little Attila." Gunner mused.

"You know what I mean." Devon rolled her eyes.

"Cody engaged confrontations. He liked things in his face." Gunner sat down next to Devon. "Cody would not want us sniveling around the ranch like two puffy eyed marshmallows, blubbering and feeling sorry for ourselves. No matter how many times your father got tossed in this arena, I never had to tell him to get back up and do it again. Cody believed that perseverance was *the mother of good luck."*

"He'd go?" Devon asked.

"For you, Devon? How do they say it, in a New York minute?" Gunner winked.

"What are they going to do?" Devon asked.

"I don't know, Devon. Could be a bunch of tongue-tied cowboys trying to tell you something you already know. It's your call. Like I said, I don't want to make things harder for you." Gunner looked out over the arena he built.

"Harder is all in your head, Gunner." Devon perked up.

"Tell me again, Devon. How old are you?" Gunner McGarrity shook his head.

* * *

Sunday was the final round of the National Finals Rodeo. The tenth round in ten days. For every rodeo junkie, rodeo fan or anyone with a passing interest in the sport, the final round was the bottom of the ninth inning during the seventh game of the World Series. Scores of eighteen wheeled semi-trailer television trucks surrounded the Thomas and Mack Center. Experienced directors scrambled to double the number of camera angles from the previous rounds.

Condescending metaphors from mainstream America played down the annual mecca to Las Vegas. In reality, the sport of rodeo embodies all that has been lost through the self-serving platitudes of wealth above competition and moral purpose so prevalent in professional sports. America is spawning a narcissistic avalanche of high-profile athletes. Cowboys are not museum pieces in costumes. Cowboys wear sportsmanship on their sleeve like a right of passage, a mantra not lost on a growing legion of parents never before exposed to bucking animals, precision roping events and hard-charging barrel racers. Dirk Johnson wrote years ago, *while cowboys may not be successful in society's measure, monetary terms...they are accomplished in their own minds and the minds of their peers.* On the final night of the 1990 National Finals Rodeo, Cody Law's peers wanted to tell him just that.

The Thomas and Mack Center was filled beyond the standing room capacity of the arena. The chaotic scramble for any NFR paraphernalia at the numerous merchandise booths began to strip the shelves completely clean. The stadium seats were filling faster than on any other night. Spectators chose not to mill around the hallways. Something was in the air.

Devon, Jacquie, Jason, Tyler and Cody arrived at the Thomas and Mack Center in a black limousine provided by the stock contractors. Gunner had requested a quiet arrival and the limousine ducked around to one of the many service entrances. Gunner, Devon and the family were escorted through the cavernous kitchens below the main floor. Dozens of white apron clad employees were organizing mountains of snacks to be shuffled upstairs to the concession stands throughout the night.

Devon's manner might have been perceived as sullen by most strangers, but Gunner knew Devon was quiet and not prone to display any emotions. Junior Mayer met Gunner and Devon at the entrance to the main floor of the arena. He asked permission to show them to their seats. Junior explained that the seats were in the first row behind the announcer's booth, which sat at the equivalent of center ice on the glass or the fifty-yard line. The short stairway led to the arena seats. With each step, Devon wondered why they came back.

Inside the arena, the scoreboard flashed the current standings at the end of the ninth round. Each event rotated on the four-sided Jumbotron, which hung from the center rafters of the stadium. Gunner greeted many fans that recognized the former world champion as they made their way to the seats. When they arrived at the designated section, Devon froze and pulled her hands up to her mouth. Devon could not speak. She took two more steps and wrapped her arms around Dana Davenport. Anna Larkin stood next to Dana Davenport. Devon looked past Dana and gasped again. Devon pulled them both together and buried herself in the only protection she had known for years. Gunner waited with a big smile across his face.

"How did you guys find me?" Devon finally came down long enough to ask.

"Devon, Cody set this up before the accident. He wanted all of us to have a big reunion after the last night of the Finals. Cody arranged all of the plane tickets and hotels for all of us. Cody offered to fly in any family members, as well. I told Cody that I would be here anyway because Justin made the Finals. He wouldn't hear of anything else. He put us all up at Caesar's Palace." Anna Larkin explained.

"I'm so sorry about what happened. Dana and I called earlier in the week, but Gunner suggested we meet here."

"Gunner suggested that we meet here?" Devon looked around for Gunner. "Where is he?" Gunner pulled his hat very low over his eyes. "I thought you told me that your old rodeo partner called and suggested that we do this?"

"He did." Gunner recounted. "I had already decided with Dana and Anna to try and see if we could put this night together. After all, it was Cody's idea." Gunner flashed that sly grin again.

"What else was Cody's idea, Gunner?" Devon knew there had to be more. Gunner looked at Devon and pointed behind her. Devon turned around.

"Say hello to Cadrell, Devon." Gunner suggested. Devon jumped into Cadrell's arms and buried her face into Cadrell Easley's chest. The former rodeo contestant and Castle Rock police officer could hug like a grizzly bear and those strong arms had Devon missing Cody, just a little bit more.

Suddenly, the lights in the arena went black. Every light in the stadium fell dark. The only remaining illumination within the arena, were the faint red exit lights above the stairwells. Twenty-one thousand people stopped talking and stood still. The Thomas and Mack Center held a collective breath. Silence enveloped the capacity crowd faster than a Marine drill sergeant calling for attention. Fans turned in their seats, searching for a clue as to what would follow. SRO ticket holders gazed blankly while standing in the aisles. Couples held hands. Parents held small children. For that moment, time was irrelevant. There was apprehension and nervous anticipation. The National Finals Rodeo never began in this manner.

After nearly one minute of complete darkness and silence, the four large screens inside the arena came alive with the triumphant likeness of Cody Law. The photograph, now more than ten feet tall on each side of the scoreboard, depicted Cody as he stood before the accident. The hat was gone. The hair was hanging on his shoulders and across his face. Cody flashed the smile of accomplishment, while his arms extended high in the air. With clenched fists, he stood erect after having ridden the ride of a lifetime. Ninety-eight points flashed across the screen between the red, white and blue chaps that Cody wore for the first time last Friday night. Devon nearly fainted. Her knees grew weak and she grabbed Gunner's hand. A muscle spasm seized Gunner's throat.

Thousands of fans sucked the air from the arena and remained silent. A single spotlight pierced the darkness and illuminated a microphone and stool placed in the center of the arena floor. The rodeo announcer spoke and the words boomed out across the hushed stadium.

"LADIES AND GENTLEMEN, PLEASE WELCOME CAPITAL RECORDING ARTIST AND THE PRCA 1976 WORLD BAREBACK CHAMPION, MASON DAYNE".

From across the neatly raked arena floor, the tall cowboy walked to the center spotlight. A warm reception greeted the former world champion bareback rider. Mason Dayne carried a Martin, six-string guitar as he strolled to the waiting stool. The black Stetson was pulled low and Mason did not acknowledge the applause. The crowd grew silent again, as Mason adjusted the lower microphone to meet the height of his guitar. Mason pulled the microphone stand closer and tapped the taller microphone near his mouth. The sweet ringing of the Martin echoed through the arena as Mason Dayne strummed once to test the sound. Mason spoke briefly to the silent packed stadium.

"I did not know Cody Law for a long time, but I knew him long enough." The public address system rang clear and loud. *"If Cody could have written a song for his daughter, the song would have gone something' like this."*

The guitar rang again and a softer spotlight threw a warm yellow light on the box behind the announcer's booth. Devon, Gunner and their guests looked stunned in the yellow glow as two spotlights creased the darkness of the Thomas and Mack Center. Devon fixed her eyes on the solitary singer she never met. Thousands fixed their eyes on the little girl they had read so much about. The lyrics read like the bright winter day when Devon met her father at the Douglas County Fairgrounds. A familiar voice pulled from the archives of the signature music and hypnotized an impassioned crowd. A Wyoming cowboy sang a song that no one would soon forget.

Badland bred with outlaw speed, a mustang tale since time began.
Grab your hat and hold on tight, I'm gonna catch that horse if I can.
And when I do, he'll be just for you.
We'll take that ride together, far beyond the doubt.
A tandem sketched against the clouds, precious memories spill about.
Trust the lines upon my face, traced and weathered by the sun,
And know that you're the reason for all I've ever done.

What happened to the saddle shoes and turned out little toes,
Nestled up against my shoulder, a pushed up freckled nose.
Never drift so far away or forget where you came from,
You will always be the reason for all I've ever done.

A debutante child soldier, too young to do it well,
Painted down in total darkness, a year of living Hell.
Lessons came too quickly and always the wrong time,
Yet a prelude to the man I'd be and all that I might find.
The elusive butterfly had landed at the sacrifice of youth,
To swallow the illusion of non-existent truth.

What happened to the saddle shoes and turned out little toes,
Nestled up against my shoulder, a pushed up freckled nose.
Never drift so far away or forget where you came from,
You will always be the reason for all I've ever done.

I may find peace among the chance of daunting scripted fate,
Ask for no forgiveness, make no apologies to date.
A daughter is the yellow stud, dressed in her father's eye,
Graceful and pretentious in all that she might try.

What happened to the saddle shoes and turned out little toes,

Curled up against my shoulder, a pushed up freckled nose.
Never drift so far away or forget where you came from,
You will always be the reason for all I've ever done.

I think of those old saddle shoes and turned out little toes,
Playing games of hide and seek, tracking altruistic souls.
A ton of Brahma fury turned out to test the gate,
Petticoats and pigtails masked a self-respecting fate.
The Grail was not the buckle, they say I might have won.
Just open up the final grade on all I've ever done.

I would settle for a carbon copy of this unpredictable short run,
Because it left one shining starlight to all I've ever done.

The Grail was not the buckle, they say I might have won.
Just open up the final grade on all I've ever done.

The soft ballad ended. The simple chords from an acoustic guitar faded softly. Mason Dayne had sung directly to Devon Law. When the song concluded, Mason stood up facing Devon. Briefly, they were alone inside the stadium. The rodeo troubadour took off his hat and slightly bowed his head toward the teary-eyed little girl. Devon stood on shaky knees, staring at the singer. The black Stetson lay across his chest. Tears ran down Devon's face like a Colorado stream filled with the melting Rocky Mountain snow. The spotlights dimmed and the arena lights returned. A standing ovation burst forth while the overhead light banks surged on.

From the riding chutes, one lone bull rider jumped from atop the chute that once held Skoal Dagger. The Final's contestant wore # 15. Norman Curry from Deberry, Texas walked to the center of the arena floor where Mason Dayne stood. The ovation continued to grow. Suddenly, all thirteen remaining bull-riders jumped from atop the same chute. Hedeman, Nuce, Gaffney, Sharp, Custer, Murray, Branger, Dunn, and all thirteen bull-riders strode to the center of the arena floor in a solitary salute to a fallen friend. The ovation climbed another notch. The noise was deafening. Suddenly, both ends of the arena opened and every NFR Finals contestant walked out toward the middle of the arena floor. Bareback riders filed out in a single line, Everyone was dressed in full competition gear.

The bareback riders lined up next to the bull-riders and behind Mason Dayne. Steer wrestlers, saddle bronc riders, team ropers, calf-ropers and barrel racers followed suit. One hundred and nineteen contestants stood in formation before Devon Law. The ovation was now thundering the foundation of the Thomas and Mack Center. Cameras flashed by the thousands. The inside of the Thomas and Mack Center became an ephemeral light show, buoyed by the ear-splitting din of those sensing something remarkable.

Finally, the faithful began to sit down and the ovation began to wane. The contestants were lined up in two lines, one directly behind the other. The lines stretched laterally across the arena floor. The rodeo announcer came back over the public address speakers.

"Ladies and Gentlemen, the 1990 National Finals Rodeo Contestant ranks and Mr. Mason Dayne."

The applause rocked the Thomas and Mack Center once again. Mason Dayne walked to the rodeo announcer's booth and hopped up on top of the announcer's table, now eye level with Gunner and Devon's box. Gunner leaned over and hugged an old friend. Mason leaned down and kissed Devon on the cheek. He smiled down at Devon and tossed his hat into Devon's lap. Mason Dayne left the arena to a second standing ovation. Devon turned the hat over and written inside the white lining were the words, *God Bless Cody Law. Your friend always, Mason Dayne.*

Norman Curry was the first contestant in line. Norman walked to the announcer's table and tossed his white Resistol toward Gunner McGarrity. Gunner caught the hat and written on the white brim were the words, *Bravo, Cody Law. Ninety-eight point ride. We'll miss you, Norman Curry.* The remaining thirteen bull riders followed suit. Each bull rider tossed their hat into Gunner's box. Each hat had a message written on the brim or the inside lining. The bareback riders followed the bull riders, each handed over a personalized message on a hat. Some contestants pinned their contestant numbers to the hat with a message written on the face of the number. The entire contestant ranks took their turns and filled Gunner's box with one hundred nineteen hats. The last contestant in line was Justin Wheeler, Anna Larkin's fiancee. Justin tossed his hat to Gunner and then climbed up on the announcer's table. Justin handed an NFR contestant back number to Devon. The canvas patch read across the front as follows:

Cody Law
NFR
Las Vegas, NV 90
1

On the back of the contestant number, a hand written message read, *To Devon, You are a part of our family now, forever. All my love, Gunner.*

Devon sat with Mason Dayne's hat resting so large on her head. Anna Larkin, Jacquie and Dana Davenport tried to assemble several dozen hats in neat stacks. Devon Law had finally succumbed to the enormity of the evening. Devon raised her knees and peered out from under the enormous hat. Devon looked for Gunner. Gunner pushed the hat down over her eyes.

"Give 'em hell, Justin Wheeler." Gunner McGarrity declared.

"Yes, sir." Wheeler replied. Anna Larkin wiped her eyes. Justin turned to jump from the announcer's table. He paused for a second. The last cowboy brought the house down. Justin raised his arms as Cody had done following his ride on Skoal Dagger. The fourth or fifth raucous ovation, Gunner had lost track, filled the arena one more time. The world's most popular rodeo gathering just became the loudest. Justin leapt from the table and raced to the exit.

The rodeo announcer's voice crackled loud and strong above the Thomas and Mack Center:

PULL'EM UP BOYS. WE'RE READY TO RODEO.

* * *

~CHAPTER VII~

Six months later

The car appeared nearly as out of place as the suits. Vague outlines amidst a swirling blanket of dust from the road, the black Ford Taurus sedan pulled to a stop on the main drive to Gunner McGarrity's ranch. Two men dressed in dark business suits stood outside the sedan looking as lost in the June sunshine as children separated from their parents at a county fair. They turned in unison, hoping the other would profess to know which direction to follow. Both men moved like molasses, waiting for someone to approach them. The early Sunday morning movement of the bulls on the near pasture caught their attention. Gunner McGarrity was expecting them. Gunner walked from the main house to greet the two men.

"I'm Gunner McGarrity. Did you have any trouble finding the place?" Gunner asked.

"Notwithstanding the large centurions guarding the road up here, we seemed to have arrived in one piece. We have seen guard dogs before, but..." Matt Turner remarked.

"My bulls like to know who's coming." Gunner smiled. "Come inside, I just made some coffee."

The three men walked into the kitchen of Gunner's home. The rough motif mirrored the grounds. Butcher block tables and iron stoves filled a kitchen cut from the archives of Red River. Stills from the commercial spots filled the walls. Gunner and a slew of cowboys were touting products from Canadian beer to Pepsi-Cola. Rodeo posters framed in carved mahogany hung alongside the bay windows overlooking the ranch. The three men took coffee and settled at the large oval wooden table just off the main kitchen. Gunner's boots hit the hardwood floors and startled two sleeping cats. The soft Italian leather shoes barely made a sound.

"My name is Matt Turner and this is Steven Sanders." The three men shook hands. "I know the phone call came out of the blue, but we appreciate your time, Mr. McGarrity."

"Call me Gunner."

"Well, Gunner." Matt Turner continued. "As I told you on the phone, Steven and I work as investigators for the Attorney General's office in Denver. I was purposely vague on the phone. It is imperative that any discussions during our visit remain private and we must insist that you do not carry these discussions further than this room until the appropriate time."

"Forgive me, Mr. Turner, but you seem to be issuing too many instructions and not enough information." Gunner was not rude, simply direct.

"Call me Matt." Matt Turner retorted. Gunner smiled and nodded. Matt

Turner continued.

"William Don Barrett has directed his attorneys to file a civil rights lawsuit in Federal District Court in Denver. The action named six defendants. They are the Douglas County District Attorney's Office, the Castle Rock Police Department, District Attorney Shana McDonough, Officer Cadrell Easley, the estate of Cody Law and you, Mr. McGarrity. Barrett claims that the defendants, while acting under the authority of the State of Colorado intentionally violated the Plaintiff's constitutional right to be free from unreasonable search and seizure. The Plaintiff is asking for ten million dollars in damages. "

"You have got to be joking?" Gunner stared at Matt Turner.

"The Federal District Court in Denver and the Attorney General do not send out investigators as a joke, Mr. McGarrity." Steven Sanders replied.

"The police and the District Attorney work under the veil of sovereign immunity and qualified immunity. What that means is that law enforcement is free from lawsuits as long as both entities have relied on information from reliable sources and they were acting within the scope of their jobs. The dismissal of charges, as in Barrett's case, based on illegally obtained information does not constitute a civil rights action in itself. The Plaintiff must show the police and the District Attorney's office acted with malice and vindictiveness. The Plaintiff may also proceed if he can show collusion between the police and the prosecutor to intentionally deprive the Plaintiff of his constitutional rights. "

Gunner became agitated, moving uncomfortably in his seat and running his hands through his hair.

"My wife and Devon are at my son Tyler's home. We have breakfast there on Sundays. I agreed to meet with you now because I knew they would be gone. Do you know the background of this case?" Gunner asked rhetorically.

"Yes sir, we know the case and we know the frustration associated with these civil actions." Matt Turner answered.

"Frustration, Mr. Turner." Gunner stood up. "When a man tortured a child for years without consequence and was finally brought to trial, you would think the system could recognize the child. Barrett was caught raping Devon Law and walked away, laughing. Perfect, now we owe Barrett for the injustice done to him? There is a twelve-year map of abuse. I thought your visit had something to do with the efforts to put this fuck away. The courts tossed the case because I ruffled some feathers to get Barrett's address. How do we go from there to this? Get Kirsten, Devon's mother to testify. Offer her immunity. Use the tapes. They fucking show what he was doing to Devon." Gunner was livid.

"Our information shows that the girl will not testify. Devon could make the case against Barrett." Steven Sanders pulled from some notes.

"Devon cannot testify. Her father laid that law and I will go to my grave to protect what Cody died for." Gunner searched for some sanity. "What are you doing here?"

"The case against Barrett was not tossed because you ruffled some feathers." Matt Turner changed his tone.

"The case against William Don Barrett was dropped because Shana McDonough enlisted the help of Cadrell Easley to do whatever it took to bring Mr. Barrett to trial. Shana McDonough was enraged by the inexcusable conduct of the police in allowing Mr. Barrett to build a decade of patterned abuse. Cadrell Easley was the one link in the Castle Rock Police Department that she needed. McDonough offered Easley carte blanche to bring Barrett to justice. You and Mr. Law, conveniently provided the tools. Had Cadrell Easley not been present at the Rascal Flats on the night you "ruffled" some feathers, then Mr. Barrett's case would have no merit."

"By allowing you to extract the information used to arrest Mr. Barrett, Cadrell Easley stripped the shield of sovereign immunity. Those actions paved the way for any dime-store law firm to jump all over the civil rights violations. A District Attorney and the police conspired to push the case against Barrett. The officer was assured no actions would be taken against him regardless of the means necessary to nail Barrett."

" Who the fuck told you this, Billy Don Barrett?" Gunner mused. "Does the Attorney General act on the fantasy of all defendants kicked on technicalities? "

"The Attorney General's office acts on the implications of all possible civil rights violations as dictated by the Civil Rights Act of 1983. Subsequent statements obtained have propelled this case to an "A" list." Matt Turner was thorough.

"You are losing me, gentlemen." Gunner exclaimed. "What subsequent statements?"

"Do you know where the easiest confessions are obtained, Mr. McGarrity?" Steven Sanders asked condescendingly. Gunner was silent. Retribution, while distant, was now tracking extinction.

"We went to talk to Cadrell Easley on a Sunday morning, two weeks ago. The family was preparing for church and the timing of our visit was planned. Under the guise of morality, police officers purge themselves of wrongdoing like scared children in confession for the first time. With a career hanging on his statements, Cadrell Easley confirmed the conversations with Shana McDonough concerning William Don Barrett."

"Why would Easley admit to anything? A police officer's word will stand against the word of an unemployed child abuser. Who would believe Barrett?" Gunner wanted to know.

"In court, Mr. McGarrity." Turner jumped in. "William Don Barrett would appear as an unemployed citizen with a relatively clean record except for a couple misdemeanor arrests. Those incidents would be explained as frustration from the inability to find work and provide for his family. There are six statements by witnesses present in the Rascal Flat's on the night in question, that place Officer Easley on the scene during the alleged civil rights violations. Any denials by Officer Easley would likely bring about the end of his career."

"You see Mr. McGarrity, in a civil action, the Plaintiff must only prove his case by a preponderance of the evidence. A criminal trial must prove the case beyond a reasonable doubt. A civil trial must show that based on the facts presented, the violations were likely or reasonable to assume they had occurred. We do not want to ruin a police officer's career or the District Attorney's career because they over stepped the law to bring Mr. Barrett to justice. The case and the Plaintiff are not worth sacrificing Officer Cadrell Easley and District Attorney Shana McDonough. We do not want to lay out the police or the DA's office for Barrett. A civil trial may accomplish that. Based on our preliminary data, we can bring the case to closure with a settlement."

"The State of Colorado is going to pay Barrett ten million dollars to drop the case?" Gunner was floored.

"The worth of the defendants will not bear in this case." Matt Turner explained.

"The estate of Mr. Law is worth millions. The wealth of the State or any other defendant is not an issue in assigning monetary damages. The case is decided on what the damage is worth. Mr. Barrett has been unemployed and the charges against him were dropped relatively quickly in relation to the time he was incarcerated. The attorneys working for Barrett are obviously on contingency, so the offer made will be tendered based on those circumstances. We believe that Barrett may go away for one or two million."

"The State of Colorado is going to pay Billy Don Barrett one or two million dollars to go away?" The question rolled off Gunner's tongue with incredulous sarcasm.

"The man has a case, Mr. McGarrity." Sanders tried to justify the flow. "Remember, don't shoot the messenger."

"Where is the case against Barrett?" Gunner was reaching.

"We are not involved with the criminal case against Mr. Barrett." Matt Turner referred to more notes.

"It is our understanding, however, that Kirsten Myers Barrett will not testify against her ex-husband. She filed for divorce and moved back in with her parents. They now live in Englewood, Colorado, just south of Denver. Without her testimony or the testimony of the child, the case is dead. Have you spoken to Devon's mother?"

"I received a request from an attorney representing the Myers family, asking to allow Kirsten visitation with Devon. The request was denied. My answer conveyed the timing was too soon and the culpability of Devon's mother had not been settled. That was three months ago. We have heard nothing since." Gunner was confused.

"What about McDonough? Isn't the D.A. pursuing Barrett?"

"We do not work for the District Attorney. She has told us that her hands are tied because Devon will not be allowed to testify. Barrett was arrested on a misdemeanor charge last month, but the case was nothing more than a public intoxication complaint." Turner recalled from prior conversations with Shana McDonough.

"We need a deposition from you Mr. McGarrity, concerning the events leading to the arrest of William Don Barrett." Turner announced.

"For what?" Gunner shot back.

"You may be a defendant in the civil trial, Mr. McGarrity. The Attorney General has asked for depositions from all parties before any monetary settlement offers are made. You will be asked to attend a formal meeting with the Attorney General in Denver next week." Matt Turner explained.

"Am I legally required to appear?" Gunner asked.

"Not yet." Turner replied. "The appearance is voluntary."

"My family is not involved?" Gunner pushed.

"No, sir."

"If they stay that way, I'll show up." Gunner offered.

"Agreed, Mr. McGarrity." Matt Turner rose to shake hands. The two men shook hands and Gunner walked with the two investigators to the black sedan on the grounds. Matt Turner got in the car behind the wheel. Steven Sanders sat on the passenger's side and closed the door. Gunner leaned in to Matt Turner.

"How well do you really know this case, Mr. Turner?" Gunner was inches from Turner's face.

"I do my job, that's it. I'm not paid to do much more. If you'll excuse us?" The black sedan struggled to turn around. Gunner McGarrity watched them pull away.

* * *

Gunner McGarrity made his final trip to Castle Rock a week after the visit from the Attorney General's investigators. On the night Gunner checked into the Castle Rock Hotel, Billy Don Barrett stumbled out of the bathroom at the Flats. Barrett wanted to get one more drink before closing. The lights at Rascal Flats had been turned up for twenty minutes and the stench of stale beer and cigarettes hung like a muggy summer night in New Orleans. Barrett was the last to leave the Flats, as usual. Curly had retired upstairs nearly an hour before closing.

The bartender pulled on a beer and waited for Barrett to make it to the front door. Two other nameless vagabonds had sucked down the better part of two quarts of Jack Daniels with Barrett. In addition, the trio chased down more than a dozen beers apiece. Barrett enjoyed his limited notoriety among the regulars at the Flats. Billy Don Barrett bragged about the potential windfall from his legal pursuits as the evening progressed. The Kentucky whiskey fueled the pontification of another mindless meeting between men who cannot find the difference between a vocation and the excuse to wake up late day after day.

Barrett heard the door lock behind him. Billy walked to the parking lot behind the Flats. Barrett was back living at his Gilbert Street address. Kirsten had left and filed for divorce months ago. The neon lights from the Flats clicked off. The summer night was quiet and warm. A thin gray cloud cover stole the moon, while the nighttime shadows disappeared. Billy fumbled to find his keys, never considering the prudent avenue to walk the three blocks home. The parking lot made him nervous ever since the terrible beating he endured last year. Barrett stopped fumbling with the keys and stared across the lot.

"Who's there?" Barrett shouted, certain that he had heard someone.

The words ran together in an unintelligible alcoholic slur. Billy's car was parked against the back row near the trees lining the parking lot. The wind kicked up and Barrett whipped around to another non-existent sound.

"Fuck..." Barrett was now mumbling to himself. He lit a cigarette and missed the door lock with his key. The window was wide open, but the effort was a reflex. Billy pulled the keys up close to his face and slowly eyed each one, searching for the right key. Suddenly, Billy Don Barrett turned toward the trees near the back of the lot. A dark female silhouette emerged.

"Got a minute, Billy?" The woman asked.

"What the fuck are you doing here?" Billy asked as he spied the figure at the back of the lot. "Are you here to congratulate me or have you come to make amends?"

The woman moved closer and did not answer. Billy laughed, seemingly at ease now.

"Man, you made some fucking bad choices and now you want to waltz back and make things right?" Barrett slipped and nearly lost his balance. The whiskey had consumed everything.

"You can't stand the fact that I'm going to walk with all the money, can you?" The silence never bothered Billy Don Barrett. Barrett began to drown in the irony before him, yet he had no clue.

"Are you here to stand up for your precious little daughter? I don't think so. I think you're here because of the money. It's not about the girl now, is it?" Barrett roared with laughter. "It's all about the money. You just can't stand it, can you?" Barrett pulled again from the cigarette in his hand.

The flames exploded from the gun barrel. The quiet summer night filled with rapid thunder as an orange glow filled the dark sky. The parking lot blinked like a lighting field with each round from the weapon. Barrett's body shook with the impact of each shot and the bullets tore through his flesh like cannons ripping into a scarecrow.

Curly King almost wet his shorts as the night sky beyond his shades ignited with the pattern of the explosions. The shots continued in rapid succession. Billy Don Barrett's body fell limp across the hood of his car and slumped to the ground. A river of blood poured over the parking lot from the ravaged torso. Curly King struggled to reach the window. The deafening repetition ceased. Curly King pulled the shades back and watched the body twitch impulsively on the blood soaked pavement. King saw no one, except what was left of Billy Don Barrett. Curly closed the shades and downed three fingers of Crown Royal. The phone would ring soon. It would go unanswered.

* * *

Gunner McGarrity walked into the Douglas County Municipal Building alone. The appointment had been made three days after Billy Don Barrett was shot. The information Gunner sought could only come from the District Attorney. While his visit may have possessed a piquant challenge, the trip was motivated from reverence. The receptionist was polite, yet formal.

"May I help you, sir?" The question came as Gunner approached the office of the District Attorney.

"Gunner McGarrity to see District Attorney Shana McDonough, ma'am." Gunner announced.

The receptionist asked Gunner to wait for a moment while she announced the visitor to the Douglas County District Attorney. After a brief wait, the receptionist led Gunner into the office of Shana McDonough. Gunner thanked the young lady and watched her leave the office. Shana stood to greet the man she had not seen for many months.

"This is an unexpected pleasure, Mr. McGarrity." Shana remarked. "I thought that I may hear from you, but I did not expect a personal visit. How is Devon? Does she know what happened to Barrett?"

"Devon is fine, Ms. McDonough." Gunner began. "She knows that her stepfather is dead, but the details of Barrett's death have not been something we have discussed at length. That time will come. I assume that the defendants in Barrett's civil case are under suspicion?"

"The evidence has not singled out anyone. We all had reason to detest Mr. Barrett, but the alibis are strong for each defendant in Billy's civil suit. The physical evidence does not point to anyone in particular. My office has focused on Kirsten, but any indictment may be difficult. Kirsten's employer and parents can put her in Denver for the entire time line of the shooting. Would they lie? Of course, they would. Can we make a case? Not, yet." Shana McDonough returned to her desk.

"The civil case has been dismissed since Billy's death. The attorney's for Barrett made a motion to continue the civil trial on behalf of Barrett's immediate family, but the judge postponed the proceedings until the homicide investigation has been completed. The Castle Rock Police Department has come up with very little. If you're here to define the culpability we all face, then I am afraid I have no answers for you. My guess is that Barrett's death will end the civil trial for good. I wouldn't worry about any ghosts, Mr. McGarrity. Billy's legal end run evaporated on the parking lot behind Rascal Flats."

"I must tell you that I am not distraught with the news that Billy Don Barrett is no longer with us." Gunner began.

"I am here because none of us need a cloud surrounding Barrett's death to linger like the Texas heat in July. I agreed to raise Devon under the eyes of a man who died trying to do the right thing. I am a simple man, Ms. McDonough, but Cody wanted a clear shot with Devon and that is all that I am asking for. Cowboys are not an aberration or a mythical misnomer associated with chewing tobacco and illiteracy. By agreeing to raise Devon, my responsibility is to that child. I will use every means available to accomplish that task. "

"Cody's wealth and stature in Chicago stretched further than either of us could imagine. When Billy Don Barrett was killed, I knew the questions would center on the defendants in his civil case. Even a cowboy could figure that out, Ms. McDonough."

"My office is not pursuing a case against you or anyone associated with Cody Law. I do not understand why you appear so defensive?" Shana McDonough asked directly.

"I asked the attorneys for Cody Law to help me after Barrett was shot. I didn't shoot him, but I knew the questions would find their way to those least likely to have an answer. Cody was connected in Chicago to more law firms than I knew existed." Gunner kept scanning the room.

"Is this room wired, Ms. McDonough?"

"Of course not." Shana McDonough rose, a bit offended.

"There are no recordings of anything we may talk about?" Gunner pushed.

"No, Mr. McGarrity. This is not the White House." Shana responded with a bit of sarcasm.

"Cody's Law's legal entourage went to work for me immediately following Barret's death. I was concerned with protecting Devon. I gave the attorneys in Chicago the information that I had pertaining to the defendants in the civil trial and the facts known about the shooting death of Billy Don Barrett." Gunner proceeded.

"Cadrell Easley provided some of the facts surrounding the crime scene. Barrett was killed by a Glock 9mm, Model 19 semi-automatic weapon. The shells from an automatic are discharged from the weapon at the time the weapon is fired. Revolvers hold the casings. The Castle Rock Police reports indicated that there were numerous shells found in the parking lot from a Glock 9mm. The gun carries a fifteen-shot clip with one shell in the chamber. Barrett was shot fourteen times in rapid succession. His death was almost instantaneous. The shooter hit every shot. The body showed more than a dozen entry wounds. One or more of the entry wounds were large enough for two shots. The shooter was very familiar with the weapon and knew how to use it." Gunner paused for some reaction from Shana McDonough. There was no reaction. Gunner continued.

"Cody's attorneys also discovered that Barrett's last arrest was for more than public intoxication. According to the initial report pertaining to the arrest, Barrett was apprehended near the Castle Rock Elementary School for exposing himself to two young girls. Barrett was drunk, but had the presence of mind to lure the girls to his car and began masturbating once they arrived. One girl could not positively identify Barrett and the other girl declined to pursue the charges. The girl's mother was adamant about protecting her daughter. The police were forced to reduce the charge to public intoxication. The young girl declining to testify was your daughter, Melissa."

"You are beginning to lose me, Mr. McGarrity. Is there anything else?" Shana McDonough inquired. "You are giving me information that I already know."

"Cody's attorneys discovered that your divorce settlement in New York was unusual." Gunner pulled from a file he carried with him.

"Your father was a New York City Detective and you followed him into the New York City Police Department. You attended NYU Law School while working as a police officer for the New York City Police Department. The accomplishment of finishing law school while working as a police officer is noted on your record throughout your career. The New York City Police Department issued Glock 9mm, Model 19 semi-automatic pistols as standard issue for all rookies that graduated the police academy. The New York City Police Department required all officers to pass rigorous firing range requirements every six months." Gunner paused and the room fell silent.

"Mr. McGarrity, I am the District Attorney for Douglas County, Colorado. When I agreed to see you, it was not to justify or clarify my past. Please remind me of how my divorce settlement and my brief tenure with the NYC Police Department have anything to do with Mr. Barrett." Shana McDonough asked.

"At any given time, there are 38,000 police officers on the New York City Police Department. Since I resigned almost fifteen years ago, there have been nearly a quarter million officers through the ranks. This does not preclude the thousands of police departments across the country employing the exact same weapon for standard issue use by their officers. Mr. McGarrity, there are many people proficient in the use of the Glock 9mm, Model 19."

"Ms. McDonough, you have a twelve year old daughter named Melissa." Gunner went on. "Melissa is your only child. Your ex-husband is a partner in one of Manhattan's largest law firms. According to the information obtained by Cody Law's legal team, your husband earned in excess of one million dollars annually for the years 1985-1987. You and your family resided at East 75th Street and Fifth Avenue, along Central Park. The building was an exclusive co-op that was home to many celebrities and wealthy tenants. Cody's legal team uncovered numerous visits to five local hospitals involving accidents associated with Melissa. Three visits to Mt. Sinai Hospital, three visits to the New York Hospital at Cornell Medical Center, two visits to NYU Medical Center, two visits to the emergency room at Bellevue Hospital and one visit to the Metropolitan Hospital on East 97th Street were all associated with Melissa. The hospital reports attribute the visits to accidents in the park. The reports do not explain however, why Melissa was taken upwards of fifty city blocks for treatment when other medical facilities were within four or five blocks of Central Park."

"On two occasions in 1986, you phoned 911 to summon the police to your Upper East Side address. The tapes from the calls indicated that your husband was making physical threats during the course of a domestic dispute. The calls were made after isolating you and your daughter in a bedroom. The voice on the 911 tapes expressed frantic concern for your own safety, the safety of your daughter and that your husband was attempting to break into the bedroom. Neither 911 call resulted in an arrest. The divorce settlement you received from a very wealthy man was expeditious, if not miraculous in duration. Sole custody was granted uncontested to the mother. Smells like a deal was closed, Ms. McDonough. Child abusers come in silk ties and foreign cars, as you know much better than I. Children are an equal opportunity target. Billy Don Barrett was an extension of your husband, minus the Ivy League education and the seven-figure income."

"When you moved to Colorado, the last thing you expected was the same crap, same cover-up, different suit. Barrett was arrested for accosting your daughter, but you would not consider letting her testify against a hometown hero piece of shit like Barrett. You knew the attorneys would eat her alive. There was no way that you would allow Melissa to be asked to describe the actions of Mr. Barrett while in his car. Barrett's lawsuit was the last crack in the damn. Billy Don Barrett's ticket had been called. Originally, you authorized Easley to go after Barrett because the case was a blown up version of your own life. The animal was going away, one way or another. Hell, you were still going after your husband. Cadrell blew it by allowing himself to be present at the Rascal Flats when we flipped Boxcar."

"The case was tossed. Barrett decided to put on a show for your daughter during a drunken joy ride to the schoolyard, which may have been a random act. You believed Barrett knew Melissa and the random encounters would continue. Then Barrett files a ten-million dollar lawsuit claiming his civil rights were violated. The Colorado Attorney General's office gave Barrett more credence." Gunner stopped.

"You have a vivid imagination, Mr. McGarrity." McDonough exclaimed as calm as a librarian.

" Barrett's dead. Is there another agenda for you that I have missed? Otherwise, your preposterous hypothesis lacks any provable facts, but it does possess an imaginative quality. "

"I didn't come here to interrogate you, Ms. McDonough." Gunner followed.

"That's a huge relief." The District Attorney replied.

"I came here to thank you." Gunner's words hung in the air.

"I'm afraid we are finished here, Mr. McGarrity."

"He got to you, didn't he?" Gunner asked as he stood to leave.

"Barrett?" Shana grimaced.

"No. The hell with Barrett. He got what he deserved." Gunner paused and headed for the door. "Cody got to you."

"Is that right, Mr. McGarrity?" Shana McDonough mused.

"Yes ma'am." Gunner turned back to the District Attorney just before he reached the door. "Cody showed us that there is a cowboy in all of us."

"Go home and take care of Devon, Mr. McGarrity." Shana recommended.

"That's a given, Ms. McDonough." Gunner pulled open the door to the outer office.

"The bible speaks of retribution in its purest form. Regrets will fade, Ms. McDonough, but virtue is eternal. Christopher Marlowe calls it "the fount whence honor springs."

Shana McDonough stood dispassionate, albeit stony. "Is it a cowboy custom to quote pre-Shakespearean authors?"

"Thank you again for all your help, ma'am." Gunner touched the brim of his hat.

Shana McDonough walked to the window of her office, turning her back to Gunner McGarrity.

"You're welcome." Shana replied staring out the window, past the mountains surrounding Castle Rock, Colorado. As soon as Gunner left, she allowed herself a small, almost secret smile.